S0-AIT-972

BEING WITH FAME

BEING WITH FAME

CAMILLE UNDINE

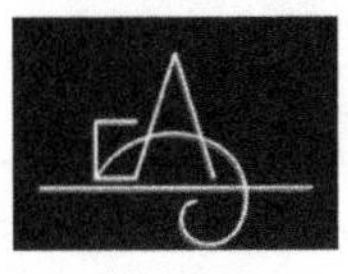

EAST AUGUST PUBLISHING

Published by East August Publishing
160 W. Foothill Parkway Ste. 105-131
Corona, CA 92882

ISBN 978-1-7346-9970-8

Printed in the United States of America

For Sharon Undine Moore

Your affection, compassion, encouragement, support, warmth, wisdom, knowledge, kindness, generosity, laughter, and sense of adventure knew no boundaries.

I could not have been placed into more loving hands.
You were what God meant for a mother to be.
I got the best, best one.

I love you, madly.

BEING WITH FAME

Chapter 1

The South of France, like years before, rumbled along its shores. It was the breezy season of spring, and droves of characters from diverse industries came to attend a beloved film festival. For most patrons, the fair was consuming, for some it was chaotic, and for a providential few, it was rewarding. Among this elite group, deals were being made, screenings were being critiqued, and carpets were being walked. Soon to walk down a red carpet of great length was Ireland Rochelle.

In a room of a posh hotel on a palm-lined boulevard, Ireland wrestled with her emotions, trying her best to pin them down. She hadn't had a moment alone since she awakened to knocking that morning. Once she opened her guestroom door to let her team inside, the day became a blur of back to back appearances. She should have been thrilled from what she had done and for what was still to come. Instead, she was literally sick to her stomach, upset that the busyness and dizziness hadn't passed.

In the restroom she'd escaped to, her warm, glistening knees quivered upon the glazed floor. Clasping a bulk of white porcelain, cold to her touch, she peered into its oval pool of shallow water. It was in the most humble of objects that she began a hazy deed. She studied the outline of her image.

Evidently, her breathing was extreme. Her chest and shoulders rose and lowered with an intensity akin to the wild sound of air scurrying to her laboring lungs. Swinging from the tugged lobes of her decorated ears were strings of borrowed diamonds. Clips jutted from her scalp, securing rows of small barrels, which converted her straightened strands into waves. Fortunately, she could not see into her perfectly contoured eyes. Fear, worry, and dread were difficult enough to feel. She had no desire to witness them as well.

As swift as a jetting arrow, the sight before her went dark. Void of her will, her eyes slammed shut while her gut churned and burned. Her neck jolted forward as her throat endured the angst of repetitious gags. Though she knew the hot contents that tumbled from her mouth were the cause of the splashes she heard, the ugliness of the moment was solidified when she saw the purée of her last meal swirling in the bowl below. Before she wiped the liquid that oozed from the sides of her eyes, she stood onto the balmy soles of her bare feet.

Ireland was a widely *unknown* actress that had only worked on low budget, independent films. One pivotal day, her persistent manager, Keith, helped her get an agent with a high-profile agency. A few months later, she got a golden audition with a very accomplished director. The director's intent in casting his film was to solely hire celebrities, but he made one rare exception and screen-tested Ireland. Due to her palpable talent as well as her intriguing look, she eventually landed the role and was the feature's supporting actress.

She adored acting in the film but promoting it brought her panic. Schmoozing and partaking of small talk were activities she despised and they seemed downright essential in recent months of her budding career. *Less Loyalty* was her first major motion picture and with it came major publicity pains. Despite the fact that it had yet to be released, it garnered anticipation and over-the-top buzz. Along with the predominantly famous cast, Ireland's presence was required in France to attend the film's premiere and its associated affairs. On just that day alone, she had been to a breakfast, photocall, press conference, meeting, and beachside luncheon.

Although Ireland had experienced other festivals, the current one was by far her most frightening. Due to its enormous attention, it was harder for her to slyly go unseen. Naturally, she feared harsh judgment, but she also feared the anonymity she was fond of would diminish or disappear. Indeed, Ireland recognized the contradiction in her dream to be a successful yet obscure actress, but it was her dream nonetheless.

As she stood at the hotel sink, staring at herself in the mirror, she grasped for last minute ways she could dodge the pending premiere. But the familiar sound of frantic knocking resumed all too soon.

On the opposite side of the door was her manager, hair stylist, wardrobe stylist, and makeup artist, all of whom were annoyed with her inconvenient trip to the lavatory. After washing her hands, she brushed her teeth and gargled with a pungent mouthwash then departed from her confinement and returned to her seat in the bedroom. Still feeling ill, she tolerated the arranging of her hair and application of gloss to her lips. Once her silk robe was removed from her body, she stepped into a glittering gown.

Created by a French designer, the dress was strapless, form-fitting, and metallic, featuring panels of ample sheen. Its most striking attribute, however, was its puzzling, chameleon-like color. It was as if it had been dipped in blush-colored wine, doused with rose gold, and blended with silver. Ireland had become the breathtaking vision her team sought to achieve. A clutch purse and high heels completed her look. With two sprays of a sweet fragrance, she was on her way to the day's main event.

As she moved through the congested lobby, she noticed a cast member approaching her. Rona Simpson was the lead actress of *Less Loyalty* and a larger than life celebrity. She maintained a stellar acting career and undeniable beauty. Four years prior, she won the most coveted award in film. It was a shiny statuette that Ireland considered earning as well one day.

In spite of all the accolades Rona received, she was warm and grounded on set, which Ireland deeply appreciated. At the same time, Rona appreciated Ireland's non-intrusive manner. Though kind and pleasant, Ireland made no inquiries into Rona's personal life, which put the star at ease when it came to sharing her past. As time went by, the two of them engaged in many discussions and fits of laughter. Even though the film had wrapped, Rona remained in contact with Ireland, and thereby, called her a friend.

"Ireland," Rona said, showing off her broad smile. Careful not to alter their hair and makeup, she passed on giving Ireland a kiss.

"Hi, Rona. You look gorgeous," Ireland replied, admiring the black beaded gown gracing Rona's frame.

"You're the one looking gorgeous. Are you nervous?"

"Am I in France?"

"I was nervous too my first time here. You'll be fine. Just try to have fun."

"Yea, I'll try," Ireland fibbed. Glancing at the entourage directly behind Rona, she asked, "Where's Dig?"

"Wasn't that the question of the hour?" Rona said, rolling her almond-shaped eyes. "He's in our suite changing because he just got back ten minutes ago. Can you believe him?"

Dig was an award-winning hip hop artist that Rona had been dating for eight years. They were the most electric couple on the planet, never mind in America. The world felt invested in seeing them together so it was practically mandatory for them to walk carpets hand in hand.

"Do you think you guys will make it on time?"

"Oh, we will," Rona said, emphatically, nodding her head.

"Okay, I'll see you over there," Ireland replied, before walking away with Keith.

Across a patterned, marble floor, and beneath grand chandeliers, Ireland proceeded to press her way past whitewashed walls. She never noticed the marveling eyes that followed each of her steps as she made it to a revolving door that eventually brought her outside.

The light of day began to fade as breezes from the bay wafted through the air. Under a canopy of the hotel's exterior, Ireland observed the nearby stretch of tan sand. Lining the dark pavement directly before her was a fleet of spotless, black vehicles. Once she and Keith climbed into one, its well-prepared driver pulled off.

Slowly, they rode along, nestled between identical cars heading to the same location. Billboards, banners, posters, and people bordered the busy road. Anxiously, Ireland examined the growing number of excited expressions, which only made her more repulsed by the festival's magnificence.

As if she were ensnared in a chokehold, the imminent premiere had her struggling to breathe. She hated that a film career required large amounts of interaction. She wished it simply entailed studying scripts, researching roles, learning lines, and acting on set. Unfortunately, that sequence of events was followed by one hobnob affair after another. She was learning that more success meant more stifling commitments.

Gradually, and unexpectedly, she felt shame for her disgruntlement. All of the years she invested into acting came shuffling back to her. Every class, audition, and performance - even every bit of rejection and glowing review of praise had led to this deserving moment. Ireland knew there was no other place she should be, but she couldn't shake wanting to be elsewhere.

Conscious her scrambled nerves were still getting the best of her, she looked out at the gentle scene of vessels sailing in the distance. As inspiring as her view was, she chose to envision another. After slow, deep breaths, she closed her eyes and saw herself on the adjacent sea.

Far from the luxury yachts, in a small, unimpressive boat, she sits in the center, staring at the sky, rich in blue like the water below it. All alone, and wearing nearly nothing, she feels the heat of the sun. As she smells the salty air, cool wind tingles her scalp and freely whips her hair about. Her body becomes one with the bobbing of the boat while she listens to the sound of waves swishing in the sea. Her breathing is easy. Her being is calm. She resolves to remain there for hours.

"There's Amanda," Keith said, rousing Ireland from her imagery. Running a hand over his slick, gray hair, he spoke the obvious. "Get ready."

Ireland opened her eyes and took in the atmosphere. The crowd's noise was riotous. The cameras lights were blinding. Her newfound relaxation descended into a dive. She had never been more relieved to be a good actress for she would have to rely on her aptitude to get her through the night. After stepping out of the car, she greeted her publicist, Amanda, then followed her onto the carpet. Adrenaline coursed through her veins as she faced a horde of cameras. Continually turning from one side to the other, she pretended she was precisely where she wanted to be.

Over the years, Ireland had grown into quite a beautiful woman. It was typical of people to do a double take when she entered a room. She was stunning, primarily because of her unconventional look. Never mistaken for another, her face was pretty, but also unique. Baby smooth and blemish free, her fudge-colored skin proved the facials she received were altogether gratuitous. Besieged by full, arched brows and long, thick lashes, her dark eyes gave off an indisputable mystery. With plump lips and perfect teeth, her smile had the power to pull people close. Although she rarely intended to be sexy, sexiness was defined by the curves of her figure, as well as the endless body within her brunette hair. Even with prominent women around, Ireland stood out. This evening was no exception.

Nearly as enthusiastic as the screaming fans across the road, the photographers waved, pointed, and yelled commands for Ireland to obey. Exuding an utmost confidence, she continued the charade of posing. Though her actions were necessary to promote the film, she couldn't wait until the preposterous grandstanding was over.

An incredibly loud cheer arose when Rona and Dig arrived. Ireland took it as the perfect cue to make herself scarce. She quickly, but gracefully, joined the supporting actor near the theater's entrance. There she watched Rona work the carpet like it was second nature. After what seemed like an eon, Rona, the director, and the male lead arrived at the entrance as well. The party of five assembled for photos then went inside the theater.

At last, away from the cameras harsh glares, Ireland gulped for the air she hadn't allowed herself to breathe. She could hardly wait to sit and take hold of her weakened knees, but first, she had to enter the auditorium and take a long walk down a sloping aisle. As she did so, she was shocked that the rows of the room were filled to their capacity. Besides an area in the center section for those who worked on the film, she saw very few vacant seats. Consumed with giving applause, the elaborately adorned audience brought the space a vibrant energy that rivaled the one outdoors.

Ireland was overwhelmed, but not just in an apprehensive way. Along with her worsening nausea, she soon felt a sense of nobility. She was reminded that her tireless work and commitment to bringing characters to life could become an inspiration to others.

Ideal Morris had been to France countless times before. Dig's closest friend of fifteen years, he was also a prominent hip hop artist, but a singer and music producer as well. In addition to his own music, he created songs for Dig and other artists within a surprising range of genres. Furthermore, he owned a fashion line, which led to collaborations with designers in Europe. Aside from his own reputation, his connection with high-powered people in the music and fashion industry allowed him to be a regular attendee to the festival. This evening, however, was his first time running late for a premiere.

Hours earlier, he along with Dig was meeting with executives aboard a chartered yacht. When the meeting adjourned, they discovered the captain had ventured further than they anticipated. Stuck on board, they continually checked the time as the boat made its journey back. When they finally reached land, they rushed to separate hotels and dressed for the screening of Rona's film.

Wearing a black tuxedo, Ideal arrived at the theater shortly before the film was scheduled to begin. Although he was in a hurry, he slowed to pose on the carpet, stirring the photographers into a tizzy. To the sound of his shrieking fans, he later advanced toward the theater's doors and was nearly the last person to pass through them. Once he took his seat, he snapped a picture of himself then proudly posted the image on social media. Seconds later, the lights dimmed and the red curtain parted. A haunting instrumental played through the speakers then *Less Loyalty* began.

Ideal was engaged in the film, when after a quarter into the hour there appeared on the screen a face he'd never seen. It was a face he found himself studying compulsively. A face he couldn't pull his gaze from. His eyes lingered on each of its features. As he watched the countenance of an actress, something roused within him. He was captivated, bewitched, but couldn't understand why. He had seen thousands of beautiful women on screen and even though he spent time appreciating their looks, he wasn't heavily impacted by them. This time he felt different. This time he felt strange. While focusing so firmly on the woman's appearance, the way she sounded, and the way she moved, he paid no attention to the meaning of her scene. Before he knew it, the scene was over and her face was gone.

His breath was cut short and disappointment set in. What he had seen of the woman was in no way enough. Feeling a wave of impatience, his fist tapped the arm of his chair as he reasoned with himself that she would resurface. The next two scenes went by without her. He grew sullen. Then a mammoth rush of alleviation came when it occurred to him she was present in the theater.

With the room nearly absent of light, he examined the orchestra section. Although he spotted the profile of his best friend, a sea of women encircled Dig. Almost unable to identify the back of Rona's head, Ideal's hunt for the unknown actress felt hopeless. His eyes roamed aimlessly. Luckily for him, she returned to the screen.

Like he'd been hit with a long-awaited dose of a drug, her presence calmed his agitation. Ultimately, he listened to the words being spoken, eager to hear the name of her character. It was *Lovely.* He sat enraptured by her, disturbed when each of her scenes would end and counting down until the next one began. In time, two hours passed, the film ended, and the credits rolled.

Generously, the audience roared with applause and gave a standing ovation. Instead of applauding, Ideal stood to his feet and tensely read the credits. Fervently, he found the name of the actress who portrayed *Lovely.* It was Ireland Rochelle. He repeated her name to himself as if it were mandatory to retain. When he brought his eyes down from the screen, the director and cast were assembling on stage. A current raced through him when he saw Ireland beneath the lights. She was far more ravishing in person. Oblivious to the cheers around him, Ideal stood motionless, centered on her movements. Unfortunately, she answered no question during the brief post-screening session. His ears were unable to relish the real-time sound of her voice, but his eyes cherished his view until she was no longer in sight.

Chapter 2

The premiere had ended, but the parties had just begun. Yet again Ireland returned to the hotel to prepare for more hoopla. She changed into a short, revealing dress made of black, satin straps. Aside from her natural beauty, her personal style was impeccable. She had a deep love for fashion, which could also be construed as a dependency. The more splendid she looked, the more splendid she felt, having lessened her chances of ridicule.

The first bash she attended was thrown by a studio. The subsequent was thrown by her agency. Both were at neighboring hotels and at both Ireland sat around itching to leave. Had she left too soon, she would have missed the many people who approached her to compliment her work. The flattery felt a bit validating, but also embarrassing. She felt awkward time and again, listening to glowing remarks about herself. They were words she thought she'd never tire of hearing, but there were only so many ways she could humbly express her thanks.

Her final party of the night was the most exclusive. Keith had done serious networking to ensure Ireland received an invitation. Hosted by a fashion publication, the party's setting was at a wondrously, luxurious hotel, propped above the rugged rocks of the sea. After posing before a wall of the press, Ireland went inside.

Compared to the huge names moving about the noisy room, Ireland was pleased to be the nobody amongst the crowd. With the exception of the celebrities Keith nudged her to meet, she was able to lie low and stargaze. Although she preferred not being at the pompous festivity, she figured she might as well smile at famous faces that passed her by.

When Keith finally left her side, she turned her gaze to the outdoors. Drawn by the ebony sky and the much smaller quantity of people, she walked onto the terrace and observed the full moon's brilliance. Bathed in its light was a small patch of sand below. While listening to the waves slap against the rocks, Ireland sipped champagne from the glass flute she held. As the sweet and sour bubbles passed over her tongue, she envisioned the alcohol plunging into her jittery nerves.

"Ireland Rochelle, right?" a male voice behind her said.

Ireland turned around to see a well-known figure in front of her. Michael Weston had made films for the past thirty years and won almost as many awards. She was shocked that such a force in the industry actually knew her name. "Yes," she answered, her voice barely present.

"Michael Weston," he replied, extending his hand.

"It's beyond nice meeting you, Mr. Weston," she said, shaking his hand in a robotic manner.

"Call me, Michael."

"Okay."

"I was really taken with your performance tonight. It was flawless."

"Thank you. That means the world coming from you."

"Listen, we're about to start casting for my next film. There's a role I'd like to have you read for. Would you be interested in seeing the script?"

"Uh . . . definitely."

"Alright, I'll have it sent to your agent. Have a good night," he said, walking away as quickly as he appeared.

The excitement that welled inside of Ireland was so fierce she felt she might erupt. Holding back her desire to scream, she smashed her lips together. Another film with another legendary director would mean another dream coming to pass. Quickly on the heels of her happiness was a voice inside of her head, reminding her that such work would further threaten her ambiguity. In spite of that truth, the anticipation of exercising her craft alongside Weston's won her over. She whispered a prayer that she'd get the role, regardless of what it was, then rushed to share her good news.

When she found Keith, he was speaking to producers who happened to look bored by him. As he introduced her to the gentlemen, they put an end to their slouched positions and zestfully stood tall. Ireland suspected it wasn't her warmth, but her dress that inspired their sudden revival. After she suffered through an additional bout of small talk, she privately informed Keith of her most recent opportunity. He was familiar with the upcoming project and immediately became overconfident.

"They won't bring in another soul after you read for that part. You've got this in the bag," he said, pointing his stubby, index finger then taking a swig of his scotch. "Well, as fantastic as this is, and this is fantastic, there's an agent I have to go speak to. Make yourself seen."

In an instant, Michael Weston had made being at the party worth it for Ireland. She ceased waiting until the time she could leave and started conjecturing when her audition would be. Perhaps a portion of her slight ease was due to the champagne she drank, but its majority was due to what she could now look forward to. Determined to try and relax the rest of the night, she stood in a dormant corner and returned to scanning the people in her presence.

As she was observing colorful artists, she soon felt as though she were being observed. From her left, she felt a commanding energy flowing loyally toward her. Carefully, she turned her head to see if someone was watching her. Indeed, someone was. She looked at the man whose narrow eyes were leaning into hers. Arrested by the stronghold they had on her, she went still for half a minute. After a few failed attempts to look away, she pulled her resistant eyes from his gaze and shifted them to the opposite direction. Wondering if she was mistaken for believing that she was the subject of such staunch attention, she glanced over her right shoulder. No one was there. As if shutting her eyes could calm the accelerated drumming of her pulse, she lowered her lids for a moment then tried to refocus on the bustling crowd.

Although her eyes moved on, her mind did not. Her thoughts were plagued by the connection she'd just experienced. The person with whom she shared the extremity of chemistry, appeared to be a celebrity, but she reasoned he wasn't. Tempted to confirm her vision had temporarily gone awry, she looked again, timidly. Halfway expecting to see a new face, the same one stared back at her. It was the face of Ideal Morris.

Ireland had always found Ideal to be a highly attractive man. Not only was he insanely handsome, but he was also amazingly talented. She long admired the music he created and his smooth yet offbeat style. That night he looked especially distinguished wearing a black tuxedo - something he rarely wore.

As if sinking in his quicksand of concentration, she turned away in order to grasp something to hold. Right on time, a server walked by carrying a silver tray of champagne. Typically, she consumed only one drink when out, but given the swirling circumstances, she decided to reach for a second.

"Great minds think alike," a fellow cast member of hers said.

"Hi, Noah," Ireland replied, watching the actor take a glass of his own.

When she kissed him on the cheek, he kindly admonished her. "No, no, no. At a party like this, you have to kiss both cheeks."

"Oh, forgive me. Where was my head?"

After her lips brushed the stubble on each side of his face, he replied, "That's much better. So, how's it going?"

"It's going. This party's interesting," she said, tilting her head.

"Always," Noah replied, referring to the times he'd been before. "How did you like the premiere?"

"It was nice, but it was hard watching myself."

"Oh, you'll never get over that. I've been in nine films and I still haven't." Shaking the curls of his head, he added, "I hate seeing myself."

"Thanks for the pep talk."

"Anytime," he said, winking one of his pale blue eyes then brushing his glass against hers. "Cheers."

As Ireland watched Noah drift away, she saw Ideal resurge into view. It seemed the sight of her back didn't prove satisfactory, because he moved to an area where he could see her features fully. Clearly, he had no interest in hiding his fixation. In fact, he appeared intent on letting her know she infused his mind. Whenever her eyes met his eyes, he never glanced away so that he and she could partake in perpetual sessions of staring.

Curious as to why he was observing her so relentlessly, Ireland concluded he either attended the premiere and felt strongly about her acting or by some glitch in good order, he was physically attracted to her. Her spirit murmured it was the latter, but her brain believed the former. Whatever his thoughts were on her choices in the film, she wished he would approach her and voice them or lose them entirely. Remaining under the weight of his steady gaze made her feel increasingly awkward.

The more time ticked by, the wearier she grew with feeling like an exhibition. Seeking a recess, she went to the only room Ideal wasn't able to ogle her. She had long understood that a restroom was also intended for rest. Regrettably, she hadn't acquired any that night. Hoping for a sliver of its rejuvenating power, she entered the gender segregating space where she was welcomed by an invisible cloud of female fragrances. Once she passed cliques of whispering women, she locked herself in a stall and leaned against one of its wooden sides. Before she could take a deep breath, she took a long yawn and felt her body begging for sleep. It was then that she realized how fatigued she was. A minute later, she decided she was through with the night. Keith would be upset by her leaving, but he worked for her not the other way around.

Back in the party's central area, Ireland scoured through the host of tight, lean bodies looking for Keith's more robust one. As much as she wanted to ditch him, she didn't have the heart to do so. Not rude by nature, Ireland couldn't vanish on anyone, much less her manager.

"There you are," Rona said, arriving at Ireland's side. "How are you holding up?"

"Barely. My feet are killing me."

"Ooh, I know what you mean. I need to sit down."

"Well, I need to lie down. I'm leaving."

Rona looked appalled. "The night's just getting started."

"It's ending for me. It should have hours ago."

"I didn't know you were a party pooper," Rona taunted, shaking her head and causing her ponytail to swing.

"Now, you know," Ireland replied, lifting her shoulders in acknowledgment. "I never got a chance to chat with Dig. Maybe next time."

"Go talk to him now. He's right over there."

Ireland followed the direction in which Rona extended her bronzed arm. Standing a short distance behind them was Dig. He was speaking with his large hands, totally engrossed in a conversation with none other than Ideal. Of all the people that were stuffed in the room, he was talking to the one person Ireland hoped to avoid seeing.

As if Ideal had a sixth sense and knew Ireland resurfaced, he turned his head away from Dig and stared directly at her. The stability of their eye contact resumed.

"That's okay," Ireland said, diverting her eyes back to Rona.

"Are you sure?"

"Yea, I've got to find Keith and get out of here."

"Suit yourself. See you tomorrow."

On a mission, Ireland hunted down Keith, debated with him about leaving, and returned to her hotel. She was way too tired to reflect on the day. She would have to do that another time.

Ideal had only gotten three hours of sleep. He made it back to his suite by five o'clock that morning but remained alert until eight. He was tempted to blame his lack of slumber on the parties he attended, but that was less than a quarter of the truth. The primary reason was Ireland. Her smile, her eyes, her hair, and her thighs haunted him unyieldingly. Eventually, it was a fantasy of him being intimate with her that finally lulled him to sleep.

Prior to his few hours of shut-eye, he recalled how seeing her for the first time was a shock to his typically calm system. Later at the party when she knew he was looking, he still failed to keep his eyes to himself. He was aware he looked foolish for never approaching her, but he wasn't sure if he could speak with his heart racing in his chest. It walloped thirty feet away from her. It may have stopped altogether had he gotten any closer.

Ideal had broken many hearts. Most often, the women he dated sought a commitment from him. Although he would tell them upfront that he had no intentions of being in a relationship, almost always they attempted to change his mind. They never did. When he met a woman he found interesting, he took her on one to three dates, slept with her one to three times then moved on. He wasn't dishonest with her nor did he mistreat her, he simply wanted nothing more.

As far as Ireland was concerned, Ideal didn't know what he wanted. He was totally inexperienced in what he felt for her. She sparked in him a reaction that made him uncharacteristically nervous, but not nervous enough to miss seeing her again. From

Rona, he learned the *Less Loyalty* cast would be having lunch on the patio of a particular hotel's restaurant. There was no other place Ideal intended to be.

Needing his presence to appear as a fluke, he got to the restaurant ahead of the cast. Upon request, he was seated inside at a table with a good view of the umbrella-filled patio. There he waited for a good view of Ireland. One by one, members of the cast arrived and were escorted to the outdoor dining area.

For some time Ideal listened to polished utensils clanking against white china, but he hadn't noticed the French music playing until Ireland walked in. Its rhythm seemed to be one with the fluid way in which she moved. He watched her as she unknowingly came his way. Seconds later, her brown eyes met his.

The surprise on her face was invaluable. Her lips parted, her eyes widened, and she nearly stopped following the hostess leading her through the establishment. Ideal could see the disbelief on her face, but he also could feel the pull between the two of them. The night had gone, but their chemistry remained.

Boldly, he looked her over. She wore silver jewelry and silver heels with a short, sky blue dress. He assumed that when she discreetly glanced over his attire, she noticed that beneath his jacket was a shirt matching her dress so perfectly it could have been cut from the same cloth. When she looked back at his face, Ideal said more with his eyes, causing her to hasten onto the patio, where she pretended not to see him examining her.

As he admired her skin's radiance in sunlight, he realized he wasn't the only one that watched her glide into the restaurant. A few men of different ages and cultures appeared at the empty seat next to her. Though they were busy speaking, it was the smiling they did that caught Ideal's attention. If it wasn't obvious to Ireland, it was terribly obvious to him that her courteous visitors were flirting.

Without warning, the thought occurred to Ideal that Ireland might have a boyfriend. He had been so preoccupied with his thoughts of her that he didn't stop to think who was on her mind. It troubled him to conceive that she could be taken. Although he may have dwelled on the disturbing possibility, the applause of a woman at the bar prevented him from doing so. Immediately, he assessed the woman's actions and saw that she was applauding Rona.

His strategy regarding Rona's arrival was a contradiction to Ireland's. When Rona waltzed in, he hid behind his menu, careful to keep his presence from her. The previous night, he noticed that Rona and Ireland were friendly, which meant if Rona saw him, she'd introduce him to the new actress. Ideal wasn't prepared for an introduction. He feared that if he spoke to her, he'd come off sounding like the intro to a rhythm and blues song from the nineties. In no way would he meet her yet. At the present time, he was content with letting his eyes feast on her beauty - no matter how uncomfortable it made her.

Chapter 3

The next day, Ireland boarded a plane and gladly returned to Los Angeles. It was evening when she opened the arched gate to the courtyard of her townhouse in Santa Monica. Placid, the area's focal point was a centralized jar fountain. Even when at rest, it welcomed her home. After passing pots of white roses, she moved to the front door and went inside. Once she stepped into the foyer, she dropped her bags and inhaled the aroma of eucalyptus drifting from a reed diffuser. With a flick of a switch, she turned on a wall fountain and to the sound of trickling water, proceeded into the living room.

Ordinarily, her house would have been beyond her budget, but she got a steal of a deal through a friend she'd met in theater. His grandparents owned the home, but when his grandfather passed, his grandmother moved in with his parents. Because of Ireland's friendship with her grandson, the widow rented the place to Ireland for a price much lower than it's worth. In five years, the rent hadn't been raised once.

After exercising her keen design ability, the two-story residence suited Ireland perfectly. A serene space of cream, each room had walls and fabrics the shade of French vanilla, which gave contrast to dark wooden floors and rustic ceiling beams. Along with several windows, glass doors brought in natural light necessary for the assorted plants that provided pops of greenery. Chaises, chairs, sofas, and beds were lined with decorative pillows, while table tops were minimal, usually dressed with fruit and flowers. Although the backyard wasn't much of a yard at all, the front courtyard was an outdoor refuge set for relaxation. Ireland so enjoyed the calm feel of her abode, she didn't plan on moving for many years to come.

Jet-lagged, she climbed the stairs and forced herself to unpack, then rewarded herself with a salt bath in a deep, claw foot tub. After washing away every layer of makeup, she ran her fingers along the smooth skin of her cheeks. She loved the feel of her face when it was totally exposed. Once all of her body was slathered in cream, she put on a nightgown, hopped into bed, and floated away for a much-needed nap.

It wasn't the ringing phones that she guiltily ignored, but hunger that caused her to rise from her rest. Barefoot, she shuffled to the kitchen and discovered that she was in desperate need of groceries. With nothing appetizing to eat, she poured herself a tall glass of peach juice and returned to the living room. After sliding back the doors of a distressed armoire to reveal a flat screen television, she sat on her sofa and scanned through a myriad of cable channels. She settled on an entertainment news show that had major coverage of the film festival.

Ireland was taking a sip of her juice when she saw herself with the *Less Loyalty* cast. She was floored. Although she knew there was proof that she had just left the festival, it was still hard to absorb that she had been part of the grand event. She wasn't sure if her work there would ever fully sink in.

The news soon shifted to Rona and Dig mania, showing clips of them posing, partying, and kissing. Ireland sat admiring the power couple, but the image she saw next, made her heart skip a beat. On a carpet, before flashes of light, Ideal Morris stood posing in his tuxedo. He looked incredibly suave and judging by the audio of high-pitched screams, other women thought so too. Intrigued, she leaned forward and viewed various pictures of him smiling with female celebrities. For some strange reason, a part of her was bothered when she saw him surrounded by a throng of beautiful ladies.

Her irritation was interrupted when the doorbell rang unexpectedly. Instinctively, Ireland knew it was her best friend, Casey. Aside from Ireland's mother, Casey was the only person who knew Ireland landed at the airport hours earlier. Casey had been a friend for over a decade, ever since Ireland moved from Philadelphia to L.A. for college. Although Ireland was a theater major and Casey a business major, they met in a political science class during their freshman year.

"I knew it was you," Ireland said, looking through the peek door of the courtyard's gate.

"Of course you did," Casey said, raising her slim shoulders. When Ireland lifted the iron latch and swung open the wooden gate, Casey presented a bag of food cartons. "I brought Chinese."

"Just what I needed."

After rushing inside, they sat at the dining table and began eating.

"So I'm dying to know. How was the festival?" Casey asked.

"Exhausting," Ireland answered, savoring the sweetness of pineapple chicken.

"Oh, boohoo. Hanging out with celebrities in France wore you out?"

"It did."

"Well, I need details."

"Let's catch up on you first," Ireland teased. Referring to Casey's boyfriend, she asked, "How's Robert?"

"Tell me everything you did," she replied, scrunching a handful of her soft, natural curls.

"Well –"

"Wait a minute. There's Ideal," Casey interjected, looking at the television screen. "He looks so good. Did you see him there?"

Images of Ideal at the party came back to Ireland. Her body grew warm as she remembered his eyes being fixated on her. She still didn't know what to make of it. She couldn't exactly feel flattered, because he never expressed any interest in her. Maybe he looked at every woman that way, which wasn't a stretch considering the socializing he did. She had no reason to feel special so she decided not to mention it to Casey. If Casey knew anything, she would spend the night dissecting his actions and hypothesizing their meanings, which would drive Ireland insane. The truth of the matter was that Ireland sometimes wondered if it was all in her head.

"Yea, I saw him," Ireland said, stirring her shrimp-fried rice.

"You did? Does he look as good in person as he does online?"

Without pause, Ireland's reply escaped her lips. "Better."

"Wow, did you meet him?"

"No, I only saw him."

"Where'd you see him?"

"At a party after the premiere."

"Hey," she said, waving her hand in front of Ireland's face. "You actually saw Ideal Morris. I can't believe you're being so nonchalant." Casey found it strange that Ireland wasn't more excited to have seen Ideal, but she figured her friend was still tired from the flight. "Anyway, how did the premiere go? I know you were sick about it."

"I had a panic attack before it started, the carpet was as batty as I expected, and watching myself on screen with that many people made me wince, but other than that the audience loved the film. It got a standing ovation."

"Yes! I can't wait to see you in it. So tell me about every event. Don't leave anything out."

Over the next hour, Ireland told Casey just about every single moment of her time in France. The only thing she did omit was the look in Ideal's eyes. She was discussing Michael Weston when her cell began ringing from the master bedroom.

"I need to see who that is," Ireland said, leaving the table.

As she hurried upstairs, she figured the caller was Keith. He was probably ready to ring her neck for not answering her phone earlier. When she reached her cell, she was surprised to see it was Rona. Thinking Casey would get a kick out of the call, she answered it the living room. "Hey Rona," she said, loudly, winking at Casey.

Casey jumped up and stood next to Ireland. "That's Rona?" she whispered.

Ireland nodded then put Rona on speakerphone. "Isn't it like five o'clock in the morning there? What are you doing up so early?" Ireland asked.

"We just got off of Gerald's yacht. We haven't even gone to sleep yet," Rona replied.

"If I didn't know any better, I'd think you did drugs."

"Good thing you know better."

"Well, I'm touched I was the first thing on your mind this morning."

"Actually, you were."

"Why?"

"While you were here, I kept forgetting to invite you to an event I really want you to come to."

"What kind of event?" Ireland asked, already feeling anxious.

"A charity event. Dig has a foundation called *You Dig* to help disadvantaged youth receive an education in the performing arts and it also provides academic scholarships. There's going to be a fundraiser with a silent and live auction, live entertainment, and a sit-down meal."

Ireland turned her back to Casey's enthusiastic expression. "That sounds really nice," she said, impressed by Dig's philanthropy, but preparing her declination.

"I know you love giving back so I figured this would be another opportunity for you to do it."

Although giving was something Ireland enjoyed, she did not want to mingle about a crowd of ritzy people, especially since she'd spent recent days doing so. "That's true," she said, committing to nothing.

"I got a ticket for you already so you won't have to pay for it. I know that I'm giving you little notice and the price is pretty steep."

"Me not paying for the ticket defeats the purpose, doesn't it?"

"No, you can still give by bidding in the auctions."

"How much is the ticket?"

"Six thousand dollars."

"Whoa," Ireland said. "Does Dig have payment plans?"

"Just say you'll come."

Ignoring Casey's wild motioning to accept the invitation, Ireland said, "I think I'll just make a donation online."

"I'm not asking you to donate online. I'm asking you to come to the fundraiser."

Feeling pressured by Casey and Rona, she stalled by asking another question. "When is it?"

"Next week."

"Next week?"

"I know. I should've sent you an invitation a month ago."

Tempted to lie and say she was busy, she asked, "What day is it?"

"Friday. It starts at five."

As much as Ireland didn't want to go, she couldn't lose sight of the fact that she had just been personally invited to an event for a good cause. It was the type of cause Ireland was truly in support of and besides that, her mother, Casey, and Keith would kill her if she didn't go. "Okay, I'll come," Ireland said, watching Casey dance with unrestrained joy. "Thanks for the invite."

"You're welcome."

"So where is it going to be?" Ireland asked, assuming it would be in Los Angeles or New York.

"At our place in Miami."

Ireland's long eyelashes fluttered with intrigue. At least she'd get to see their home, which would satisfy her curiosity for knowing how Rona and Dig lived. "I haven't been to Miami in a long time."

"Then stay awhile and we can run the streets."

"No, I'll just fly in on Friday morning and head back home on Saturday."

"Well, if you're only going to stay one night, why don't you spend the night at our house?"

Ireland and Casey stared at each other in disbelief. Ireland finally managed to say, "What?"

"You heard me."

"Rona, there are plenty of hotels in Miami. I'm not going to stay at your place." As appealing as it was, Ireland dismissed the idea.

"Oh, come on. We have three guest rooms with their own bathroom. You won't be in our way. We won't even have to see you if we don't want to."

"Shouldn't you check with Dig first?"

"He won't care."

Even if Dig didn't mind, Ireland couldn't stomach coming off like a moocher. "Look, I'm going to treat myself to a luxury hotel and when the time comes, I'll head over to your house."

"You'll head over to my house when my driver picks you up from the airport."

"You stay hard-headed."

"So do you," Rona retorted. "When someone is being kind to you, accept their kindness."

Persuaded by Rona's insistence and Casey's glaring eye, Ireland gave in again. "Fine, I'll stay at your place."

"Good. Now, book your flight and send me your itinerary."

"Yes, Ma'am," Ireland said, preparing herself for the next adventure headed her way.

Chapter 4

When the driver entered the gate to Rona and Dig's Miami home, Ireland was awestruck. A massive structure of white stucco stretched to meet a clay roof. It was ten o'clock in the morning and the grayness of the day surrounded the Spanish home enchantingly. The exterior was unquestionably grand and the interior was an impressive match.

Among seventeen thousand square feet were vaulted ceilings and floors of terracotta tile. Beautiful wooden pieces, the color of pecan, were peppered throughout each room and the earthy palette of beige and sand allowed the home's best feature, the view of Biscayne Bay, to remain the worthy focal point of nearly every space. Rona assigned Ireland to a room with a full view of the bay then led her to the kitchen, once breakfast had been prepared.

When they entered the kitchen, Dig was there. He welcomed Ireland with a hug then threatened to put her in jail if he caught her stealing anything. After making himself a plate from the spread upon the island, he headed to his office for an important conference call.

While vendors roaming the backyard, looked through the windows for glimpses of Rona, she and Ireland filled their plates then settled at the breakfast nook. As they began gulping food, they laughed about how they ate like birds during the film festival. At great length, they discussed sitcoms and books they'd love to see made into films. With plenty of opinions to share, time dashed by. Before they knew it, Rona's style team had arrived and the event was scheduled to begin in a few hours. Quickly, the new friends parted ways as Rona needed time to get ready physically and Ireland needed time to get ready mentally.

In her borrowed bedroom, Ireland sat at the window and watched ripples of waves run atop the bay's surface. They seemed symbolic of the rippling of her nerves. She reflected on the fact that in a short matter of time, the waterfront property would be crammed with people and she would again be in the midst of a crowd, impatiently waiting for it to disperse. Already regretting not having made a donation online, she chose to replace her fearful thoughts with a pleasant one. She closed her eyes, and with deep breaths, conjured up an image.

On a flat mountaintop, she watches dawn let light emerge and darkness slip away. Ethereal strands of mist glide from side to side. The air is distinctly cool. As fog escapes her mouth with each, blessed exhalation, she feels a chill on her cheeks. Low squawks and high tweets of flying creatures ring pleasingly in her ear. She glances down at the brown of her boots, firmly planted on earth, then lifts her head to the dim sky. An eagle soars by. She follows its magnificence and smiles at its outstretched wings. With a full heart, she looks out at the town and the bordering ocean below and is grateful for the gift of love.

It was an hour past the start time of *You Dig*'s annual fundraiser when Ideal arrived. After having the valet park his silver sports car, he took pictures on the black carpet. In addition to diamond stud earrings, he wore a gray blazer, white shirt, black jeans, and gray sneakers. Beneath the bill of his black cap were light-tinted shades, which gave an unhindered view of his entrancing eyes.

When he entered the backyard, he scanned the familiar space. The water of the bay shimmered from the sun's blazing light. Musicians in white jackets played mid-tempo jazz on an open-air stage near a pool. Floral arrangements of orchids and freesia towered on tables dressed in pressed linens. Most notable, however, were the famous faces that occupied sections of the manicured lawn.

Although the place was crawling with likable personalities, there was only one person Ideal wanted to see. Unfortunately, she wasn't there. Days before the fundraiser, he drilled Rona on the list of attendees. The name he wanted to hear, Rona never mentioned.

Ideal had been thinking of Ireland ever since he saw her in France. He hoped when he returned home, he could put her out of his mind. He failed. Even during his busiest days, he stalked her social media accounts. The more he looked at her, the more he missed her, which troubled him greatly.

Ideal was a celebrity among celebrities. With every few steps he took at the event, men and women approached him. The former sought his advice on their so-called original schemes. The latter sought an invitation to keep him company. When he finally got a moment free, he looked around for Dig. He spotted him at the bar, taking two glasses of cognac from a bearded bartender.

"You can pass me one of those," Ideal said, walking up to the counter.

Knowing the voice all too well, Dig turned around with a smile. "Here," he said, passing Ideal a glass.

Ideal got a whiff of the sweet smelling drink then took a swig. "You got a good turnout."

"You know it," Dig said, proudly. He leaned his back against the counter to face the numerous guests then glanced over Ideal. "That's a smooth looking jacket."

"I do what I can. You know what I'm saying?" Ideal said, giving his lapel a tug.

"Those are some nice kicks too. They're not as nice as mine, but they're nice."

"You better take a break from gulping that yac. It's impairing your vision."

"Oh, I see just fine," Dig said, lifting up his shades and looking down at Ideal's shoes.

"Then you should see that my kicks are embarrassing yours."

As the two of them smiled, an authorized photographer rushed over and snapped pictures of them. "So do me a favor," Dig said, changing gears. "Take a walk around here and buy everything."

"As always," Ideal replied, prepared to make a significant contribution as he had done many years before. He began to walk away but then turned back to Dig. "Hey, where's Rona?"

Dig shrugged his big, broad shoulders. "She's running around here somewhere with Ireland."

Ideal's lean body froze. He must have heard Dig wrong or maybe Dig had it wrong. Perhaps Rona was with someone else and Dig mixed up the names. Ideal had to be sure. "Did you say, Ireland?" he asked, listening intently for Dig's response.

"Yea, a weird name like yours, right?" Dig replied. Believing Ideal had no idea who Ireland was, he went on to clarify. "She was in Rona's movie at the festival. She played the main guy's sister. Remember?"

The pace of Ideal's pulse could have surpassed the speed of a trained mustang. The realization that Ireland was there sent his head spinning in several directions. Seeing her again was something he had been wanting for days. Although he became excited, he also felt tense. He still didn't know what to say to her, but he did know one thing. He would no longer put off meeting her. They would soon stand face to face. "Yea, I remember," he replied.

"Rona's all into her."

"Why?" Ideal asked, wondering what Rona saw in her.

"I don't know, but she likes her so much she's letting her stay with us tonight. Now, you know that's serious."

"She's staying here?"

"Yep."

Ideal was shocked. Rona had to thoroughly trust Ireland if she was letting her stay in their home. No one stayed in their homes except Dig's mother. Fortunately for Ideal, Ireland staying there meant he could see her all night. He instantly made plans to do so. "Alright, let me go spend this money."

With a nod, Dig tapped his glass against Ideal's. "Do it well."

When Ideal walked away, Ireland was the only thing on his mind. He was determined to find her immediately. His eyes darted from left to right and zoned in on every inch of the yard until at last, he saw her.

Never did the sight of someone cause Ideal to feel so consumed. The look of her lit him up. She was standing with Rona, admiring a piece of art and looking as attractive as she had before. Wearing a shredded, white dress, her feet were in a pair of indigo heels that played well with her mix of cobalt jewelry. He didn't know if it was Ireland's own taste or the work of her personal stylist, but as a man in fashion, Ideal thought she had incredible style.

With pure pleasure, he stood perusing her until all of a sudden, her eyes met his. Needing her to feel the vigor of his desire, he sharpened his ravenous stare. Second upon second crept by as they became entrenched with each other's gaze. An entire minute later, Ireland ended their engagement and redirected her eyes to the painting before her.

Desperately wanting back the attention she had just bestowed, Ideal delayed no more. Confidently, he walked over and stood right beside her. When she happened to look up, he could tell she was surprised to see him inches from her shoulder. Being close to her made it clear that she was more mesmerizing than he thought. His eyes could do nothing but peer deeply into hers. Her eyes returned the favor. Silently, they stood still, fascinated by each other.

Soon Rona looked away from the painting and noticed Ideal. “Hey, Deal,” she said, taking a few steps toward him and giving him a hug. “How are you doing?”

“I’m good,” he said, giving Rona a fleeting look before staring back at Ireland.

“I’m sure Dig’s glad you and your wallet are here.”

“Yea, he gave me that impression.”

“So what have you bid on?”

“Nothing yet.” Still focused on Ireland, he added, “I’m just getting started.”

“Well, you should look at this painting. It’s so gripping. Ireland said it reminds her of a play. Oh, wait,” Rona said, shifting gears. “Have you met Ireland?”

Ideal stared into Ireland’s dark eyes. “No.”

“This is my friend, Ireland Rochelle. She was in *Less Loyalty* with me.” Rona then turned to Ireland. “Ireland, this is Ideal.”

Ireland’s body grew so hot, she hoped Ideal couldn’t see the perspiration building on her cheeks. He had finally made his way over to her and she was taken by him. His eyes were seductively narrow and the look in them was tempting. Aside from his lips being handsomely shaped, his brass colored skin was the smoothest she had seen on a man with such masculinity. His presence was irrefutably powerful. “Hi,” she managed to say softly.

Oddly enough, hearing Ireland speak to him, made Ideal feel special. Just as softly, he replied, “Hi.”

“I’m sure you know who he is, right?” Rona asked Ireland.

Of course, Ireland knew who Ideal was. She had loved his music and his looks for years, but she didn’t need him to know that. “Yea,” she answered, simply.

“It’s nice to meet you,” he said, restraining himself from reaching for her hand. He knew he’d hold it too long.

“You too.”

"So, Deal, I think you should bid on this painting," Rona said, sliding her arm around his neck. The painting was of a small boy sitting alone in a boat in the middle of a river.

Ideal glanced at the painting then watched Ireland studying it. "Do you like it?" he asked.

When Ireland didn't hear Rona respond, she got the feeling he was seeking her opinion. "Who, me?" she asked, looking back at the serious look in his eyes.

"Yea, you."

"Yea," she said, eyeing the large work of art again. "It seems bittersweet."

"Buy it, Deal," Rona piped in.

"Alright."

"Thank you," she said, adding a bow. "Come on Ireland, let's go get a drink."

Ideal watched Ireland glide all the way to the bar. As she waited for her wine, she glanced back in his direction, and he made it clear that his examination of her would be ongoing. During the next few hours, their eyes continued to meet and each time they locked, they were more difficult to release.

The live auction was great fun and tremendously profitable. Among the donated items, was an autographed motorcycle, dinners at upscale restaurants, and a seven-day stay at a Caribbean resort. Whereas Ideal won a few times, each opening bid was out of Ireland's budget, therefore, she stuck to the silent auction.

After a lavish six-course meal was served, guests were given a treat. What they thought was a break for the jazz musicians turned out to be a performance by Dig and a few of the teenagers benefiting from the event. Alongside their idol, the teens rapped some of Dig's hits as well as their own songs and impressed the accomplished crowd.

Once the show was over, Dig thanked everyone for attending and participating in the bidding. His staff then announced the highest bidders of the silent auction. Ideal obtained more objects, one being the painting he viewed with Ireland, while she won tickets to an orchestra and ballet. The fact that she won two tickets for each event made Ideal wonder who would accompany her. He had to find out if she was dating someone or even worse, in love with someone.

The winner of the raffle won a tour of Napa Valley and was so ecstatic with her prize, Rona and Ireland laughed deliriously, determining the woman was a drunk. It amused Ideal to see Ireland laughing so hard. She actually had to wipe tears from her eyes. Even though she was beautiful, she knew how to let loose and have fun.

He had gone out with many beautiful women that took themselves much too seriously. They walked around boulder-faced, not wanting to do anything because it would somehow mess up their hair, nails or clothes. They wouldn't put on a pair of sneakers in order to ride a bike or slip on a pair of flats to take a long walk, and they certainly didn't laugh out loud. Ideal couldn't stand women like that. Though he enjoyed the finer things in life, he had always been a guy with a knack for having fun. On the minuscule chance that he'd ever get a girlfriend, she would have to be a woman that loved his playfulness.

When the guests were wished a good night, they left lugging gift bags, centerpieces, and winnings. After all of them had gone, only one guest other than Ireland remained. Ideal stood at the bay's edge talking with Dig, who puffed on a cigar. As the staff broke down the last of the equipment, Ideal watched Ireland and Rona make their way toward a door to the house. Rona quickly turned around and yelled, "Goodnight, Deal!"

Ideal thought of yelling back the phrase, but knew it was pointless. He wasn't going anywhere.

"I'm going in too," Dig said, extending his hand to Ideal. "I'll get with you later this week."

"Hey, I'm going to come in for a while. I need a favor from you."

"After the money you spent tonight, name it."

"It's going to sound crazy," Ideal said, preparing him.

"What's up?"

"I need you to leave me alone with Ireland."

"What?" Dig asked, thrown by the statement that had come from left field.

"I need you to leave me alone with Ireland."

Dig looked at his friend then cracked a smile. "Why would you need me to do that?" he asked, suspecting the reason.

"Come on, Dig," Ideal said, knowing Dig was giving him a hard time.

"No, you come on. Why would you need me to do that?" he asked with a wider smile.

"Why do you think?"

Torturing Ideal was too fun to resist. "Look, I don't know if I'm going to be able to help you out tonight if I don't have a clear understanding of why you want to be alone with her. You know what I'm saying? I mean, Rona's attached to her hip so it might be hard for me to pull my girl away."

Giving in to Dig's game, Ideal offered more information. "I want to talk to her for a while."

"About what?"

"Come on, Dig!"

"Alright, alright," Dig said, laughing at Ideal's impatient reaction. "I'll get you some time with her. But just so you know, you're going to have problems with Rona if you mess over Ireland."

"It's not like that."

"Uh huh," Dig said, dismissing Ideal's comment. "Let's go."

"Hold up. Give me a minute," Ideal said, removing his blazer and sunglasses then taking a deep breath.

"I know you're not scared to go talk to some girl."

"No, I just need a minute."

Chapter 5

The day had been long and loud, which made Ireland weary. Sitting alone on the family room sofa, she felt heavy like a wheelbarrow weighed down with steel. Grateful the guests were gone, she waited for Rona to return to the room so she could bid her goodnight. While she tried to channel her thoughts on the success of the evening, they insisted on darting back to stirring images of Ideal.

Although she was shocked he finally spoke to her, she was puzzled when he so quickly reverted back to silence. He managed to make her feel both desired and ignored. Because of their never-ending eye contact, she wondered if he felt a rare connection with her or if he engaged in the same eyeballing sport with other women on other occasions.

"I'm glad you came," Rona said, sitting beside Ireland.

"So am I," Ireland replied. Even though she went kicking and screaming to events, she usually ended up having a nice time.

"Now, I know you saw what Sylvia had on. Tell me what you thought about it."

Ireland covered her mouth with both hands then spoke through them. "My lips are sealed."

"Tell me," Rona demanded, grabbing Ireland by the wrists and trying to pull her hands down. "Tell me."

As Ireland held on tight and shook her head, they laughed uncontrollably. They were still screaming with amusement when Dig and Ideal walked into the room.

"I see you guys are still at it," Dig said, referring to their mirth, which halted the moment he spoke.

Ireland was floored to see Ideal. She figured he'd gone and taken his hypnotic eyes with him.

"I thought you left, Deal," Rona said, releasing her hold on Ireland.

Answering on his behalf, Dig said, "I told him to stay and hang out for a while."

"Oh," Rona said, watching them sit on the sofa across from her and Ireland. "Well, everything turned out really nice."

"And really profitable," Dig added with a wink. Knowing Ideal was observing Ireland, Dig decided to get her to talk. "So did you enjoy yourself, Ireland?"

Ireland was surprised she heard a word Dig said. The beating of her heart seemed so loud it should've drowned him out. Ideal's gaze still hadn't let up. Nervously, she answered, "I did, especially your performance."

"Aw, you don't have to say that."

"It's true. I love that I got to see you in a smaller setting."

"You'll have to see Deal do his thing next," he said, looking at Ideal slyly. "Where's your next intimate spot?"

"Vegas," Ideal answered.

"You should get Ireland a ticket."

Ireland didn't want Ideal to feel any obligation to her. Immediately, she spoke up. "No, you don't have to do that."

Pleased she was addressing him, he replied, "I wouldn't mind unless you wouldn't want to come."

Though she was hesitant to reassure him, she did. "I would come."

"Have you ever been to one of Deal's shows?" Rona asked.

Ironically, Ireland hadn't. On three separate instances she had intentions of going, but each time something prevented her from making it. "No."

"You're going to love it. Maybe me and Dig can go too."

"Yea, maybe. I got to go check on something," Dig said, rising to his feet and strolling out of the room. He went into his office, grabbed his laptop computer, and carried it into the master bedroom. A few minutes later, he yelled, "Rona!"

"What?" she yelled back.

"Come here for a second," he replied, knowing full well he planned to keep her from returning.

Ireland felt pure panic but hid it with all her might. The thought of being left alone with Ideal terrified her. She wanted to fall on her knees and beg Rona not to go, but she knew the action would look ludicrous.

"I'll be right back," Rona said, before leaving the room.

Up until that moment, Ireland found safety in glancing at Rona and Dig. With them gone, she stared at the floor, but could only do so for so long. Eventually, she lifted her chin and looked straight ahead at Ideal. In his eyes was the trenchant stare he had been consistent in giving her.

Although Ideal could go longer without uttering a word, he ended the cumbersome silence by asking a question he knew the answer to. "So what did you get from the silent auction?"

It was hard to believe that Ideal's popular voice was actually speaking to her. "Tickets to an orchestra and a ballet."

"An actress going to an orchestra and a ballet. You must really like the arts."

"I do."

"Why?"

"I like lovely things. I think about them and pay attention to them whenever I can."

"So what else is lovely, besides your character's name?"

"You remember my character's name?" she asked, thrown by his knowledge.

"There's no way I could forget it."

Although it took a moment for her to get back on track, eventually, she did. "Well . . . a ton of things are lovely."

"Like?"

"Cathedrals, sculptures, paintings, clothing, pieces of furniture. But I think nature is the most beautiful. It keeps me happy to be alive and well." Feeling a rise of self-consciousness, Ireland wondered if she had bored him by rambling. "Was that too much?"

"Not at all. I asked." Ideal felt even more drawn to her. She had a depth that he found alluring.

"Well, let me ask you something," she said, feeling a bit more at ease with him.

"What's up?"

"Have you ever been to a ballet?"

"No, but I'd go if I was invited."

A flash of heat hit Ireland's body. It sounded like he wanted to go with her, but she couldn't risk inviting him and getting rejected. "Well, that's good, you're not closed off to it."

"Did you get two tickets to each show?"

"Yea."

Needing to know if she had a boyfriend, he asked a logical question. "So who are you going to take?"

"I'll probably take my best friend to the orchestra and if Rona has the time, I'll go with her to the ballet."

Ideal wasn't satisfied with the answer. It was still possible that she had a man. In a manner more straightforward, he asked, "You're boyfriend doesn't like the arts?"

The question had little finesse. It was obvious he wanted to know if she was single. Leery of what he'd ask next, she answered him honestly. "I don't have a boyfriend."

Ideal was filled to the rim with relief but determined to hide his elation. "How does a pretty woman like you not have a boyfriend?"

Ideal Morris called her pretty. She wanted him to repeat it. "I don't have time for a relationship."

"If Dig and Rona have time, you have time," he challenged. If he ever chose to pursue her, he wouldn't accept her not making time for him. Deciding not to press her, he moved on. "So you're staying here tonight?"

"Yea, Rona kind of made me."

"Kind of how she made me buy that painting?"

Ireland couldn't stop herself from laughing and Ideal couldn't stop his heart from falling for her smile. When it faded he knew he had to see it again.

"I guess so," she said, agreeing Rona had a knack for twisting arms.

"Glad you know your new friend is bossy."

Smiling at the validity of his statement, she added, "She's kind and generous too."

"She must think the same about you for her to invite you to stay here."

"Maybe."

"It's no maybe. Rona doesn't let anybody stay with her and Dig except his mom."

"Really?" Ireland had assumed Rona extended the invitation to plenty of people since she was so quick to offer her one.

"Yea, she doesn't really have any family or friends."

"Well, I know that she was an only child and her adoptive parents died in a car accident when she was seventeen."

"And at eighteen her career took off and she's been working ever since. She's been famous for years so it's hard for her to trust people in order to make friends."

"I get that."

"So what is it about you that makes her like you so much?"

"I don't know."

"You have that effect on everybody you meet?"

"What effect?"

"Having them really like you."

"No. Everybody doesn't like me," she said, recalling people in the past that didn't care for her.

"That's hard to believe."

"Why? You don't even know me."

"There's just something about you," he said, studying her face.

Ireland didn't know if she was supposed to feel flattered or teased. She did know, however, that Rona had been gone too long.

Noticing her discomfort, Ideal moved to simpler territory. "I'd never seen you before France. Is this your first movie?" As a result of his dutiful, online research, he already knew it wasn't, but wanted to hear her talk more about herself.

Thankful for the new topic, Ireland answered, "No, but the others were low budget films so they didn't get media attention."

"How long have you been acting?"

"All of my life. I did a play in elementary school and never stopped. Well, actually, I stopped for a while when I was twelve, but I ended up going back to it."

"So you're living your dream?"

"I am. It's crazy being able to."

"Yea, it is."

"When did you get into music?"

"I've loved it ever since I can remember, but I started creating it in high school."

"Do you remember your first song?"

"Yep, I sang it in a talent show during my freshman year. It was called *Mind Your Business.*" Ireland began giggling and although he loved the sound of it, he wondered why. "What's so funny?"

"It was called *Mind Your Business*?" she asked.

"Yea."

"Are you any good at that?"

While smiling at her smile, he saw the irony. He had been interrogating her with endless questions. "I'm very good at that when I want to be."

"Oh, okay. When you want to be," she said, sarcastically.

"You think you're cute don't you?"

"No," she laughed.

"I do," he replied, sincerely, surprising them both with his admission. The lighthearted mood they had been enjoying instantly departed.

Sitting alone with Ideal, conversing with him and being flattered by him was hard to accept as a true experience. More unsettled, Ireland pulled her eyes away from his and focused on the bracelets encircling her wrist. "Thank you," she whispered, unsure of what else to say.

"Well, since you think I'm already in your business, I might as well keep going. I have a personal question I'd like to ask you." Ideal noticed the subtle way she held her breath in anticipation. "What's your favorite color?"

Tickled by his inquiry, Ireland smiled again. "Chartreuse," she joked.

"Chartreuse. That's mine too."

"It's black," she answered, honestly. "What's yours?"

"Black."

"Tell me the truth."

"I am."

"You're just trying to be like me."

"For real, it's black," he insisted, admiring the way she teased him. Being there with her felt like a destined moment in time. He had visualized them talking, but didn't know how it would actually turn out. It was better than he ever imagined. It was beyond incredibly good. Although their sexual chemistry was inconceivably strong, they spoke to each other and laughed with each other in a way that felt supportive, like best friends were meant to be. "Why do you like black?" he asked.

"Other than the fact that it's beautiful, it can be elegant, classy, and chic, but also sexy, strong, and edgy. It has complexities other colors don't have."

"That's well put," he said, appreciating how seamlessly she explained herself. "So if you weren't an actress, would you be a superhero, wild animal trainer, or professional whistler?"

Ireland took another look at Ideal and observed how gorgeous he was. Before they had spoken, he was insanely intimidating, but now she knew he was fun. "You're silly."

"Is that okay?"

"What do you mean?"

"You mind me being silly?"

"No, I don't mind. I like it."

Her confessing that she liked something about him put him on cloud ninety-nine and gave him more confidence to share what he felt. "I like a lot of things about you. Like your style, your smile, and your eyes." He stopped himself from mentioning her body but allowed her to see him look it over.

"That's sweet of you to say."

"I mean it," he said, nearly cutting her off. He didn't need her thinking he was being nice.

Ireland turned her head for a much-needed break from his dominating eyes. "I don't think Rona and Dig are coming back."

"It doesn't look like it," he said, hoping with all of his heart that she wouldn't end their time together.

"Well, I'm going to turn in. I have a flight tomorrow," she said, standing to her feet.

Ideal was crushed. The time he dreaded had arrived. "What time is your flight?"

"Three o'clock."

"You live in L.A.?"

"Yea, you live out here?"

"Sometimes. I have a few different places. I'm usually in New York."

Recognizing he was still sitting, she asked, "So are you leaving?"

"Yea, you mind walking me to the door?"

"No," she said, relieved he was going. It became scary getting to know such a painfully handsome man. She couldn't afford to develop feelings for him. They would only lead her to unrequited devotion. No amount of flirting could cause her to lose sight of that.

Side by side, they walked as if being led to their rightful execution, but rather than their hands and feet feeling bound, it was their hearts that seemed grasped by the heavy thread of iron links. The only sound heard was the gradual tapping of Ireland's blue heels.

After reaching the foyer, Ideal turned toward Ireland. When he felt the unyielding urge to kiss her, he knew he had to go. Through his shuddering breath, he said, "It was cool talking to you tonight."

"It was cool talking to you too."

Right away their desire made them afraid. Ideal afraid of what he might do and Ireland afraid of what she might allow.

"Goodnight," Ireland added, determined to hurry him along.

"Goodnight," Ideal replied. He then opened the door and closed it behind him.

Chapter 6

Dig awoke the next morning to the sound of his cell phone ringing. Lying next to Rona in their king size bed, he turned to look at the clock on his mirrored night table. It was nine o'clock and too early for him to rise. After the long day of fundraiser activities, he had been up all night having a romantic time with Rona. He reached for his cell, which sat next to the clock, and checked the caller I.D. It was Ideal. Dig wondered if something was wrong since Ideal never called him in the morning. Concerned, he answered the call. "What's up Deal? You alright?" he asked, gruffly.

"Am I alright?" Ideal mumbled. At his Miami penthouse, he stood in a pair of pajama pants, looking out at the bay from his master bedroom window. "I don't know, Dig."

"What's wrong?" Dig asked, letting the sheets slide down his bare chest as he sat up against layers of crisp, white pillows.

"All morning, I've been trying to convince myself not to call you, but here I am ringing your phone. I'm sorry, man."

"Don't worry about it. What's up?"

"I need to come over," Ideal said, cringing at the sentence he had just spoken.

"For what?"

"It's hard to say."

"What did you do?"

"Nothing. I haven't done anything crazy."

"Then why do you need to come over?"

"I'm messed up," he said, walking away from the window in frustration.

Dig didn't know what to think. Ideal was in no way acting like himself. He wasn't making any sense, which he always did. Dig hoped he wasn't having some kind of late surfacing breakdown. "Alright, come over. We'll talk when you get here."

"Alright." After hanging up, Ideal rushed to the bathroom and took a steaming hot shower, although, he could have used a cold one.

With a twitching hand, Ideal rang Dig and Rona's doorbell, which resonated loudly throughout the home. Shortly after, Dig opened the door and welcomed his friend inside. Right away, he examined Ideal's appearance. Fortunately, he looked healthy and well. Dressed meticulously, he wore a pair of blue shorts, a blue and yellow t-shirt, bright sneakers, and a baseball cap. Dig hadn't known what to expect and was calmed to see that Ideal looked his normal self.

"Come on," Dig said, leading the way to his office.

As Ideal walked through the house his senses grew sharper. Keenly alert, his eyes scanned each room he passed, but he saw only the grand furniture and accessories that filled them. Other than plants, he saw no sign of life. His nose smelled the mix of seasonings floating from the kitchen, where he heard food sizzling. When his ears picked up the distinct sound of high heels on the floor above him, his heart passed over a beat.

Dig closed the door to his wood-paneled office and sat in the tall, leather chair behind his desk. Ideal sat in a chair across from him, looked down at the area rug, and zoned out.

"What's going on with you?" Dig asked.

Ideal looked up from the floor. "You're going to think I'm crazy."

"Maybe, but I'll let you know after you tell me what's going on."

Reluctant to say the words, Ideal finally did. "I had to come over because I have to see Ireland again."

"Is that it?" Dig asked in disbelief.

"What do you mean, is that it?"

"Man, you're right. I think you're crazy," Dig replied, leaning back in his chair.

"Yea, well, I think so too."

"You had me thinking you got caught up in something serious or that you were losing your mind."

"I am," Ideal said, resting his head in his hands. "I am losing my mind. I haven't been able to get her out of my head since the premiere."

Surprised, Dig asked, "You were feeling her then?"

"Yea."

"Did you talk to her out there?"

"I didn't know how to approach her. I couldn't figure out what I wanted to say."

"What do you mean you couldn't figure out what to say? You talk to women all the time."

"Yea, but that's when I want to just take them out."

"So what do you want to do with Ireland?" Dig asked, raising his eyebrows.

"I don't know," Ideal said, shaking his head.

"You got to know, Deal."

"I don't."

"You've been thinking about her since the premiere. You saw her four hours yesterday and you still wanted time alone with her last night. You talked to her last night and then you wake my ass up this morning to get over here today. You got to know what you want."

"I don't," Ideal repeated in an aggravated tone.

"Alright, then go home."

"What?" Ideal said, alarmed.

"Go home. Leave without seeing her today."

"I can't."

"Why not?"

"I have to see her."

"Why?"

"I don't know, Dig!" he shouted. "I never felt like this before."

"Like what?"

"Sick to my stomach and out of control. I feel desperate like some chick. I hate this." Ideal noticed a broad smile stretch across Dig's face. "What the hell are you smiling at?"

"You talking like this," Dig said, chuckling. "Honestly, that's how I felt when I met Rona."

"So what am I supposed to do?"

"It depends on what you want."

"I don't know what I want."

"Yea, you do. You know exactly what you want you just don't want to admit it. Admit it."

Ideal fell silent. Struggling to say the words, he finally did. "I want to be with her. I want her to be mine - only mine."

"You willing to be only hers?" Dig asked, pointing out that Ideal had never been committed to anyone.

"You know that I've been to tons of countries and to every state in our own. I've seen thousands of beautiful women and I've gone out with a hundred of them. But I can honestly tell you that if I'm able to have Ireland, I won't touch anybody else."

"Damn, Deal. You might be in love."

"I can't be in love."

"You sure?"

The realization hit Ideal hard. He could be in love. He supposed many would say loving Ireland wasn't possible, but he knew his feelings were true. Dig knew they were true. After all, Dig had felt the same feelings for Rona and had been in love with her for years.

"So how did you get Rona to fall in love with you?" he asked, recognizing he needed Ireland to reciprocate his feelings.

"I went after her and didn't let up. You can't let up. This is real talk. You have to stay consistent. You have to keep going after her and even when you get her, you got to keep up what you did. If you're sporadic, you'll seem like every other dude she dated. When you tell her you're going to call, call. When you tell her you're going to be there, be there. When you tell her you're going to help out, help out. You got to blow her mind. She has to know you're serious if you want it to last."

"Alright," Ideal said, taking mental notes.

"Now, when you're with her, you have to cherish her and treat her like you'll never see her again. But when you're not with her, you have to give her room to do her thing. You've been at your dream, but she just got to hers, so you'll have to let her climb the ladder without getting in the way. If you get in the way of what she's striving for, she'll stop wanting you around. But like I said, whenever you are with her, you have to make her life better and more passionate and she'll want more of you, which is what you want. You feel me?"

Listening intently to every word Dig spoke, Ideal replied, "Yea." He knew Dig had a wonderful relationship with a wonderful woman and he made it look easy. If there was any man he should listen to about having a successful relationship it was Dig. The rest of his boys were still bachelors and wanted to keep it that way.

"We're about to have brunch with her before she leaves so you can eat with us."

"Should I ask her for her number?"

"Hold off on that until you get more time alone with her."

"What if that never happens?"

"It will," Dig said, moving to the office door. "Let's go to the other room. They'll be down in a minute."

Ideal and Dig walked to the family room and sat on the same sofa they had the night before. When Dig discussed a new hip hop artist that was on the horizon, Ideal tried hard to listen, but failed. All he did was anticipate seeing Ireland. When he heard the clicking of heels coming down the stairs, his pulse quickened.

"Dig, who was at the door?" Rona asked, stepping into the room. Before Dig could respond, she noticed Ideal. "Deal, did you spend the night on that couch?"

"Yea, it's pretty comfortable," he joked.

"I had him drop something off for me," Dig lied.

"This early?" Rona said, rolling her naked eyes. "Deal, you should've told him he was crazy. He could've waited a few more hours."

Another set of heels made their way down the staircase. Ideal held his breath until his heart jumped at the sight of Ireland walking into the room. She looked sexy wearing blue jeans, a tank top, and chunky-heeled sandals. Her hair was slightly pulled up in the front, showing more of her face that was framed by gold earrings. Her expression had been relaxed until she saw Ideal was there. She almost seemed frightened to see him.

"Hi Ireland," he said, standing to his feet, exhibiting he knew how to be a gentleman.

"Hi," she replied.

"Deal's going to eat with us," Dig said.

"Oh, good," Rona said, leading them all to the dining room.

Strategically, Ideal walked behind Ireland to get a full view of her moving in her jeans. When they arrived in the dining room, he sat across from her at the long table. On display were waffles, bacon, and eggs, turkey croissant sandwiches with avocado, mandarin salads sprinkled with shaved almonds, as well as a tray of kiwi and berries.

The conversation between the four of them was as vibrant as one would expect. Besides music, they spoke of restaurants, charities, politics, and design. While some moments of the discussion were motivational, many were downright funny. Through it all, the desire between Ideal and Ireland remained as steady as the flow of a full stream.

Ideal turned somber when it came time for Ireland to leave. He was tortured by the fact that he didn't know when he'd be near her again. Worried that it would be long, he hung his head low as he and his friends walked her outside. Rona's driver then whisked her away.

Chapter 7

Fresh from an orchestra's concert inside a striking hall, Ireland and Casey were all smiles as they entered a late-night lounge in Los Angeles. The harsh music was a vast contrast to the soft symphonies they had just enjoyed. Both wearing dresses accented with gold, they moved through the space of brick walls and concrete floors, until they reached a circular bar. Once they received their order of raspberry martinis, they sat on a dark, leather sofa and dove into conversation.

After talking candidly with Casey about work, dreams, friends, and family, Ireland could no longer justify omitting the mind-boggling experiences she had in France and Miami. She tried to convince herself that they were unnecessary to mention, but she couldn't shake the persistent feeling that she was keeping something from Casey. "I hate to even tell you this, but I know I should," Ireland began.

"What?" Casey asked, intrigued by the choice of words.

"I don't even know where to start. I could just state the facts, but then there's what I feel, and then there's what I think might be my delusions."

"And then there's confusion," Casey added, sarcastically. "What are you talking about?"

"Remember when you asked me if I saw Ideal in France?"

"Yea, you said you saw him at a party."

"Yea, but I didn't tell you that when I first saw him he was . . ."

"He was what?"

Rethinking her delivery, Ireland began again. "Do you know how sometimes you can feel somebody looking at you before you actually see them looking at you?"

"Yea."

"Well, I felt that way and when I turned to see who it was, it was Ideal. He was looking at me like . . ."

"Like what?" Casey said, hurrying Ireland along.

Ireland didn't want to sound like some young girl in a fantasy world. Carefully, she replied, "Like, intensely."

"Intensely how?"

"This is just how I felt. It doesn't mean it's how it was."

Fed up with her friend's delays, Casey spoke, sternly. "Intensely how, Ireland?"

"Intensely, like he was attracted to me," she said, embarrassed to have made the statement.

Casey's brown eyes widened as far as they could. "Are you serious?"

"I thought I was seeing things so I kept looking away, but every time I looked back at him, he was still staring at me."

"Are you serious?"

"I'm serious."

"Oh my God," Casey whispered, closing her eyes. "Did you stare back at him?"

"Most of the time."

"Oh my God. What was that like?"

"Outrageous. There were so many people at this party, I couldn't believe he noticed me."

"Now, wait, you told me you didn't meet him."

"I didn't. He never came over to talk to me."

"You should've gone over and talked to him."

Ireland fixed her face into a scowl. "Have you forgotten who you're talking to? You know I don't approach men."

"Ideal Morris isn't just some man. You should've made an exception to your little rule." Casey took needed gulps of her martini. "Well, at least you had a whole, dreamy night of him watching you."

"I'm not exactly finished," Ireland said, raising her glass to her glossy lips to take a sip.

"What do you mean?"

"I saw him the next day and he did the same thing."

"Tell me you're lying."

"I'm not. I was at a restaurant and he stared at me from the time I walked in to the second I walked out."

"You'd think a man like Ideal would at least walk over and say something since he spent so much time admiring the view."

"Well, I saw him two more times after that."

"What?" Casey shrieked. "I cannot believe you saw Ideal four different times and you didn't tell me. We're supposed to tell each other everything, especially, things like this."

"I know. I'm sorry. I was scared you'd think I was crazy," Ireland said, feeling bad that she had doubted her friend.

"I think you're crazy because you didn't tell me." In exasperation, Casey covered her purple rimmed eyes with her right hand then dropped it into her lap. "So he never spoke to you? Not even the third time?"

"Actually, the third time he did."

"What did he say?" Casey asked, leaning in closer to Ireland.

"I'll give you the short version."

"I don't want the short version. I want the long version, the extended version," Casey said, adamantly.

"If I give you that we'll be here all night."

"And?"

"And, I have an important audition tomorrow, I can't be tired."

"You have already held out on me. If you don't tell me every detail tonight, I'm going to strangle you right here in public."

Ireland replied with a drawn-out sigh. "I was at the fundraiser, looking at a painting with Rona –"

"Hold up," Casey interjected. "I need another drink for this." Leaping onto her spiked heels, she rushed over to the bar. When she returned, Ireland spilled every detail about the fundraiser, the conversation afterward, and the next afternoon. Casey was flabbergasted. "Wow, he really likes you," she said, her eyes abstaining from blinking.

"No, he doesn't."

"Don't play modest. You have to know he wants you."

"Wanting me and liking me are two different things."

"If he didn't like you, why would he ask if you're okay with him being silly?"

"I don't know," she said, fiddling with the clasp on her sequined purse.

"Well, if he asks you out, I'm going to pass out."

"He won't."

"How do you know?"

"Because he's had plenty of opportunities to and he hasn't. He hasn't even asked for my number."

"Maybe he's dating somebody that we don't know about and he needs to dump her first."

After smiling at Casey's joke, Ireland became grim. "I don't think he's really interested in me. Like a lot of guys, I think he enjoys flirting for the thrill of it. Maybe he was flirting with other women all along and I just didn't notice."

"I highly doubt that since every time you took a peek at him he was looking at you. But let's not forget the most important thing. If he was flirting with other women at the fundraiser, he could've left with one or two or a few of them and had a very interesting night. Instead, he stuck around to talk to you."

"But we don't know where he went afterward."

"But we do know where he went the next day. He went back to that house to see you."

"Okay Case," Ireland said, lifting up her hands. Any debate with Casey was a never-ending journey and Ireland wanted to skip the trip.

"If you ever hear from him or see him again, you better tell me ASAP."

"I will," Ireland acquiesced, certain neither would occur.

In the small, quiet office of a major Hollywood studio, Ireland stood in front of a panel steered by Michael Weston. In addition to Weston, there was a producer, a casting director, an assistant behind a camera, and another holding a script. There to audition for the role of an older businessman's girlfriend, Ireland was grateful the jitteriness she felt had transformed into an odd sense of calm. Wearing a sexy, on the brink of sleazy, short dress with a plunging neckline, she was as prepared as she could possibly be.

The male assistant holding the script adjusted his black-framed glasses then read aloud the very first line. Ireland replied softly, slightly restraining her flirty behavior. Without hesitation, she moved fluidly from one line to the next. After a few minutes of sweet gentility, she let forth a chilling strength then concluded with three words at an exceptionally low volume. When she was finished, the panel remained silent, tilting their heads in observation of her.

Ireland expected to be routinely thanked for coming in to read, but she wasn't. The only thing she heard was the ticking of a black and white clock that hung on a beige wall. She didn't know what the panel's silence meant, but she did know she had given her all. She kindly thanked them for the opportunity, gathered her things, and exited the room.

Jumping to his feet was Keith who had been sitting in the waiting room. "How did it go?"

"Good. They didn't say anything, but it felt right to me."

"Silence could be a good sign," he replied, before glancing at his watch. "Alright, get changed. We've got to get over to the agency."

Ireland went into the restroom, changed into a cream blouse and pant, and wiped away the red lipstick she had piled on for the audition. With a lack of time to pat herself on the back for an audition well done, she glided a gloss onto her lips then rushed out.

In the passenger seat of Keith's convertible, she watched as he meandered through traffic, intent not to keep her agent waiting. In the end, they were the ones that sat idly by while her agent finished a meeting with a more established client. Keith was upset that his time was being wasted, but Ireland couldn't have cared less. Her adrenaline had been pumping all day and she welcomed the unexpected time to be still. Thirty minutes later they were called into the office.

At an oval, glass desk, Ireland sat across from her agent, Rick, who grilled her about the audition. After the interrogation, she was relieved to hear him discuss other films she was being considered for. All peaked her interest until he introduced the role of a woman that was a nanny during the day and a prostitute at night.

"You have to be joking," she said, giving him a cold stare.

"I'm not, but hear me out," he said, raising his thin arms, on which the sleeves of his dress shirt were rolled up. "This is the kind of role that can get you recognized during award season."

"No, thank you."

"Let me tell you more about it before you shoot it down."

"You've told me enough."

"Think of how complex the character has to be."

"I am not portraying a prostitute this early in my career. Now, if years from now when I have two of every award then maybe I'll consider it."

"I'm going to hold you to that." Rick said, furrowing his blond eyebrows.

"Yea, be careful," Keith piped in. "Those awards will be here sooner than you think."

Soon Rick's fashion-forward assistant interrupted their meeting with a call from Michael Weston's office. He quickly picked up the line. "This is Rick."

Once Ireland heard who the call was from, she wondered which of Rick's other clients had business with Michael Weston. She listened for a name, but never heard one. When Rick hung up the phone, he smiled at her.

"What?" she asked.

"You did good, girl."

"What do you mean?"

"Weston wants you to come in again."

"Yes!" Keith said, pumping his fist.

"You're serious?" she asked.

"He wants to see you next week," Rick said, rocking in his leather chair.

"I've never gotten a call back this soon."

"Which means they liked what they saw so whatever you did, do it again. Don't go changing things," Rick warned, determined for Ireland to avoid shooting herself in the foot.

"You're going to get that part," Keith declared.

"Let's just take it one step at a time," Ireland replied. The prospect of being hired for the project was entirely exciting, but it was also becoming scary.

Ignoring her suggestion, Keith repeated himself. "You are going to get that part."

Chapter 8

In a Midtown Manhattan high rise was the bustling office of Ideal's fashion line, *Try Real.* At the head of the conference room's metal table sat Ideal, studying sketches for a new collection. He approved half of them, many of which he had personal input in designing. Several others, he directed to be embellished, simplified, or scrapped altogether.

Ideal was never on the fence when it came to his work. He knew exactly what he wanted and had no difficulty making decisions. Although he delegated plenty of responsibility and took accountability very seriously, his staff felt he was an appreciative person to work for. He gave them the utmost respect, freedom, and trust to do their jobs. He also never lost his temper. Like a pendulum, his mood swung steadily from quiet and contemplative to excited and energetic. His behavior was simple to predict and that particular day he was predominantly quiet.

After pushing away from the table, he walked over to a long rack, stuffed with colorful clothing. Routinely, he shoved hangers aside to inspect each article they held. When he came to a pink-collared shirt, he paused then lifted it from the rack. With a sliver of a smile, he promised his team they'd see him in the piece a few times. He continued on, periodically assigning tasks to various employees until he reached the rack's opposite end. Before adjourning the meeting, he thanked everyone for their dedication then ordered them to enjoy happy hour on the company's dime.

Once he reached his private office, he stood at the window and looked out at the city. His staff believed his mind was on the current collection, but in actuality, it was on his plans for the upcoming evening.

In a slender, softly lit hallway, Ideal anxiously examined the condition of his appearance. Relaxed were his black jeans and unblemished were his exclusive, red sneakers. Harshly, he removed a lone piece of lint from the t-shirt he wore beneath a thin jacket. As he tilted the bill of his bright, red cap toward his right brow, his left earring gleamed from the lighting overhead. After glancing at the time on his watch, he knocked on the prominent door before him. A minute later, it was opened by Dig.

"Is she here?" Ideal whispered.

"Good to see you too," Dig replied. "No, she's not here yet."

"Good," he said, exhaling sharply. "I wanted to get here first." He hadn't seen Ireland in weeks but in a matter of minutes, he would.

"Come on," Dig said, leading him into the large living room with views of the Hudson River. They sat side by side in taupe, chenille chairs. "So are you ready to see her?"

"I'm dying to see her, but I don't know if I'm exactly ready," Ideal said, rocking his leg from left to right. His feelings were deeper than he wanted them to be and he worried they wouldn't be reciprocated. He even began to doubt the chemistry he shared with Ireland. Maybe she was simply a really nice person and was being polite the night they talked in Miami. Maybe she was attracted to him, but would never bother dating a musician.

"Don't worry about it. Whether she's feeling you or not, you just have to be persistent. I don't have to tell you how far that gets you in life."

"I guess."

"You guess? Who's in the other room?" Dig asked, referring to Rona.

"You're right."

"Speaking of Rona, you should tell her."

"Tell her what?"

"Tell her why you're really here. She could be a big help to you."

"I don't know," Ideal said, rubbing his chin.

"I think she'll be happy about it. She'll probably put in a good word for you."

"Well, I could use that."

"Tell her."

Right on cue, Rona walked into the room wearing a trendy teal dress. "Tell who what?" she asked, walking over to Ideal to give him a hug.

"Deal needs to tell you something."

"What is it?" Rona asked, sitting on the sofa.

Slowly, Ideal spoke through his apprehension. "The night of the fundraiser, I didn't stick around afterward to talk to Dig. I didn't go back to the house the next day to give something to Dig. And I'm not here right now to see Dig."

Fixing her lovely face into a frown, Rona asked, "You came to see me?"

"No."

"Then who are you here to see?" The only other person at the home was the chef and Ideal had his own.

Ideal glanced over at Dig then answered, "Ireland."

"Ireland? Why do you want to see her?" she asked, squinting her eyes.

"I have feelings for her."

Rona was as alarmed as she was dumbfounded. "What?"

"I have feelings for her."

"What kind of *feelings*?" Rona asked, her irritation unmistakable.

"Real ones."

"Do you even know what real feelings are, Deal?"

In an instant, Dig jumped in. "Come on, Rona. Listen to him."

"I am listening," she replied without looking Dig's way. "Deal, I love you, but I know you. Your *feelings* lead you to take a girl out, screw her, and move on. Then she sits around somewhere pining away for you. I'm not letting you do that to Ireland."

"That's not what I want to do to her."

"Then what do you want to do?"

Feeling pressured, Ideal struggled to say the right words but ended up saying nothing.

"See," Rona continued, "You don't even know. Keep going out with those random chicks and leave Ireland alone." Standing up, she added, "You should go."

Ideal shook his head. "I can't. I need to see her."

"How did you even know she would be here today?"

"I told him," Dig admitted.

Rona shot Dig a glare. "You told him when to come over here so he could play my friend?"

"He doesn't want to play her. You'd know that if you'd give him a chance to explain."

Not done with her sarcasm, Rona sat back down. "Would you like another chance to explain, Deal?"

Leaving his seat, Ideal sat on the sofa next to Rona. "I understand why you're acting the way you are. I change women like I change shoes. I've never been serious about anyone, so you're being a good friend to Ireland. You don't want me to hurt her. But I can guarantee you, I won't hurt her. I'm serious about her. I've never felt anything like this for anybody and I've been feeling it since I was in France. I truly want to be with her - only her."

Utterly surprised by how genuine he was, Rona didn't know how to react. She had never once in all the years she had known Ideal, heard him speak of a woman in such a way. Studying the look in his eyes, she stated the obvious. "You're serious."

"I am."

"He is," Dig confirmed.

"I can't believe it," she said, throwing her lean arms around him. Joyously, she swayed her shoulders then released him. "You guys are going to be so good together."

Though he was relieved with the change in Rona's attitude, Ideal was careful not to get his hopes high. "Well, first, I've got to see if she's willing to give me the time of day."

"Why wouldn't she? You're good looking, crazy talented, fun, and filthy rich."

"I think Deal needs you to tell Ireland all of that," Dig relayed.

"You want me to?" Rona asked, her eyes scanning Ideal's expression.

"You don't have to say that exactly, but you could talk me up so when I ask her out she doesn't turn me down."

"I'll talk to her, but even if I didn't, she wouldn't turn you down."

"How do you know?" Ideal asked, hoping it meant Ireland had said flattering things about him.

"How many women that you've asked out, have rejected you in the past twenty years?"

"None," he answered. He hadn't experienced rejection since he'd made his first hit.

"I rest my case."

"But Ireland seems different."

"Oh, she's different, but not *that* different."

After listening for a while, Dig made a suggestion. "So how about me and Deal join you guys at the restaurant tonight? That way Deal can spend some time with her."

"That's perfect. I'll text you when the ballet's over," Rona replied, her matchmaking wheels turning. "Then after dinner, we'll split and have Deal take her to her hotel."

"See Deal, she got your back," Dig said with a nod.

A second later, the doorbell rang and Ideal's heart began to wallop.

Rona sprung to her feet. "That's her. I told him to let her up," she said, referring to their building's concierge. In great haste, Rona left the room and let Ireland inside. Once Ireland took a few moments to admire the foyer, she followed Rona into the living room and immediately saw Ideal. Shocked, she gasped and froze in her tracks.

With feeble knees, Ideal stood and restrained himself from hugging her hello. He was amazed that he could continue to be stumped by her face. He grew more attracted to her each time he saw her. She looked especially pretty due to the light pink dress she wore. Its short skirt was filled with frills, balanced by silver pumps and her hair, which hung sleek and straight.

Amused by the two of them gazing at each other, Dig winked at Rona then ended the silence.

"What's up, Ireland?"

Shaking, she looked at Dig. "Hi."

"You remember Deal, right?" he asked, pointing at his best friend.

Looking back into Ideal's eyes, she said, "Yea. Hi."

Filled with fire, Ideal replied, "Hi," staring at the woman he had longed to see for weeks.

"So how have you been?" Dig asked her.

"I've been good. What about you?"

"I can't complain."

Looking around the room, Ireland said, "No, you can't. Not with a place like this." While moving toward the window, she added, "And not with a view like that. What do you guys do, hog up all of the waterfront views wherever you go?"

"We do what we can. You know what I'm saying?"

"What time did you get in today?" Rona asked.

"Seven."

"That's early. Did you get some sleep?"

"Well, I got some rest. Luckily, there was a room ready when I checked in."

"I still say you should've stayed here."

"I'm not imposing on you again."

"Blah, blah, blah," Rona said. "Let me give you a tour and then we'll go."

"It was good seeing you guys," Ireland said, before turning to exit the room.

"You too," Ideal replied, pleased she had no clue they'd see each other in a few hours.

As Ireland and Rona, along with Rona's bodyguard, Sampson, waited outdoors to be admitted into the theater, they listened to the shouts of Rona's fans in the plaza. After leaving the loud admiration behind, they presented their tickets, entered the curvy-lined lobby, and were directed to the right corridor. Happily welcomed by a crooked-toothed usher, the ladies were then escorted to their secluded, box seats while Sampson remained near the section's slim door. Unlike the yells heard outside, there was a steady rumble of murmurs as fellow attendees noticed Rona's presence.

Because she'd only spent time with Rona on the set of their film and during work-related engagements, Ireland hadn't experienced Rona's fame in the normal world. The thought of hanging out with a celebrity was so daunting, it nearly discouraged Ireland from inviting Rona to the ballet. Though she summoned up the courage and did so, she worried the concentration on them would be unrelenting. It was. As practically every head in the theater was lifted and focused to the right, Ireland felt as if she were a part of the show people came to see.

After pretending to read the program, Rona closed it and turned toward Ireland. In the most open and innocent fashion, she asked, "So what do you think of Ideal?"

Taken aback by the random question, Ireland became flustered. The two of them had never discussed Ideal. She was unsure of how to answer, but there was no way she was going to unleash the many things she thought about him. "He's nice," she replied at last.

"Nice? That's all?" Rona prodded.

"He's silly."

"He's silly and nice. That's all?"

Due to Rona's dissatisfaction, Ireland grew skeptical. "Why are you asking me about Ideal?"

"You've become my friend so I was wondering what you thought of my other friend," Rona said with a smirk.

Ireland watched the twinkle in Rona's eye. "I don't think that's why you're asking."

"I don't think that's all you think of him," Rona said, challenging her. "So you tell me more and I'll tell you more."

"Never mind," Ireland said, uninterested in sharing more of her opinions.

"It's funny," Rona said, slyly, "every woman I know thinks Ideal is really attractive and sexy. Every woman except you."

"I didn't say I didn't think he was attractive and sexy."

"But you didn't say he was. You didn't say one word about his appearance. Why is that?"

"What are you a detective?"

"Just answer the question."

"Why are you questioning me?"

"Do you think Ideal's attractive?"

"This is a ridiculous conversation," Ireland said, turning her attention to the audience members she'd been trying to ignore.

"Do you?"

Looking back at Rona, Ireland casually lifted her hand. "Yes."

"Sexy?"

"Oh, come on, Rona. That's the same thing."

"Sexy?" Rona repeated, not missing a beat.

"Yes."

"Then why did you only say he was nice when I first asked?"

"Because he's your friend, I figured you would rather hear something about his character than his looks."

"Uh, huh."

"Why don't you answer a question? Why are you asking me about him?" For the first time, Ireland worried she was doing a terrible job hiding her reaction to him.

After taking a beat, Rona said with a smile, "He likes you."

Ireland shivered at Rona's words then swallowed to alleviate her suddenly parched throat. "What do you mean, he likes me?"

"You know what I mean."

"No, I don't." Despite what she hoped Rona meant, Ireland needed urgent clarification.

"I mean, he likes you. He's feeling you. He's into you."

"Where did you get that from?" Ireland asked, assuming Rona had noticed the eye contact between them.

"He told me."

As Ireland's jaw dropped, a bolt of heat surged through her. "He told you what?"

"That he has real feelings for you."

The concept was far too improbable for Ireland. If Rona had said he was attracted to her or wanted to go out with her, she could've believed it, but she couldn't accept that he had *real feelings* for her. It sounded like some tired line, which made Ireland suspicious. Immediately, her guard went up. "He's lying."

Rona was appalled at the accusation, "No, he's not. He wants to be with you."

The plethora of women she'd seen with Ideal entered Ireland's mind. She hated the thought of being another face in his expanding portfolio. "Me and who else? Half of Hollywood?"

"Oh, I totally get how you would think that. I thought the same thing. I've watched Deal date so many chicks that I really didn't think he'd ever get serious about anybody, but now he is." Rona paused for a moment of reflection. "You probably know that Dig was just like Deal. He messed with ten women at a time, but somehow for me, he changed. And Deal wants to change for you."

"That can't be true," Ireland said, doing her best to drown out the fluff Rona was talking.

"Why can't it?"

"He doesn't even know me."

"Okay, let's test your theory. Do you have any feelings for him?"

Ireland instantly looked away. As torturous as it was to admit to Rona and herself, she replied, "I guess."

"Now, how can that be? You don't even know him."

"Okay, you made your point. But having feelings doesn't mean he wants to change for me."

"Trust me, he does. He already has."

"We've only talked twice."

"Well, after dinner tonight, you guys will have talked three times. Deal and Dig are going to meet us at the restaurant."

"What?" Ireland said, her eyes widening with panic. The house lights then flickered and people rushed to their seats. "When did the two of us going to dinner turn into four of us going?"

"When I found out Deal has a major thing for you."

"Don't tell me you're going to be in matchmaker mode from now on."

"I just want you to give Deal a chance. Don't be scared."

"That's easier said than done."

"You don't think I know that? I'm speaking from experience."

Within minutes, the lights went out, the curtain opened, and tutu-clad ballerinas appeared onstage. Throughout the performance, Ireland's heart mirrored the leaps of the dancers.

At an upscale, Italian restaurant on the upper east side of Manhattan, Dig and Ideal joined Rona and Ireland for a late-night dinner. Miniature flames wavered from rock-cut candle holders, and the sound of opera could faintly be heard among clanking goblets.

Resembling the last meal they shared, Ideal sat across from Ireland, but on this particular night, he felt a different vibe. Though their mutual attraction was as vital as ever, it seemed she was examining him. At one point, as he went to steal a glance at her, he discovered her attention was already fixed on him. He supposed her intrigue was due to Rona's flattering words.

The hour went by too quickly and dinner was over in a flash. When the dessert plates were gone, Ideal paid the bill then offered to drive Ireland to her hotel. With no time to create an excuse as Rona and Dig urged her along, Ireland accepted the offer.

Upon exiting the restaurant, they encountered paparazzi that had grown within the last half hour. Sensing Ireland's tentativeness, Ideal put his hand on the small of her back and guided her around the corner. When they reached his black sports car, he opened the passenger door and watched her ease into the seat. He then moved to the other side, got behind the wheel, and drove away.

The woman who had taken charge of his mind was now in his car, riding next to him. Ideal was amazed by that fact, but the private time he'd just gained with her was short and critical. He chose not to turn on any music, letting the muffled sounds of the street serenade them. Holding his breath, he looked over at her. She kept her focus straight ahead.

"So you've been to New York before?" he asked, pleased the question caused her to look his way.

"Yea, a lot of times."

"For work?"

"Pleasure."

"Too bad I never ran into you." He gazed at her so seductively, she directed her eyes to the passenger window. "So you must like it out here."

"I love it."

"Would you ever live here?"

"I've always wanted to, but I need to keep my place in L.A. If I could afford two homes, I'd get a place here in a heartbeat."

An unexpected thought occurred to Ideal. He could buy her a New York home and get it done in the heartbeat she mentioned. As excited as it made him, he knew better than to voice his idea. It was a sure way to have her run for the hills. "Well, if you keep on your grind with acting, I'm sure you'll be able to."

"Thanks," she said. "I hope so."

"Had you been to France before the festival?"

"No, that was my first time. It was beautiful from what I could see."

"You didn't have time to see much?"

"Every single thing I did revolved around the film so all I saw were hotels and theaters."

"You'll have to go back then," he said, picturing the two of them there together.

"Yea, that would be nice."

As Ideal got close to the hotel, he realized he had to see her again before she returned to Los Angeles. "How long are you going to be here?"

"Three more days."

"You have a lot of plans?"

"Not a lot," she answered, cautiously.

Not far from the front entrance of the hotel, Ideal found a space along the curb and parked. He hoped he could talk longer with Ireland, but when he turned toward her, she picked up her purse.

"Would you like me to walk you to your room?" he asked.

"Uh . . . no. I'm fine."

Her alarmed expression was easy to read. He couldn't let her think he was being presumptuous, assuming he could get into her room then get into something else. He was purely being protective. "It's late. I just want to make sure you get back safely."

"Well, thanks, but I'm okay. Thank you again for dinner and for driving me here."

"Anytime."

"Have a good night." Ireland turned and reached for the handle.

"Ireland?" Ideal said, interrupting her action.

"Yea?" she replied, turning back to him.

"Can I see you again before you leave?"

She hesitated. "Maybe."

Maybe was in no way an acceptable answer for Ideal. Just as he began to pry, his cell phone rang.

"I'll let you get that," she said, turning to leave again.

"It can wait," he replied, ignoring the call. "What are you doing tomorrow?"

"Having a spa day."

"All day?"

"All day."

"And then?"

"I'm going to walk the city and pop into a few stores."

"Alone?" he asked, hoping she wasn't meeting someone.

"Yea."

"Do you want some company?"

"You mean, you?"

"Yea, me," he confirmed, fearing for the first time in a long time a woman wouldn't want him around.

As much as Ireland liked his presence, she didn't want a repeat of the media circus she had just experienced leaving the restaurant. Walking the streets of New York was a favorite past time of hers. She loved floating freely amid the hustle and bustle. Somehow she found the weirdest stream of calm while watching the hectic pace of everyone else. Her goal was to disappear into the crowd not be at the center of its attention. "Well, I like to just roam around. I don't see how that would work walking with you."

"I walk the city a lot."

"But do you go unnoticed?"

"Not usually," he said, disappointed in her responses.

"I know this might sound crazy, because of all the noise, but I like to take peaceful strolls out here. I won't be able to do that with you," she said, gently.

Ideal felt a sharp pang. Hurt by her decision, he concluded that becoming her man would be a steep, uphill battle. "Alright," he said, attempting to hide the rejection squeezing his heart. "Let me get your door."

Once he held her door open, Ireland stepped out of the car. "Thank you," she whispered. When she looked into his sad eyes, she almost regretted her decision. To soften the tension between them, she stepped closer and gave him a hug.

Caught off guard by the unexpected action, Ideal froze for a second then slipped his arms around her body and held onto her. With his face buried in her hair, he inhaled her floral scent. He no longer heard horns or tires upon the pavement. He saw not one other soul. All else was nonexistent while he was wrapped in her essence. Unwilling to let go, he soon felt her pull away. Before he knew it, she had spun around and gone into the hotel.

Ideal stood there in a daze until the gasp of a young woman brought him back to where he was. Due to her animations other pedestrians emerged by his side. For the next ten minutes, he took pictures with his fans and understood Ireland made a valid point.

Chapter 9

Five days of the previous week, Ireland drug herself out of bed at five o'clock in the morning to take spinning and yoga classes at her local gym. Just one day before, she left her home at four in the morning to catch an early flight to New York. So when her eyes opened at eight o'clock that morning, without the assistance of an alarm, the extra hours of sleep were just what she needed. Lying in layers of white bedding, she felt ready to take on the tough schedule of being pampered at the hotel's spa.

Once she rose out of bed, she walked over to the window and looked down at its standard view. A sea of yellow taxis whizzed through narrow lanes and herds of people, clad in black, rushed through crosswalks. The scene made her smile. She was definitely looking forward to being in the thick of the streets that evening.

Casey never understood why Ireland, a person who avoided crowded parties, always wanted to go to New York. Casey was a California girl, bias to year-round summer dresses while dining al fresco on the sunny sidewalks of famous communities. It was on those very sidewalks that Ireland felt on display. It seemed the average person there had prying eyes and judgmental minds, rating what others drove and wore.

What Casey failed to realize about New York was the ambiguity it provided. For the most part, millionaires blended in with everyone else. There weren't gawking sessions of possessions on the trains or avenues. There could be a seedy politician on your left and a well-known actor on your right and people went on about their business. Unless, of course, there was someone of immense international fame like Rona, Dig or Ideal nearby. They were the type of celebrities that sometimes drew mobs. People couldn't pass them by and keep it moving. They wanted autographs, pictures, even conversations.

After resting at the window, Ireland ordered room service then took a quick shower. Once she was dressed in light jeans and a white t-shirt, she wanted to do some reading but knew she had to call Casey. Dutifully, she sat at the desk and placed the call, hoping to leave a voicemail at Casey's place of business.

"This is Casey," Casey answered on speakerphone, typing intensely on her computer.

"You are such a workaholic. You have no business being at your office this early," It was just six o'clock on the west coast.

"First of all, that tells me you were trying to avoid speaking to me live. Secondly, Miguel and I both have presentations to make today and if he thinks he is going to do better than me, he's crazy." Casey punched the enter key on her keyboard then leaned back in her ergonomic chair. "So how was the ballet with your new best friend?"

"Stop," Ireland said, thrown by Casey's remark. "You know only you hold that title."

"I know that I normally would've been invited to both the orchestra and the ballet, but I wasn't."

"You're joking, right? You never want to go to New York."

"But you invite me anyway."

"And you always decline."

"That's not the point."

"Look, Rona lives here so I invited her. But I didn't call to talk about Rona. I called to talk about Ideal."

Casey paused from swaying in her chair. "What about him?"

"When I got to Rona's place yesterday, he was there."

"No," Casey whispered. "Was he there to see you?"

"That's what Rona said."

"Wow."

"And when we got to the ballet, she told me that he has feelings for me," Ireland divulged, surprised the words lifted from her tongue.

"Are you trying to give me a heart attack?" Casey asked, unbuttoning her suit jacket.

"I had one so you might as well have one too."

"I'm going to need a drink."

"You are because there's more," Ireland said, bracing Casey. "After the ballet, Ideal and Dig crashed my dinner with Rona so it turned into sort of a double date. And just when I thought the night couldn't get any crazier, a bunch of press was outside when we left the restaurant."

"The press was there? You might be online," Casey sat up and reached for the mouse of her computer.

"Newsflash, they weren't there to see me."

Feverishly, Casey typed a phrase into an internet search engine. A minute later, she exclaimed, "There you are!"

"What?" Ireland said, hopping onto her feet in dismay. She assumed any shots including her would've been disregarded.

"Ideal was holding your back? Wait, you were in his car?"

"That's on there?" Ireland asked, beginning to tremble. A picture of her being posted when it had nothing to do with her career was beyond bothersome to her. Her work was the only online presence she was remotely interested in having. At that moment, she realized going unseen would be impossible if she hung out with her three new acquaintances. If she continued to do so, she'd have to remind herself that she was simply an insignificant bystander.

"You better tell me what happened."

"That's what I'm doing," Ireland said, reciprocating Casey's impatient tone. "When dinner was over, Ideal offered to drive me back to the hotel and Rona and Dig accepted on my behalf."

"That was a setup. Rona and Dig must want Ideal to be with you."

"I think they want Ideal to be with anybody. They want him to settle down."

"Can you imagine if he settles down with you? What if he falls in love with you?" Casey asked, getting chills from her own question.

"That's not going to happen."

"It might."

"Don't you know when things seem too good to be true, they are?"

"Wasn't your last role too good to be true? Becoming friends with Rona too good to be true? Going to France too good to be true? All of those things were very true and very real so I don't see why love with Ideal can't be added to that list."

"Love with Ideal is way more out of reach than any of those things."

"It's not out of reach - not from the pictures I'm looking at," Casey said, pulling back from her computer screen. "Listen, the day is going to come when Ideal reaches out to you. Be smart enough to take his hand when he does."

Ireland's guilt from the night before resurfaced. "Well, I wasn't exactly smart last night when he dropped me off."

Casey's nose wrinkled with a scowl. "What did you do?"

"I already know that you'll think I did the wrong thing so don't beat me up about it."

"What did you do?" Casey repeated in a lower tone.

"Well..."

"Ireland."

"He asked if he could walk me to my room and I told him no."

"You did not."

"But the main thing is that he asked if I wanted company tonight while I walk around the city and I pretty much told him he was too famous to do that with."

"Ireland! You shot him down twice?"

"There was no way I was letting him in my room and I walk to get rid of headaches not bring them on."

"Ireland, I know you love your privacy, but your privacy's not going to love you back. It's not going to keep you warm at night so if that means you lose some of it in order to be with a man that wants you, so be it."

Ireland pondered Casey's words until a knock came at the door. "Room service is here. I'll talk to you later."

"Wait," Casey instructed. "I know what you've been through so I know you're scared to get close to Ideal. But don't push him away or you'll always wonder what could've happened with him."

Ireland mulled over Casey's last words and murmured, "Okay." As she ended the call, she heard a second knock then went to open the door. An employee of the hotel stood beside a cart topped with a huge vase of flowers.

"Ireland Rochelle?" the plump bellman asked.

"Yes?"

"There was a flower delivery for you."

"Uh, you probably have the wrong person."

"No, they're for you," he said, strenuously lifting the vase. "Where would you like them?"

"The desk is fine," she said, confused as to why she would be receiving flowers. Ireland pulled out her leather wallet from her bag.

The bellman raised his right hand. "The gratuity has already been taken care of. Enjoy your stay," he said with a nod, before promptly leaving her alone.

Ireland marveled at the flowers. The colorful arrangement was gigantic and stuffed with several types of blooms. After smelling a variegated rose, she opened the adjacent envelope and slid out its card. The note read:

Ireland,

Just a thank you for letting me drive you to your hotel last night. Hopefully, I can learn your favorite flower. That way I won't have to send you every kind there is.

Respectfully yours,
Ideal

Ireland stared at the personalized note. In addition to stunned, she was touched. The gift was a very thoughtful thing to give. It was something she didn't envision Ideal giving anyone. He didn't seem the type to send flowers, but she admired that he was. She felt even worse for not allowing him to keep her company on her walk.

Room service arrived minutes later. Although Ireland attempted to eat, she couldn't. Ideal's grand gesture had her stomach swarming. She couldn't get his cute smile and smooth skin off of her mind. After pointlessly picking over her meal, it was time for her first spa treatment. She grabbed her bag and room key and headed down the hall toward the elevator.

For hours, Ireland was fortunate enough to put her thoughts of the press on hold. A sweltering sauna, jetted tub, body scrub, facial, and massage worked wonders on her frazzled mind. With less stress, she returned to her room and was welcomed by the fragrance of fresh flowers. Drawn to the display, she floated over to it and ran her fingers along the head of a pink hydrangea.

Once she removed her attention from the flowers, she noticed she had received turndown service. The decorative pillows had been removed from the bed, the sheets were expertly exposed, and two dark chocolate truffles sat strategically atop a fluffed pillow. The treats made her realize how hungry she was. Quickly, she unwrapped one and popped it into her mouth. As her teeth glided into its silky smooth texture, her cell phone rang.

"Hello?" she answered, not recognizing the number. For a moment there was silence.

"Hi," a soft voice said.

Instantly, Ireland felt stuck to the floor. The voice sounded like Ideal's. With one hard gulp, she swallowed the chocolate. "Hi," she replied, uncertain of the caller's identity.

"Hi, it's Ideal."

Before her knees could buckle, Ireland allowed her body to sink onto the edge of the bed. His voice sounded more commanding over the phone. "Hi," she repeated.

"Hi."

Needing time to process being on the phone with one another, neither said a word for a while. After Ireland reminded herself to breathe, she thought of the flowers. "Oh, thank you for the flowers. They're really pretty."

"You're welcome."

"They got here this morning and we were out late last night so I don't know how you had time to do all of that, but I'm impressed."

"So what's your favorite flower?" he asked, referring to the note.

"It's a tie between lilies and tulips."

"Cool, both of those are in there."

"Yea, I noticed," she giggled, looking at the arrangement. "I don't think there's a type missing."

"I didn't want to take any chances."

The call fell silent as Ireland clutched the phone. There was a nagging question within her and against her better judgment, she decided to get it answered. "Can I ask you something?"

"Anything."

"Why did you send them? I didn't do anything to receive flowers."

"You don't have to do anything for me to send you flowers. But like I said in the note, I wanted to thank you for letting me drive you to the hotel."

"But you gave me the ride. If anything, I owe you flowers."

"You know what? You're right. Where are they?"

"I didn't have your address."

"You could've gotten it from Rona."

Though Ireland laughed, she hoped her questions hadn't made her sound ungrateful. "Anyway, I honestly appreciate the gift. Thank you again."

"You're welcome again. So did you go on your walk?"

"No, I was about to get ready when you called."

"Oh, I'm sorry. I didn't mean to hold you up."

"It's okay."

"Well, I wanted to make sure you got the flowers, but that's not the main reason I called. I wanted to ask you something."

"What?"

After an extended pause, he asked, "Will you go out with me tomorrow night?"

Though Rona and Casey tried to prepare Ireland for his question, she wasn't prepared in the least. It echoed in her head as she struggled to absorb it. Ideal Morris asked her out. It was a reality far more jolting than its concept. The intense thrill she experienced was a clear sign that she wanted to accept, but the immensity of his notoriety and fear of the unknown tempted her to decline. She contemplated what to say then remembered he was waiting. "Yea," she heard herself say.

Ideal grabbed his forehead and let out the breath he had been holding in. "How about I meet you in the rear lobby at eight?"

"Okay."

"Please be careful on your walk," he said, sternly.

"I will."

"Alright, see you tomorrow."

When Ireland set down her phone, she fell back on the bed and kicked her legs with joy. But all too soon her happiness of holding the interest of a spectacular musician was dampened by the same fact that he was a spectacular musician. Because of his gifts and good looks, she had adored him for years, but so did millions of others. She wondered how they would react to her dating him. She wondered if she should go through with dating him.

After wondering for too long, it dawned on Ireland that she was jumping the gun. Her past had taught her, time and again, that a date was just a date. Often times, it didn't lead to another but remained a single occurrence. She spent a minute trying to calm down then sat up with alarm. She had nothing to wear for what would possibly be the most memorable date of her life. She peered at the clock and recognized most stores would be closed in a few hours. The night was supposed to entail a nice, peaceful stroll but turned into a search for a great dress and accessories.

Ideal arrived at the hotel lobby fifteen minutes early. Annoyed with himself for being nervous, he felt like a preteen, taking a girl to a middle school dance. As he sat in a leather chair, a few people approached him. Luckily, they were older, more mature fans and were satisfied with a handshake and hello. When he was left alone, he shifted the shirt he wore underneath a dark, V-neck sweater. Soon after he scanned his jeans for lint, he spotted Ireland.

Right on cue, his heart raced at the sight of her. In his favorite color, she wore a dress with a slight shimmer and an asymmetrical neckline. Silver spikes protruded from the heels of her black, peep-toe pumps, and along with a silver clutch, she modeled an array of turquoise jewelry. Unlike the straight hairstyle she had two nights before, her hair was full of soft, subtle waves.

When he rose from the chair, her eyes met his. With purpose, he walked toward her then gave her a hug.

"Hi," he whispered in her ear.

"Hi," she replied.

"You stay beautiful," he said, looking her over and shaking his head. "So do you like Japanese?"

"I do."

"Good. Let's go."

When they exited the building, Ideal led her to his most extraordinary, luxurious vehicle. In the front passenger seat, was his bodyguard, Chase, and behind the wheel was his driver, Greg. Once Greg held open the gray doors for his passengers, he resumed his position behind the wheel and drove away. It was only a short while later when he parked in front of a popular, upscale restaurant and opened Ideal's door. As Ideal was being photographed by the paparazzi, he followed Greg to the other side of the car and observed him opening Ireland's door. Realizing he had the perfect excuse to hold her hand, Ideal stepped in front of Greg and helped Ireland out of the vehicle. Once she was on her feet, he kept hold of her hand while following Chase to the front door.

Within seconds, they were standing beneath the monstrous chandeliers of the bar-lined entry. Prepared for Ideal's arrival, a hostess led them further inside the bamboo-accented establishment and seated them at a table for two against a nature-inspired wall. With stifled excitement, the hostess handed them their menus, wished them a great meal, and walked away.

"Is he going to sit over there the whole time?" Ireland asked, examining Chase, who was sitting at a table twenty feet away.

"Yea," Ideal answered.

"Do you think he should sit with us?"

Ideal chuckled and lowered his head. "I didn't ask to take him out, I asked to take you out. The only people that should be at this table are me and you."

"But won't he be lonely?"

"Chase is working. He's getting paid to sit there alone. Don't worry about him. You should be worried about me." Although, he thought her concern was kind, he didn't want to spend another minute discussing his bodyguard.

"Why should I be worried about you?"

"Because I'm persistent. When I really want something, I don't stop until I get it."

"That still doesn't tell me why I should be worried."

"Oh, it doesn't?" Ideal asked, playing along.

"No. What does that have to do with me?"

Ideal knew Ireland was an intelligent woman. He figured she was pressing him for sport. Amused, he answered, "I think you know." For a minute they remained occupied, staring into each other's eyes until a waiter arrived and interrupted their public display of attraction.

They ordered white wine from Bordeaux as well as sushi rolls, tuna, black cod, and yellowtail. Considering the full house and the selections they made, the wait for their meal was short. With chopsticks in hand, they ate from the beautifully designed plates.

After sampling everything, Ideal was able to ask questions he had been wanting to ask Ireland for some time. "So did you really know who I was when you met me in Miami?"

"You can't be serious," she said, lifting her wine goblet to her lips and giving a good view of the turquoise bangle on her left wrist.

"I'm serious."

"Of course I did," she said, setting her glass back down.

"Well, I didn't know who you were when I got to France, but once I saw you I knew I had to find out."

"Is that why you kept staring me down at that party?"

"I couldn't help it. I couldn't help it in Miami and I can't help it tonight," he said, the intensity in his eyes doubling. When he saw her glance away for a break from his gaze, he moved the conversation along. "So you know my music?"

"It would be really hard not to know your music. It's everywhere."

"Do you like it?"

"Are you asking if I'm a fan?"

"I guess so. I'm hoping you are."

"I am. I've bought most of your music. I think you're really talented and so does my father, by the way."

"For real?"

"For real," she said, smiling.

"That's cool."

"So when are you going to put out some new songs?"

"In a few months. I'm working on tracks right now."

"I'm sure yours aren't the only ones you're working on."

"No, I'm working with four other artists. Dig included."

"Wow, I'm surprised you even have time to be out tonight."

"I'll always have time for you."

"No, you won't."

"Here we go."

Ireland acknowledged she was challenging his statement. "I just mean you're a very busy man with gigantic responsibilities. I don't think there's a way you could always have time for anybody."

"I didn't say, anybody. I said you."

"Don't you have a clothing line too?"

"Yea, but with my line, like with everything else I do - I decide when things happen. I'm in charge of my own time. So if I want to move a deadline, I move it. If I want to spend time with you, I do it. You know what I'm saying?"

"I guess," she answered, before having more sushi.

"Let's forget about me. I want to talk about you. Are you working on a movie right now?"

"No, I'm unemployed, but I had an audition with Michael Weston and he wants me to come in again."

"Michael Weston. That's big."

"I'd love to work with him."

"You will."

"What do you know that I don't know?"

"It's not something I know, it's something I feel. I have a feeling you'll get the part and I'm usually right. When do you go back in?"

"The day after tomorrow."

Being reminded that Ireland would leave soon irritated Ideal. He hated that she would be back in California, but he refused to dwell on it while he was with her. "When do you fly back?"

"Tomorrow evening."

"Were you raised in California?"

"No," she said, adamantly. "I grew up in Philly. My family is there. You're from Queens, right?"

"Yea," Ideal replied, assuming she knew from the many times he spoke of his upbringing in his lyrics. "So when's your birthday?"

"April."

"Aw, man, it already passed," he grimaced.

"When's yours?"

"September first."

"How old are you?"

"Thirty-seven. You?"

"Thirty-four."

"So when my birthday gets here will you celebrate it with me?"

Ireland was surprised by the question. "Uh...yea, if we still know each other."

"Why wouldn't we still know each other? You planning to stop talking to me?"

"No, but people lose touch all of the time."

"Then let's make sure that doesn't happen." Once his serious expression softened, he added, "Now, since you're going to spend my birthday with me, you'll have to go out and get the best champagne and cake."

"Okay, red velvet it is."

"What? No," he protested, shaking his head. "Carrot cake is the best."

"I'm pretty sure red velvet is."

"No, red velvet is chalky and bland."

"This coming from someone that has to weed through carrots, raisins, and walnuts to even taste his cake."

"You might as well gnaw on a dry sponge."

"You might as well toss back some trail mix."

Ideal laughed at her comparison. "You're quick."

Amidst the stares and whispers of fellow diners, the two of them enjoyed an extensive conversation and finished a delectable meal.

After Ideal paid the check, three young women came close to approaching him, but Chase sprang into action and prevented them from reaching the table. He then led Ideal and Ireland out of the restaurant.

When they returned to the hotel, Ireland allowed Ideal to escort her to her room. As they walked briskly through the lobby and corridors, they passed delighted faces but arrived at her door without being stopped. From the moment Ideal saw Ireland retrieve the room key from her purse, he was yearning to go inside.

"Thanks for spending time with me tonight," he said.

"Thanks for asking me to."

"How are you getting to the airport tomorrow?"

"A cab."

"Can I take you?"

"No, I'll be fine."

"I want to take you," he said, the look in his eyes reaffirming his words.

"I'm sure you have better things to do tomorrow than to drive me to the airport," Ireland said, tucking a few strands of hair behind her ear.

"What time should I pick you up?"

"You're hard of hearing, huh?"

"What did you say?" he said, leaning his ear toward her mouth as if he couldn't hear.

"You can pick me up at three o'clock, but I'm paying for the gas."

"You're funny."

"I'm for real."

"I'm not going to let you give me gas money. Trust me, I'll be alright."

"I know you'll be alright, that's not the point."

"I love the way you are," he said, silencing her the way he had hoped to. Wanting to lean over and kiss her, his heart pounded as he examined her face. "I love the way you look."

Shaken from the appeal in his eyes, Ireland glanced away.

"Ireland," he said until she brought her eyes back to his. "I love the way you look."

"Thank you."

Stepping incredibly close to her, he brushed his nose along the side of her neck. "I love the way you smell." As if feeling the effects of a blizzard, the touch caused them to shiver even though they were on the verge of overheating. Just when Ideal found the courage to try to place his mouth on hers, Ireland promptly stepped away.

"I should get some sleep," she said. "I'll see you tomorrow."

Deeply disappointed, Ideal could only mutter, "Alright."

"Goodnight," she said, before turning away, rushing inside, and shutting the door.

Bitter the night didn't end the way he had dreamed, Ideal hung his head and slumped his heavy shoulders. Desperate for the taste of her lips, he considered having Ireland open the door so he could kiss her anyway. A minute later, he released the urge and made his way down the hall.

Chapter 10

Walking beside a bellman, Ireland entered the main lobby ten minutes prior to her checkout time. She was glad to see that Ideal had already arrived. His repetitive punctuality was impressive, among other things.

Although she escaped affection with him the night before, she sat up thinking about him into the wee hours of the morning. She loved that he behaved like a gentleman toward her. His conversation was thought-provoking and his humor, uplifting. He was intriguingly smart, which she found admirable. Last, as well as least, his handsome looks made her feel more alive than she thought was possible. At the end of the night, Ireland climbed into bed and admitted to herself that she was smitten with Ideal.

Contrary to how she felt about him was how she felt about going out with him. Dining with him at a crowded spot was a slice of hell she never wanted to have again. It took her a million breaths just to calm down her heart from being photographed by paparazzi and gawked at by other diners. Only periodically was she able to give Ideal her undivided attention.

"Look at you," Ideal said, pleasantly surprised by how cute Ireland looked wearing a t-shirt, jeans, and sneakers with her hair in a ponytail. "I thought you only wore heels."

"That shows how much you know," she said, accepting his hug.

After turning down Ideal's persistent offers to pay her bill and tip the bellman, Ireland slid into his matte black sports car and was on her way to the airport.

Unlike the silent car rides before, this one had plenty of conversation. They were desperate to enjoy their last minutes together, knowing it could be long before they saw each other again. Their laughter was constant until they drew near to the airport. Then their conversing came to a halt.

Once Ideal parked along the curb, the two of them got out of the car. Grudgingly, Ideal retrieved her bag from the front trunk and sat it next to the rubber soles on her feet. As young men with thick New York accents began shouting greetings to Ideal, Ireland hoped he knew kissing her in public was out of the question. Fortunately, he gave her a long, gentle hug. With uncertainty about their future, they finally parted ways.

During the plane ride home, Ireland's mind went back and forth from Ideal to Michael Weston. They both held such promise for wonderful experiences in her life, experiences that would be thrilling as well as frightening. Eventually tired from excessive pondering, she fell asleep mumbling the lines for her upcoming audition.

Ireland felt great about her second reading for Weston. Since she had a better idea of what to expect, she was much more comfortable than the first time she went in. In the end, the audition went so well, she earned herself a third.

For the third time, she arrived at the same office and performed the same scene, but was also asked to read from additional areas of the script. Always prepared to do more, she acted out the other scenes without a glance at her lines, proving her vigilance as an actress. Soon after, she expected to be excused from the office. Instead, she learned that she'd be doing one last scene with the actor cast as the male lead.

When the actor entered the room, Ireland was shocked to see it was the legendary, Alberto Domingo. Immediately, after shaking his hand, she was asked to begin. She had no time to remain starstruck. She couldn't see him as the sexy, talented, and distinguished man that he was. She had to view him as an average working actor, that she was there to play with. Thankfully, they played well together and the scene was electric. She felt she had great chemistry with Alberto, but she'd have to wait and see if Michael agreed. After thanking everyone in the cold, cramped room, she met Keith in the lobby, gave him a report, and bid him a happy farewell.

The following Saturday, Ireland and Casey, shopped at their favorite mall in Orange County. Shopping was an exhilarating experience that Ireland had gotten the hang of by the time she was eight. Inhaling the aroma of new merchandise, gliding her hands atop an array of fabrics, trying things on in elegant dressing rooms, and selecting items to ultimately purchase, all contributed to one great high. After achieving her latest buzz from retail therapy, she and Casey stopped to have lunch at a department store's bistro.

"So Robert was in meetings all day long then came to your place and cooked you dinner?" Ireland asked.

"I'm blessed, I know," Casey said, taking a sip of lemonade.

"That's why I call your man, *Romance*."

"Guess I'll have to come up with a name for Ideal," Casey replied, jutting her full eyebrows up and down. "How is he?"

"He's fine."

"We all know that. How is he really?"

At that very moment, Ireland's cell phone rang. She reached into her camel colored bag and pulled out her phone. It was Ideal. He had called her every single day since she left New York. Because of their consistently long and intimate phone conversations, they had gotten to know each other on a much deeper level. "Hi," Ireland said, answering the video call.

"Is that him?" Casey whispered, dying to jump up and stare at the screen. When Ireland discreetly gave confirmation, Casey listened to what was said. Although it was typical chit chat, she noticed how good Ideal sounded and how cheerful Ireland seemed. Unfortunately, the call ended too soon. "Why did you get off so fast?" Casey asked, frowning with disapproval.

"Because I'm having lunch with you," Ireland replied, stirring her salad with a fork.

"You did not have to hang up on my account. I would've much rather listened to Ideal."

"I wouldn't have talked to him in front of you anyway."

"Ooh, why is that? What does he talk about?"

"None of that," Ireland said, shaking her head at Casey's naughty insinuation.

"Not yet," Casey teased. She looked Ireland over and noticed the light in her eyes. "You look happy."

"I look normal."

"Trust me, I know your normal. This isn't it."

"Well, it's probably because I've had three great auditions with Weston."

"That's maybe forty percent of it, but sixty percent is Ideal."

"Maybe," Ireland said, smirking.

"I'm so happy that you're happy."

"I always start out happy. It's later that things fall apart."

"Don't go looking for that to happen. Just enjoy each day that things are good."

During their quick bite to eat, they discussed their families then rushed back to Los Angeles to beat the impending traffic. While Casey headed to Robert's home, Ireland went to her local gym. Following an intense workout, she decided to take a yoga class.

On a soft, purple mat, she sat with her eyes closed, palms up, and feet crossed in her lap. Along with sixteen other students, she imitated the instructor and stretched both arms above her head then pushed her body into various poses. In a moment of stillness, where only a wooden flute was heard, a cell phone began ringing boisterously. Everyone in the room was disturbed.

The once peaceful expression that was on the instructor's face was replaced with a look of disdain. "Phones are to be placed on silent," she yelled, looking around to find the culprit.

Ireland knew the disruptive ringtone all too well. Embarrassed, she hurried to her bag, grabbed her phone, and ended the call. Instantly, regret made her wish that she'd gone home and done yoga alone. "I am so sorry. I forgot to turn it off."

"Obviously," the instructor said, giving Ireland a cruel stare.

"I'm sorry," Ireland repeated. Because she saw that the call was from her agent, she raced out of the class to call him back. "Hi Rick," she whispered after he answered.

"Are you sitting down?" he asked.

"I was. Why?" she asked, expecting to hear that her luck had finally run out.

"Because Weston wants to see you again, but he wants to meet with you at his house."

"His house? Are you serious?"

"That I am. He wants you there Thursday evening."

"Wow."

"Wow, is right. I'll shoot you and Keith his info."

Hope, fear, excitement, and doubt set up residence in Ireland's core. Although she could benefit from yoga, there was no way she was returning to the class.

Chapter 11

Ideal was thrilled when Ireland accepted his offer. Her acceptance, however, didn't come easy. It was one of the hardest sells he ever had to make. He invited her back to New York for an all expense paid trip on him. It was his intent to cover her first class flight, five-star hotel, and all of her meals. From Ideal's point of view, she would be coming at his invitation, therefore, he should handle the finances. Unfortunately, it took a great deal of time to get Ireland to see things his way.

She argued that she was blessed enough to take care of her own costs, even though it meant flying in coach, staying in a standard room, and ordering less expensive items from the room service menu. Aside from the dates he'd take her on, she didn't want him to pay for anything. She held on tightly to her arguments but finally released her grip when the severity of his insistence surfaced and showed no sign of leaving.

Although Ideal refused to let her pay for the trip, he secretly admired her stubbornness. It was a trait that would serve her well in her blossoming career. It would prove ineffective, however, in regards to him spending money on her. When she was with him, she would pay for nothing. He had achieved his childhood dream of becoming tremendously wealthy and that made him fortunate enough to be able to take care of her. In addition to her not taking out her wallet, Ideal had one, last, demand concerning her week there. She would have to see him every day.

Her arrival came with a slowness that rivaled an elderly turtle's pace. When she walked out of the airport and into the cool of the night, Ideal was overtaken by warmth. He might as well have drooled on his raspberry-colored shirt with the way his mouth hung open. She wore a pair of navy pumps, dark blue jeans, and a white, silk blouse. She also wore a trio of long, silver necklaces and matching skinny bracelets. But what she wore best, Ideal thought was the glow on her face and the gleam in her eyes.

Along with everyone in the vicinity, Ireland spotted Ideal's sedan then made her way toward it. As Greg stepped out to seize her luggage, Ideal stepped out to seize her body. He kissed her on the cheek and with a tight hug, lifted her feet off of the ground. He knew that random people could take pictures of them, but he didn't care in the least. He had already seen plenty of pictures of himself with Ireland and he adored the online images. It was like having a chronicled photo album of his favorite times.

When they were settled in the car, Greg drove to the midtown hotel where Ideal had reserved a luxurious suite for Ireland. Initially, he considered choosing a remarkably modern hotel, but because of the one she had chosen during her last visit to New York, he concluded that she preferred more classic accommodations.

They soon entered an opulent, gold leaf-trimmed lobby where a magnificent mural enlivened the ceiling. At the marble reception desk, Ideal assisted Ireland with check-in by handing the front desk manager a weighty credit card on which everything was to be charged. He kindly gave the gentleman strict orders to ensure that Ireland's service was exceptional. After giving Ireland a wad of cash to tip her butler and maid, he handed the bellman a generous tip in the most discreet manner.

While the bellman showed Ireland to her suite, Ideal sat alone in a room of rich moldings and imagined her discovering the red calla lilies he had sent to her suite an hour prior. He had never done so much for a woman and hoped she noticed the effort he put into making her feel special.

She returned to the lobby wearing the same shoes and jewelry, but had changed into a navy dress. Initiating their second hug for the night, she told him she loved the flowers then scolded him for booking an insanely large room.

In no time, they were on the Upper East Side at a French restaurant with a contemporary feel. White columns framed colorful artwork that brought white walls alive. Fresh flowers were plentiful and the music was infectious. Ireland found herself swaying to its rhythm, aware the activity disguised her nervous trembling. Soon Ideal followed her lead and the two of them were moving in unison when their steaming plates arrived. Paired with a bottle of pinot noir, they savored meals of venison and chicken coq au vin.

"I have something to tell you," Ireland said, coyly.

"What?" Ideal asked, intrigued.

"I got the role in Weston's film."

"Whoa, you did?"

"Yea."

"That's so big," he said, smiling at her from ear to ear then reaching over to squeeze her hand. "Congratulations."

"Thank you," she replied, touched by his support.

"I knew you'd get it. When did you find out?"

"A few days ago."

"A few days ago? Why are you just now telling me?" he asked, letting go of her hand.

"I thought it would be nice to tell you in person." Ireland sat watching him ponder her words. "Are you mad?"

"No, I'm not mad. I could never be mad at you."

"You'll change your mind about that sooner than you think."

Ideal ignored her remark. "I wish I was with you when you found out."

"Well, you're with me now."

"Yea, I am," he said, taking her hand again. "I know getting the role meant a lot to you and what means a lot to you, means a lot to me. Since acting is what makes you happy, I'll support you in it always."

"Thanks, Ideal," she said, aware that he spoke as if he would know her for quite some time.

Ideal refused to leave until they celebrated with champagne. Once they downed their bubbly with mango sorbet, they prepared to weather the paparazzi storm that awaited them outside. Following behind Chase, they exited the restaurant, walked past the chaos, and got into the car.

A short while later, Greg dropped them off at the park and removed a cashmere blanket from the trunk. As he handed Ideal the blanket, he gave assurance that he would return by midnight. Ideal and Ireland then climbed into a horse drawn carriage. The light in Ireland's eyes and the excitement of her smile, gave Ideal a jolt of joy. She more than approved of his mindful plan to take a romantic ride.

To keep her from feeling the fifty-degree weather, he removed his blazer and helped her put it on. As the carriage began to roll, he opened the blanket and wrapped it around the two of them. He now had the perfect excuse to hold her. Unable to resist, he put his arms around her waist and pulled her back against his chest. He closed his eyes, feeling as though he was as close to happiness as he had ever been.

Under the influence of affection, they rode in silence, listening to the sound of the horse's slow, steady trot. The hooves against the pavement were calming, as were the vocal vibratos of the crickets they passed. Although the park's beauty was much less visible in the dark, they had privacy that they wouldn't have had during daylight.

Tucked behind Ireland, Ideal went unrecognized. It was as if they had the park to themselves and they loved every minute of it.

Greg picked them up right on time and arrived at the hotel much too soon. Dreading the end of their night, Ideal and Ireland passed through double, French doors then walked slowly down the lantern-lined hallway until they reached her room.

"I can't believe you have me staying in this huge suite."

"Believe it."

"There's no way I can thank you enough for everything you did today, but thank you."

"You don't have to thank me. I invited you here. You're doing me a favor."

"It doesn't feel that way," Ireland said. She was the one receiving all of the perks.

"It feels that way to me. You're here. I got to spend time with you and I'll get to spend time with you tomorrow."

"I don't think that was part of the deal," she said, pretending not to remember.

"Oh, it was," he said, flashing his famous grin. "I'll meet you in the lobby at ten."

"Where are we going?"

"Don't worry about all that."

"I need to know what to wear."

"You'll make a good choice. You always do."

"Should I wear heels or flats?" she asked, knowing the pain of fashion was primarily centered on the feet.

"Whichever you want."

"Thanks a lot," she said through gritted teeth.

With a sly wink, Ideal returned her sarcasm. "You're very welcome."

There was nothing left to say. The two of them stood there impeccably still and perfectly quiet. As they stared into each other's eyes, their chemistry began to climb. Perhaps from anxiety of what would happen next, Ireland again, ended the moment that felt far too overpowering. "Well, I'll see you in the morning," she said, turning to face the door.

As she attempted to slide her key into the lock, Ideal grabbed her right arm and turned her back around. Filled with longing, he spoke sternly. "Stop running from me."

Embarrassed he could see through her tactics, she nervously replied with a lie. "I'm not."

"You are," he insisted. While staring down at her, he prepared to do what he'd been craving to do for weeks upon weeks. He took a firm hold of her waist, pulled her against him, bent his head down, and kissed her. He kissed her slowly, tenderly, deliberately, loving the feel of her lips between his. Then an insatiable passion leaped inside of him and he kissed her hungrily, searching her mouth as if it contained the oxygen he needed to breathe.

The next morning, Ireland awoke to a wakeup call from her trusty butler. When she rose from the canopied bed, she walked around the lavish suite. Although she admired its amenities, she reflected on the ridiculousness of its price. She realized her total stay would equal many people's annual salary.

Ireland had never once dated someone with extraordinary means. Her past dealings were with lower or middle class men, two paychecks away from financial ruin. That reality didn't bother her. In fact, she had much respect for those men. They were hardworking people who got up every day to ensure they led dignified lives. Strategically, they saved for months to enjoy rare luxuries or a week-long vacation.

Ideal was part of an entirely different world. A world that she knew was vastly small. His great wealth was incredibly scarce and it afforded him things most people only dreamed of. He could go where he wanted, he could buy what he wanted, and he could take off from work whenever he chose. Whatever he spent was rapidly replenished, solely from the hits he had on the radio. The other millions he raked in were all icing on his multi-layered cake. He freely spent his disposable income, which Ireland suspected, satisfied the brashly materialistic side of his personality.

Dating someone like Ideal was nothing short of bizarre. Ireland believed the odds of a woman being courted by a millionaire were not only miniature but barely existent. In no way, did she ever think she'd be with a rich man, nor did she strive to be with one. Her longtime goal was to have an acting career that brought in a comfortable six figure salary, which she assumed would always make her the breadwinner in her relationships. Now that she was seeing Ideal, she realized her assumption couldn't have been more wrong.

Regardless of the amount of money he made, he was making her feel invaluable. She felt wanted, adored, cared for, and heard. His listening skills were stellar, as were the dates he took her on - not due to the money he spent, but the time he spent being thoughtful.

Still, Ireland knew all too well that people put their best foot forward in the early stages of dating. Time would tell if he was as fantastic as he seemed. Until plenty of weeks passed by, she wanted to refrain from becoming overly excited, which was now excruciatingly difficult to do since he'd given her the most delicious kiss. She continued to melt from it, replaying it in her mind and afraid to receive another. She presumed the more of them she got, the more of them she'd need.

Nevertheless, she fantasized how a second kiss might be, until the notion of others witnessing it swooped in and shook her up. She hoped he had enough sense to not kiss her in public. In fact, she hoped their next date would forego being in public altogether. Private time with him was what she wanted. Sadly, something told her they'd be visiting another jam-packed eatery, where panels of eyes would be admiring him and evaluating her.

Foolishly, she began imagining awful scenarios, which filled her with so much fright, she doubted her ability to go out with him again. To slow her speeding thoughts, shaky limbs, and hard-beating heart, she sat on a chaise, closed her eyes, and deepened her breath.

Tangerine and cranberry leaves fall along a trail and crunch beneath the soles of her sheepskin shoes as she walks in the autumn air. Her gloved hands rest in the deep pockets of her marigold coat while the soft fringe of her wool scarf tousles in the wind. Smoke rises from red chimneys in the distance, granting her a woodsy scent to inhale. She has nowhere to be, nowhere to go. Her steps are slow. A hump of rugged branches interrupt her straight path. She alters her course. Toward the steeple of a tall, white church, she begins to move with intention. Her eyes linger on the pointed tip, protruding from the pigments of richly hued foliage. She draws nearer and nearer. As she licks her cold lips and swallows the taste of cherry, she arrives at the place of worship. The wreath-adorned door is open. No one is inside. Down a center aisle of wine-colored carpet, she moves to a pecan pew closest to the altar. It squeaks when she sits. She stays a wonderful while as beams of natural light pour through stained glass. She keeps her mouth closed and lets her spirit speak.

Ireland was clueless as to where she and Ideal were going when they entered a high-rise building in Times Square. Although Ideal's olive green cap, matching shirt, and army fatigue shorts, should've made her feel more than comfortable, she worried her cream dress wouldn't be appropriate for the day's outing. After riding an elevator up several stories, the doors slid open. What she saw was a large sign that simply read, *Try Real.* Surprised to be at the headquarters of his fashion line, she smiled then bit her lip with intrigue. Once they greeted a warm receptionist who seemed taken aback by Ireland's presence, they passed a multitude of occupied cubicles where curious eyes were all too visible. Soon after, they headed down an empty corridor lined with closed doors. Just before reaching Ideal's private office, he stopped to introduce Ireland to his leggy assistant, Danielle.

Danielle, Ideal explained, was not simply his executive assistant at *Try Real.* She was also his personal assistant in every area of his life.

She handled all of his doctor appointments, travel arrangements, household staff, and dinner reservations. He felt she was a magician.

Long and lean without a hint of a grin, Danielle looked Ireland over from the shine of her hair to the heels of her shoes. "Hello," she said, blandly.

"Hello," Ireland replied, turned off by the cold expression emanating from Danielle's green eyes. Wise enough not to mistake her for being the friendly type, Ireland had nothing more to say. She made her way through the open door of Ideal's office and was glad when he followed and closed the door behind him.

His office appeared far more serious than Ireland expected. It had no sign of his playfulness. In fact, it looked nothing like his fashion line, which was predominantly bright and colorful with both quirky and classic styles. Instead, the office had an air of sophistication with an unrelenting color scheme of black and white. The contrasting tones were implemented by an expansive desk, streamlined sofa, two tone chairs, and framed sepia prints. Complementing the room's large size was a grand window positioned behind Ideal's desk. Oddly enough, it showcased a white window seat that looked as though it had never been sat on. When Ireland received the green light to recline in the unblemished nook, she did just that, resting her back on a herringbone patterned pillow.

When Ideal stopped communicating in order to read documents, Ireland was pleased his attention was diverted to something other than her. She needed a moment to recoup the calm she had found before leaving the hotel. Though she'd only been at the business mere minutes, she felt she was an object of study. Regrettably, she wondered what Danielle and the other employees thought of her. Were they viewing her with pity? Did they feel she was a fool that would be replaced shortly? Just how many women had Ideal brought to the office?

To the helpful sound of silence, she stared out of the window and allowed herself to be lulled by the beauty of the morning's grayness. Minutes later, architectural details of neighboring buildings held her interest until she heard Ideal speaking on the phone. As she listened to him give specific instructions and convey his expectations, she was impressed with his professionalism. Though she figured he had to be an astute businessman, it was a side of him she hadn't seen.

It was Ideal's intent to stop at the office and sign a bit of paperwork, but two hours had passed when he finished scribbling his signature and forwarding emails. The primary reason for the delay was an unscheduled conference call. While conducting the call, he repeatedly placed his phone on mute to make sure Ireland was okay. When he finally stepped away from his desk, he apologized for taking long, but Ireland wouldn't accept his apology. She learned long ago that life was always met with the unexpected.

Before leaving, Ireland received a tour of the office with Ideal as her guide. The conference room, lounge, and kitchen were very nice, but nothing piqued her interest like the exhibition rooms. For a fashion lover like herself, they were an exciting place to be. Akin to miniature boutiques, they displayed the company's merchandise and more importantly, Ideal's creative style. In a room for women's accessories, Ireland hid her glee but somehow was gifted with what mainly caught her eye - a buttery soft, leather handbag with a rose of large, curled petals.

When they were on their way out, Ideal introduced Ireland to Brian. He was the Chief Operating Officer and had just entered the lobby.

"This is a first," Brian said, shaking Ireland's hand.

"What is?" Ireland asked, puzzled by his comment.

"Ideal bringing a lady to the office. You must be pretty special," he said, winking at Ideal.

The words gave Ireland a well-needed dose of relief. It seemed Ideal didn't have women there all of the time. Before she could respond, Ideal shoved Brian aside and escorted her out of the building. Brian had no clue how grateful she was for their brief encounter.

Ireland knew better than to ask where they were going next. Ideal would only give her a silly response so she did her best to try and enjoy the ride. Much to her surprise, the car dropped them off at a sandwich shop. Loud and crowded, it's casual atmosphere was a big change from the posh restaurants they'd been to.

Despite the long line, they were seated quickly at a table Ideal requested, which placed them beside a group of girlfriends. Queasy from the closeness, Ireland's stomach did somersaults at the probability of her neighbors listening in on her conversation. As with the past few times she dined with Ideal, she tried to handle being the center of attention by staring squarely at him or the walls of the room. It wasn't until she finished ordering that she noticed a picture of him on the wall.

"Now, I see why you wanted to sit here," she said.

"Yea, it's a good spot," he said, scanning every surface except the wall closest to them.

"You are such a show-off."

"What do you mean?" he asked with false modesty.

"I mean, you better get your headshot off of this wall before the manager notices you put it there."

"That's cute," he said, laughing. "Real cute."

When a young boy attempted to approach Ideal, Chase stopped him instantly. "It's alright," Ideal said to Chase while reaching out to shake the boy's hand.

The handshake was the start of fans arriving at Ideal's side. Ireland watched as he was friendly and gracious to everyone he met, including the women offering him their most alluring smiles. So far, Ireland had observed Ideal being nothing but a good man. He was known as being musically talented, but much wasn't reported about his character. He seemed consistently kind. In truth, he was far kinder than she could've been in that situation. If people came at her from every side, she would feel the need to escape, by any means necessary.

"I'm sorry about that," Ideal said, after taking pictures with a couple of visitors.

"It's okay."

"If it wasn't for them, I wouldn't have what I have."

"It's good you remember that. A lot of people forget."

"I don't. That's why it's hard for me to turn them away sometimes." Their huge pastrami sandwiches then arrived with a thud. "I'll make you VP of *Try Real* if you finish that."

"Bet," she replied, taking her first bite. Sadly, she only ate half and missed out on a fabulous job opportunity.

The next stop on Ideal's agenda was a recording studio in lower Manhattan. They passed through a vacant lobby then entered one of many dimly lit rooms, which emanated the smell of wood polish. The room was dominated by a massive board with a dizzying number of buttons. Witnessing Ideal at work would grant her an extraordinary education.

She first met a male engineer, who assumed she was an artist Ideal was working with. Once he was set straight, Ideal introduced her to the R&B singer, Lance. He was a popular, twenty-year-old heartthrob, who just so happened to be shorter than he appeared on television.

There was a leather couch in the room, strategically positioned out of the way, where Ireland made herself comfortable. When Ideal sat in front of the board, he pressed a few buttons and music began playing. Ireland was then able to see the unleashing of his musical mind.

For the next three hours, he picked apart every section of the song. While humming, singing, and writing lyrics, he added instrumentations, gave vocal instructions, and listened to playbacks. Not only was Ireland amazed by his creativity, but she was drawn to him because of it. The work was tedious and incessant yet he was brilliantly in control. He waited patiently for his suggestions to be precisely followed by Lance and when they were, he was nothing short of jubilant. Joy radiated from his face and Ireland felt privileged to see him so blissful.

It was the first time Ideal paid Ireland very little attention. He glanced at her a few times, but remained diligent at work. Music was clearly the love of his life and Ireland found his passion for it enormously appealing.

Chapter 12

Ireland could tell by Ideal's silence that he was taken by what she wore. The class and style of her dress wasn't much different from others before. It was flattering, form-fitting, and stopped above her knees, but it did have one outstanding component. Its fabric was an amazing red.

It was common knowledge the color red grabbed a great deal of attention. Often times, the wrong kind. The wrong kind was precisely what Ireland shied away from garnering. She never wanted to appear too obvious, forward, or even seductive, which is why she didn't wear the hue frequently on dates. Tonight, however, she decided not to worry about being overly attractive. She convinced herself she was simply wearing a romantic color for a romantic dinner. But as she and Ideal approached his two-seater, she couldn't ignore his concentration on her garment. Several times, he looked it over. He either loved it or hated it. Perhaps one day in the future, she'd work up the nerve to ask him which it was.

As Ideal maneuvered his car into the thick of traffic's scarlet glow, Ireland was disappointed that Greg and Chase weren't present. Getting in and out of a restaurant without the extra help would be much more of a hassle. Immediately, she started the night off more afraid than usual.

They hadn't been riding long when Ideal stopped the car at a curb on *Central Park West.* Wearing all black, from his sweater to his sneakers, he exited the vehicle and helped Ireland do the same. When a valet attendant got behind the wheel, Ideal led Ireland onto the sidewalk.

"Where are we going?" she asked, noticing they weren't near an entrance to a restaurant.

"Just come with me."

"I thought we were going to dinner."

"We are."

"Where?"

"A good place with great food."

Ireland had on six-inch heels and hoped he hadn't planned for them to take a long stroll before reaching their destination. "Is it far?"

The question had barely left her lips when she froze in sudden fear. Out of nowhere, two photographers jumped directly in front of them and began taking pictures. Unable to keep walking, Ireland felt Ideal slip his arm around her waist and push her along. The cameras were closer than they had been before and undoubtedly were capturing her anxiety. In that moment, Ireland learned the paparazzi weren't merely an awful nuisance, they were a real danger.

"Who's your new girl, Ideal? What are you going to do with her tonight?" one of the men asked.

Ireland was horrified by the question. The insinuation was disgusting and demeaning. Discreetly, she took slow breaths and tried to keep her face from expressing anger. A wave of relief washed over her when she heard Ideal whisper, "It's right here."

The two of them turned and walked through the revolving door of a limestone building. After stepping into the lobby they were greeted by a doorman. "Welcome back, Mr. Morris."

"Welcome back?" Ireland said. "Where are we?"

"Wait and see."

"Well, I can already see this isn't a restaurant. It looks like an apartment building. A very expensive one."

"Does it?" he asked, ushering her across the floor to a private elevator.

Ireland then asked a question that she already knew the answer to. "Is this where you live?"

"Maybe."

"I hope not."

"Why?" Ideal asked, pausing with worry.

"Because you didn't ask me if I would mind coming over to your place."

"Ireland, would you mind coming over to my place?"

"I have to think about it."

"Think about it on the elevator," he said, shoving her on ahead of him then inserting his access key.

They rode past many floors until they arrived at the penthouse, which consisted of the top two floors and the rooftop. When the doors slid open they walked directly into the foyer.

The sound of a piano playing slow jazz quickly caught Ireland's attention. The soothing music flowed into her soul then gradually carried away the tension she had just experienced. Knowing they would be out of the public eye was wondrously healing.

The L-shaped foyer with black, wooden floors expanded from a short hallway into a much longer one. Along both halls were white paneled walls and on each side hung frame after frame of the most intriguing artwork. Many were colorful, some were black and white, but all were modern and bold. This place, Ireland thought, looked like Ideal. It was what she expected to see in his office at *Try Real.*

Along the chair rail were black lacquered benches that led to a spiraling, marble staircase accented by a dark iron banister. Just beyond the staircase was a pair of roman columns that preceded another corridor, which ran perpendicular. Several doors lined this corridor and Ireland was eager to go through them all, but Ideal had other plans. He escorted her up two flights of stairs then onto a green-filled, rooftop terrace.

The warm air was kind to Ireland's nude arms as she marveled at the quantity of potted plants and topiaries. A flat stream of water poured from a square, stone fountain and flames rose high from a gas fire pit table. Due to perfectly positioned speakers, the jazz that played inside was clearly heard outdoors. Three seating areas consisted of pillow-lined couches and chairs made of solid teak wood. Although a dining table was present, a plate of hors d'oeuvres, green bottle of champagne, and crystal flutes sat in front of the fire.

Ireland tried her best to take in every detail. An immeasurable amount of treetops in the city's beloved park and dazzling lights in the distance made the scene all the more special. "It's beautiful up here," she said, walking to the ledge of a brick wall.

"You're beautiful in that dress."

"Thank you," she whispered over her shoulder.

"You stay beautiful," he said, arriving at her side.

"You wouldn't keep saying that if you saw me wake up in the morning." It wasn't until she had spoken the words that she realized how provocative they were. As if images were running through his mind, Ideal went silent. "So we're eating up here?" she asked, hoping to guide his thoughts to another topic.

"We'll have a starter up here and dinner downstairs. Is that okay?"

"Yea, it's fine. Although, I would've worn something more casual if I had known we were going to be here."

"Then I'm glad you didn't know," he said, scanning the dress yet again. Taking her hand, he led her to the couch where they sat before a tray of crème fraiche blini. "Do you like caviar?"

"I wouldn't know. I've always passed on it. It seems to be something people serve when they're trying too hard. Are you trying to impress me?" she teased.

"Maybe."

"Oh, maybe. Not definitely."

"Give it a taste," he said, holding one of the miniature pancakes to her mouth.

Ireland paused for a moment then allowed him to feed her. As she chewed the delicacy, she watched him wait for her verdict. "It's interesting. Salty like I've heard."

"It'll grow on you. I didn't like it either when I first had it."

"I don't dislike it. It's just different," she said, not wanting him to think serving it was a waste of time and money.

"Let me get you some champagne," he said, picking up a linen napkin then removing the bottle's foil. "We need to have a toast before dinner."

"Speaking of dinner, did you cook?"

Smiling back at her, he replied, "No, I didn't cook."

"I didn't think so. You probably don't even know what to do in a kitchen."

"Actually, I do. The question is whether or not you know what to do in a kitchen," he said, popping the cork from the chilled bottle.

"Maybe you'll see for yourself one day."

"I hope so."

After Ideal filled her glass, she sipped the champagne then let him feed her another hors d'oeuvre. "You're right, it's growing on me."

"Raise your glass," Ideal said, already holding his up.

Ireland followed his order. "What are we toasting to?"

"You."

"Me?"

"To you agreeing to come here and letting me spend every day with you. You don't know how much it means to me. I just pray you're enjoying our time together at least half as much as I am. You're such a good woman. So here's to how good you make me feel and how good you make me want to be."

Ireland's heart was stirred in a way she didn't expect. He shared his feelings so eloquently. She cursed the unavoidable day when he would somehow screw up. "I don't know what to say," she said, studying his face.

"Say, cheers," he said, tapping his glass against hers.

"Cheers." As she took another sip of the champagne, she saw him reach behind a pillow and pull out a small gift bag. Ireland looked back and forth from the gift bag to Ideal. "Tell me you didn't buy me something."

"I can't tell you that." Handing her the gift, he added, "This is for you."

"You shouldn't have done this."

"Open it."

Noticing Ideal wasn't fond of waiting, Ireland put down her glass and reached into the bag. She gasped when she pulled out the recognizable red box of a famed jeweler. Her body shivered at the thought that he'd purchased something costly, but then she remembered who she was dealing with. Ideal was a silly guy and he liked to have fun. The box must have been a prank. "This is a joke, right?" she giggled. "You put a candy necklace in here, right?"

When Ideal chose not to answer her, she stopped laughing and opened the box. Ireland fell speechless. With parted lips, she gazed at a white gold, diamond encrusted, bangle style bracelet. It was a bracelet she had recently seen in the pages of a fashion magazine. It was undeniably gorgeous and undeniably expensive. Moments went by and she said not a word.

"Do you like it?" he asked.

Staring at the gift in disbelief, she murmured, "You're crazy."

"What?"

"You're crazy," she said louder, standing to her feet.

"Why?" he asked, rising from his seat.

"This is why," she said, lifting up the bracelet. "You can't buy me something this expensive."

"Why can't I?" he asked, disturbed by her upset tone.

"It's too much. It's too serious."

"Even if I'm serious about you?"

"You can't be this serious," she said, glancing back at the bracelet.

"Obviously, I am." Ideal took a step closer to her. "I know this is sudden to you, but it's not to me. I've thought about you every single day and night since I first saw you in France."

Disregarding his rationale, Ireland closed the box and held it out for him to take. "I can't keep this."

"I'm not taking it back," he said, sliding his hands into his pockets.

"Take it."

"No."

"Take it."

"Don't you know it's rude to refuse a gift?"

"Can't you see that it makes me uncomfortable?" she replied, setting the box down and walking away from him.

Puzzled by her statement, Ideal stared at her back until it occurred to him that she viewed the gift as him trying to buy her time, or even worse, her affection. Straightaway, he walked over and faced her. "Why does it make you uncomfortable?"

"It just does."

Though she wouldn't confirm his theory, Ideal believed it to be the truth. He had to let her know how wrong she was. "Ireland, I don't expect anything back from you. I won't feel like you owe me."

"That's what you say."

"That's what I mean."

"Well, even if that's the case, I'm not the kind of woman that needs a man to buy her shiny things in order to be happy. I don't like that you think I'm that way." Him viewing her as a needy friend that he had to spoil made her feel cheap.

"I don't think that about you. You had already been in two of my rides and I still had to beg you to let me pay for this trip. I didn't buy the bracelet because I thought you needed it. I bought it because I wanted to. I care about you and I wanted to get you something special. That's it."

"A thirty dollar bracelet would have been good with me."

"But that's not what I wanted to get you." Ideal walked over to the bracelet, removed it from the box, and walked it back over to Ireland. "This is what I wanted to get you." Lifting her left arm, he slid the bracelet onto her wrist then kept hold of her left hand. "Do you at least like it?"

"Of course I like it."

"Will you please keep it and wear it? For me?"

Ireland wanted to say no, but how could she? She could see the disappointment in his eyes as well as a flicker of hope. "I need a day to think it over."

"Okay," he said, before turning her hand over and kissing her palm. "Listen to me. Don't ever think that when I buy you something, I'm expecting something in return." When she looked away, Ideal moved to stand before her. "You hear me?"

"Yea."

"You believe me?"

"I believe, you believe what you're saying."

"Well, I need you to believe it, because I plan on buying you more things."

"I know I should've already said this, but, thank you."

"You're welcome," he said, leaning over and kissing her the way he'd been waiting to for hours. Enraptured in each second, he was ever so grateful when he felt her kissing him back.

As they both became lost in their intimate exchange, Ideal's chef, Tut, arrived on the roof. Of all of the women he had seen with Ideal, Tut had never witnessed Ideal kissing any of them. Dazed, he couldn't resist watching the passion Ideal exhibited toward this particular woman. When the feeling of shame finally arose within him, he made his presence known. "Pardon me, Mr. Morris," he interrupted, amused by the woman's obvious mortification, "The table is set."

"Thanks, Tut. You have a good night."

"You as well," Tut replied, certain Ideal was already having one.

Back on the main floor, they entered a handsome dining room. Its mood was serious, quiet, and cool. On walls the color of clouds during rain were photographs depicting the beauty of fog. Silver metallic drapes framed sliding glass doors overlooking a terrace with another astounding view. Rather than one, long table, there were multiple round tables with seating for eight. They were skirted in thick linens the color of ash and surrounding them were velvet chairs, trimmed in nickel nail heads.

"Do you entertain a lot?" Ireland asked.

"No, I just like the way this looks. I only come in here when my family's over for a special occasion."

Ireland was thankful to hear he didn't have dinners frequently. "So who are you closest to in your family?"

"My mother and my sister, Honesty."

"Honesty? That's your sister's name?"

"Yea, our mother gave us odd names."

"You mean, Ideal is your real name?"

Grabbing his chest as if he'd taken a bullet, Ideal said in an English accent, "And you call yourself a bloody fan."

Playing along, Ireland held her heart. "My lord, I am disgraced." Then on the verge of tears, she whispered, "Please grant me your mercy."

"Damn, you're in the right business," he replied, stunned by the depth of her sudden emotion. As he watched her smile and return to herself, he asked, "So who are you closest to?"

"My parents. I'm an only child."

"Another thing you have in common with Rona."

They walked to the table closet to the terrace, where Ideal pulled out a chair for Ireland to sit. Taper candles glowed beside a centerpiece of white flowers and a bottle of cabernet sauvignon. Most prominent, however, was the dome-shaped cover of a scalloped, silver platter.

"Are you hungry?" he asked.

"I shouldn't be after having that sandwich today, but I am."

"Good. I hope you like what we're having," he said, swiftly removing the platter's cover. Spread on the polished surface were paper-wrapped cheeseburgers, chicken nuggets, and fries from a famous, fast food restaurant. Beyond tickled, Ireland covered her face and laughed as Ideal explained the menu. "Now, this is hands down the best cuisine I have ever had, especially the fries, you must try the fries. And for dessert, we'll be having apple pie. How does that sound?"

"Really good," Ireland said. "But, you know, if I keep eating with you, I'm going to get huge and Michael Weston is going to fire me."

"No, he won't. That would make him a fool and Mike didn't get as far as he is by being a fool," he said with a wink. "So come on, enjoy this meal with me."

Later in the night, after their dinner was well-digested, Ireland received a full tour of the home. She saw the gourmet kitchen, where black cabinetry encased a host of stainless steel appliances. She was then shown the library, which was dominated by high gloss, red paneled walls. While the red shelves were filled with classic and contemporary works, the sofa and chairs were upholstered in a mustard yellow fabric, ensuring the room was a stimulating space for reading, writing, and snacking.

Next, she visited a large living room. Against white crown moldings and baseboards were pitch black walls. Although the walls were dark, the room was surprisingly bright due to various rows of canned lighting. Surrounding two seating areas of red and yellow furniture were paintings, sculptures, and statues, from Africa, Asia, and Europe. A wide, colonial style fireplace was the focal point of one wall and a large, framed picture was the focal point of another. In Ireland's opinion, the best wall in the room was comprised of glass doors that gave expansive views of the park.

Though she had seen more than enough, her tour didn't stop there. She viewed a miniature music studio, three guest rooms, and the master suite. Throughout much of the home there had been bold colors, but in Ideal's bedroom, there was a noticeable shift. Calming shades of beige and caramel were mixed with tones of gray, while materials of silk and leather played off of paisley prints. Across from his king-size bed, sat a tufted sofa, which faced a fireplace and table, flanked by striped chairs.

When they eventually stood next to his bed, the mood between them changed. Gone was their dialogue about design and architecture. Their eyes were the only things talking and the temptation of falling into bed was clearly the topic of discussion.

"So is this your closet?" Ireland asked, distancing herself from him and his bed.

"Yea," he answered, watching her walk away. "The right side is pretty empty."

"The great fashion icon, Ideal Morris, has empty space in his closet?" She opened its double doors then moved into the huge area. "Are you working on filling it?"

"Actually . . . I am," he said, following her inside.

Ireland discerned the closet was nearly as large as the bedroom and though heaps of clothes hung on its racks and loads of shoes rested on its shelves, there was ample space for another wardrobe. Why an image of her dresses occupying the vacant space flashed before her eyes, she did not know.

As much as she liked the closet it was the master en suite that stole her heart. An environment dominate in chocolate marble and ultra sleek fixtures, it exuded simplicity and thereby tranquility. "That tub must be paradise," she said, imagining herself diving into its pond-like size.

"I never use it, but you're welcome to whenever you want."

Recurrently bathing in Ideal's master bath was the most lavish idea Ireland could think of. "Well, your place is really incredible. Thank you for showing me everything."

"You haven't seen everything. There's one last room."

"Your workout room?"

"No, I don't work out."

"You don't work out?"

"Nope."

"Are you serious?"

"Yep."

"Oh, now I see. You're naturally thin and cut so you're okay with us eating pastrami and burgers. Never mind my sluggish metabolism."

"From what I see, your metabolism is just right."

The last room was an actual arcade. It made Ireland feel as if she had stepped back in time. There were air hockey, skee ball, and pin ball machines as well as a variety of video games. It was when Ireland spotted her favorite game of all time that a war ensued with Ideal. The two of them battled, trying their best to beat the other's score. When Ireland was close to victory, Ideal yanked her away from the game.

"Let me go!" she screamed.

"You smell so good. What is that you're wearing?" he asked, not releasing her until the game's song of defeat began to play.

"Cheater."

"What? I just wanted to know what perfume you were wearing."

"It's called, *I Won.*"

"No, you didn't."

"Yes, I did."

"I clearly heard the sound of you dying."

"You wouldn't have heard that sound if you hadn't pulled me away."

"The key word here is *if.*"

"*If* your ego wasn't so big, you would've been able to stand there and take your loss like a man."

"Well, you got one thing right. I definitely got a big ego," he said, walking her out of the game room.

They returned to the living room, where Ideal dimmed the lights then picked up a remote control. With a press of a few buttons, a grand painting slid away to reveal a flat screen television. Ireland never pictured Ideal watching television. She figured his daily to-do list prevented him from indulging in the popular past time. "What do you want to watch?" she asked, sitting in the middle of the nearest sofa.

Once he sat very close to her, he pressed one more button then asked, "How about this?"

At a blaring volume, a cooking show came on where a pastry chef was instructing how to bake a carrot cake. Ireland hollered with laughter. Being alone with Ideal was endless fun. It most certainly trumped being out with him with endless people around.

After watching an entire episode on her least favorite cake, Ideal turned on a dramatic film that had just been released in theaters. The story was about a young, wise man and an older woman, trying their best to deny the attraction they felt for each other. During a heated scene, Ideal turned to Ireland. The look in his eyes was so compelling that she felt a twinge of desperation. He positioned his face directly in front of hers then paused. What she first thought was a tactic of torture, she shortly recognized was a moment of tenderness, as he slowly ran his right hand along her left cheek. Then he kissed her.

Ongoing and intoxicating, the kiss was warm, wet, and wild. Ideal's craving for Ireland grew so strong that he pressed her down onto her back and laid his body on top of hers. With his hand in her hair, he ran kisses down her neck, like he had envisioned many times before. Now, that it was real, he couldn't contain himself.

After encouraging each touch of his lips by gripping the back of his head, Ireland realized Ideal had no intention of stopping. She'd have to stop him herself. Nothing more could happen between them. It was far too soon. "Wait," she said, pressing her hands against his chest.

Ideal's body came to a screeching halt. A command he hadn't heard from a woman in years, he had just heard from Ireland. Although he wanted her badly, he listened to the wisdom of his mind rather than the pleading of his body. With biting difficulty, he pulled himself off of her.

"Are you okay?" he asked, panting.

Slowing her breath, she responded, "Yea, but I need to go."

As much as he was tempted to ask her to stay, he looked at her and said with a respectful nod, "Alright."

Chapter 13

Word on the streets of Harlem was that Ideal would be coming through. It was a place he went to often in order to get his haircut. His visits were so consistent that the locals grew to expect him. Whenever his barber mentioned the day the musician would arrive, supporters gathered outside of the barbershop's front door.

During the times Ideal turned up, this crowd didn't push and block his path. They also rarely requested pictures, videos, and autographs. All they wanted was to shake his hand, give him a hug, and offer their praise or criticism. With vigor, they would advise him on what he should do or never do again. This group kept him grounded. They kept him solid and real. He needed time with people that were the heartbeat of a community, the heartbeat of New York, and the heartbeat of hip hop. He treasured them and in return, they treasured him as well.

It was morning when Ideal stepped out of his car and familiar faces greeted him. He shook the hands of boys and men, gave hugs to women and girls, and pinched the soft cheeks of round-faced toddlers. After minutes of conversing and overlooking a few women's advances, he waved everyone a goodbye and walked inside.

Aside from Clarence, Ideal's barber, there were customers sitting near the door and four barbers working on the tilted heads of clients. Once Ideal shook hands with each male present, he made himself at home in Clarence's black leather chair. Clarence was a tall man in his late fifties with salt and pepper hair and a sweet smile.

"How do you keep coming up with shoes that look crazier than your last pair?" Clarence asked, looking down at Ideal's turquoise and yellow sneakers.

"It's all about vision, man. You have to have a vision."

"I know a whole lot of people with vision and they still don't come up with the craziness you come up with," he replied, wrapping a thin paper strip around Ideal's neck.

"That's because they're not as deep as me."

"Or they're not as high as you. You got to be on something to come up with shoes like that," Clarence joked, sliding open one of his drawers.

"The only thing I'm ever high on is my brilliance. You know what I'm saying?"

A fourteen-year-old boy with waves in his hair and enthusiasm in his eyes decided to join the conversation. "Ideal, I think your sneakers are hot."

"You think so?" Ideal asked.

"What's your name?"

"DeMarius."

"DeMarius, you do what your parents tell you to do?"

"Yea, my father's right over there. You can ask him," he said, pointing at his father who sat a few chairs away.

"He's a good boy," the father said, looking Ideal squarely in the eye. "Stays out of trouble."

"Alright, DeMarius. How about I bring you a pair of these shoes the next time I roll through?" Ideal said.

"Huh?" DeMarius uttered, unable to believe his ears.

Ideal pulled out his cell phone and entered the boy's name on his calendar. "What size do you wear?"

"A ten."

"Alright, I'll leave them with Clarence if I don't see you."

"Whoa! Thanks, Ideal," DeMarius said, going to shake the musician's hand again.

"You're welcome. Keep being a good dude."

"Since you're in the mood to give things away, I could use a new car," Clarence said, draping a cape over Ideal.

"Man, you're doing just fine up in here. You can buy your own damn car."

"Well, I could use one of your ladies," a younger barber interjected. "So when you're done with the one for this month, pass her on over this way."

"That's not going to happen, man. The woman I'm with now is going to be the woman I'm with from here on out."

The collective sound of clippers buzzing instantly came to a halt as each barber froze.

"Say what?" the young barber replied.

Clarence stared at Ideal through the mirror. "Don't tell me after all these years, you went and fell for somebody."

"Alright, I won't tell you," Ideal said with a smile. "Go ahead and get started. I got somewhere to be." Eager to resume courting Ireland, Ideal hurried Clarence along then arrived at his next appointment right on time.

In Queens for a photo shoot with the most successful fashion magazine, Ideal would be modeling pieces from the fall collections of top designers. The shoot was to take place outdoors with an iconic bridge in the background. Once Ideal met with his manager and the publication's team, they went through racks of clothing looking for ensembles for him to try on.

When Ideal emerged from his trailer for the third time, the creative director nodded emphatically. "That looks good," he said, pleased with the combination.

"I like it too," Ideal replied, studying himself in a full-length mirror. He wore a tan, wool coat over a burgundy, cashmere cardigan on top of a light blue shirt, balanced by a navy pant and wingtip shoes.

Once the attire was approved by all, tailors placed pins in a few areas of the clothing and quickly sewed the fabric by hand to ensure the best fit on Ideal. After more looks were selected, Ideal put on a robe and went to the make-up trailer. While getting made up and powdered-down, he met the female models he'd be working with.

As gaunt as to be expected, both models had porcelain skin, piercing blue eyes, and platinum blond extensions. One stood six feet tall and the other stood five feet, ten inches. Although one was quite friendly the other was remote. She seemed angry and exhausted as if she would faint at any given moment. Ideal thought she surely needed a double cheeseburger with a side of fries.

An hour later, in humid, hot weather, Ideal posed in heavy, warm clothing, draped by nearly nude models. To the sound of his own music, he began another long day of work.

Initially, Ireland declined Rona's invitation to go shopping, but with Rona's highly skilled arm twisting, Ireland gave in. All too soon she was kicking herself with regret. With each store they entered, photographers bogged them down on both sides. Forced to take baby steps along the congested avenue, the two-hour shopping excursion felt more like two days.

As they were inching toward their final destination, Ireland's phone rang. Still bordered by paparazzi, the last thing she wanted to do was pull out her cell, but she was expecting an important call. When she retrieved the phone, she saw the caller was Casey. "Hey, Case," she answered in a rushed tone.

"I haven't talked to you in days," Casey shrieked. "What in the world is going on?" Even when either of them was away working, the best friends spoke every day.

"I'm sorry, but I can't talk right now. I'll call you back," she mumbled, ending the call.

A minute later, she went inside a restaurant, gleaming in gold and ruby, where she and Rona were seated expeditiously.

"Was that Ideal on the phone?" Rona asked.

"No, it was Casey."

"I'm going to have to meet her. What is she up to today?"

For the first time in years, Ireland didn't know the answer to the question. Out of habit, she answered, "Work."

"That's good," Rona replied. After leaning forward, she said in a lowered voice, "So I want to know what you and Ideal have been doing?"

"I told you we've been having lunch, having dinner -"

"But have you had breakfast?" Rona asked with a sly grin.

"No, we haven't had breakfast."

"No, I mean, *breakfast* as in breakfast in bed."

"I know what you mean, Rona."

"So do you think that'll happen this week?"

"Definitely not," Ireland replied, opening her menu.

"No?" Rona asked, looking puzzled.

"No."

"Well," Rona said, following Ireland's lead and opening the menu. "I really want you two to work out so it's probably a good thing for you to wait a while."

The entire day, Ideal wondered how Ireland was, where she was, and what she was doing. He also wondered whether or not she was thinking of the previous night they had shared. Images of them kissing on the sofa flashed in his mind just as constant as his blinking. It was all he wished it to be. Electric, fervent, and relentlessly arousing. If holding and kissing her was that sensational, he trembled to think how making love to her would be.

"This neighborhood belongs in a magazine," Ireland said, sitting in the passenger's side of Ideal's sports car. It was an hour past nightfall and they had just entered an upscale community in

Connecticut. The homes looked like illustrations in a fairy tale. "Are you ever going to tell me where we're going ahead of time?"

"I don't know," Ideal answered, conscious of how much he enjoyed surprising her.

Wearing the bracelet he'd given her, Ireland's left wrist sparkled as she tucked a few strands of hair behind her left ear. "Thank goodness I can read. At least I know I'm in Greenwich."

After making two more turns, Ideal pulled into the long driveway of a splendid, Tudor style mansion of brown brick with four chimneys. "We're here," he said, turning off the engine.

"We're where?"

"Where we're going to have dinner," he said, before going to open her door.

"Who lives here?"

"Get out of the car and come see." Smiling down at the cold stare she gave him, he pulled her out of the vehicle then admired how she made simple look sexy. A clear contrast to his pink and purple hoodie, she wore a gray sheath dress with a skinny, black belt.

When Ideal led her up the porch steps and rang the doorbell, Ireland tried to hide behind him. Clueless as to who to expect, she was intrigued when a beautiful woman in her sixties answered the door. The woman seemed happy to see them, but not surprised.

"Hi, baby," she said to Ideal, waiting for him to step inside. Once they stood in the foyer, the woman took Ideal's face into her hands and gave him a kiss on the cheek.

"Hi, Ma," he replied, giving her a long hug. When he released her, he reached behind himself and pulled Ireland forward. "Ma, this is Ireland. Ireland, this is my mother."

"Ideal was right. You are beautiful," she remarked, beaming at her son's date.

Uneasy, Ireland said, "Thank you. I'm not sure what to call you."

"You can call me, Sheila," she replied, giving Ireland a hug.

"I'm sorry. I didn't know I was coming to meet you. I would've brought you a gift."

"Trust me, you being here is my gift. Let's go sit," she said, ushering them into an elegant, traditional style living room with a palette of pale greens.

Ideal pretended not to see the daggers being darted from Ireland's dark eyes. He could tell she wanted to strangle him, but he was too happy to care. He sat with Ireland on a tassel-fringed sofa while his mother sat in an armchair. "Ooh, it smells like peach cobbler," he said, grinning.

"It'll be done in thirty seconds," Sheila replied.

"You cooked for us?" Ireland asked, horrified that Sheila would have gone through the trouble.

"Yes, but don't worry about it. I love to cook."

"And cook she does," Ideal chimed in.

Ideal's mother was the female version of Ideal. She had the same smooth, baby soft skin, narrow eyes, and jet black hair. She also had the slim physique her son inherited. The epitome of chic, she wore classic black flats, a black pant, and a white blouse, which was impressive considering she was in the process of preparing a meal.

"So I haven't spoken to Honesty since she landed in Atlanta. Did she make it to your house okay?" Sheila asked.

"Yea, she was there when I talked to her, but I'm sure she's running the streets now."

"You have a place in Atlanta?" Ireland asked.

"Yea," Ideal answered, taking her hand in his. "I had another place in Malibu, but I sold it. I wouldn't have done that if I had known I was going to meet you."

Sheila was astounded to see her son smitten. "I can't get over this," she said, shaking her head. When Ideal looked over at her, the two of them began laughing as if sharing an inside joke.

"What?" Ireland asked, eager to be clued in.

"I'm just so happy to have you here. Ideal's never brought anyone to meet me.

"Never?"

"Never. You're the first."

Ideal gazed at his mother. The joy on her face was priceless. She had always wanted him to meet someone that would knock him off of his feet. Patiently, she waited for many, many years. Because Ideal didn't believe he'd ever fall for someone, he often felt a twinge of guilt when she asked about his love life. It didn't feel good having to consistently tell her that it was non-existent. Not wanting to give her any false hope, he didn't waste time introducing her to the women that came in and out of his bed. They were women he quickly got tired of. Ireland, however, he couldn't get enough of. She was the woman his mother prayed would one day come along.

When Sheila excused herself from the room to take out her cobbler, Ireland scowled at Ideal. "How could you bring me here to meet your mother?"

"I wanted her to meet you."

"But this is too soon."

"I don't do anything too soon. *Anything*," he said with a snarl.

Ireland couldn't stop herself from smiling at his sexual innuendo. "You could've at least told me."

"But then I would've missed that riveting look on your face. How do you manage to still look beautiful when you're terrified?"

"A ton of practice."

"Okay, everything's ready," Shelia announced, returning to the room. "Follow me."

While feasting on soul food at the kitchen's farmhouse table, Ideal listened closely as the women in his life conversed. Between stories, they shared laughs, often at his expense. Excited by how well they got along, he took pictures of them talking and posted them on his social media. In the end, the two ladies seemed like friends, which made Ideal look forward to them meeting again.

Before leaving, Ireland praised Sheila for her outstanding cooking ability, warm hospitality, and great style. After giving her a tight hug, she and Ideal were off.

Throughout the remainder of their week together, Ideal did things he dreamt of doing as a child and scarcely did as an adult.

With Ireland by his side, he enjoyed mornings at parks and gardens, days at museums, and evenings at live shows. When the time came for her to return to Los Angeles, he was ailed with an acute case of the unwanted emotion called sadness.

Chapter 14

Standing at the front door of Casey's Culver City home, Ireland watched her friend stare at her with a dull expression.

"Can I help you?" Casey asked.

"Can you help me? Uh, yea, you can let me in."

"Why would I do that?"

"Are you serious?"

"Do I look serious?"

Ireland refused to pretend she didn't know what was bothering Casey. Humbled, she said what was necessary. "Case, I'm sorry I didn't get a chance to talk to you while I was gone."

"Yet you got a chance to go shopping with Rona."

"No, she shopped and I watched. Then I got shuffled along in her photo storm. It was terrible."

"I guess that's when you should've been talking to me."

Feeling another layer of guilt, Ireland muttered, "You're right. I'm sorry."

At last, Casey stepped aside, allowing Ireland to enter.

Dominated by lilac, Casey's home had the feel of a feminine cottage. After sitting on her sofa, she folded her arms across her chest. "Well, thanks to the internet I know exactly what you did on your trip."

"You think so?" Ireland said, sinking into an overstuffed chair.

"I know so. You went to a ton of upscale restaurants, one casual deli, musicals on Broadway, museums, two gardens, and of course, Ideal's penthouse. His penthouse! You should've told me that," Casey said, growing angry again.

Ireland was appalled at what Casey knew. "I was going to tell you all of that."

"When? Today? I can understand you being busy with Ideal. That's the classic case of a woman finding a man then ignoring her friends, but hours with Rona at designer boutiques then sitting with her to have lunch and mandarin tea?"

"How do you know we had mandarin tea?"

"I told you, the internet."

"That's insane," Ireland said, more disturbed.

"This is not about your business being online. It's about you not making time for me, but making plenty of it for your new best friend."

Ireland couldn't help but feel that Casey was acting like a jealous girl in high school. "You know Rona's not my best friend," she said, sounding juvenile to her own ears.

"The media says she is."

"You know what Casey? You're paying too much attention to what other people are saying."

"Look who's talking. You can't make a move without worrying about what people are thinking of you."

"That's not the point," Ireland said, attempting to stay on track. "People in the press don't know the truth. They take a picture then make up a story. Quit reading their stories."

"Maybe I would if you'd keep me informed."

"From now on I'll keep you informed."

"Where have I heard that before?"

"I know I should have made time to call. I'll do better next time."

All of a sudden, Casey grinned with anticipation. "Is there going to be a next time?"

"He's making plans for me to come back next month."

"Yes!" Casey yelled, leaping blissfully from the sofa then throwing her arms around Ireland. "I can feel it in my soul. Ideal is the man for you."

When Ireland crawled into bed that night, she waited for her visit from the Sandman. He never came. In the moon's white light, she reached for her hand painted carafe from which she poured herself a glass of purified water. While taking brief sips, she considered what to do with the extra time she'd accumulated. Though she was positive she should remain in bed and study the screenplay that lay beside her, she felt a pull from across the room. Gradually, she made her way over to her desk, where she hovered above her laptop. Before long, she was logging on.

At a hurried pace, her fingers led her to an online search of herself and Rona. Sure enough, site after site declared the actresses were best friends. Supporting the false claims were pictures and videos of them together at the film festival, fundraiser, and ballet. It was reported that because of the deep bond they formed on the set of *Less Loyalty*, Ireland was Rona's most trusted confidant. It was Ireland who knew the classified information regarding Rona's relationship with Dig. This, of course, made her a person of great interest.

Within the dozens of articles she read, most made mention that she was Ideal's girlfriend. A gut-wrenching, nausea settled inside of her when she reflected on her current romance. Because there was substantial coverage on her hanging out with Rona, there had to be more information on her dating Ideal. The thought made her skin crawl.

Jittery with anxiety, she searched her name beside his and found the very news that she feared. An absurd amount of images of almost every one of their dates was posted on countless pages and in an abundance of articles. Magnified shots showed them holding hands and cuddling, which made it perfectly clear that they were much more than friends. Though everything shown was a source of embarrassment, she genuinely felt exposed by a photo of them kissing. At a botanical garden, they stood beneath a rose-covered arbor, where they foolishly thought they were out of sight. A picture really was worth a thousand words and in the media's case, thousands of dollars.

As upsetting as the photographs were, the video clips were creepy. Seeing so much footage of herself was like watching an unauthorized documentary on her personal life. She felt violated as if a group of strangers had put their grimy hands through her private things. Her times with Ideal were organized online for the whole wide world to see. But there was no one else to blame.

Against her better judgment, Ireland got involved with Ideal, and thereby flung herself underneath the microscope. Ignorance, however, had been bliss the past week. Although she noticed the cameras around, she persuaded herself to believe in a comforting fantasy. A fantasy that reasoned, the lenses in her midst were mostly focused on Ideal and any communication regarding the pictures taken would solely be about him. After all, he was the millionaire. He was the musician. He was the celebrity.

It turned out, her helpful fantasy was nothing more than an awful delusion. It was a crutch that allowed her to exist in denial. She had avoided the internet like the plague, preferring to keep outside voices outside. Unfortunately, loud voices, sooner or later, whether spoken or written, have a way of being heard. The comments of various blogs read:

Why in the hell is he with her? He could have any celebrity.
Ugh, she is so ugly. And she's fat on top of that.
She's using him to get famous and he's falling for it.
Ireland has to be the dumbest name I have ever heard.

What in the hell does he see in her?
She must be great on her knees and an acrobat in the sack.
He needs to dump that gold digger and find somebody worthy.

Line after line of mean-spirited comments crowded the pages of popular sites. Considered too unattractive to be with Ideal, there wasn't a thing about Ireland that went unexamined. Her walk was all wrong. Her hair was too long. Her body was out of shape. Her eyes were dull. Her skin was rough. Her nose needed serious work. The dresses she wore and handbags she carried, showcased her horrible taste, and the bracelet Ideal had given her was deemed unflattering on her wrist. The bloggers then took time to list female singers Ideal should be dating instead.

It was as if creating put-downs was a high paying sport and these people were competing to win. They invented or searched for flaws then spent their time and energy expressing their warped opinions from the comfort of their keyboards. Their insults were fiercely brutal and though Ireland knew it was their idleness and insecurity that caused them to write degrading things, she was unbearably hurt. Overanalyzed, criticized, and scrutinized, she had been picked apart in the most grotesque way. Her greatest fear of harsh judgment on a large scale had lastly been realized. Though half of the comments were complimentary, it was the wicked ones that stayed with her. Her feelings had been pulverized and her ego, which she worked diligently on diminishing, had been slaughtered.

A mass formed in her throat. A sting spread through her nose. Then tears poured from her eyes. Continuously they came and continuously they fell as she struggled to keep her cheeks clear of their trails. In that moment, she learned more profoundly what she'd always known. Unkind words cut her deeply.

Without warning, an experience she had at twelve years old raced into her mind.

"Stop it! Hey, I'm talking to you, little girl! Stop it!"a middle school teacher yelled, as Ireland stood with friends in a crowded cafeteria, reciting her lines for an upcoming school play.

"Who, me?" Ireland asked, intimidated by the man she'd never seen or spoken to.

"Yea, you!" he said, glaring at her. "Everybody, be still and be quiet!" he shouted, scanning the room to ensure every student followed his orders. Turning his attention back to Ireland, he sneered, "You think you're tough stuff, don't you?"

"Huh?" Ireland asked.

"You think you're tough stuff! You think you're so cute and smart and talented! You think you're the best thing around here, but I got news for you! You ain't! You ain't in charge of nothing and your family ain't in charge of nothing! You think because you wear fancy clothes you're something special? Well, I got fancy clothes and I drive a fancy car!"

It was the scariest moment of Ireland's young life. She stood there petrified while the adult male towered over her. As he spewed his venom, she was utterly clueless as to what he was ranting about. Mortified couldn't begin to describe what she felt as the entire student body listened to him and stared at her.

"You walk around here like you're so mighty, but you ain't! You ain't nobody! I run things around here!" he roared, just before storming away.

Though the vicious man had gone, the effect of his absurdity remained. Reduced to a puddle of tears, humiliation became Ireland's companion. Seeing the look of pity and curiosity in classmates eyes, made her prefer to go about unseen. The following days and months, she did her best to disappear. Escaping into a protective shell, she abandoned acting, withdrew from leading, and stopped participating in class. As a result, her good grades disintegrated, as did her self-love and confidence.

It was three o'clock in the morning when Ireland shut down the computer and stumbled back to bed. Desperate for peace, she played the recorded sounds of a wooden flute then fell asleep.

As Ireland entered the library of her college alma mater, she listened to a voicemail from Amanda. Naturally, Amanda was thrilled to see her newest client on outings with Ideal. She then requested prior notification of their future activities. Ireland had no intention of granting the request. Reporting her plans to her publicist was a guaranteed ticket to disaster.

Once she reciprocated smiles to friendly faces, she passed through the rotunda and crossed into the reading room. Beneath a beamed ceiling with round lighting fixtures, she sat at a table and began studying the revised script for Weston's film.

Set in New York, Ireland's character, *Lena*, discovers that her lover, *Lorenzo*, has a serious gambling addiction. After months of broken promises, she gives him an ultimatum - he either quits gambling or lets her quit him. It's an ultimatum that even she isn't sure she can live with. Well-educated with a successful career, she knows she should walk away, but is deeply attached to the relationship.

Ireland was an hour into dismantling her scenes when she was disturbed by incessant whispering. Curious to see who the culprits were, she looked over at the table adjacent to hers and found two young ladies looking back at her. One was very pretty with wavy, red hair and freckles along her nose. The other had dark brown hair styled into a pixie cut. When they saw that Ireland noticed them, they immediately stopped talking, but continued with their murmuring when Ireland returned to her reading. Annoyed, Ireland looked at them a second time, which fortunately resulted in a prelude to them rushing away.

Grateful they were gone, Ireland went on marking some of her lines with an orange highlighter. Amongst her monologues, there was one in particular that felt incredibly layered. She recognized she'd have to do more research on male, gambling addicts and the women who loved them. Why did the women stay? What excuses did they make? How did they handle their fears?

The squeak of a chair's wooden legs, sliding across the floor, pulled Ireland's focus from the note she was scribbling. The two ladies had returned. This time, however, they sat at Ireland's table, directly across from her. After another session of staring and whispering, the redhead finally spoke. "Excuse me," she said, apprehensively.

"Yes?" Ireland replied, looking into her hunter green eyes and wondering what she could possibly have to say.

"Are you Ideal Morris' girlfriend?"

A bolt of energy zipped through Ireland and her elbows became glued to her sides. Oddly, she felt caught, as if she had been hiding something. The thought didn't cross her mind that she would encounter such a question at the library. It then dawned on her that she didn't know how to answer. "Uh, no. I've just hung out with him a few times."

"You were just on a date with him in New York, right?"

Not interested in lying, Ireland answered, "Right."

"That is so cool. We love him."

Giggling as if they'd just won the jackpot, the brunette asked, "Your name is Ireland, right?"

"Right."

"Well, we're sorry for bothering you, but we just had to know if you were you."

"It's okay," Ireland replied. Clearly, she was in the mood to lie after all.

Chapter 15

Alone in a dark, vocal booth with headphones covering his ears, Ideal moved his head to a soulful track and rapped:

"She got me feeling like I don't know what I'm about
Had a place I was headed, somehow she changed my route
Got my focus so fuzzy it's hard to see myself
All I see is she's crucial to giving me good health
I can't stand going day after day without her
My heart's been whispering love and it's getting louder
Excessively, you'll see me calling her number
When her plane touches down I'm a roadrunner
Oh no, security can't keep me from her gate
Because I'm shaking and faking like I was all-state
Her pretty face lights me up like the brightest tower
I never knew that a woman could have this power. . . over me."

Ideal pulled off the headphones, stepped away from the microphone, and walked out of the booth.

Boards, the engineer, stood to his feet. "That was hot."

"Play it back," Ideal replied.

"Hold on. You got to let me take a leak at least one time tonight," Boards said, exiting the room.

Just as Ideal was about to play the recording himself, Dig grabbed his arm. "Hold up, hold up. Does Ireland know you're rhyming about her?"

"No," Ideal answered, grinning at his best kept secret.

"Are you going to let her know?"

"I don't know. I got four songs about her and I was thinking about not letting her hear them until the whole project is done or even released."

"Well, when you shock her, you're going to shock your fans. They haven't heard you spit lyrics like that."

"First time for everything."

"Damn, Deal. She got every ounce of your heart for you to be writing songs about her."

Ideal decided to give Dig more news. "I took her to meet my mother."

"Whoa, this early?"

"I want her to know I'm serious."

"Well, you are certainly on your grind. Keep spoiling her."

"I will."

"Don't start slipping."

"I won't. As a matter of fact, I should call her now."

Ideal left the room for privacy and placed the call in an empty hallway. After three rings, he was warmed by the sight of her face.

"Hey, Carrot," Ireland answered.

"Hi, Velvet. How are you doing?"

"I'm good. How are you?"

"I'm good."

"I see you're at the studio," she said, recognizing the wall he often leaned against during their video calls.

"Yea, what are you doing?"

"Reading about high-stakes gambling."

"Oh, I can tell you all about that."

"Oh, now, you tell me. After I'm on the last chapter."

Ideal smiled for a moment then paused. "There's something I've been wanting to ask you."

"What?"

"When you get here, would you mind staying a few days with me at my house in the Hamptons?"

"Um . . ." she said, glancing away. "I don't think I should."

Ideal's shoulders began to slump. "What about for just two nights?"

"That'll probably be two too many."

Ideal knew she was thinking he'd want to make love if she spent the night with him. He couldn't blame her for the assumption. It was exactly what he wanted to do. But he would never pressure her if she wasn't ready. "Look, I have guest rooms there. You can stay in one of those if it'll make you feel more comfortable."

"That's thoughtful of you, but, I'd rather not. I'm sorry."

"That's alright. Maybe another time."

"Maybe."

"Well, I got to get back to the booth. I'll call you tomorrow," he said, afraid she'd see his dejection.

"Okay."

"I miss you."

"I miss you too."

"Bye."

"Bye, have a good session."

When Ideal went back to the studio, Dig noticed his mood had changed. "What's wrong?" Dig asked.

"Nothing," Ideal replied. He then turned his attention to Boards. "Play it back."

Ireland was in New York for a total of six hours when she felt bullied by exasperation. After having lunch at a Jamaican restaurant in Harlem, she and Ideal caught a movie at a theater in the Bronx. Both outings she was surreptitiously against. While she only pretended to feel comfortable being the subject of gapes and advances, Ideal actually was. He had the same cavalier attitude Rona had when she was out shopping. Their continual indifference to being swarmed was nothing short of baffling to Ireland. Though Chase kept most admirers an arm's distance away, Ireland couldn't wait to retreat. When, at last, she hid her face behind the curtains of Ideal's automobile, she closed her eyes and remained silent until they arrived at her hotel.

"Can you come inside for a minute? There's something I need to tell you," she said, as she and Ideal stood outside the door to her suite.

"Is everything alright?"

"Not really," she said, opening the door and walking into the room. When she felt him behind her, she faced him.

"What's wrong?" he asked, his voice cracking.

"I hope you didn't make big plans for tonight."

"Why?"

"Because I don't want to go back out."

"Did I do something wrong?"

"No."

"Then what's going on?"

"I just need some quiet time."

"Quiet time?"

"Yea, like alone time."

Ideal's face arranged into an unmistakable wince. "You feel like I'm crowding you?"

"Huh?" Ireland replied, puzzled. "No."

"But you need time away from me?"

"No, I don't need time away from you. I need time away from everybody else. The photographers, your fans, Greg, Chase. I'm just not up for going out tonight."

"Is that it?" he asked, cautiously.

"Yea."

"You sure?"

"I'm sure. Why are you second-guessing me?"

"I'm just wondering if you're not feeling me anymore."

"That's not it." She could see the fear in his eyes and it astonished her. Ideal Morris fretful about her not being interested in him was strange to comprehend. It seemed ridiculous. Still, she had to convince him that his fear was unfounded. "Seriously, I just can't stomach walking through a maze of cell phones and cameras and being watched all night tonight."

"Okay," he said, deciding to trust her explanation. "Since you don't want to go out, you want to have dinner at my place?"

"Your place has paparazzi sometimes."

"How about the restaurant downstairs? It has a private dining room."

His knowledge of the hotel's restaurant made her wonder how many women he had taken there. "Okay," she agreed, just as his cell began to ring. Grateful they were interrupted, she sat on a chair and listened to him speak.

"Yea, what did Mike say?" he asked. "Alright. That's fine. Uh, make it for a Monday morning. Alright. Wait. I need you to cancel all my plans for tonight. All of them. Get us a dinner reservation at her hotel's private dining room. Okay, let me know." Though he'd been looking at the floor, he turned his focus back to Ireland after ending the call.

"What?" she asked, noting the way he was carefully looking her over.

"I'm just thinking that if you really want some quiet time you should take me up on my offer to go to the Hamptons."

After the trying day she had, getting out of Manhattan was an appealing thought. But spending the night anywhere with Ideal could wreak havoc on her self-control. "I don't know."

Ideal moved over to her chair and spoke tenderly. "We can walk around town and once the paparazzi knows we're there, we can go back to the house and relax. A private beach is my backyard so we can sit on the sand for hours, watch the sun set then get up in the morning and watch it rise."

Ireland was immediately calmed by the picture he painted. "I see why people do business with you."

"Smart people know a smart deal when they hear one and you're brilliant so . . . I guess we're leaving tomorrow."

Ireland smiled at his presumption then confirmed the most important detail. "You said you have guestrooms?"

"Yea, you can stay in one of them."

"Okay, let's go."

More glorious than usual was the sunshine of July when Ideal approached a farm stand vivid with colorful produce. Relaxed from the drive to East Hampton, Ireland remained in the car as Ideal examined rows of flower-filled buckets. In a flash, he returned and handed her a bouquet of fragrant, white lilies. The spotless, star-shaped petals held her attention until a short time later when he parked in front of his home. Ireland was literally amazed. The house was gigantic. Adorned with gray shingles, white columns, and French windows, the colonial structure's sprawling, square footage appeared to be a resort.

With her red sandals atop the circular driveway, she gawked at the home's dimensions while Ideal grabbed their bags. Looking like an advertisement for couples along the coast, they both wore bright white jeans. Ireland's was paired with a skinny, red belt and a blue and white, diagonal-striped shirt. Ideal's denim was teamed with a custom red polo and white canvas sneakers. Though Ideal's ensemble was previously part of his wardrobe, he had a rack of clothes and boxes of shoes sent to Ireland's hotel for her to prepare for their getaway.

At a leisurely pace, they made their way to the mansion's front door then walked inside.

"This can't be your house," Ireland said, softly, in awe of her surroundings.

"Why can't it?"

"It's beautiful."

Ideal laughed at her response. "Are you trying to say my other place isn't nice?"

"No," she said, smirking. "It's very nice in a strange sort of way."

"Oh, so you think it's strange?"

"Back to this place," she said, pointing to the room in which they stood. "I love it. It is so nautical and traditional."

"And normal?" Ideal asked.

"Yea," she giggled. "And do you see how well I match your decor? It looks like I belong here."

"You do," he replied, enjoying the way she posed against a couch. "Let me show you more."

The home was the epitome of beach elegance. Between base and crown moldings were thick layers of white wainscoting that dominated faint colored walls. Overhead were white beams of coffered ceilings and below were ebony, wooden floors accented by beige, sisal rugs. The color scheme was cool with a constancy of navy and white fabrics that embellished sofas and chairs as well as tables of dark wood. Paintings of sailboats and islands invited viewers to breathe while watercolors of smiling sharks invited them to laugh. The kitchen dazzled with white marble and the dining room charmed like a seaside restaurant.

The most phenomenal feature of the property was what could be seen through the many glass doors that lined the sides and rear of the home. Past the Adirondack furnishings of the terrace and beyond the green lawn embedded by a pool, was an expansive view of the ocean.

When it came time for Ireland to see the guestrooms, she kept in mind she had the privilege of selecting one to sleep in. After viewing three, she came to the fourth, which was lovely, airy, and exquisitely designed in icy blues and grays.

"I'll stay in this room," she said, admiring its feminine feel. "I bet your mother stays in here."

"She does."

"It's really pretty," she said, before noticing an odd expression on Ideal's face. "What's wrong?"

Ideal was deeply conflicted. He told Ireland on more than one occasion that she could choose to stay in one of his guestrooms. Although he could see she was thrilled with her choice, he wanted her to stay in the master bedroom with him. He worried that stating his true feelings would not only make her feel pressured, but make her believe his word was worthless. But the need for her in his bed was so terribly strong, he decided sharing the truth was worth the risk. "Are you really going to stay in this room?" he asked, beginning the discussion with a harmless question.

"Is that not okay?" Ireland asked, concerned she'd made a misstep. Perhaps the room was reserved just for his mother.

"You're not going to stay in my room with me?"

Ireland appeared confused. "We agreed, I wouldn't."

"I know, but will you change your mind?" he asked, his eyes pleading like a puppy just put out into the cold.

"I think it'll be better if I stay in here."

"I won't try anything, Ireland. I just want you next to me."

Ireland's legs began to weaken. The beseeching look in his attractive eyes was hard to ignore. All she could do was turn away.

Finding himself behind her, Ideal slid his arms around her waist. "I want to hold you like this all night." He then whispered one word in her ear. "Please."

Her willpower withered like a hydrangea in heat. Once a silent moment of tension went by, she replied, "Okay."

The master bedroom felt akin to a Caribbean suite. Its mahogany, four poster bed, ceiling fan, and doors framing the sea, gave Ireland a feeling as if she'd traveled thousands of miles away. After placing her flowers in water and setting the vase on a bedside table, she unpacked her things then prepared to head into town.

Delighted photographers weren't present, Ireland glided out of the house. The ability to move freely to the car and ride away like a normal couple put her in the greatest mood. Combined with the social hiatus she'd taken during the night before, her uplifted state gave her the gumption needed to face the public.

After entering a quaint village of shingle and brick buildings, they pursued their craving for ice cream by stepping into a sweet-smelling parlor. Their time inside was an unexpected treat as they stood in line, behind a group of funny children, indecisive on what flavors to choose. Ireland and Ideal, however, promptly selected double scoop cones of bubblegum and black cherry. While holding hands, they strolled sidewalks, licking their cones until the frozen food vanished. Floating from sugar, they roamed antique shops as well as designer stores selling a wide range of goods. It was like pulling teeth, but Ideal's companion coached him on the art of contented browsing in lieu of compulsive buying.

Exploring the area for the first time, Ireland realized it lived up to its great reputation. She loved the character of the roads and walkways, the exquisite designs in storefront windows, and the casual attitude of the affluent people. Ideal had been asked to take just seven pictures and cell phone filming of him was very discreet. Fortunately, the paparazzi didn't begin hounding them until two hours went by. Unable to fulfill their desire to ride bicycles with addictive bells, the couple got away from the cameras and hurried back to the house.

To Ireland's surprise, Tut was there, preparing dinner in the kitchen. Rather than wait on their meal indoors, Ideal suggested they take a walk on the beach. Ireland jumped at the chance. The serene sound of the surf met them the moment they departed the living room. They walked barefoot across the freshly cut sod, beside the swaying sea grass, and down his private staircase onto the soft sand. There wasn't another soul nearby. They stood motionless, staring at the rolling body of blue water. Ideal took hold of Ireland's hand and led her further out, where they walked along the shoreline and watched white foam gathering at their feet. As they enjoyed one of life's simplest pleasures, the feel of cool, wet sand gushing between their toes, they had no desire to speak. There was no need to interrupt the songs of the seagulls or the low roars of the waves.

Minutes later, they arrived at a table and two chairs, nestled in the moist sand of the shore. Undoubtedly arranged by Tut, the table presented a platter of cheese, crackers, fruit, and crab cakes, as well as a cold bottle of white wine. Once seated, they enjoyed the appetizers as they observed the splendor of the ocean beneath the sun setting in the sky. It was the most speechless time they had spent together and their connection deepened because of it.

Dinner was in the dining room, where they ate sourdough bread, New England clam chowder, and buttery, steamed lobster. After washing dishes together in the kitchen's farm-style sink, they dropped onto the family room sofa. When Ideal opened the tufted ottoman before them, Ireland spotted her favorite board game, which she insisted they play. Although Ideal warned her that he was the master of the game, Ireland promised he would have to eat his words, no matter how full he was from dinner. Both determined to crush the other, they raced back to the dining room table and played by candlelight. For an hour, they alternated taking the lead until Ireland reached a total of points so far ahead of Ideal's, it was clear she was the victor.

"Just how I knew this would end," she boasted. "Now do you know what m-a-s-t-e-r spells?"

"No, I don't," he lied while laughing at her.

"Of course you don't. If you knew how to spell you would've won this game."

"Why don't you school me on what it spells?"

"Why don't you look it up? You'll retain more that way."

"You know what?" Ideal said, his gleeful expression growing serious. "I've never laughed like this with someone I've dated."

They had been acting so silly that his comment threw Ireland for a loop. She had to admit, she'd experienced a lot of things in her past relationships, but never the amount of fun she had with Ideal. "I don't think I have either."

"I've never been this happy with anybody before."

"Me either."

Perhaps it was the peace and quiet, salty air, or feel-good chemicals from laughing so hard that caused Ideal to speak the truest emotion he felt for her, but before he could consider censoring himself, he said three words he couldn't retrieve. "I love you."

Ireland supposed the prickling sensation traveling rapidly throughout her body was from Ideal misunderstanding his feelings. Though she heard his words, they didn't ring true. "No, you don't," she replied.

"Yes, I do. I have for a while."

Ireland struggled to find an appropriate response. It was hard for her to label the feeling she had for him. She worried it could be an intoxicating level of infatuation. "I don't know -"

"You don't have to say it back. I just want you to know that I'm in love with you. You're the one and only person I've ever been in love with."

Ireland stared into the eyes that were staring into hers and was relieved he alleviated her need to speak. It was something she simply couldn't do at that moment.

"Let's go relax in the hot tub," Ideal said, certain they both needed to recover from what he'd just divulged.

Thankful for the avenue to go elsewhere, Ireland darted to the master bathroom. Before changing, she sat on the vanity's chair and looked at herself in the mirror. There was such irony in the moment. Just as she stared at her image in a bathroom in France, afraid of how visible the premiere would make her, she now stared at her image in a bathroom in New York, afraid of how visible Ideal's feelings would make her.

A man of her actual dreams had just told her that he loved her. As exhilarating as that truth would be, she had to question the authenticity of his sentiment. How could she know it was real? Was he simply feeling something he'd never felt before, and mistaking it for love when it wasn't? On the other hand, wasn't he an extremely sharp man? Wouldn't he, if anyone, be able to recognize if he were in love?

Her early line of questions led to more alarming ones slithering into her mind. Was it a coincidence that the night he first told her he loved her was also the first night she would be in his bed? Did he tell her he loved her so that she'd be so giddy with flattery and so blinded by stars that she would release her inhibitions and sleep with him? Perhaps he routinely used the heart-clenching line on women who weren't quick to have sex with him. Ireland hated to think Ideal could be so calculating, but she knew it was a trait he must've possessed to succeed in his many endeavors. It was possible he thought it was high time he used the trait on her. He was, after all, a man.

As she contemplated moving her things to a guestroom, Casey and Rona's reprimands filled her thoughts. She was reminded she wasn't to think negatively when she was with Ideal. If she'd been enrolled in the *University of Fear,* she would've earned a P.H.D. Instead of beaming about Ideal's love for her, she was searching for hidden agendas. It took some time, but soon she resolved not to sabotage what was one of the most blessed days of her life.

In loose-fitting, plaid swim trunks, Ideal stood in the family room, anticipating Ireland's return. He was a sight to behold. Adding to the magnetism of his good-looking face was a smooth chest, defined abs, and lean, cut arms, marked by tattoos below each one of his shoulders. Though his appearance was sure to entrance Ireland, it was hers that he couldn't wait to observe. His satisfaction was delayed, however, when she arrived in a cover-up. Hurriedly, he escorted her to the hot tub where she, alas, disrobed and revealed what he had been waiting to witness. It was as if she lit him on fire.

In a white monokini with various cutouts, she showcased much of her shimmering bronze skin. Her body was a lovely collection of curves and Ideal found them to be breathtaking. As he helped her into the bubbling water, he examined every inch of her frame then climbed in beside her. Unsure if the steam rising was from the tub or his body, he realized his initial plan to relax was illogical. In an attempt to distract himself from how sexy she looked, he brought up the subject of water sports. Surprisingly, they shared a fondness for surfing, jet skiing, and even whitewater rafting. Amused by their mutual appetite for adventure, they planned to surf the next morning.

Once half an hour passed, Ideal helped Ireland out of the tub then restrained himself from drying her off. Unfortunately, she quickly wrapped her body in a beach towel, making him mentally replay his newly favored vision. Assuring her it was time to prepare for bed, Ideal stayed on her heels as she walked to the master bedroom, but was confused when he saw her grab a tote of toiletries then turn to leave the room.

"Where are you going?" he asked.

"To use one of your bathrooms."

"Why don't you use this one?"

"I figured you were going to use it."

"You stay in here. I'll use one of the other ones."

"Ideal, I'm a guest. I'll be fine using a guest bathroom."

"I said, use this one," he said, lowering his voice.

"How did I know you were going to insist?" she asked, shaking her head and walking toward the master bath.

"Will you do me one more favor?" he asked, stopping her in her tracks.

"It depends on what it is."

From a tall chest of drawers, he pulled out a red t-shirt. "I'd really like it if you slept in my shirt." Ideal watched her hesitate and contemplate then finally shrug her shoulders in acquiescence. Fearing she'd change her mind, he placed it in her hand and walked away. After leaving a window ajar, he gathered a few things, a pair of black shorts, and left the room.

Though Ideal took a great deal of time brushing his teeth, he had never showered so fast in his life. He also applied lotion and deodorant at a lightning speed. Being back in the bedroom prior to Ireland was of the utmost importance. He had to see her emerge in his shirt. He had to see her get into his bed. Wearing just shorts and diamond stud earrings, he rushed back to the master bedroom, but the very moment he stepped inside, Ireland did as well. Unprepared to see her so soon, he came to a halt. In light of how quickly he had showered, he was convinced she had done the same, which he concluded meant she also planned on returning to the room first. Luckily for him, she hadn't.

With a concentrated look in his eyes, he wondered why he found such a sexy woman adorable. Grateful the shirt wasn't too long on her, he admired her rounded thighs and nearly lost his mind when it coerced him into speculating if she had gone without a bra and panty. Though he overflowed with desire, he noticed she hadn't moved an inch. "That's a hot shirt. Where did you get it?" he asked, attempting to put her at ease.

"This guy I know let me borrow it."

"He must be a nice guy."

"He is."

"It looks good on you."

"Glad you like it."

Looking at her face, Ideal discerned it appeared even smoother than usual. It had a dewy glow as if she had received a facial. He was dying to run his thumb along her cheek. "You're pretty without makeup," he said, impressed by her lack of dependency on it.

"Thank you," Ireland replied, relieved he didn't run like hell at the sight of her bare face.

Eager to touch her, Ideal went to the bed, pulled back the covers, and climbed in. "Are you going to sleep standing up tonight?"

"Huh?"

"You want me to tie a pillow to that door?"

"No," she smiled, walking over to the bed and getting in. Straight away, she turned her back to him to lie on her right side.

The soothing sound of the waves had no soothing effect on Ideal. He grappled with choosing the perfect time to move. A few minutes later, he positioned himself behind Ireland, wrapped his left arm around her waist, and allowed his thighs to feel the softness of hers. The moment felt sacred.

As he lie spooning her, he had little doubt the hardness of his chest and abdomen were all she could feel. Involuntarily, his body announced that he craved closer contact. No longer able to resist the urge, Ideal removed his arm from around her waist and permitted his left hand to take hold of her left thigh. Squeezing it gently, he glided his fingers along its suppleness.

Though his mind implored him to stop exploring her limbs, he couldn't. His hand had to take advantage of her body lying in front of his. After caressing the entirety of her arm, the tips of his fingers traveled to the slope of her hip, and unfortunately, came across the cotton fabric of an undergarment. Although he discovered her garden was concealed, he desperately hoped her breasts hung free. Over and over, he pleaded with himself not to reach for them. He had told her he only wanted to hold her. How would he explain failing to live up to his assertion? Why did the answer to that question no longer matter?

He began kissing her neck and shoulder. Interpreting her moans as a form of approval, he had her lying on her back in a flash. Once he lowered his lips onto hers, he clutched what he had been yearning to hold. He and she gasped simultaneously. As he handled her with the utmost care, it was the closest he'd been to bliss, yet all too soon, he felt her pulling away.

"Ideal," she managed to say.

He wanted so much to pretend he hadn't heard the urgency in her voice, but somehow, he did and released her shortly after. "I'm sorry," he said, regretfully.

Ireland sat up beside him. "I should go to the other room."

"No," he responded, quickly. "Please, don't go."

"It'll be easier for us."

"I want you in here with me. I'm sorry for getting out of control. It won't happen again," he said, trying to figure out how on earth he could prevent it from happening again.

Once more, Ireland lie on her right side, Ideal placed his left arm around her waist, and this time, after a long time, the music of the waves lulled them to sleep.

When Ireland opened her eyes the next morning, she smiled. She could hear the loud sound of the ocean, but even better, she could feel Ideal's arm still wrapped around her. She loved the feel of him holding her, however, the position did prevent her from sneaking off to the bathroom to look herself over. She didn't want her disheveled appearance to frighten him when he woke up. Delicately, she began smoothing her hair.

"Good morning," Ideal whispered in her ear.

Ireland looked behind her to see his bright eyes grinning at her. Her assumption that he was sleeping was clearly wrong. "Good morning," she replied.

"So you do stay beautiful at the first sign of daylight."

"If you say so," she said, moving to lie on her left side in order to face him more comfortably.

"Did you sleep okay?"

"Better than okay."

"Good," he said, brushing his lips across her neck. "I was going to wake you to watch the sunrise, but I figured I'd let you sleep."

"How long have you been up?"

"About an hour."

"Are you serious?" she asked, hoping she hadn't been snoring and wondering what he'd been doing in all of that time. "You don't seem the type to lounge in bed."

"I'm not, but I never have a good reason to. I've never had a woman I love lying next to me." Ideal gave her a few short kisses then got out of bed. "Guess what?"

"What?"

"Surf's up."

"Oh yea," she said, remembering they were supposed to go surfing. Sitting up in bed, she asked, "Where's my board?"

"I'll show you after we eat breakfast."

"You don't know how to surf on an empty stomach?"

"I do, but I'm looking out for you. You're going to need some nourishment to keep up with me."

"I'll get some nourishment after I ride."

"Alright, I'll make breakfast when we get back."

"*You* are going to make breakfast?"

"Yes, *me*. I told you I could cook."

"What are you going to cook?"

"Shrimp omelets and grits and it's going to taste like the truth. Ugh!" he shouted, kicking his leg in a way that would've made a rowdy musical group proud.

Ireland laughed while walking toward the bathroom in order to freshen up. "We'll see."

"No, you'll see," he replied, heading out of the room to do the same.

Sooner than later, they sauntered over to the pool house, put on wet suits, and grabbed yellow boards. In the wind, they ran to the sand then swam into the rising sea.

The following days of their getaway were similar to the first. There were fun-filled, relaxing times under the sun and passion-filled, tempting times under the moon.

Chapter 16

After laying out his arguments like a trial lawyer, Ideal convinced Ireland to spend the rest of her time in New York at his Manhattan place instead of the hotel she originally checked into. In the living room of his penthouse, she stood at a glass door, fixated on the view of the park. Conversely, Ideal sat in a chair, fixated on his view of her.

"You really do like looking at things, don't you?" he asked.

"What do you mean?"

"In Miami, you told me you like to pay attention to lovely things."

"I forgot I told you that."

"I catch you all the time staring at bridges, buildings, and trees. You barely took your eyes off the ocean the last few days. You liked looking at the water more than you liked looking at me."

"That's not true," she said, going to lean over his chair. "Your pretty face is my favorite thing to look at."

"I feel the same way."

"About your face?"

"No, about yours," he laughed, pulling her into his lap. "Why don't you let me take you out to dinner tonight then you can sit across from me and look at my pretty face?"

"I can do that here. Let's stay in and have dinner."

"We stayed in the last three nights. We need to go out."

"I don't want to," she said, aware she sounded like a toddler.

"Why?" he asked, puzzled by her lack of interest. When he didn't get a response, he repeated himself. "Why?"

"I don't want to deal with any photographers."

"Baby, you're going to have to. They're not going anywhere," he reasoned, surprised her attitude hadn't changed after she spent days at his beach house.

"I know, but can't we just stay in tonight?"

"No, I want to take you out. I'm not going to let you let photographers keep us from having a good time."

"Scrambling to get in and out of a restaurant is not a good time."

"We don't need to scramble. We'll walk in and walk out like we always do."

"As they snap away at every step we take."

"Why does that bother you so much?"

"Why doesn't it bother you enough?" she asked, standing up and taking a few steps away from him.

"It's not something I can control. I only have three options. One, I can get furious, destroy their cameras, punch them in their faces and spend my time, energy, and money in court. Two, I can get scared and worried and start hiding out and staying in. Three, I can go about my business and enjoy living my life to the fullest. Which one do you think is the wisest choice?"

Knowing Ideal made perfectly good sense, Ireland couldn't resist asking, "Are you sure those are the only options?"

"I'm positive," he said, walking over to her.

"It's not just the photographers in our way that bothers me. It's the pictures and videos that they post. They tell everybody where we go and it's nobody's business."

"Well, they feel entitled to shoot everything, because honestly, people want to see it."

"Well, it drives me crazy."

"You can't let it. You can't let what other people think or say, matter to you. It'll ruin you. You have to grow rhinoceros skin, especially for when your career gets crazy and for when everybody knows that I'm in love with you."

"Nobody needs to know that."

"I don't plan on hiding it or denying it."

"You don't have to deny it, but you don't have to acknowledge it either. If somebody ever asks you anything about me you could choose not to comment."

"I could."

"Don't comment, Ideal."

"Is that an order?"

"Yes, it is. People know enough about us. I don't need you offering up extra information. As much as I love Dig and Rona, they talk too much about their relationship. So let's take a lesson from the smart couples in the media and stay quiet."

"Alright."

"And please stop posting pictures of me on your social media."

"Why?"

"Because, I don't like it. I don't like your millions of followers getting weekly pictures of me."

"Fine," he said, not fine with it at all. "Now, you do something for me."

"What?"

"Go get dressed so we can go out."

As far as Ireland was concerned, their time away went away too soon. She was back in the thick of a sick celebrity world. In the master bedroom's oversized closet, she picked out a dress and shoes to wear. As nausea had its way with her stomach, her heart skipped a few beats. After dropping to the floor, she closed her eyes, and grappled for a portion of peace.

A handsome resort, resembling a castle, is crowned with fresh fallen snow. It hugs the edge of an ice-covered lake. Steadily, flakes fall atop an expansive mantle of white, brightening all she can see below the clear sky. There is an awesome absence of sound. Through the open windows of her feminine suite, she delights in the quiet. The room's stream of warmth nurtures her core, while her eyes take in the sight of the cold outdoors. Inspired, she bundles up and goes outside. Each of her steps sink into layers of spotless snow upon the ground. A dazzling bevy of powdered trees dominate the distance. She ties on skates. and on thin blades, glides along the slippery surface of shiny ice. Wind scuttles over her and she gladly shivers.

Later that night, Ireland climbed into Ideal's bed and into his waiting arms. The moment she exhaled, her cell rang. "Who's calling me this late?" she said, retrieving the cell from the nightstand.

"So is this what you do? You have me take you out on dates and then you go back to the hotel and take calls from your other boyfriend?" Unfortunately, Ideal was only half-way joking. The late call made him wonder if there were other men she spent time talking to on the phone.

"For me to have another boyfriend, I would have to have one in the first place."

"Oh, you don't have one?" he asked, stung by her comment as well as concerned about her delay in answering the phone.

"I don't know. You tell me. Do you consider yourself my boyfriend?" She honestly had no idea of what to label him.

"Definitely," he answered, but not before noticing her phone stopped ringing. "Am I wrong?"

As Ireland prepared to answer, her phone rang again. Annoyed by the noise, she identified the caller and quickly answered. "I'm not on California time."

"I know, but I had to tell you this," Casey replied. "Wait, you're not hot and heavy with Ideal right now, are you?"

"What if I am?"

"Then you shouldn't have answered your phone."

Not surprised by Casey's candor, Ireland hurried her friend along. "What's going on?"

"Guess who is in this week's issue of *Enter* magazine?"

"Do I want to know?"

"You and Ideal," Casey answered. "There's a really good picture of you guys with an article that says Ideal's been dating you for nearly two months, which is the longest he's been seen with a woman ever."

"Great," Ireland said, rolling her eyes.

"Oh, come on, Ireland. There's nothing wrong with this article," she replied, picking up the magazine.

"It's in there, isn't it?"

"Would you get over it? If the article was promoting a movie you were in, you'd be fine right now."

"Yea, because they'd be talking about my work, not my boyfriend." The second the word slipped out of her mouth, Ireland looked over at Ideal. There was no doubt she used the term as a result of their recent discussion, but she was still embarrassed. Ideal, however, was more than pleased.

"Ooh, your *boyfriend,*" Casey giggled. "Well, I'm going to let you go have a great night with your *boyfriend.* I just wanted you to know you made it into *Enter.*"

"Thanks so much for keeping me informed."

"Oh, one more thing."

"What?"

"Did you let Ideal *enter*?" Casey asked, before cackling uncontrollably.

"Case, hang up and call Robert," Ireland said, ending the call.

"So you do have a boyfriend," Ideal said, in an accusatory tone. "Now, I just need to know if it's me because if it's not, I have to figure out who to kill."

"It's you."

"It better be," he smiled. "So is everything alright with Casey?" he asked, relieved he heard Ireland say her name.

"Yea, she wanted to let me know that we're in *Enter* magazine. She loves us in the spotlight."

"But you don't," he said, observing her disappointed expression.

"Not at all."

"Come here," he whispered, pulling her closer then pressing her head to his chest. "Keep your focus on me and you and how happy we are together. Alright?"

"Okay," she whispered back, not wanting him to let her go. All seemed right in the world when she was in his arms.

"I love you," he said, rubbing the back of her knee.

It was in that tender moment that Ireland knew she loved him too.

Chapter 17

It had been four weeks since Ideal had seen Ireland. They were four weeks he despised. Each of the days insisted on dragging by. Although he called and spoke to her daily, conversing on the phone didn't come close to being with her physically. As he predicted, sleeping alone was no longer a luxury. It was a sad reminder of who and what he was missing. Fortunately, the day had come when he would share a bed with her again.

Over the past thirty-six hours, he was in Las Vegas, consumed with his work as he prepared for a show. But everything came to a halt when Ireland finally joined him. From the time he picked her up from the airport to him escorting her through the hotel's private entrance, he couldn't stop sizing her up. He admired her white and black tank dress, accented with mysterious writings, and the studded belt hanging loosely around her hips, which complemented the sandals on her feet. Above all, he loved that with silver accessories, she wore the diamond bracelet he'd given her.

When he opened the door to his suite, she was just as enthused as he assumed she would be. Although he was offered a mountain view villa, he chose a tower suite, knowing Ireland would appreciate the enthralling views of the strip. A luxurious space with three bedrooms, the two-story suite encompassed the finest amenities. Designed in red and coffee browns, it was warm yet lively. Marble floors, the color of mocha, extended from the entry to the living areas, while the floors of the bedrooms were covered in patterned carpet. The master bedroom was upstairs, where massive windows showcased the splendor of their surroundings. Positioned on a bedside table was a vase of red tulips that Ideal acquired for his girlfriend.

As he watched her empty her luggage, he was struck by a particular item. The dress she planned to wear to his show had a serious, edgy vibe. Short, black, and strapless, it was covered in eccentric, square flaps. A drastically different vibe from the casual clothes she'd worn in the Hamptons, he could hardly wait to see her in it.

As they rode the suite's elevator down to the first level, the doorbell began to ring. When they answered the door, they were humored by the flabbergasted expression of the room service attendant. Clearly, the man hadn't been told that Pierce Wentworth III was an alias for Ideal Morris. Keyed up, he rushed in, arranged their breakfast on the dining table, and left with a generous tip.

"I'm so excited to see you perform," Ireland said, feeding Ideal a piece of cantaloupe. "Do you get nervous before you go on?"

At that moment, Ideal realized Ireland rarely asked about his work. His shows, photo shoots, interviews, and appearances clearly didn't interest her much. All of the women he dated, drilled him about his schedule and asked to tag along whenever it was possible. Ireland, on the other hand, asked about his childhood, his family, his political views, and his spiritual beliefs. She wanted to know him aside from what he did. Even now that she was asking, she was inquiring about his feelings, not where she would be sitting in the auditorium.

"A little," he admitted. "A lot if I haven't had enough time to prepare and things are shaky."

"Well, after you eat, you don't have to stick around here and babysit me. Go do whatever you need to do."

"I need to spend time with you."

"You don't have time for that."

"You seriously think I'd know you were coming in this morning and not have time for you? Didn't I tell you I'd always make time for you?" Instantly, his phone began ringing. Laughing at the caller's ironic timing, he looked at the caller I.D. "I need to take this," he said, sheepishly.

Playfully, Ireland whined, "No, don't. Make time for me."

Although Ideal knew she was joking, he continued to let the phone ring. "May I please take this?" he asked.

"Yes," she said, throwing up her hands.

Abruptly, he answered the phone. "What did you find out?" After listening for a moment, he hurried the caller along then gave them a few instructions before ending the conversation.

When his attention returned to Ireland, they finished eating breakfast, listened to New Orleans jazz, and watched a popular series of fantasy films. Hours later, they detached themselves from the living room sofa and freshened up for an early dinner.

With two of Ideal's bodyguards, they journeyed on foot to one of the hotel's restaurants. Ideal had walked through Vegas casinos one hundred times and although he was often accompanied by a woman, his mind was always focused on how well he appeared. But this time, as he passed slot machines and game tables, he enjoyed each step of the walk because the woman he loved was by his side.

Because their steps became mirrored by a growing number of followers, the wood-paneled restaurant they entered, acted as a shelter. After being greeted by a hostess, they were led down a staircase to a private dining room. Inside the room, cocooned by flowing curtains, was a pleasant surprise Ideal arranged for Ireland. Seated at a table for four were Rona and Dig.

"There's the world's best couple," Rona said, standing to her feet and prompting Dig to do the same.

Walking into Rona's open arms, Ireland replied, "The world would much rather see you and Dig than me and Ideal."

"Hey, you don't know that," Ideal interjected. "I think the world's going to find us more interesting than these two."

"If that happens, put me on suicide watch," Ireland warned.

As Dig shook Ideal's hand, he said to him, "You're already lying to your girl, huh? You know that next to me, you're about as interesting as golf."

"Yea, a hole in one," Ideal shot back, before turning to embrace Rona.

After hugging Ireland, Dig decided to give her some advice. "If Deal's not talking about his relationship with you, music, or fashion, don't listen to a word he has to say."

"Dig, get out of her ear," Ideal said, pushing him away from Ireland.

Once they were all seated and given time to study the menu, Ideal was unwilling to keep his hands to himself. He reached under the table and began stroking the inside of Ireland's knee.

"Let's take a picture," Rona said, lifting her cell phone and snapping the four of them. "Ooh, it came out good. I'm going to post it."

"Please, don't," Ireland said, glaring at Rona as she tapped away on her touch screen.

"Too late," Rona said, tapping a final time.

"So Deal, I know you're ready for tonight so I won't ask if you are," Dig said.

"I'll be on like the lights on the strip," Ideal replied.

Sweeping her braids to the side, Rona added, "Anybody that knows anything knows that you will be on so let's talk about what people don't know. Like how good Ireland is for you."

"You are so biased," Ireland declared.

"I sure am. So how have you guys been?"

Ideal grinned at Ireland. "How have we been, baby?"

"Oh, she's your baby?" Rona asked, her eyes sparkling like a glass of champagne. "I guess I have my answer."

"I guess you do," Ideal said, pulling Ireland closer to him and kissing her on the forehead.

Though Dig was aware of Ideal's love for Ireland, he was shocked to see him being affectionate toward her. It was adoring behavior he didn't know Ideal was capable of displaying. "Who is this dude?" he asked Rona.

"I don't know, but I like him," Rona replied, smiling up at the love of her life. She then returned her gaze to Ideal. "Hey, there's something I want to ask you."

"What's up?" Ideal said, slightly lifting his chin.

"What do you think about you and Ireland going on vacation with us after the holidays?"

"You guys always go alone."

"That's because we haven't had a cool couple to go with," she said, tilting her head to the side and causing one of her long earrings to sway. Conscious of the fact that she, like Ideal, loved spending time with Ireland, it made perfectly good sense that the four of them should travel together. Ireland felt like the sister Rona always wished for.

"Now, I know this wasn't Dig's idea," Ideal said, glancing over at Dig.

"No, it was Rona's, but I'm good with it," Dig replied.

"You sure?" Ideal asked, surprised Dig would give up private time with his girl.

"You're my boy. It's not like you're somebody I'd have to tolerate. You know what I'm saying?"

As the matter was discussed, Ireland remained silent. She was shocked and perplexed by the offer. Vacationing with Dig and Rona sounded like a circus waiting to happen.

"Where are you guys going?" Ideal asked.

Dig was the first to respond. "The French Caribbean."

Because Dig was okay with a third and fourth wheel tagging along, Ideal was fine with going, but he knew he needed to consult with Ireland. "What do you think?" he asked her.

"I don't know."

"It'll be really private. I know you'll like that."

"The three of you would be on vacation together and you think it would be private? Does the French Caribbean have a hotel on the moon?"

Smiling at her remark, Ideal clarified the situation. "We'll be on a yacht."

"A what?" Ireland asked, becoming still in her seat.

"A yacht. It'll be just the four of us and the crew."

"Are you serious?"

"Yea."

"So we won't be crowded by fans and photographers?"

"Not unless we walk around some towns, but if you don't want to we can stay on board."

"I've never even imagined vacationing on a yacht."

"So you'll go?" Rona asked, eager to interpret Ireland's statement.

"I don't know," Ireland replied, unsure if she would still be dating Ideal in future months.

"Just say, yes, Ireland," Rona demanded.

"I have to think about it."

"Who in their right mind would have to think about this? You're going on a fabulous yacht with your fabulous man and two fabulous friends. Don't you ever do anything without thinking it to death?"

Ideal could only smile at Rona's assessment. He had noticed the very same thing about Ireland. She was often a slow mover and exceedingly cautious. "Let's go," he said, gently nudging her to accept the offer.

"Are you sure you want to?" she asked.

"I'm sure."

Ireland took a long, deep breath. "Alright, I'm in."

"Yes," Rona said, stretching out her arms. "We are going to have such a good time."

The night was strikingly hot and so was Ireland. Exuding an essence of sex appeal, she glided upon a mosaic tile floor, after making her way through the casino. Accompanied by security, Rona, and Dig, she eventually approached the theater and saw something peculiar. Despite the summer's triple-digit temperature, middle-aged men wearing velvet jackets marched around in dark suede shoes. Their look alone could make somebody sweat.

After entering the crowded venue, Ireland was ushered down the center aisle. Feeling like a bowl of sourdough bread, floating in the midst of a duck pond, she returned the many nods and waves she received until she reached her seat in the front row. Relieved the stares were behind her, she kept her focus on Rona and Dig and on the stage before her.

As the time drew near for the performance to begin, Ireland started to shiver. She realized that she wanted everything to go according to Ideal's plans. He had put so much time and effort into the show, the thought of it not going well, made her ill. She hated to think he could experience rejection. Soon she felt obligated to assume the role of his personal cheerleader. If the show wasn't a success, she would comfort and uplift him. If it went off without a hitch, she'd repeatedly sing his praises. Executing those actions were her new responsibilities.

Without warning, the lights went out. Cell phones glowed in the darkness. Hands slammed together in claps and murmuring voices were concealed by high-pitched screams. When a group of musicians began playing one of Ideal's platinum hits, everyone roared.

Ireland's heart pounded. Her throat tightened. Then her eyes saw her boyfriend stroll onto the stage. The audience lost all forms of inhibition and completely went wild. With a baseball cap dipped low, shading his narrow eyes, Ideal walked about in his t-shirt, jeans, and sneakers with unwavering confidence. The hand Ireland had learned so well, gripped a black microphone, and the voice she had heard so often, spoke beloved rhymes. The ease in which he flowed was hypnotizing. He was so smooth. He was so cool. He had such control.

At certain moments, Ireland felt as if she hadn't met the guy moving before her. He seemed like a famous stranger. It was hard to merge the superstar on stage with the man that said he loved her. Did she truly know this person causing everyone to rock with joy? He was enveloped by an outpouring of adoration and she felt humbled to be a part of his personal life.

She was still sitting, watching him roam from one side to the other when she was pulled onto her feet by Rona. Trembling, Ireland watched him walk to the center of the stage and when he smiled at her, she nearly swooned. As excited as the other fans in the crowd, she and Rona danced to the chart-topping single, blasting through multiple speakers.

Ireland was grinning from ear to ear when something startling appeared. An ensemble of nine women in midriff-baring tops, extremely short shorts, and gold high heels paraded onto the stage. Round and round they swirled their hips and jerked their torsos forward and back. Seductively, they leaned over then swayed their buttocks from right to left. It wasn't long before two of them arrived at Ideal's side and skillfully gyrated next to him. Within a matter of seconds, their amazing bodies were pressed against his.

Ireland's mouth fell open. She hadn't expected any women onstage, let alone nine half-naked ones. She would have been lying to herself if she didn't admit the scene bothered her. In fact, the visual turned her stomach.

Throughout the song, she coped by glancing away or lowering her eyes. Aggravated when the women were too close to him, she anticipated the time their pronounced butts would bounce back into the wings. Jealousy arose, hung on for a while then escorted anger to the foreground of her emotions.

It wasn't until she incurred several minutes of her sickened state that dissimilar thoughts came to mind. She had seen, many times, Ideal perform on television with scantily clad female dancers. Why should this performance be any different? Why should he stop doing shows the way he had done them for years? His performances were a major key to his worldwide success. She would have to allow his work to be his work, the way she'd want him to allow her work to be hers. After all, in a matter of months, she would be getting extremely physical with Alberto Domingo.

Doing her best to ignore distractions, she zeroed in on Ideal who was rapping incredibly sexual lyrics. It was a song Ireland knew well and had enjoyed in the past, but hearing the words live and delivered with such commitment, made her realize just how vulgar they were. Needless to say, she was happy when the song ended and the nine ladies surrounding him exited stage right.

The many songs that followed contained many expletives. Because Ideal refrained from cursing around Ireland, it was the first time she saw such words escaping his lips. If she'd ever forgotten that he used foul language, it certainly came back to her as he brought forth his hip hop repertoire. Though she truly enjoyed those tracks, her heart skipped beats and took huge leaps whenever he sang his rhythm and blues songs. He would transform from a smooth, skillful rapper to a soulful, mesmerizing crooner. His voice sounded so beautiful, it sparked within her hope that he'd one day sing privately to her.

When all was sung and done, Ireland had an amazing time. In the midst of wandering, neon lights, she moved with the crowd and observed their ability to conclude every lyric Ideal began. His fans were clearly devoted. They loved him. So did she. It was time she let him know.

Champagne flowed as celebrities and fans fortunate enough to have backstage passes, made merry with Ideal. Aside from chatting with the baritone, the group listened to the glowing commendations he received from his team, musicians, and friends. Uncomfortable voicing her praise in public, Ireland remained silent like the stone-faced Danielle. The dedicated assistant only uttered a word when swiftly interrupting an embrace between Ideal and Ireland. Apparently, it was at that very moment he needed to hurry to his after party.

In sport utility vehicles, his entourage caravanned down the strip to a glittery casino with a rowdier reputation. Upon entering one of its nightclubs, they were escorted to an elevated VIP section, where Ideal waved to cheering clubbers. Though the majority of people stood shoulder to shoulder on the floor, women wearing g-strings hung from the ceiling. Undeniably limber, their oiled bodies appeared red due to ruby lights flashing in time with the music's rapid beat.

As tipsy female actors and singers approached velvet ropes to compliment Ideal, each of them eventually asked how Ireland managed to snag the guest of honor. Their clever use of words seemed strangely similar to comments Ireland had read online. The similarity led her to wonder just how many bloggers had famous faces.

The party had been going for a little more than an hour when Ideal looked at Ireland and tilted his head toward the door. "You ready to go?" he asked.

The question was music to her ears. She had been dying to go since the moment they arrived. "If you are," she replied, trying her best to remain supportive.

"We're taking off," Ideal announced, standing to his feet.

"Already?" Dig asked, accustomed to partying with Ideal for hours after their shows.

"You just got here," Danielle said, enunciating every word.

Supremely confused, a publicist of his added, "Everybody here came to see you."

"And they've seen me," Ideal replied.

"Hey, if Deal wants to go then he can go," Rona said, assuming he wanted to be alone with Ireland. After smiling at the couple, she gave them a wink. "You guys have a good night."

Rona's words were the last they heard. After dashing toward the door, the shouts and greetings of others were nothing but noise. They made it to their vehicle, rode the short distance to their hotel, and entered their suite without a hitch.

Looking out of the tall window, Ireland studied the city lights brightening the living room.

"The whole time I was on stage I had to force myself not to stare at you," Ideal said, gazing at her profile while standing beside her. "I love the way you look."

Ireland redirected her eyes to Ideal. "Well, I have a confession to make."

"What's that?"

"I love the way you look."

"Do you?" he asked. He had noted the times she called him pretty and handsome but wasn't sure she loved his physical appearance.

"I do."

"Well, I love the way your lips feel."

"Do you?"

"I think I do. Wait, let me see." He moved closer to her, planted brief kisses on her red lips, and nodded his head. "Yea, I do."

Ireland smiled at his smile. "You were incredible tonight. I couldn't believe how good you were."

"Are you for real or are you just saying that?"

"I'm for real. You really impressed me."

Her compliments genuinely made him bashful. If his skin could have blushed, it would have. "You impressed me with all the songs you knew. I saw you singing along."

"I told you I was a fan."

"I know," he said, glancing at the floor.

"Your voice sounded so good it literally gave me chills."

"That's good." Her raving about the show had him feeling like he was the greatest man alive.

"Actually, your show helped open my eyes to a few things."

"Like what?"

"Like, how proud I am of you, how proud I am to be yours, and how much . . ." she said, slowing herself, "I love you."

Ideal's eyelids refused to blink. The banging of his heart, blared in his ears. Dazed, he stared back at her. "What?" he whispered.

"I love you."

Ideal closed his eyes. After dropping his head, he found his breath. Joy, relief, gratitude, and arousal came over him at once. "I love you, Ireland," he said, looking into her eyes. Happier than he'd been in years, he gave her a long, prodding kiss then surprised himself by leading her in a slow dance. Initially, they moved without music, but then he began to sing:

"I'll love you just how you want me to, baby
I'll love you just how you need me to, baby
I'll love you just how you ask me to, baby
You'll see, I'm the man for you
No other dude will do all that I'm willing to
My love's the truth."

Touched by the romantic ballad, Ireland pulled back to look at him. "What song is that?"

"A song I wrote for you," he replied. "You like it?"

"I more than like it."

"Then come take a shower with me," he said, taking her by the hand and tugging her in the direction of the stairs. "I'll sing it while I wash you up."

"No, you go ahead. I'm going to take a bath."

"Then I'll take a bath with you."

"I want to take it alone. There's a lot of things I have to reflect on."

Doing a poor job at disguising his disappointment, he conceded. "Alright," he said, looking away. He knew that she liked her quiet time to think about various things, but he didn't know why it couldn't wait until morning. "I'm going to be quick so don't you take long."

He hurried to the bathroom, stripped down to his diamond stud earrings, then stepped into a steady stream of hot water. After lathering a white washcloth with a thin bar of soap, he rubbed the dripping suds across his hard chest. Throughout the short time he stood on wet tiles, he continually relived the instant Ireland told him that she loved him.

When women in his past spoke the same three words, the phrase had an irritating effect on him. At no point in time did his heart return the feeling so he typically went mute when the expression was imparted. As a result of his earlier experiences, he found it astonishing that he reciprocated the words and the emotion that went along with them. Although he disclosed his love weeks prior, the fear that it would be unrequited, resided within his soul. Hearing her declare that she loved him as well, launched him into a state of awe. He was officially a member of a loving relationship, filled with honesty, respect, attraction, and passion. Because the two of them laughed incessantly, reoccurring physical affection on an incredibly intimate scale was all their union needed.

For more selfish than kind reasons, Ideal ran Ireland's bath as soon as he stepped out of the shower. He then wrapped a towel around his chiseled waist and returned to the living room. With beads of water sliding down his body, he led her to the bedroom, handed her a t-shirt, and watched her disappear into the bathroom.

After drying off and pulling on a black boxer-brief, Ideal lie in bed, begrudging every minute that Ireland was gone. Luckily for his heart, she came back sooner than he expected.

"Thanks for drawing my bath," she said, hanging her dress in the closet.

"You're welcome."

When she settled herself between the sheets, he glided his hand along her arms and intertwined his legs with hers. Following a minute of feeling her breathe, he asked, "What are you thinking?"

"I'm thinking you smell better than you did backstage," she replied, making herself laugh.

"Aw, that's wrong. That's really wrong."

"I'm just kidding."

"No, you're not," he said, sniffing her neck. "Everybody can't smell like sweet, hot, happiness at the end of an autumn feast."

"What in the world did you just say?"

"I said you smell like dessert after Thanksgiving dinner."

"You are such a lyricist. Look how you put things."

"You know I'm right."

"For your information, it's a cinnamon nutmeg body potion."

"Well, that potion is working," he said, becoming still. "It has you smelling like you're good enough to eat."

"Turn over," Ireland ordered.

"What?"

"Turn over," she said again, guiding him onto his stomach. Once he was face down, she sat on his lower back and began massaging his neck and shoulders.

Ideal groaned from unexpected pleasure. He had massaged her many times, but she hadn't returned the favor. Though her hands were soothing, he failed to focus on their kneading. Her thighs straddling his waist and her crotch resting on his back were all he could concentrate on. While she put in great effort to ease his tightness, the tension he felt could only be released in one way.

At once, he reached behind himself, pulled Ireland down onto her back, and lay on top of her. Kissing her lips, he slid his hand up the back of her thigh and held her backside. Desperate to have every inch of her skin bare, he grabbed her one piece of intimate apparel and started to pull it down.

With a quickness beyond fierce, Ireland seized his hand. "Don't," she said with unmistakable clarity.

"Ireland," Ideal groaned, continuing on with his agenda.

"Don't."

"Baby, I want you."

"I want to go slow," she said, flinging his grip from her body, then rolling out from under him.

"We have been," he replied, clobbered with confusion. From his high school years to his musical success, Ideal hadn't waited longer than five days to have sex. With Ireland, he had been waiting three months. Although they didn't see each other daily, they spoke every day and most of their conversations were deep discussions. During the nights they were together physically, he respected her choice not to go further. But that night, waiting was intolerable.

"I'm sure I can guess why eight nights together seems like waiting to you, but it's not."

"Eight nights? We've been together three months," he replied, sitting up in disbelief.

"But in those three months, we've only had eight nights."

Quieted by a mental shift, Ideal stared at Ireland with intense curiosity. "What's wrong?"

"What?"

"What's wrong?"

"What do you mean?"

"I mean, what's wrong?" he asked, sternly. He had to know what was keeping her from him.

"Nothing's wrong."

Feeling plainly unwanted, he wondered what about himself repelled her so. "Why won't you let me make love to you?"

"I just want to go slow. I don't know how else to explain it."

Ideal couldn't believe with the visceral passion they had just shared, Ireland was capable of stopping him from loving her. She had the discipline of a Catholic archbishop. Uncertain of what to do with his hurt and humiliation, he sat against the padded headboard and stared into the sea of lights.

Chapter 18

On the wraparound terrace of a penthouse in Miami, Ireland lounged on a contoured chaise. With sweeping views of endless sky and aquamarine water, she alternated her attention between the balcony's spectacular scene and a fat September issue of a fashion magazine. Wearing a colorful scarf dress, she sipped cold grapefruit juice, rippling its pink, sweet bitterness with her tongue as she waited for Ideal to join her in the hot, moist air.

The whirlwind Ireland was caught in often left her dizzy. The previous morning, she awoke in Las Vegas to Ideal massaging her feet. Though she was thankful for his touch, most of her gratitude stemmed from the fact that he was his usual self. Due to her refusal the night before, she feared things would be strange. Fortunately, they weren't. With a view of swaying fountains, they shared a lovely lunch then headed to the airport for a plane bound for Florida.

Ireland was prepared to leave one sizzling destination for the other. Two weeks prior to his show, Ideal reminded her that she agreed to celebrate his birthday with him. He then decided he wanted the celebration to take place in Miami. Why he preferred Florida during its hurricane season, she did not know.

Following a turbulent flight, they arrived at his place soon after midnight. Entirely art deco, his home's dominantly white interior was splashed with sea foam and sea green accents. Somehow, the art of the two-story pad managed to be more bizarre than those of his Manhattan residence.

"Conference calls and emails. You really know how to celebrate your birthday," Ireland jabbed, watching Ideal walk outside with a laptop and cell phone in his hand.

"The biggest week in fashion's about to jump off so things get crazy now," he said, sitting on a chaise identical to hers.

As Ideal opened his laptop, Ireland returned to inspecting the pages of her magazine. Minutes later, she was caught off guard when she came to a gorgeous photograph of Ideal. Appearing sexy and assured in an unbuttoned shirt, he was modeling for a cologne advertisement. Not until that moment, did she recall he was the face of a French designer's male fragrance campaign. "I don't know what this editor was thinking throwing this tacky ad in here," she asserted, holding the page up for him to see.

Ideal looked up and saw his image staring back at him. Smirking, he went along with her. "Trash," he remarked.

"Filth," she agreed, dropping the publication to the ground. Trying not to giggle, she walked over to the terrace's glass railing.

As she stood before a vision of beauty, she reflected on her good health, loving family, perfect home, and mounting career. In addition, she had the most loyal best friend, generous new friend, and extraordinary boyfriend. Ireland felt embarrassingly blessed. She did not know what she had done to deserve prosperity in life. What she did know with all of her heart was there were thousands of individuals that worked just as hard, hoped just as hard, and had just as much faith as she did, yet their dreams hadn't come true. Who was she to have received such riches? Lacking an answer, the question rattled in her thoughts until she felt Ideal hug her from behind.

"This is nice," he said. "I've never been in love on my birthday."

"I thought you've never been in love any day."

"I haven't."

"I still don't get how you dated so many women and never fell in love with one of them."

"You sound like my mother," he said, as Ireland turned around to face him. "I can't say why I didn't catch feelings for anybody, because I don't know why I didn't. All I know is that once I saw you, I wanted to be wherever you were. I want to go wherever you're going."

"Good thing your schedule doesn't permit that or some people would say you're suffering from an unhealthy love."

"And they'd be wrong because that's a contradiction in terms. True love is healthy love and that's what I have for you."

"Well, since I was your catalyst to having true love I think I deserve a really good kiss."

Happy to oblige, Ideal took her sweet, cold lips into his mouth and ran his hands along her back. A bright, white light flashed around them. A roar of boisterous thunder soon followed. "See how powerful our love is?" he joked, before rushing his lips back to hers. Though they were deeply involved in their kiss, they were interrupted and pummeled by a downpour of rain.

"Whoa!" Ireland screamed, laughing at how promptly the water came down. As Ideal grabbed his things, she scooped up her magazine then ran through the glass door he held open for her. She was still laughing and patting herself dry when the doorbell rang. "Who is that?" she asked.

"Go open the door and see."

"You, go open the door. This is your place."

"And you're my girl so go open the door."

"Right away, my king," she said, performing a curtsy. "I'll be sure to bring you back a ham sandwich too."

When Ireland answered the door, she saw a male member of the concierge staff, holding a vase of hot pink calla lilies.

"Good afternoon. These were delivered for Ireland Rochelle."

"That's me," Ireland said, raising her hand in a humble manner. The moment she took the arrangement from the man's gloved hands, he dashed away. Not the least bit surprised, she carried the flowers into the living room. "This is your birthday, not mine," she reminded Ideal, who was sitting on a sofa, eyeing an email.

"You're welcome."

"Thank you. They're really pretty," she said, setting the vase on a coffee table. Glad Ideal wasn't the only one with a gift to give, Ireland jogged upstairs, pulled shiny packages from her suitcase, and returned to the living room. All too pleased with herself, she placed each present on the white leather cushion he sat on.

"What's all this?" he asked, his face fixed into a scowl.

"Happy Birthday."

"You didn't have to get me anything."

Doing her best imitation of him, she replied, "I know I didn't have to. I wanted to."

Chuckling at her impersonation, he said, "That's pretty good."

"I can't afford expensive things, but hopefully you'll like what I got you."

"I don't need expensive things."

"Ha!"

"What?"

"You could've fooled me."

"I enjoy expensive things. I don't need expensive things."

"You would die without them, Ideal."

"You really think that?"

To prove her point, Ireland ogled the many extravagant pieces in his home. "Uh . . . yea."

"I can't believe you think that about me."

"I can't believe you don't know that about you. Let go of denial and admit it."

"It's not true."

"You don't do anything cheap. You don't own anything cheap. Oh wait," she said, patting one of his gifts, "You do now."

"Alright, fine, I'm not thrifty. I splurge on a lot of things, but I wouldn't expect you to do that for me."

"Even when I'm making millions per film?"

"Even then. It's my job to spend good money on you, not the other way around."

"That is not your job," Ireland said, throwing up her hands in frustration. "How many times do I have to tell you that?"

"Fine, I'll buy you cheap crap." Picking up his first box, he shook it like a child then ripped it open. "Carrot!" he yelled, reading the personalized baseball cap. "It's hot," he said, placing it loosely on top of his head.

"I came close to having them engrave the word, Velvet."

"Then you came to your senses," he said, opening the next box. True to his style, the second gift was a pull-over, print hoodie. "Whoa, this is nice. I like the wild color."

"Of course you do. It's your favorite."

Ideal tossed his head back and let out a laugh. "Chartreuse," he replied, recalling their first conversation.

Ireland felt a great sense of relief that he seemed to like the items she'd gotten. Buying gifts for someone, who literally had everything, was a daunting task. "Okay, open the last one."

"One was more than enough," he said, opening his final box. Unprepared for what was inside, he froze upon seeing two objects. Sparkling in a stylish case was a pair of black and white diamond stud earrings. After staring at them, Ideal stared at her.

"What do you think?" she asked, nervously. Other than things for herself or her parents, it was the priciest gift she had ever purchased.

"How much were they?"

"I'm not telling you that."

"That means you paid too much."

"Will you tell me if you like them? I'll return them if you don't."

"Baby, I love them. I really do. I would've picked them out myself, but I know this designer so I know you spent too much."

"You've spent so much on me, I'm actually afraid to think about what the total could be so don't bother me about buying you something for your birthday."

"Don't spend this much on me again."

"You're welcome."

"Thank you," he said, remorseful he hadn't expressed his gratitude. "Thank you for every gift, including being here with me." Burying his hand in her hair, he pulled her close and kissed her.

Once he freed her lips, Ireland rested her legs in his lap. "So what do you want to do tonight?" she asked.

Running his fingers along her shins, he replied, "You really want me to answer that?" Although he had never been in love on his birthday, he had never been celibate on the day either.

"No," Ireland said, realizing she knew his answer. "Well, one thing you're going to do is let me take you out to dinner. I made reservations."

"You, what?" he said, astounded she'd taken such initiative. "I can't figure you out. I thought you would want to stay in tonight."

"What I want is to give you what you want. You normally want to go out so I'm taking you out." While squeezing one of his shoulders, she added, "But you're driving."

"Wait, if you're taking me out, why aren't you driving?"

"I'm not driving that sports car you have downstairs."

"I also happen to have a top of the line turquoise scooter."

"Oh, you want to hold on to my waist while I drive around, dodging puddles?"

"Hey, if you're going to take me out then take me out."

In the midst of metallic walls, magnificent lighting, and contemporary seating, a dark waiter carried a dessert through the dining rooms of a Miami Beach restaurant. Ultimately, he placed it on the table Ideal and Ireland shared. After enjoying the establishment's glamorous ambiance, red wine, and tender steaks, the couple prepared to taste their final course. Once they took an additional sip of their full-bodied wine, she sank her polished spoon into a chocolate soufflé, while he moaned, enjoying his first taste of a triple-layered carrot cake.

"So what was the best birthday gift you got as a child?" Ireland asked, savoring a strawberry topped with powdered sugar.

"Other than cakes my mother would bake, we didn't have enough money to buy gifts."

Ireland regretted asking. "Oh," she replied, softly. She had no idea what it was like to go without as a child. On each of her birthdays, presents were piled high.

"But I did get a remote control car once. I was so excited."

"Was it chartreuse?"

"No, it was blue," he answered, flashing his famous smile. "Today's been perfect, baby. I couldn't ask for . . ." After his voice trailed off, he continued a moment later. "Actually, there is one more thing I could ask for. It's what I want more than anything. I want to make love to you."

"Shhh," Ireland urged, her eyes darting around the room.

"Let me make love to you when we get home."

"I don't want to talk about this here."

"I don't want to talk about it at all. I just want to go home and be with you."

The sound of Ireland's cell phone ringing interrupted their discussion. "I'm sorry," she said, reaching into her tiny purse. In normal circumstances, she would've ignored the call, but during that moment, she was desperate for a distraction. Though she didn't recognize the phone number calling, she answered anyway. "Hello?"

"Ireland, this is Danielle, Ideal's assistant. Don't let him know you're on the phone with me," Danielle said in an authoritative tone.

"Okay," Ireland murmured, hiding her irritation and maintaining a straight face.

"Are you guys out right now?"

"Yes."

"Good. We're throwing him a surprise party at *Club Six Seventy Straight* in South Beach. Everybody's here so I need you to get him over here now."

Ireland didn't want to spend any time in a club, especially since she had just visited one in Vegas. "Uh . . ." she said, stalling.

"The valet will tell me when you guys pull up. Get him here now. It's *Club Six Seventy Straight.* You got it?"

With a room full of people waiting on Ideal, Ireland felt she had no choice. "Yea," she said, ending the call.

Wondering if Ireland's brief responses were due to her conversing with a male friend, Ideal asked a question he hated to be asked. "Who was that?"

"My agent."

As if buying gifts, arranging dinner, and seriously attempting to pay for the dinner, didn't stun Ideal enough, Ireland wanted to go to *Club Six Seventy Straight.* Although he claimed she wanted to experience Miami's nightlife, he presumed she was trying her best to give him an unforgettable birthday. In spite of him reassuring her that he preferred to go back to his place, she insisted they swing by the noisy venue.

Wet palm trees leaned from strong winds as he stopped his silver car at the club's valet parking. After exiting the vehicle, he opened his giant umbrella and hurried to the passenger side. As an attendant helped Ireland out of the car, Ideal placed the umbrella over her head, allowing himself to get temporarily doused. Once he pulled her against him, he guided her toward the entrance while paparazzi photographed their faces and apparel.

Looking particularly handsome, Ideal stepped along in tan shoes, a gingham shirt, and a cream suit and tie. Gleaming were his cufflinks, wrist watch, and new diamond earrings. As appealing as he appeared, his pride was centered on Ireland. She wore her diamond bracelet, an orange dress, and gold heels.

When they made it out of the rain and into the vestibule, Ideal was struck by how quiet it was. He heard no music whatsoever. A few steps later, he pulled open a door and realized not only was it quiet, but it was also too dark. Something wasn't right. His breathing ceased. Not being able to see or hear was never a good situation. It was a recipe for danger.

In a matter of seconds, he sensed there were other bodies in the room. Even though his bodyguard was a few feet ahead of him, he lamented over not being armed with protection of his own. Years prior, he made the decision to forego carrying his firearm and to rely solely on those of his security. Frightened for Ireland's safety, he now wished he hadn't made such a choice.

Cursing himself for putting her in harm's way, he squeezed her hand tightly and prayed she would stay quiet and follow his lead. Rapidly, he whipped around, yanked her body in front of his, and pushed her back into the vestibule. Suddenly, the lights came on and loads of people began to sing a classic birthday tune.

It took seconds for the song to register with Ideal. Not until Ireland returned to his side, smiling and singing along, did he comprehend the moment. Waiting for his adrenaline to subside, he watched as a huge, carrot cake was wheeled toward him by his sister. Behind Honesty was a horde of friends, family, and colleagues, including Dig and Rona.

When it came time for him to blow out the candles, he made his deepest wish for that night then blew out thirty-eight flames. While smoke snaked into the air, Ireland gave him a hug, which pleased the photographers allowed inside to document the event.

As one of his bass heavy songs began to play, Ideal gripped Ireland by the waist. "So this is why you wanted to come here. How long have you been planning this?"

"I didn't plan this. This is Danielle's doing."

"Yes, this was all my idea," Danielle said, planting her feet beside Ideal. Impressed with her own well-executed plans, she awaited praise from her boss.

"Wow, this is really amazing. Thank you so much," Ideal said, giving her a bear hug.

"You're very welcome. You deserve something really amazing on your birthday."

As his sister threw her slender arms around him, she shrieked, "Surprise!"

"Hey!" he yelled back, beyond excited to see her. "Ma called me this morning. You couldn't get her to come tonight, right?"

"You know she wasn't stepping up in here."

Honesty was attractive but looked nothing like her brother and mother. Her hair was slicked back into a tight bun, her pouty lips were covered in a flattering red, and her full eyebrows were professionally arched. She wore a solid white dress with white heels. Cheerfully, she looked at Ireland and extended her hand. "Hi, Ireland. I'm Honesty."

Ireland smiled and shook her hand. "Hi, I'm so happy to meet you."

"No, the pleasure is all mine. When my mother told me my brother was smitten over somebody I called him right away. And when he told me he was in love with you, I fell to the floor. I don't know what you're doing, but please keep doing it."

"I'll try."

"You don't have to try anything," Ideal said, pulling Ireland against him and kissing her neck.

When flashing lights ensued, Honesty asked, "Has the media been driving you crazy?"

"Out of my mind," Ireland answered.

"I figured. I've seen a million pictures of you two together."

"Yo, you're not helping," Ideal interjected.

After elbowing his and Rona's way into the main mix, Dig shook Ideal's hand. "Hey, Happy Birthday, man."

"Happy Birthday, Deal," Rona added.

"You two could've at least told me about this surprise," Ireland said, glaring at both of them.

"Danielle thought it would be easier for you not to spill the beans if you didn't know about it either," Rona explained. She then turned her attention to Honesty. "How have you been, little sister?"

"Fine, movie star."

"You still with that guy you met in Atlanta?"

"Yea, he's right over there," she said, pointing.

"Ooh, I want to meet him."

"Trust me, he wants to meet you." Rona's presence was lost on no one there. "Come on."

Before following Honesty, Rona grinned at Ideal. "Would you mind parting with your woman for five minutes?"

"I would actually, but I'll deal with it," he said, removing his arm from Ireland's body.

After watching his girlfriend glide to another area of the club, Ideal went to the corner reserved for him and sat on a sofa with a few of his friends. While examining the room, he observed there were numerous women in attendance. Many he knew, many he didn't, and many were attractive. Clad in tight dresses with plunging necklines, they moved around in packs, trying hard to be noticed. As he glanced at several of them, he couldn't help but see the seductive stares consistently sent his way. In the past, he would have chosen two women to take home, but now his mind was expended with thoughts of only one.

He directed his eyes back to Ireland. Although there were plenty of beauties in the club, she failed to blend in with their common, commercial looks. Ireland's beauty was anomalous, which was why he was shaken to his core the very first time he saw her.

Out of nowhere, a figure emerged before Ideal and blocked his riveting view. When he looked up, he saw a tall, young woman staring down at him. He didn't remember her name, but he did remember she was a model that he had slept with twice.

"Happy Birthday," she said, placing her hand on her narrow, right hip.

"Thanks," he mumbled, ready for her to scurry along.

"So how have you been?"

"Good."

"Good? That's all?"

Her thinking he owed her small talk aggravated him. "Who are you here with?" he asked, confident Danielle hadn't put her on the guest list.

"Hill invited me," she said, rolling her eyes as if she were bothered by the director she'd come with.

"Well, go find Hill."

After sucking her bleached teeth, she said, "I haven't heard from you in a year."

"And?"

"Did you lose my number?"

"Yea, intentionally."

"Why?" she asked, hiding how hurt she was.

"I was through talking to you like I am now."

"You didn't even give us a chance."

Ideal was done. In no way, shape, or form, would he risk Ireland seeing him talking to a woman he'd slept with. He stood to his feet, leaned forward, and in a tone as cold as refrigerated steel, whispered in her ear. "You can go find Hill or get put out. Which one you want to do?"

Once she stormed away and unblocked his view, he saw Ireland and Rona surrounded by men. Three of the guys were singers and two of them were rappers, but all of them appeared far too pleased with their female company. With greedy eyes, their heads swayed from one woman to the other, assessing every inch their eyesight offered.

When one of the singers made Ireland smile, Ideal felt robbed. Whether his feelings were right or wrong, they were real. Infuriated, he was tempted to interrupt the conversation and pull Ireland away, but the fear of seeming controlling caused him to delay. "You see these dudes talking to Rona?" he asked Dig, seeking validation for his anger.

"Yea, I see them," Dig replied, carelessly, adjusting the charm on his chain.

"How do you stand that?"

"I don't worry about it. Rona's going home with me." Sensing Ideal's fury, he added, "And Ireland's going home with you."

Ideal couldn't hear the wisdom Dig was imparting. Though it made sense, it didn't stop the overpowering jealousy coursing through his veins. Boiling with possessiveness, he rose from his seat, and ignoring protests from Dig, rushed over to Ireland. Right away, he took her by the hand and led her to his reserved area. With her sitting securely between himself and Dig, he stared into her eyes. The thought of her ever leaving him for another man was excruciating. He never wanted to know the horrible pain it could cause.

"Are you okay?" Ireland asked, noting his steadfast concentration on her.

He wasn't okay. He wanted to know she would be his always. He wanted reassurance that she was his now. He placed his palm on the back of her head then kissed her tenderly.

"Ideal, not here," she said, wobbly with embarrassment.

"I want to kiss you."

"They're taking pictures."

"I said I want to kiss you. Can't you at least give me that on my birthday?" he snarled, upset by her increasing denials. He knew his question was a bit of a low blow, but he meant it. As shock then remorse crossed her face, he saw she would change her mind. Hurriedly, he kissed her again, and all the while photographers prepared for colossal paydays.

Chapter 19

Swathed in abundant, late morning light, Ideal and Ireland stood at separate sinks, brushing their pearly whites. Expecting a call about her future film's schedule, Ireland rinsed her mouth and ran to the bedroom when she heard her cell phone ringing. "Hey, Case," she answered, after viewing the name of the caller.

"Hi, Ireland. How are you doing?" Casey asked, softly.

"I'm good. What about you?" Ireland replied, glancing at the painting Ideal bought at Dig's fundraiser.

"Me? I'm fine. I want to know how you're doing."

"I just told you, I'm good."

When Ideal entered the bedroom he took hold of Ireland's hips. "I'm going to go make us some breakfast."

"Was that Ideal?" Casey asked, overhearing his voice.

"No, it was the milkman," Ireland joked, causing Ideal to grin at her flippant reply. As he left the room, she asked, "Who else would it be?"

"Are you guys okay?"

Ireland paused at the odd and careful way that Casey spoke. "Case, what's wrong with you?"

"I'm worried about you guys."

"Why?"

"The blogs say you guys had a fight."

"What?" Ireland said, facing the window in time to see the sky turn dark.

"They say you had a fight at a club because he was flirting with another girl."

"That's incredible."

"So you guys made up?"

"No, we didn't make up. We never had a fight."

"You didn't?"

"No."

"So you're saying this story isn't true?"

"No, it's not true," Ireland snapped.

"Alright, calm down. I just wanted to make sure you were okay."

To the rumble of thunder, Ireland replied, "I am fine, Casey. There was no fight and the only person Ideal was flirting with last night was me."

Casey could hear the disgust in Ireland's voice, but she had to ask one last question. "Then who's the girl in the pictures?"

"What girl? There was a ton of girls there."

"Well, this one he was whispering to."

Flinging her body into a chair at the window, Ireland asked, "When are you going to stop going online and overanalyzing everything you see?"

"I don't think I can," Casey said, admitting she was a slave to her curiosity. "I guess, I'm too nosy." Delaying herself before diving into the next touchy topic, Casey let seconds of silence pass by then got down to business. "Now, in keeping with my nosiness, please tell me you made love to Ideal last night."

Ireland winced and twisted her lips. "I didn't."

"Not even on his birthday, Ireland?"

"Why does everybody act like there's a rule saying you have to have sex on your birthday?"

"Because there is. But you can even put his birthday aside. You two have had amazing times together and he's shown you how much he loves you. You have to let go of your issues and be with him."

"You know I can't do that yet."

"I know you can't let the past wreck the present."

"Why don't we talk later, Case?"

"What? You haven't even told me about last night."

"It sounds like you already know all about it."

"Oh, come on."

"Love you. Bye."

Ireland closed her eyes in aggravation as the peace she felt prior to answering the phone, faded like a puff of smoke blown into a wind storm. Besides compounding the pressure she felt to have sex with Ideal, Casey brought her the bad news of a fictionalized fight headlining the blogs. Ireland wished rumors would roll right off of her back, but they stomped on her shoulders and ruffled her core. It became perfectly clear that blatant mistruths would be created whenever she went out with Ideal. Most disheartening was the fact that not only strangers but her best friend would believe the gross tales.

Luckily, in a matter of minutes, Ireland succeeded in dismissing Casey's questions. All except one. One of them lingered in her mind with a brash insistence.

"Then who's the girl in the pictures?"

Casey's query seemed absurd at first. There was a multitude of girls at the club, therefore, a multitude of them would be featured in photographs. For that reason, Ireland couldn't fathom why Casey and the media would hone in on one. Following a subtle urge to investigate, Ireland opened her laptop and went online to view pictures of the party.

Among typical celebratory shots were also detailed depictions of Ideal kissing Ireland, her pulling away, and the tense look on both of their faces when he reproached her for objecting. Somehow, an instant looked like an hour-long spat when numerous images of the same moment were posted side by side. Displeased, she scrolled further down until she saw what she had failed to see the night before.

A very beautiful woman, standing directly in front of Ideal, presented him with an amalgamation of naughty smiles and seductive stares. So overt were her expressions, it seemed she was posing for a nude centerfold. Although the woman's actions annoyed Ireland, they certainly didn't surprise her. She had seen countless women exhibit similar behavior when in proximity to Ideal. What she had not witnessed was him responding in such a cozy way.

Though she could not confirm the interpretation of her eyes, it appeared that Ideal's lips rested snugly on the woman's ear. Just as it was hard for the media, it was hard for Ireland to imagine that the words Ideal murmured were chaste in nature. Anyone with half a brain, one good eye, and life experience would have concluded the tête-à-tête centered on mutual, sexual attraction. Perhaps a tryst had even been arranged.

Ireland found it heartbreaking that in the small amount of time she left Ideal's side, he managed to flirt and be affectionate with another woman. His conduct was underhanded and spoke volumes of how he most likely behaved when she was away in L.A.

Feeling exceedingly nauseous, she also felt like a fool. She had fallen for someone that didn't exist. The Ideal she knew was a role he played. He was someone else when she wasn't looking. It turned out, his acting was better than hers.

Livid that she overlooked her initial judgments of him and illogically expected loyalty, she closed the screen then glared at the subtropical storm raging outside. Consciously focused on water splattering against the window, she paid little attention to the dinging of his footsteps jogging up the metal staircase.

"Velvet, you want pancakes or waffles?" he asked, standing under the door frame.

Not only did Ireland not respond, but she also didn't look his way.

"Velvet," he called a second time.

Yet again she ignored him.

"Ireland!" he said, loudly, marching into the room.

"What?" she replied, looking at him with newfound antipathy.

"What were you thinking about?"

"Stuff."

"What kind of stuff?"

"What do you want?"

"I want to know if you want pancakes or waffles," he asked, assuming he had disturbed her rehearsing lines.

"Why don't you make both? You're good at doing two things at one time."

"Alright, both it is," he said, heading to the door.

"Oh, before you go," Ireland said, lifting the laptop's screen and angling it to face him. "Who is this?"

Ideal looked at the image then dropped his head in distress. After grunting, he walked back over to Ireland. "That's just some girl I went out with twice."

"And slept with twice?"

Grimacing, he answered, "Yea, but she didn't mean a thing to me."

"So you don't have any feelings for her?"

"No, none," he said, alarmed that she didn't know his answer. "You're the only woman I have feelings for."

"It doesn't look that way."

"I don't care how it looks."

"It looks like you were very happy to see her."

"I wasn't."

"And it looks like she was thrilled to see you."

"It doesn't matter. I don't want her. I haven't talked to her in over a year."

"So why was she invited to your party?"

"She wasn't. She came with Hill."

"Well, you should thank Hill for giving you the chance to get close to her again."

"I didn't get close to her."

"Clearly, you did," she retorted, glancing back at the screen.

Gesturing toward the maximized image, Ideal tried to clarify its details. "That's me telling her to leave me alone."

"Oh, wow. Has that one worked before?"

"I'm dead serious. I told her if she didn't leave me alone, she'd have to leave the club. She was bothering me, asking why I quit talking to her."

"She didn't know it was because you were done with her sexually?"

Guilt-ridden at the accuracy of Ireland's assumption, Ideal took a pause from speaking. He then sank into the chair across from her. "I'm sorry that I used to be that way, but I can't change the dirt I did in my past. There's going to be a lot of times when we're out somewhere and somebody I've been with will be there. I know it won't be easy, but when it happens, you have to remember that I'm all yours. I've been all yours since France. You got my mind, my heart, my soul. . . and my body if you'd let me give it to you."

"I think your body needs rest. You've given it to so many people."

"Not the way I'll give it to you."

"Don't turn this conversation into *that* one. We're talking about you and this girl."

"The bottom line is, I don't give a damn about her. I didn't want to see her last night and honestly, I didn't want you to see her last night. That's why I whispered to her. I was pissed off, but I didn't want to end up yelling and have you hear me."

Ireland wanted to accept his account, but she knew liars were prompt at giving good explanations. Still hesitant about him, she had to make one thing clear about herself. "I am not going to be with a man that's unfaithful so if that's what you are, tell me now."

"I haven't spent any time with any other woman since the first time I saw you. Normally, I would've had women from the film festival and the fundraiser. But I didn't do anything, because all I could think about was you. I love you. I thought you knew that."

"I thought I did too," she replied, setting her laptop aside.

"Don't doubt my love for you, Ireland," he implored, abandoning his chair to crouch at her feet. "I'm not lying to you. I need you to believe me." With his heart having received an unexpected thrashing, he asked, "Do you?"

The hot seat had just been jostled beneath Ireland. At an important crossroads, she now had to choose between being insecure and suspicious or confident and trusting. Leaving Ideal altogether, without solid proof of wrongdoing, felt extreme and impulsive. Then again, ending things with him was perhaps the wise thing to do. Women so often failed to follow their instinct when it told them to bolt. Was her ailing gut a sign that she should move on or was it a result of her fear interfering?

"I don't know," she answered, eventually.

"Baby, you have to know. You have to know I'm real with you."

"I don't know what I know right now! Just leave me alone so I can figure it out!" Glaring at him in frustration, she waited for him to leave. He didn't move an inch. Desperately needing time to think without looking at his face, she added in a low and certain tone, "If you don't go, I will."

In a matter of minutes, she heard him get dressed, withdraw from the bedroom, and leave his own home. In a state of confusion, she beheld the shifting clouds while grappling with what to do next. At the forefront of her mind was returning to California and choosing never to see Ideal again.

If only she could have persuaded her sickened heart to agree with her mind, Ireland would have been on a flight approaching Los Angeles. Instead, she remained in Miami.

Over the course of several hours, slowly, but surely she recognized she misspoke before Ideal left her alone. She wasn't unaware of what she knew. She was tormented by what she wondered. As her mother had told her years before, she could make herself miserable with her imagination. The decision she needed to make couldn't be based on her speculations. She had to rely on her knowledge, which undoubtedly proved Ideal treated her with the utmost respect and sensitivity. Day after day, without fail, he demonstrated how much he cared for her, which led to their relationship growing stronger. She wasn't willing to allow photographs of an unknown conversation to dismantle what she and he had built. Despite the fact that the ear in which he whispered, belonged to someone from his past, it seemed obtuse to choose jealousy over joy.

After what was hours, but fortunately, just before nightfall, Ideal returned home and wobbled his way over to Ireland. She was sitting at the bedroom window as if she hadn't moved since he'd left. In a moment of quiet awkwardness, he resumed his earlier position by sitting in the chair across from her.

"I believe you," she managed to utter, watching relief appear on his face. Immediately, he took her hand, pulled her into his lap, and kissed her tenderly.

When at last their lips went separate ways, Ireland presumed it was an appropriate time to raise another thorny subject. "Since we had a difficult discussion today I think we should have one more and get it out of the way."

"About what?"

"My premieres."

"What about them?"

"I want you to skip going."

"What?" he said with a frown. "Why?"

"I just don't think you should go."

Her comment dazed him. "Is this about the picture?"

"No, I was going to tell you this last week." Detaching herself from his lap, she stood to her feet. "I want the premieres to be about the film. I don't want attention on us being a couple."

Ideal nodded his head with a sore realization. "So basically, you don't want to be seen with me."

Ireland could see the hurt in his eyes. She didn't want to cause him any pain, but she knew the press would focus on her arriving with him. Avoiding his penetrating stare, she turned and gazed at the blue-gray sky stretched above the teal bay. "If you go with me, the media's going to turn it into a big spectacle."

"It won't be a spectacle when Rona shows up with Dig? It won't be a spectacle when that curly-haired dude shows up with that Australian actress or when the director shows up with that twenty-year old?"

"None of those spectacles will involve me."

"So everybody else is willing to deal with a spectacle, but you can't be bothered with one for me."

"It's not like that."

"It is like that. You'd rather go to the premieres alone than to have me by your side." Lifting his hands, he asked, "You ashamed of me or something?"

"What?" Ireland asked, turning to look at him. His question was beyond puzzling.

"Are you embarrassed to be with me?"

"No, how could you even think that?" Ireland asked, shocked someone as attractive and successful as Ideal could think anyone would be embarrassed by him.

"Maybe you don't want people in the acting industry to know that you're with a rapper. Maybe you think they'd rather see you with somebody more polished or wholesome."

"Would you get real? When you're not being praised for the cool way you dress down or for the weird stuff you make work, magazines call you the most polished man on the planet. And I can guarantee you, most of my peers admire you even though your image isn't wholesome."

"I'm not talking about your peers. I'm talking about the people making careers."

"You think I don't want you around because it'll hurt my opportunities?"

"You tell me."

"That's backwards, Ideal. Being with you would help my career, not hurt it. Keith, Rick, and Amanda, love that I'm with you. They want the studio heads to see us together."

"So why don't you?" he asked, his pride lessening. "I want to tell the world we're together, but you don't want anybody to know."

"I just went out to dinner with you last night."

"And later at the club, it killed you to kiss me."

"There were cameras there."

"Cameras," Ideal said, rising out of his chair. "That's all you talk about. You're so worried about what other people think that you don't care what I think."

"I do."

"Well, I think I should be at the premieres, but I'll go with Rona and Dig and pretend I don't know you if that'll make you feel better."

"That's not what I want."

"What do you want then?"

"I want you to know how much you mean to me."

"Then show me," he said, peering back at her. "Show me." After grabbing her waist, he began kissing her, all the while walking her back toward the bed. When the back of her legs touched the side of the mattress, he pressed her down and lay on top of her.

Ireland wanted to show him. She wanted to show how fulfilled and overjoyed she was to be his. Her body ached to feel him. With every kiss he placed on her body, she became weaker. As his hand dashed underneath the shirt she wore, and caressed the softness of her bare mounds, she considered giving in. But when he tried to proceed further, she heard herself say, "Stop."

"Don't do this, Ireland. Don't do this to me."

"Stop," she repeated, pushing his chest.

"Show me, baby."

"I can't."

It still was too soon. Ireland needed more time. The reoccurring wave of guilt washed over her as Ideal moved to the other side of the bed. Subdued by sexual and emotional frustration, they both lie on their backs, staring at the ceiling, and listening to the steady sound of sudden rain.

Chapter 20

Much to Ideal's dismay, he was unable to escort Ireland to Italy for her Venice premiere. His *Try Real* show in Manhattan happened to be the same day. Though he was scheduled to fly to Europe a day after her film debuted, Ireland chose to leave the continent prior to his arrival and traveled to Toronto earlier than what was expected of her.

He had asked that she remain in Europe to accompany him to a few runway shows. He knew she adored fashion and assumed she'd jump at the chance to see the unveiling of new collections. However, she compared going places with him to running on a high-speed hamster wheel then informed him she needed to hop off in order to catch her breath. Ideal knew there was a bit of truth to the excuse she aligned with her declination, but he predominately believed she was seeking a reprieve from the strain she felt to make love to him. His ongoing attempts to change her mind on the subject were taking a toll on them both.

Ideal had spent countless hours racking his brain on why Ireland was insistent on not making love. One night, as he rode through the Bronx, the reason raced into his mind like a leopard escaping a cage.

His busy sexual history frightened her. She must've felt being with him would be a major risk to her health. She had no way of knowing that each and every time he was with any woman, he protected himself.

When Ideal first became famous, he noticed with delight, the enormous amount of women chasing him down and lifting their skirts. Without pause, he made an oath to himself to always wear protection and never put himself in a position where he could get someone pregnant. He had a suspicion women wanted to have his child so he didn't trust any of them to take birth control.

Although he was confident he was STD free, he had himself tested the following morning, before heading into his SoHo store. By the time he left for Europe, he had received the results he expected and was pleased he would be able to give Ireland peace of mind.

While abroad, he took part in the fast-paced lifestyle and jam-packed agendas he had indulged in for years. He attended shows, meetings, and parties with people from all walks of life. Even though he thrived on activity, he found himself awaiting the end of every engagement, as each of them brought him closer to the day he'd see Ireland again. He hated missing her and was defenseless to the lovesick feeling trailing him ubiquitously.

On a foggy day in the town of London, he was hours into shooting a music video with an English band called *Gold Yarn*. The group, made up of four blond, lanky guys and one brunette, curvaceous girl, had been eager to work with Ideal. Eventually, he agreed to produce two songs that were on their current album. One of the songs was topping the charts and because he was featured on the hit, he was asked to make an appearance in their upcoming video.

In the midst of gliding cameras, he stood before a green screen while the band's female member danced next to him. At the director's instruction, Ideal flirted with the girl, displaying a look of lust whenever she leaned forward. Soon the time returned for him to sing along to the playing song. He stared into the camera's lens the way he had for dozens of videos. Then he sang with ease:

"One day, like on a Friday
You can get with me, I can get with you
We can go ahead and do what we've been wanting to do.
One day, maybe on a sly day
I'll work it hard like this, turn it around like that,
Hit that homerun with my long, wooden bat."

In a split second, he altered his flow and rapped:

"I see you looking and looking and looking at me.
While I'm pushing and pushing you're looking happy.
I got that body of yours feeling so thankful.
The way you screaming and shrieking, I know you're grateful.
Now, you're begging and begging for me to never stop.
You like me dripping with sweat, it keeps you burning hot.
You want it over and over all day long.
But once I'm done with this deed, I'll be long gone."

"Cut!" the director yelled, cueing the music to be turned off. "Ideal, you're a pro. We got what we need. Take care."

Excused from the set, Ideal returned to the lounge and began to gather his things. Laughing at an adjacent table were the male members of the group.

"What's so funny?" Ideal asked.

"We met an American girl yesterday," the guitarist answered, tugging on the lapel of his magenta suit. "We were all doing these wild things, trying hard to impress her, but she couldn't have cared less. I don't think she fancies white guys."

"She's American. She doesn't *fancy* anybody."

"Hey, speaking of American girls," the drummer said to Ideal, "there's been a lot of pictures of you out and about with just this one. Are you in love with her?"

As Ideal considered whether or not to answer him, the group sat with bated breath, waiting for the response reporters would have shaved their heads to hear. "Yea, I am."

"Wow, that's incredible. She's smoking hot."

"I second that," the guitarist said, raising his hand.

"Sorry to end this little chat, guys," Danielle interrupted. "Ideal needs to get going."

Once Ideal shook each of their hands, he pulled Danielle to the side. "I'm only going to stay in Milan for two nights."

"You're scheduled for five," she said, scowling.

"Change it to two."

"Why?"

"I want an earlier flight to L.A."

"You're leaving Milan early to go to L.A.?" she asked, certain he was running off to see Ireland. Over the past few months, most arrangements she made revolved around the actress.

"Yea."

"You have work," she reasoned, still tired from the many scheduling conflicts she had to resolve to organize his meeting with an Italian designer.

"Change my meetings to conference calls. Then schedule morning studio times with Lance in L.A."

Opening an application on her cell phone, she asked, "You're still going to go to Paris, right?"

"I'll let you know later."

"You cannot miss Paris!" she barked. Attending shows in Paris with Ideal was the best perk of her job.

"Relax," he advised, sliding his hand into his pant pocket. "I said, I'll let you know."

***

Though it was nippy and dreary, Ideal removed the chartreuse hood from his head as he approached Ireland's townhouse. Examining his surroundings, he was relieved to see that the suburban street was not only immaculate but attractive with plenty of pruned plants. The palm-lined lane provided the perfect appearance of safety.

With a leather bag hanging from his shoulder and a suitcase parked at his feet, he rang the gate's bell then pounded the door knocker. When the peek door came ajar, he plugged its slot with the tulips he held then gestured to his waiting driver that it was okay to leave. Seconds later, the gate swung open and his eyes met the eyes of Ireland.

Both of them rendered speechless, Ideal took advantage of their muteness and absorbed the feminine vision before him. Her face was as pretty as ever and her legs begged him to come-hither as they were on display in a short, gold romper. Though charmed by seeing her bare feet on the ground, he was most fond of her amazed expression. "How was Toronto?" he finally said with a roguish grin.

"Fine," she replied, grinning back. "What are you doing here?"

"This," Ideal answered, stepping into the courtyard and kissing her. Fortunately, the kiss was returned just as enthusiastically as it had been given. It was sweet, warm and smooth, like folds of melted fudge being scooped by a heated spoon.

Their private moment soon ceased as Casey ventured from the kitchen to the front door and witnessed what she could not believe. Who she saw and what she saw were both thoroughly bizarre. Although she had read multiple articles, viewed innumerable images, and heard firsthand accounts of Ireland's romance with Ideal Morris, the love affair never seemed one hundred percent real. As delicious as it was, it was stored in the spine-tingling fantasy section of Casey's mind. But after stumbling upon live, undeniable evidence, reality set in. She didn't know whether to be more in awe of the fact that Ideal was standing twenty feet away or that he was kissing her best friend.

"Oh, wait," Ireland warned. "Casey's here."

At once, Ideal looked up and found Casey eyeing him with a sharp look of intrigue. Though she was pretty, she looked intense. Unapologetic for the awkward moment, he walked over to her and extended his hand. "Hi, Casey. I'm Ideal."

Shocked Ideal Morris was speaking directly to her, Casey shook his hand and replied robotically, "Uh, yea, I know."

"I've heard a lot about you. It sounds like you're a good friend."

Forcing herself out of her trance, Casey looked down at the bouquet he held. "So you brought me flowers?" she asked, causing him to expose his famed smile. "You shouldn't have."

"These are actually for your girl," he said, moving back over to Ireland and handing them to her.

"You had me thinking you were the florist. You're supposed to be in Milan," Ireland declared.

"I was. I left early," he said, observing the courtyard and the fountain it encased.

"Why?"

"Why do you think? I wanted to see you."

"But aren't you supposed to be in Paris in a few days?"

Retrieving his suitcase from outside of the gate, he replied, "Baby, I know how to handle my business. Don't worry about it."

"Okay," she replied, taking him at his word. Following a glance down at his bag she gave him a crafty smirk. "So now that you're in L.A. where are you going to stay?"

"I was hoping I could stay here."

"Hmmm, I don't know. You didn't make a reservation."

Casey quickly chimed in. "If she's all booked, you're more than welcome to stay at my place, Ideal."

Laughing, Ideal replied, "Thank you, Casey."

"And how would Robert feel about that?" Ireland asked.

"Who's Robert?" Casey countered.

Shaking her head at Casey's response, Ireland turned back to Ideal. "Well, good luck getting comfortable here. It's nothing like the castles you live in."

The moment Ideal was led inside, he was entertained by the wall fountain, but enchanted by the scent of jasmine. "Man, it smells good in here," he said, taking a deep breath. Struck with how beautifully the first floor was decorated, he insisted upon immediately being shown the second. In the end, he was so impressed with the appearance of the small home, it took a moment for him to grasp that Ireland designed it herself.

As much as Casey wanted to stick around and gawk at Ideal's gorgeous face, she assumed he wanted her to scram. "I'm going to go and leave you guys alone," she said, picking up her purse.

"You don't have to do that," Ideal said, hoping to reassure her. He wanted Casey to know he wasn't bothered by her presence. In fact, he enjoyed getting to know her. She had a fun personality that meshed seamlessly with Ireland's. "I'm going to have dinner delivered. Stay and eat with us."

"Since you're twisting my arm, I'll stay."

Two hours later, when hunger reared its habitual head, meals arrived from a Malibu restaurant. While eating, the three of them laughed and debated the thrill of things under the sun.

Quite sometime after sunrise, Ireland cooked grits, bacon, and eggs accompanied by buttermilk spice muffins. While wolfing down the breakfast, Ideal told stories that made her cackle and when the time came for them to part, she left her home appreciative of the morning cheer he had given her.

As he was driven to a recording studio, she drove herself to an acting studio, where she had an appointment with her beloved coach, Clark. Ireland began working with Clark when she graduated from college. Whenever she landed a role, she went straight to him for guidance. Gifted, well-educated, insightful, and kind, he continually inspired her to plunge deeper into characters. Even when there was just one line to say, he convinced her that a line was just as important as a page. He simply brought out her best.

"Come on, you know how that made her feel," Clark said, staring at Ireland with earnest, brown eyes. Dressed in a corduroy pant and cardigan sweater, he awaited her response.

"Unheard," Ireland replied.

"And what else?"

"Ignored."

"And what else?"

"Irrelevant."

"And because she's unheard, ignored, and irrelevant he does what with her wants?"

"Dismisses them."

"Dismisses them. Have your wants ever been dismissed?"

"Yes."

"Of course they have. So show us. Show us the hurt and anger that manifests when what you want is shoved aside," he said, his voice filled with zeal.

After closing her eyes and taking a breath, Ireland returned her gaze to Clark. She recited:

> *"I have never mattered to you. I have never been more than an audience to applaud your firmly expressed views. What I had to say never penetrated your thoughts. What I happened to feel never penetrated your heart. And do you know why? Because you can't see or hear anybody but yourself. You are incapable of learning how to love someone else. God knows I've tried to show you for years. But I am done. I only have one thing left to say. Go to hell."*

As she delivered her monologue, she was suffused by a wad of vigor. The enormous feeling was the primary reason she loved her work. Living courageously in the safety of a scene was a liberating action and while she planned to continually experience that freedom, she'd do all she could to dodge its supplemental fame.

Ireland's hope had always been to become one of those ever-working actresses, hired year after year due to their steady string of powerful performances. Though the women were recognized by their peers and gifted with awards, they somehow managed to fly just below the radar of crazed celebrity status. They had grand bodies of work with grand compensation to match, but they weren't chased by the public or hunted by paparazzi. In conversation, their names were rarely recalled. Appreciated for talent and not exalted for beauty, they were labeled with petite descriptions: *The one with the cold stare, the one with red hair, the one always revered, and the modest one from England.* A name forgotten was insignificant when a face and artistry were remembered.

Among all of their achievements, their ability to lead ordinary lives was what Ireland respected most. A flash of them basking in the spotlight was impossible to find. They didn't dine at the trendiest restaurants or drink at the busiest clubs. They weren't present during brawls and had no mug shots or close calls. At the end of special events, after-parties were skipped, because returning home to their children was their top priority.

An enviable balance between work and family was orchestrated by these women. They were the examples Ireland planned to follow with each step she ascended in her field. How she wound up intertwined in the limelight lifestyles of Rona and Ideal, she could hardly understand.

Chapter 21

Slowly, Ideal crept into Ireland's home, careful not to allow a sound from the squeaky soles of his sneakers. Returning earlier than he said he would, he intended to amuse himself by scaring the tranquility out of her. Ironically, he was the one taken by surprise.

Above the sound of the foyer's fountain, he heard something that struck him still. It was a remarkably beautiful voice singing a familiar song. When he was certain he wasn't hearing a recording, an awareness smashed him like a big rig into a brick wall. The voice belonged to Ireland.

As a professional in the music industry, Ideal knew he was hearing a gift. Strong yet sweet, her tone was a pleasure to his stimulated ears. Her pitch was perfect as she mastered the highs and lows of various notes in a cappella. His vocal ability had nothing on hers.

Recognizing she was on the second floor, he moved up the stairs and into the master bedroom. Though he didn't see her, the splendor of her voice flowed past the open door of the en suite. Seconds later, he heard in the background, a subtle shift of water.

Up until that moment, Ideal was solely concerned with Ireland's singing. The instant he knew she was bathing, he was concerned with her nude body. With a twinge of guilt and a heap of hope, he stood beside the bathroom door and peered inside.

As beautiful as the sheen of her face, the wet of her neck, and the gleam of her shoulders appeared, he was greatly disappointed he could see nothing more. The rest of her was concealed in a deep, vintage-style tub. In an effort to see more of her form, he blew his cover by going into the private space and standing over her. Unfortunately, she remained hidden by a shroud of froth, seemingly latched onto her skin.

"You scared me!" Ireland shrieked, abruptly straightening her back and causing the bathwater to swish violently. "What are you doing here?"

"What are you doing here?" he replied, catching a glimpse of her cleavage through the water's rocky current.

"Excuse me?"

"You didn't tell me you could sing."

Ignoring his statement, Ireland sank lower into the tub. "I didn't give you permission to come in here."

"The door was open."

"Yea, the door was open. I was supposed to be alone for hours."

"I'm so glad I came back early," he said, doing nothing to diminish his smile.

Smiling back at him, Ireland replied, "Get out."

"Why didn't you tell me you can sing?"

"I don't tell anybody I can sing."

"I'm not anybody. I'm your man. I'm a musician that's in the studio every day."

"So?"

"So, you have a voice like that and you kept it from me."

"I didn't really keep it from you. I just kept it for me."

"How would you feel if you caught me doing a phenomenal job acting out some two page, tear-jerker monologue?"

Ireland took a beat to think. "Okay, I should've told you."

"Yea, you should've told me. I could've put you on my album," he said with regret.

"Oh, no, you couldn't have," she declared, adamantly.

"I'm putting you on my next one."

"No, you're not. I don't want to be a singer."

"You already are."

"I'm a singer for myself. I sing when I'm alone."

"Start singing for the world."

"I'll stick to my acting career," she said, lying back to rest her head again.

"You can do both. I'll produce your music."

Ireland sat back up. "I am not going to have any music."

"I think you will."

"I think you're crazy."

"What's driving me crazy is you naked in that water," he said, kneeling beside the tub. Picking up her ylang-ylang salt scrub, he scooped a portion into his palm. "Let me exfoliate you."

"I can manage."

"So can I," he replied, swirling the grains onto one of her damp shoulders. Continuing a circling motion, his hand traveled to the back of her neck then moved to the shoulder closest to him. After buffing the delicate skin above her chest, he plunged his arm into the bubbles below. Slowly, his hand slid underneath her thigh and down to her ankle. Lifting her leg out of the water, he placed her foot on the edge of the tub and rubbed more scrub on her knee.

With nearly every inch of skin he glazed, he kept his focus on Ireland's face, trying to engage her in eye contact. Confident she was too nervous to look at him directly, he caressed all of her limbs then made sure she was well rinsed. Only when he returned his hands to himself, did she look him in the eye.

"Thank you," she said, convinced he was done.

"Stand up so I can do the places I missed."

"I already did those places."

"Then stand up so I can dry you off."

"I'm not done soaking."

"Actually, you are. You have to get ready to go."

"Go where?"

"Out," he said, rising to his feet. "I have an appointment and I want you to go with me."

"I was going to cook you dinner tonight."

"Thank you, baby. Do it tomorrow," he said, grabbing her white bath towel. With his eyes twinkling at a rapid pace, he held the towel up and taunted her to stand. "Come on."

"Get out."

Deciding to forego the rear entrance, Ideal had his driver park directly in front of a Beverly Hills jewelry store. After assuring Ireland the appointment had nothing to do with her, he helped her out of the car and looked her over once more. At his request, she wore a pink and red dress to complement the pink and red shirt he wore with denim. Pleased that they appeared to be a perfect match, he escorted her across the sidewalk and beyond a gold door.

They were welcomed by an elderly, slick-haired jeweler who was more than prepared for the meeting. Straight away, he led the couple to a private room where a display of jaw-dropping jewels had been carefully assembled. A dozen dark velvet cases presented extraordinary works of art with the most amazing brilliance. As the stones of each exquisitely designed piece glittered from a system of high-intensity lighting, Ireland was awestruck.

Jovial that he succeeded in blowing her mind again, Ideal watched as she stood bedazzled, scanning the sparkling treasures. All the while, he wondered how long it would be before she perceived the most telling aspect of the assortment. Every case contained earrings and every pair contained diamonds, but also blue sapphires. Soon enough, she noticed the collection's distinctions and accused him of rummaging through her closet. Proudly, he confessed that he had taken a peek at the dark blue gown she planned to wear to her next premiere.

When he made an attempt to usher her to one of two empty chairs, Ireland wouldn't budge. Holding her ground, she informed him that she didn't want a gift from the store. To pacify their stand-off, he claimed he brought her there solely to browse. It was a claim she knew wasn't true.

Once they were seated, she planned to glance at the merchandise, but the lure of the gems proved too powerful to resist. At the jeweler's strict insistence, she tried all of them on and as they hung from the lobes of her ears, Ideal monitored her reactions. Eventually, when her modeling came to a close, he asked her to choose a pair for him to buy. Without delay, she refused.

Although he knew she'd be uncomfortable with the jewelry-picking process, he hadn't anticipated her being unreasonable. No matter how hard he reasoned with her, she wouldn't voice her preference. The more stubborn she grew, the more frustrated he became. Done with bickering, he ultimately made a selection himself and purchased long, drop, diamond-filled earrings accentuating eight-carat, pear-shaped, sapphires. With a velvet box shoved deep into his pocket, he and Ireland left the store and re-entered their awaiting car.

After traveling a few blocks, they pulled up to a Chinese restaurant then walked beside photographers, beaming with satisfaction. Once the cameras were behind them, they entered the eatery and were shown to a small table near the rear.

As they sat in the loud, heaving room, the silence between them festered. She was genuinely angry that he bought the earrings and he was disillusioned she wasn't thrilled about it. Although he remained perplexed, her lack of speech had him feeling deprived.

"Are you going to talk to me tonight?" he asked, softly, aware the ogling couple beside them looked eager to eavesdrop.

"You don't listen to me when I speak so why bother?" Ireland replied, her focus fixed on the menu she held.

Seeing her undaunted by their neighbors overhearing was a clear indication of just how angry she was. "You know that's not true," Ideal murmured. "I always listen to you."

"You didn't today."

"I did. I just didn't do what you wanted me to do." Fed up with her avoiding his eyes, he said, impatiently, "Look at me." The moment her gaze met his, the perpetual heat between them surged. "I wanted to buy you something really nice for the premiere and I thought sapphires would look good with your dress. What's wrong with that?"

"What's wrong is that you think everything nice has to equal a surgeon's salary. You could've found sapphires at a department store."

"What?" Ideal replied, tightening his face. "I'm not going to some mall to buy you jewelry."

"See, that's what I mean. You always feel this twisted compulsion to buy top of the line things at top of the line stores. Life is not about labels."

Before he had a chance to respond, a young waitress arrived at their table. "Good evening, Mr. Morris," she said, keyed up to be waiting on him.

"Good evening," Ideal replied.

"My name's Jessica. I'll be your server tonight. Is there anything I can start you off with? A drink or an appetizer?" she asked, her teal eyes never once looking at Ireland.

"Give us ten minutes."

"Okay, sure. I'll be back in ten," she said, her streaked ponytail swinging as she pranced away.

Aiming for enlightenment, Ideal resumed their discussion with an earnest question. "Baby, why won't you let me try to take care of you?"

"You already do. You take care of me better than any man I've ever been with, but it's not because of the things you buy me."

"Then the things I buy you should be the icing on the cake."

"They're too expensive."

"Not for me," he said, bluntly. He'd grown accustomed to his exceeding wealth and spent what he could afford.

"I know you have a lot of money and you've been handling it just fine for years, but when you're spending it on me I feel like I have a right to say something."

"You can say all you want as long as I can buy all I want." Reaching across the table, he pulled the menu from her grasp, set it down, and took her hand into his. "Buying things for you makes me feel good. Allow me that."

Tense from his public display of affection, Ireland watched his thumb caressing her fingers. "Can I ask you something?"

"Anything."

"How important is money to you?"

"Extremely," he answered, unapologetically. "I didn't have any growing up and when you don't have any you learn early that money is power."

"So you think you'd feel powerless without it?"

"I know I would. I already lived like that. I had to start working when I was ten. We went years living check to check, worrying about bills, getting our electricity cut off, not being able to go somewhere or buy something because we couldn't afford it. I could never go back to that. It's not a life," he said, staring down at the white tablecloth.

"It is a life. It's a much more difficult one, but it's a life. Good people live that way every day."

"Well, I have to stay successful."

"So successful means rich to you?"

"Yep, rich doing what you love." Ideal knew Ireland didn't agree with him. She felt success was having peace. Whether it was on the white sands of a beach or the cold floors of a studio apartment, she felt if peace was present, one was well off. Ideal didn't buy her philosophy. He believed he had lots of peace because he had lots of money.

"What about just doing what you love?"

"It's not good enough if you can't afford things you want."

"Things like a home and a car or five homes and five cars?" she asked, raising her voice above the rise in chatter as a television actor entered the restaurant.

"If you want five homes and can't get them, you're not as successful as you need to be."

"That is ridiculous," Ireland blurted, slipping her hand away.

"Why?"

"Because you talk like people should be able to afford every single thing they dream of."

"They should," he replied, furrowing his brow.

Ireland, as well as the woman sitting beside her, looked at Ideal as if he had grown two heads. "The sad thing is you aren't joking. You are actually serious."

"I am. I know you say that peace brings joy, but I say money brings peace."

After taking a beat to breathe deeply, Ireland leaned forward with worry in her eyes. "Here's the thing," she whispered, "I need to know that you know, people without money are just as important as people with tons of it. A homeless man isn't less human than a millionaire."

"I can't believe you're trying to tell me this," Ideal muttered, shaking his head. "You don't think I know that?"

"I don't know what to think. Throughout this conversation, you have been talking crazy. A second ago, I realized I need to get clear on some things and make sure I know the real you."

"Look, the real me has been homeless more than once. My mother was homeless right along with me. Even though I envied people driving fancy cars and living in fancy mansions, I knew back then that they couldn't hold a candle to my mother's worth. Today, the real me spends a lot of time with the filthy rich and the really poor. I still know the size of a wallet has nothing to do with the size of a heart. Money doesn't give you character or kindness or compassion or love. It just gives you diamonds and sapphires," he said, amused by his final words. When he saw the corners of Ireland's mouth turn up, he asked, "Do you like the earrings?"

"You know I do."

"I know you're ungrateful. You didn't say thank you."

"Thank you, Ideal. I can't believe you bought such an incredible gift for me."

"I can't believe how incredible you make me feel." After adoring the touched expression on Ireland's face, Ideal detected similar looks on the faces of their neighbors. Turning toward them, he asked, "Did you guys catch all of that?"

"Yea," they admitted, with a timorous laugh.

The Santa Ana winds grew so strong that high-pitched howls were audible through the sealed windows of Ireland's bedroom. With the exception of a thin creek of moonlight, the room was dark, yet Ideal could see Ireland's figure moving about. When she turned on the soft light of a small, glass lamp, his eyes gripped hers immediately. Compacted in their stare was the weighty, lustful attraction that consistently streamed between them.

Without a second to spare, Ideal kissed her so frantically, he crashed her against the desk. After yanking off his shirt and exposing his hairless chest, he whirled her around, took hold of the zipper at the nape of her neck, and slid it to her waist. Turning her back around to face him, he tugged on the top of her dress until he revealed the entirety of her crimson bra. Below her neck, his lips descended then paused upon the brink of her breasts.

Temporarily abandoning her upper body, he drove her dress to the floor and hoisted her up with a grip on her backside. Step by step, he carried her to the neatly made bed. When her dangling legs wrapped around his waist, he knew she was ready at last. In a matter of minutes, he would love her completely. In a matter of moments, he would feel her completely.

It was horizontal heaven, hearing no protests, as he moved his boxer-clad pelvis atop the panty that shielded hers. After tending to her bosom, he moved down to her lower limbs. Soon they both were delirious, she from his mouth exploring her thighs, he from the scent that lingered between them. Choosing to no longer delay their gratification, he drifted to her body's most secluded part.

"Don't," Ireland said, unexpectedly.

Assuming she thought he felt obligated to please her, he reassured her it was one of his deepest desires. "I've been dying to. Let me."

"No."

"Let me, baby."

"No," she said, reaching for his shoulders.

"Please," Ideal, grunted, pressing her back down to lie flat. What he so badly wanted, he was so close to having.

"I said, no."

When her stubbornness failed to convert into surrender, his desperation ruled his judgment. Intent on obliterating her resistance, he swiftly detained her wrists.

"Ideal, stop it," she insisted, kneeing him in the chest.

"You, stop it," he retorted. Staring up at her, he realized that in spite of everything, she failed to comprehend how dire his yearning was. At a loss for original words, he whispered "I need you."

"I know. . . but I still want to wait," she said, her eyes soliciting understanding.

Although it was the painful phrase he'd heard from her too many times, it had never been so excruciating. Writhing, he reached out to her again. "Ireland, I need you."

"I'm not ready."

Exploding into a rage, Ideal sprung to his feet and roared, "Why the hell not? I told you I got tested! I'm healthy!"

Scared into silence by his unpredictable reaction, it took Ireland a while to voice her response. Following a visible gulp, she finally murmured, "That's not it."

"Then what the hell is it? Tell me."

"How many times do I have to tell you? I want to wait."

"I can't wait anymore!"

"Well, you have to," she said with an unplanned sass that seemed to leap from her previously held tongue.

The look in Ideal's eyes shifted from anger to defiance. "Do I?" he asked. He knew that if he made the decision to have her that night, he could very well have her that night. Never in his life had he thought of forcing a woman, but at that moment he considered it. Ultimately, his love for her impeded him from acting brutally. As much as he wanted Ireland, he didn't want her in that way. He needed her ready and willing.

The speed of the winds grew faster, causing the rustling of leaves to sound like rushing water. Feeling warned by the weather's abrupt interference, Ideal spoke in a hushed tone. "I hate not being able to make love to you. I hate it. So I don't understand how it's easy for you not to be with me."

"I never said it was easy."

"But it is."

"It's not."

"Then stop," he said, sitting back on the bed and leaning over her. "Stop keeping us from each other. Let me make love to you."

"I can't."

Instantly, Ideal's rage resurfaced. Back on his feet, he yelled, "Why didn't you tell me you wanted a sexless relationship?"

"I don't. I just want to wait awhile."

"Until when? When? Give me a date," he said, picking up his cell phone to enter it on his calendar. When she gave him no answer, he slammed the phone down. "That's what I thought."

"Ideal, I'm not trying to hurt you. I just need to make sure . . ."

"You need to make sure of what?" he asked, terribly curious.

"I need to make sure that we're going to be together."

Ideal couldn't figure out what she was talking about. They were already together. He struggled in thought for a minute then had a startling epiphany. "You mean you need to make sure we're going to *stay* together," he said, dismayed by what he uncovered. "You don't know that I love you."

"Yes, I do."

"No, you don't. You're worried that I'm going to be with you a few times and then leave."

"Isn't that what you do?"

Ideal gripped the top of his head and lowered it in disbelief. Determined to be clear, he glared at her and articulated himself relentlessly. "How about I tell you what I don't do? I don't worry about approaching a woman. I don't lose sleep over a woman. I don't send flowers to a woman. I don't date her more than three times or call her every day for months. I don't buy her jewelry -"

"Jewelry," Ireland interjected as if she'd had her own epiphany. "Did you think I'd change my mind tonight, because of the earrings?"

"This ain't about the damn earrings. This is about you not knowing how I feel about you. I don't fall in love, and I for damn sure don't go without sex. I can have it anytime I want, any way I want."

"I'm sure you can," she said, looking away.

"Yea, I can. But here I am going months without it. So how in the hell can you think sex is what I'm here for? If that's all I wanted, I would've never wasted my time being with you."

With her eyes remorseful, Ireland managed to utter, "I'm sorry."

"I don't want to hear that."

"I don't know what else to say."

"Then don't talk to me," he advised, turning his back to her. In the middle of the night, he stood motionless, hearing no more than the wailing of winds.

Chapter 22

After parking her body on Ireland's sofa, Casey pulled from her tote a stack of magazines. "I had to stop by and show you these."

"Ugh," Ireland replied, sinking into a chair. "You know I don't want to see those."

"These you do. They have some beautiful shots of you."

"Casey, please. Not today," Ireland moaned, dragging out each syllable. She was still reeling from the night before. Although she and Ideal exchanged apologies that morning, she felt unsure of where he stood with her. Worry had her stomach in a muddle of knots.

"What's wrong with you?" Casey asked, observing Ireland's drained demeanor.

"Nothing."

Casey wasn't fooled by Ireland's white lie. Something was clearly wrong. Although Casey hoped it had nothing to do with Ideal, her intuition told her it did. In fact, she had a hunch the problem was due to how ridiculously long Ireland had been holding out. A man could only take so much. A celebrity man could take even less. "You're telling me before I leave," Casey warned, thumbing through pages until she found photographs of Ireland in Las Vegas. Passing the periodical, she whispered, "Look at this."

"I'm not impressed."

"Are you serious? That's a whole spread on you."

"That's the problem," Ireland said, tossing the magazine.

"You should be flattered."

"Well, I'm not."

"Like I've told you a million times, the actor that doesn't want attention is working in the wrong field."

"That spread isn't about my acting, it's about my boyfriend."

"And your fashion," Casey added with a wink. "Look, somewhere down the line you were going to get famous from movies anyway so look at all of this as an orientation."

The chiming tune of the gate's doorbell was mercy for Ireland's mind. "Saved by the bell."

"Who is that?"

"Rona," Ireland said, standing to her feet.

"Rona? You didn't tell me that she was coming over here."

"I just found out thirty minutes ago. She checked into her hotel then called and said she wanted to come by."

"So she just invited herself over?"

"Uh, yea, like you just did."

"Excuse me. Do not compare me to Rona. I've been coming over here for years."

"You're right," Ireland agreed, before turning to leave the room.

"Well, I don't want to crash your girl time," Casey blurted, halting Ireland in her tracks. "Should I go?"

"Quit talking crazy. Don't you want to meet her?"

Casey answered, wryly, "Sure."

At the sound of the bell ringing a second time, Ireland hurried off to open the gate.

All too soon, Casey heard high heels coming down the hall. A moment later, she laid eyes on Ireland's famous acquaintance. There was no denying that the actress was even more beautiful in person than she appeared in her films. Though admiring her beauty, as well as the fierceness of her attire, Casey managed to disapprove of one thing. Her lipstick was much too bright.

"Hi," Rona said, warmly, strutting over to Casey with a whitened smile. "Ireland just told me you were here. She talks about you all the time. I feel like I know you."

"I feel the same way," Casey replied, rising from the sofa with a forced grin. After accepting Rona's hug, Casey eased into a remote chair with the grace of a Siamese cat.

Observing the design of the living room, Rona remarked, "This place looks so nice."

"Well, that's rich coming from you," Ireland replied.

"It's elegant and classy, plus it smells like a spa. All you need is a massage table in here."

"She wouldn't use it," Casey interposed. "We go get massages every month. Actually, we're going tonight."

Rona looked at Ireland and giggled. "Why are you paying for a massage, when you can put Deal's hands to work?"

"You make a good point. Maybe I should cancel my appointment," Ireland joked, omitting the fact that Ideal touching her was a very sore subject. "You want something to drink?"

"No, I'm good," Rona responded, settling herself on the sofa then noticing a tabloid on the coffee table. "You buy this stuff?"

"No," Ireland said, adamantly.

"Then what's it doing here?"

"That would be Casey's doing."

"Oh," Rona said, looking over at Casey. "Be careful of what you read. Nothing they print is true."

Casey didn't appreciate the admonition. She was a grown woman who had been capable of choosing what to read for years. "The pictures are true, right?" Casey asked.

"Well, yea."

"Yea, I buy them for the pictures so you don't have to worry about me. I'll be fine."

Although Ireland had described her best friend as a joy to be around, Rona failed to feel a delightful vibe. There was a judgmental look in Casey's eyes. "Okay," Rona replied, nodding her head to keep the peace. "So are you excited to go to the premiere with Ireland?"

"I am. I'm really proud of her."

"So am I."

"Hey," Ireland said, in order to get Rona's attention. "Did you finally choose a dress?"

"I've narrowed it down to three," Rona said, playfully swinging her hair.

"Oh, just three. Not bad, considering the premiere's tomorrow."

"Let me see your dress."

"You'll see mine when I see yours."

"Then show me the rest of your place and I'll just happen to go in your closet and find the dress myself."

"Wow, you really are Ideal's friend."

"Come on," Rona said, jumping onto her feet and rushing toward the stairs. "Where's your bedroom?"

As Ireland chased Rona up each step, the two of them laughed frenziedly. To a rigid Casey, their hysterical squeals were like sharp fingernails moving across the length of a chalkboard.

It was dusk when the black limousine drew near to the eminent Hollywood theater. Hundreds of fans, blocked by portable gates, lined a starry sidewalk. While Ireland's focus was fixed on the crowds, Ideal's was fixed on her.

From the moment she emerged from her bedroom that evening, Ideal had been mesmerized. It had been a long while since he'd seen her dressed formally and the vision of her hit him as hard as it had in France.

A deep hue of blue, her long, satin gown fit her beautifully. An abundance of fabric upon her shoulders plunged into a cowl-neck positioned atop the perfumed space between her breasts. Although her side-swept bangs were sleek, the remainder of her tresses were loosely tucked into a low, lateral bun. Her makeup was alluring, atypical in a way, and as her dark eyes gleamed so did her extraordinary sapphire earrings.

Having held her hand on the way to the theater, Ideal felt her flinch when she saw people along the boulevard. She immediately went still and shut her eyes. Assuming she regretted her choice to make an official appearance with him, he told her all would be well then humbly hoped it would be. When she eventually took another look, he sensed she remained uneasy, but she appeared to be a portrait of calm. Her best friend, however, resembled the total opposite.

Sitting across from Ideal and alongside Keith was an animated Casey. Dancing in her designer, black dress, she happily absorbed each enthusiast she saw. Their energy was enormous and she was eager to envelop every ounce of it. In her opinion, anyone who didn't welcome such lively encouragement, needed their head examined - Ireland included.

When the limo came to a complete stop and the driver went to open the rear doors, Ideal made himself keep something in mind. Although he wanted everyone to see that he was with Ireland, he didn't want his presence to overshadow hers. He was there to support her work, therefore, he needed to do his best to keep her in the foreground.

After Keith and Casey stepped outside, Ideal came into view. Like a tidal wave, cameras rose and screams swelled to great heights. He looked impeccably debonair in a dark gray suit, white shirt, and navy, silk tie, accented with the diamond studs he'd gotten for his birthday.

When he helped Ireland out of the vehicle, he took hold of her hand and began walking her down the carpet as Keith and Casey followed behind. Once they passed posters featuring images of Rona, they were met by Amanda, who'd been awaiting their arrival.

Amanda was beyond pleased to see Ideal at the premiere, and as a result, tried to usher him toward the clamoring press. As Ireland was asked her first question, which ironically regarded Ideal, he took several steps back and away from the microphones. Although his action disappointed Amanda, it granted Ireland much-needed relief. Every single interviewer motioned for him to come forward, but repeatedly, he refused. Strangely enough, standing far back put him in the perfect spot for photographers.

Forcefully, they shouted, "Ideal! Ideal! Look to the left! Ideal, look this way!"

Perhaps him ignoring their boisterous demands, put Ireland more at ease, because ten minutes later she succumbed to Amanda's groveling and posed with Ideal before a backdrop. To the sound of cheers, he slid his arm around her waist and pulled her against him. "You can act like you know me," he whispered, smiling at her sweetly and blessing the press with a beguiling shot.

A shrill sound of cries arose when Rona and Dig appeared. Rona had settled on a chocolate brown, sequined dress while Dig wore a taupe suit. Rather than immediately trekking down the carpet, they sauntered over to uproarious fans and started signing autographs. Before long, the fans began chanting Ideal's name, hoping he would make his way over. Normally, he would have, but he passed on doing so that night. Instead, he continued on gratefully, escorting Ireland between velvet ropes and into the theater's entrance.

The film was well received and the after party a stereotypical scene of glitz, glamour, and business. In the midst of exotic flowers, flanked with elaborate feathers, celebrities clutched cocktails and managers huddled like helmet wearers. While Casey was having the time of her life, watching the parade of stars glide by, Ireland couldn't wait for a suitable time to dash for an exit. Unfortunately, her sprint was regularly postponed by members of Hollywood royalty, approaching her under the guise of wanting to discuss her character. But all too quickly their crafty words morphed into praise of the musician by her side. Seeing such accomplished actors overjoyed to meet Ideal was a jolting reminder to Ireland of just how esteemed her boyfriend was.

When the Ideal worship came to a close, Ireland made haste and headed for the door, impatient for the seclusion her quiet home provided. Prior to diving into her limousine, Dig and Rona asked if they could stop by her place before returning to their hotel. Much to Casey's chagrin, Ireland approved the request.

The moment the limo driver pulled up to her gate, Keith hopped into his parked car and went home. Once Ireland led the way into her living room, she and Casey kicked off their heels as Ideal shrugged out of his jacket. When Rona and Dig arrived twenty minutes later, the five of them sipped on ginger ale and argued about jazz. As Dig gave his opinion on the trumpet, they were all caught off guard when the doorbell rang.

"Who is that?" Ideal asked, sternly, bracing himself to pounce. "It's two o'clock in the morning."

Puzzled, Ireland replied, "I don't know."

"Uh-oh, Deal," Dig said, reading the worry in Ideal's eyes. "This must be when her other man comes by."

"Dig, stop," Ireland said, standing onto her sore feet. When she left the room and walked to the foyer, Ideal remained right on her heels. He then nearly knocked her over as she moved outside to the gate. Noticing his clenched fists only burgeoned her apprehension. Slowly, she pulled open the peek door then saw the spray-tanned face of one of her neighbors. "Cindy?" Ireland said, teeming with perplexity.

Cindy's cool, blue eyes grew alive with surprise. "Wow, he's really here," she said, staring at Ideal.

"Cindy, do you know what time it is?" Ireland asked.

"I'm so sorry, Ireland. But when they told me Ideal Morris was here, I had to see if it was true." Gazing back at Ideal, she said with a frozen smile, "Hi."

"Hi," Ideal replied, downright relieved Cindy wasn't a man.

"Wait a minute. Who told you Ideal was here?" Ireland asked, her stomach as tight as a newly made drum.

"The paparazzi. They're all up and down the street," she said, just as a few of them converged around her. Positioning their cameras next to her head, they proceeded to take pictures of the couple in the courtyard.

Ireland went speechless.

"They said Dig and Rona are here too. Is that true?" Cindy asked, trying her best to peer into the home's foyer.

"I have to go," Ireland whispered, slamming the peek door shut. Weakened by fright, she turned to run back inside, but her knees completely gave out. Fortunately, Ideal seized her waist and held her up, before she hit the ground. Carefully, he helped her make it back to the living room.

"What's wrong?" Casey asked, immediately observing her friend's distress.

Still holding Ireland, Ideal sat on the sofa and answered. "There's paparazzi at her gate."

"Oh no," Casey replied.

"How did that happen?" Rona asked.

"They followed your limo over here," Casey said, certain that if Rona had returned to her hotel, the media wouldn't be at Ireland's home.

Accepting the responsibility Casey was quick to assign her, Rona said with regret, "I'm sorry, Ireland."

"Rona, get her some water," Casey ordered.

When Rona went to the kitchen, Casey knelt beside Ireland and squeezed her trembling hands. "It'll be okay. You can stay with me for a few days if you want."

"That's alright," Ideal interceded. "I'll stay with her until she goes back to New York."

"Don't you have to go to Paris?" Casey asked.

"Not anymore."

Chapter 23

Ireland didn't want to answer one more question. Two days prior, she endured a never-ending press junket. In a well-appointed hotel suite, she watched one journalist after another, sit down before her and ask the exact same thing. Twenty-four hours later, she responded to identical inquiries on the red carpet of her New York City premiere. Currently, on the set of a Manhattan television studio, as she prepared to do the first of three interviews for the day, she wished she was one of the tourists waving wildly outside of the window she'd been conspicuously seated next to. The ability to choose when to be watched was a freedom they weren't aware of.

Previous interviews for promotion, although difficult and draining, never felt as monumental as the one she was about to give. She wasn't going to meet with a magazine where an article would later be written. She wasn't going to be recorded where the footage would later be edited. She was going to be on live television. In real time and without a character to hide behind, her look, traits, phrases, and tone would be up for assessment by much of the nation. Like the lifting of a tight lid on a deep, dark jar, she would be opened and peered into.

As her crossed legs rocked involuntarily, she tugged on the long sleeves of her black dress. Unwilling to appear as a jittering mess, she drew air into her lungs then slowly let it flee from her rosy-stained lips. When she closed her eyes, she saw herself being showered with sunshine.

It is the cool climate of spring. Hot pink heads of oleander fall freely from their shrub and into the turquoise-tinted swimming pool in which her feet are submerged. Scalloped, white clouds seem to whisper soft words as she dwells on their position above her uncovered head. Upon tan flagstone and glitter specked cement, she sits perfectly still, soaking in the soothing hum of a nearby filter system. In the distance, she sees three trees, almost as high as sequoias, dangling their innumerable leaves from smooth, pewter branches. Her gaze lowers to look ahead at fuchsia bougainvillea that has wound itself into the prettiest of patterns. As if hidden in a French garden's manicured maze, hedges and tall walls of ivy surround her, while orange sepals on a bird of paradise plant, point toward her warm back. In this space, she has no need. In this place, she has no want. She is divinely content. Her spirit is home.

"Are you ready?" a host of the show asked, easing into the chair across from Ireland's.

Ireland opened her eyes to see the face of Erica, a chic brunette with a calm demeanor who smelled of mild soap. "Yes," Ireland fibbed, watching powder be applied to Erica's cheeks. A minute later, they were live on the air.

"In the highly anticipated film, *Less Loyalty*, which opens this Friday, Ireland Rochelle plays, *Lovely*, the sister of a malicious man, but she's also the friend of her cruel brother's lover. Things become complicated when she, like others in the film, gets pulled in different directions." Looking away from the teleprompter, Erica smiled at her guest. "Ireland, Good morning."

"Good morning," Ireland replied evenly.

"I was fortunate enough to see this film last night. It is gripping, to say the least, and you were wonderful to watch."

"Thank you."

"So there you were a new actress surrounded by a slew of big names. What was it like working with such an incredible cast?" Erica asked, her brown eyes brightening.

"It was wonderful. It took a while for me to be able to absorb the reality of working with people I had admired for years. It was definitely surreal, but eventually, I had to jump down from the clouds so I could get to work."

"I bet. Now, it appears that you're quite close with your costar Rona Simpson. Did you guys know each other prior to this film or did you meet on the set?"

"We met on set."

"How is it having a superstar as a friend?"

"Well, Rona's a really warm, and down-to-earth person so I honestly forget that she's a superstar until we go out. Then I remember instantly."

After glancing down at the blue card she held, Erica lifted her head and smiled. "Well, I can't have you sitting here and not ask about another high profile celebrity that you seem close to. In fact, you seem *very* close to him. There are many photos, some of which are intimate, of you out and about with a special someone. For the few clueless viewers we have, would you care to share who that someone is?"

At that moment, Ireland discovered just how hard her heart was capable of pounding. Her nerves hurdled within her. She had hoped the show would respect her wishes and forego any questions about Ideal, but Amanda warned her they wouldn't. "I'd rather not," Ireland replied, circling her ankle with nervous energy.

"Then I'll do the honors. It's Ideal Morris the rapper, singer, songwriter, producer, designer, entrepreneur, and even model. Did I leave anything out?" Erica joked, pretending to be out of breath. "How long have the two of you been seeing each other?"

"I'd rather not discuss that."

"You can't exactly deny that you're seeing each other."

Ireland felt as though her chair had been lit on fire. "Again, I'd rather not discuss that."

"We know for a fact that he escorted you to two of your premieres. How did he feel about your performance?"

"You'd have to ask him," Ireland said, suppressing her desire to scream.

"He didn't share his feelings with you?" Erica asked, tilting her head as if Ireland's response was peculiar.

"His feelings aren't for me to share."

"Well, I'm sure he feels the same way that everyone else does. You are brilliant in this film."

"Thank you. It was gratifying to play a character so deeply torn. I think it's something most people can relate to."

"That's true, but we certainly can't relate to dating Ideal Morris."

In front of an applauding audience of a mid-morning talk show, Ireland walked out in blue and burgundy python heels that balanced the balloon hem of her burgundy shirt dress. After she shook hands with the two hosts of the show, she waved at the audience then adjusted herself in an uncomfortable stool.

"Wow, I love your ensemble. You look great," Kate said.

While straightening his tie, Doug remarked, "I have to agree with that."

"Thank you," Ireland replied.

"So Ireland, where are you from?" Doug asked.

"Philadelphia."

"Oh, brotherly love."

"Yes, I was born and raised there then I moved to L.A. to attend college and I've been there ever since."

"Hey, I bet you don't miss the cold," Doug said, waving his index finger.

"I don't."

"Well, to the world this is your very first film, but I'm assuming you've been in others, right?"

"I have. I've been in a few independent films, but they had much lower budgets so -"

"So you weren't a virgin, so to speak, to being on a set with a director and so forth," Doug interjected.

"No."

"Speaking of not being a virgin," Kate said, leaning on the arm of her stool, "let's cut right to the chase. We the public, don't know a lot about you, but we have seen a lot of you because you've been dating the enormously sexy, Ideal Morris for months. So are things serious?"

Deflated, Ireland's shoulders sunk sharply. Less formal than the first interview, she appreciated her free-flowing conversation with Doug, but just when she became hopeful all would go well, things went south. Searching for a response, she murmured, "Uh . . ."

"And spare us with the whole, *we're just friends* speech, because if you kiss your friends the way you kiss Ideal there's a problem," Kate warned, causing the audience to laugh heartily.

"I'd rather not talk about him," Ireland answered, running her hand lightly along her freshly waxed knee rather than clenching it the way she wanted to.

"Are you guys in love?"

"I think we should skip talking about him," Ireland said, straining to remain polite.

"We can't do that. The ladies in our world are dying to know. Are you guys in love?"

"No comment."

"That means yes! That means yes!" Kate shouted to a whooping crowd.

"No, it doesn't," Doug said.

"It most certainly does," Kate replied, perfectly sure of herself. "If they weren't, she would've denied it."

"That's not necessarily true," Doug countered.

Rolling her eyes at Doug then flashing a sneaky smile to Ireland, Kate continued. "Tell us. How do you get a man like Ideal Morris to fall in love with you?"

"Now, I can answer that," Doug declared. "Look at her. She's beautiful."

"Doug, a man like Ideal sees beautiful women all the time. I want to know what Ireland did to make him plunge into the depths of love." With every word, Kate tickled the audience. Studying Ireland, she whispered, "What did you do? What did you say?"

"Will you give her a break? She clearly doesn't want to discuss, what's his face."

Watching the two of them was like watching a tennis match. Back and forth they went like teenage siblings. Fortunately, the more they spoke to each other the less Ireland had to speak. She was grateful Doug wasn't pressuring her to discuss her relationship. Unfortunately, Kate had yet another intrusive question.

"So how did you and Ideal actually meet? Was it one of those love at first sight moments where everything stops, the music swells, and the people fade away?"

On the set of a late night talk show, Ted, a wiry-haired host, sat behind a wooden desk as his band performed during a commercial break. When the break was over and the last note was played, Ted read the teleprompter before him.

"Our next guest is an up-and-coming actress who you can catch in the film, *Less Loyalty*, which hits theaters this Friday. Ladies and gentlemen, please welcome to the show, the beautiful, Ireland Rochelle."

Ireland took the deepest breath of the day and emerged in a short, silver dress. Carefully, she walked along the slippery floor, making her way to the platform on which Ted stood. He seemed miles away. The live music and audience were blaring. She couldn't hear one scary thought in her head. When she eventually reached Ted, she placed her hand in his and permitted him to assist her onto the stage. After receiving a fleeting kiss on the cheek, she acknowledged the crowd and took her seat.

"Ireland, welcome," Ted said, centering himself perfectly behind his desk.

"Thank you," she replied, trying her best not to shake.

"You truly are a lovely woman," he said, admiring her appearance as random men whistled. "I mean, *Lovely* is your character's name in the film, but you as a woman certainly do the word justice."

"Thank you."

"You smell great too."

"Thanks," Ireland repeated, wearing a frozen smile.

"You're very welcome. Now, you know, you're real name is an uncommon name for someone to have. It's nice but uncommon." Chuckling generously, he then asked, "Are you Irish?"

Ireland couldn't help but laugh with Ted and the audience. Clearly, her features didn't scream Irish ancestry. "No, but I was conceived in Ireland," she answered.

"Whoa! I see," Ted shouted before laughing harder. "So have you been there since your conception?"

"I haven't. My parents and I had plans to go when I graduated from college, but I ended up booking a lot of jobs so we never went. But I still want to go."

"Then you should go. You should just pick up and go. And I'm sure there's someone in your life that you could just pick up and go with, right?"

Although immediately bothered, Ireland wasn't surprised. Recent experience had been the best teacher. She expected Ted to talk about Ideal, but she had no plans to join him. "Yea, there are quite a few people that I could go with."

"Well, I guess you could go with people, but it would be a lot nicer to go with someone special." After taking a quick sip from his mug, he asked, "Do you have a boyfriend?"

"I'd rather not answer that."

"Oh, come on," Ted moaned. "You can at least say if you do or not."

"Or I can say what I just said," she replied, provoking more laughs. Aware that her response amused the audience, she realized avoiding Ted's questions was the best strategy.

"Come on. It's a simple question. Do you have a boyfriend?"

"You know, *Less Loyalty* is an exceptional film."

Appreciating Ireland's wit, Ted nodded his head. "I'll tell you what. If you will just admit to having a boyfriend then I promise I'll move on to the film. What do you say?"

Ireland thought the proposition over. She knew she wasn't fooling anyone. If stating the truth steered the discussion away from her personal life, it may be worth it. "Okay," she agreed.

"So Ireland ... do you have a boyfriend?"

"Yes."

"Anyone, we know?" Ted asked, reneging on his word.

Without warning, a slideshow of Ireland with Ideal began playing on a nearby screen. Although the audience rejoiced, Ireland struggled to find her breath as her body trembled from embarrassment. Trapped in a foreign room, she listened to foreign voices hooting over images that made her feel small. Clearly, her confession only made things worse.

"Ah, yes," Ted said, smugly, studying the screen. "Now, if my memory serves me correctly, this guy is Ideal Morris. Ideal has been on my show numerous times over the years and I get the distinct impression that he's rolling in dough. I'm sure he can fly you first class to Ireland."

When Ireland crossed the threshold of Ideal's penthouse, she heard him singing in the library. Hoping to rush past the open door, she removed her shoes and hurried down the hall as fast as her cold feet could carry her. They weren't fast enough.

"Hey, how did it go?" he asked, stepping out in front of her.

"Fine," she answered, cleverly walking around him.

"Wait, slow down," he said, turning to face her. "Where's my kiss?" Disappointed with the half-hearted kiss she placed on his cheek, he asked, "What kind of kiss is that?"

"A tired one," she replied, walking away again.

"Baby, wait. I want to hear what happened."

"I'll tell you later."

"Later?" he said, puzzled by her procrastination. "I made sure to be here when you got home so you could tell me how it went."

"I said, I'll tell you later."

"Did something happen?" he asked, noticing her crossness.

"Ideal -"

"If something happened, I want to know."

For the very first time, Ideal's voice was driving Ireland berserk. "I don't want to talk about it right now."

"If somebody did something to you, I need to know now so I can handle them now."

"Nobody did anything to me," she said, squelching his rampage before it began. "I just don't feel like talking."

"Why not?"

"I'm all talked out. I've been talking all day and not about me," she said, bitterly.

"What does that mean? Who have you been talking about?"

"You!" she shouted, losing her patience. "All everybody wanted to talk about, was you. How I met you. How long I've known you. What I do with you. On and on and on. Never mind about when I started acting or how I prepared for my role or what I felt about my character." Once her sight was fogged with tears, she lowered voice. "I've worked so hard and so long to build a career and I gave everything in that film, but none of that mattered. It was all ignored because I'm with you."

Ideal bowed his head and stared at the floor. "I'm sorry you had to go through that," he said, his voice barely there.

As soon as she watched him walk away, Ireland felt cruel. It was a hurtful reminder that she was capable of engaging in ugly behavior. Recklessly, she took her frustration and unleashed it onto Ideal. She did so because it was easy. She did so because he was there. She made him feel like he was a hindrance to her happiness, when in fact, he was the chief cause of it.

Needing to make things right, she followed him into the living room and found him hunched over a table, blowing out candles. Adjacent to the pillars was a deep dish pizza, patterned plates, and goblets prepared for a pour from a nearby bottle of wine. Tulips and lilies prettied up the table and matched the orange flames springing from the fireplace.

"Ideal," she muttered, feeling worse than before.

Caught off guard, he stood up straight. "Yea?"

"What happened today wasn't your fault. I shouldn't have gotten mad at you."

"It's alright."

"No, it's not. You were here to support me and I acted like you were a problem."

"You were hurt. I understand."

"Don't give me a pass. Tell me I was wrong or something."

"I'll do something," he said, walking over to her. Taking the shoes and bag from her hands, he set them down and removed the jacket she wore. He then led her to the sofa, where he leaned her back against his chest. Once his fingers traveled to her temples, he rubbed them with a pleasing pressure. With each circular rotation, he lessened her tension, proving his technique was superb. When his hands moved deep into the strands of her hair, he gripped and kneaded her scalp. Minutes later, her body went limp. "I just want to make you happy," he whispered, still massaging her head.

With her stress stripped away, she pulled his hands into her lap. "You already do."

Chapter 24

Snow began to fall from the dark evening sky above Philadelphia. Recently saturated with soft powdery piles, the city's scene was picturesque. In the town square, trees were spruced with golden-white lights, while warmly dressed residents gripped mugs of steaming beverages. Bordering the square were smiling sightseers, riding in carriages pulled by white horses. All appeared festive as men in tartan kilts, showcasing muscular calves, created joyful sounds from bagpipes.

As Ireland drove through the city, Ideal sat on the passenger side of their compact rental car. Wanting to be as inconspicuous as possible, she refused to rent anything considered a luxury vehicle. Eventually, Ideal went along with her proviso and kept to himself that he hadn't seen the inside of an economy car in years.

To the squeaky, rhythmic sound of the windshield wipers waving, they made their way onto a narrow road and rolled along its cobblestones. Illuminating the blanketed sidewalks were black lamp posts from which velvet ribbons hung low and blew high in the crisp, patchy wind. Most charming, however, were lofty row houses made of red brick, where green wreaths graced each door.

At the end of a search for a parallel parking space, Ideal watched as Ireland eased the car between a snowcapped van and truck. Impressed with her maneuvering, he slid on his wool coat and knit cap then exited the car. Once he retrieved every piece of their luggage, he let her lead the way.

In a winter-white pea coat, Ireland walked at a pace both amazing and amusing. Considering she was wearing knee-high, stiletto boots, Ideal thought she would take her sweet time. Instead, she moved like she was wearing a pair of non-slip cleats.

After cutting through a residential alley and proceeding down two blocks, they headed up the steps to a four-story row house with shiny, black shutters and a black door. It wasn't until Ireland pressed the bell that Ideal became too scared to breathe. With his diaphragm still and his heart walloping, he halfway hoped no one would be home. Far too soon, the door swung open, jingling a bunch of bells hanging from its handle.

"Merry Christmas!" Ireland screamed.

"Merry Christmas, baby," Ireland's mother sang, launching forward to take her daughter into her arms. "Oh, I've missed you so much."

"I've missed you too."

Their love for each other was largely apparent in the tight embrace they would not end. Remaining silent, Ideal observed them, especially Ireland's mother. He had known she was pretty from the pictures he'd seen, but quite frankly, she was lovelier in person. Her long, layered hair was glamorously coiffed. Her hazelnut skin was firm and smooth. Make-up enhanced her bright, cheery eyes and her perfectly painted lips matched her maroon sweater. She was a bona fide beautiful woman, which cemented what he already believed. Ireland would be beautiful for decades to come.

When Mrs. Rochelle finally released her child, she looked at Ideal and smiled. "Ideal, I am so happy to meet you."

"I'm happier to meet you," he said, snatching off his cap in spite of the cold.

"Then give me a hug," she said, opening her arms.

Gladly, he stepped into them. It was like stepping into a beloved bakery. Wondrously warm, comforting, and sweet, an avalanche of aromas swaddled him. Chocolate, cinnamon, vanilla buttercream, gingerbread, nutmeg, coffee spiked with syrup streams. In addition to the faint fragrance of fine, French perfume, Mrs. Rochelle's scent was heavenly.

"Okay, you guys come on inside."

After walking through a wallpapered vestibule, Ideal parked the bags near the inner door. He then heard Ireland exclaim, "Daddy!" A shiver rushed along his spine. Meeting Ireland's father was what he feared most about the evening. Denying his desire to cower in the corner, he lifted his head and looked at the man responsible for Ireland's being.

In a slow, deliberate manner, Mr. Rochelle moved down the steep staircase. Tall and intimidating with broad shoulders, his hair was a blend of onyx and gray. Along with his plaid pajamas, he wore a sleek robe and slippers. All the attorney needed, was a pipe between his teeth.

"Hi, Gorgeous," he said, grinning at Ireland. Without so much as a glance at Ideal, he reached the foot of the garland-lined stairs and gave her a hug. "How was your flight?"

"It was short, which was nice for a change."

"That's good. I'm glad you're home."

"Me too." A moment later, Ireland shuffled back to stand next to her guest. Smiling broadly, she made an introduction. "Daddy, this is Ideal."

"I know who he is," he replied, lastly looking Ideal's way.

"Ideal, this is my father."

Feeling like he was auditioning for his first recording contract, Ideal took a step closer and stretched out his hand. "It's an honor to meet you, Mr. Rochelle."

"Is it?"

"Yes, sir. It is."

Shaking Ideal's hand with a strong grip, he sized him up. "Likewise."

"Ideal, call us Jonah and Janet," Janet said. "You can drop the Mr. and Mrs. Rochelle, okay?"

"Speak for yourself, baby," Jonah interjected.

Ignoring her husband's instruction, she gave the couple one of her own. "Give me your things," she said, extending her hands in order to lighten their load. While taking coats, scarves, hats, and gloves, she admired how well they looked together. Though impressed with Ideal's cashmere sweater and tie, she was enchanted by her daughter's shimmery cowl neck and accessories. "Ireland, you look so pretty."

"She does," Ideal agreed. "I kept telling her over dinner."

"Nice to know you're not blind," Jonah remarked, wrapping his arm around Ireland's shoulders and ushering her away.

"Just leave the bags here, Ideal," Janet said. "Let's go sit down."

Designed in deep tones of green and gold, they went into the living room, which smelled of fresh pine. Flickering lights and sparkling bulbs garnished a pair of topiaries that stood between the parted draperies of the room's twin windows. A much larger tree, adorned with ribbon and memory-filled ornaments, rested in a corner near an enclosed fire. On the mantel of the fireplace were thick strands of greenery as well as brass hooks, which dangled opulent stockings. As jazzy carols played, the flames of scented candles swayed around a stunning nativity scene complete with bronze figurines. Prolific with red poinsettias, the room was refined and lush.

While Janet and Jonah sat in wingchairs near a box of assorted candy, Ideal sat beside Ireland in the center of a camelback sofa. "Thanks for letting me crash your Christmas Eve and Christmas Day," Ideal said, hoping her parents didn't mind his presence.

"You're not crashing anything. You're welcome here," Janet said. Pointing at the fireplace, she added, "I even got you a stocking."

Speechless for seconds, Ideal eyed the velvet item and recognized it spelled his name. "Wow, that was really nice of you. Thank you."

"So would you like eggnog, hot chocolate or hot cider?"

"Uh, I'll have eggnog."

"I want hot chocolate," Ireland said. "It was freezing outside."

"California's made you soft. You used to be able to handle this cold," Jonah teased, popping peanut brittle into his mouth.

When Janet stood to her feet, the oven timer went off. "That's my ham."

"I'll take it out for you," Ideal offered, happy to help Janet and eager to escape Jonah.

Passing underneath a swag of evergreen, they walked through the separate dining room, where the table was topped with fine dinnerware and a centerpiece of red roses. Before exiting the space, Ideal appraised the buffet, appointed with a mouthwatering display of pies, cookies, and cakes.

Infused with modern amenities, the updated kitchen had an old world feel. Suspended from an overhead rack were copper pots and iron pans, beneath distressed cabinetry was a red brick backsplash, and above the stove's gas range, gleamed a copper hood. Offering holiday cheer upon the cooking quarter's counters was a classy collection of glossy nutcrackers.

"Thank you," Janet said, as Ideal pulled out a ham embellished with cloves, pineapples, and cherries.

"You're welcome," he replied, carefully placing it in the center of the slim island.

"You know what?" she said, removing the pot holders from his hands then staring at his face. "Everybody goes on and on about how handsome you are. I have to admit, they're right."

Embarrassed by the unforeseen compliment, he glanced at a pedestal bowl of pinecones and said with a soft smile, "Thank you."

Janet found his shyness appealing. There was a sweet quality about him. In the public eye, he was the model of confidence. He exuded self-assurance and even sometimes came off as cocky. Janet soon realized it was a shield of bravado. If he allowed her to see past his shield in just a matter of minutes, she could only imagine what Ireland had seen. "Ireland told me you like banana pudding so I made you some last night."

"Aw, you didn't have to do that."

"You've been taking care of my daughter so while you're here, I'm going to take care of you."

"That's not necessary, Mrs. Rochelle."

"Who?"

"I mean, Janet."

"Would you like some pudding now?"

"I don't want to seem greedy."

"That sounds like a yes to me."

"It is," he laughed.

Janet pulled the pudding from the refrigerator and placed it beside the bowl of homemade eggnog. "I'm sure your mother is missing you."

"She is but my sister and relatives are with her."

"Well, you'll meet Ireland's relatives tomorrow and I'm giving you fair warning. You will be mobbed."

"That's alright," he said, watching her fill a bowl and glass with creamy confections. "Ireland got mobbed at my place on Thanksgiving. My family had never seen me with a woman."

"Why is that?"

"Nobody was ever special enough - special at all, really."

"I learned a long time ago to observe a person's actions. Your actions seem to say Ireland is very special to you."

"More than you'll ever know. I love her."

Their eyes latched unexpectedly and all of their movement ceased. While gazing at one another, a feeling deep within them swelled. Their souls shared a connection from the overwhelming affection they had for the same person. In that brief, powerful moment, they somehow formed a bond. A bond based on their ambition to keep Ireland happy, healthy, and safe.

When they silently agreed to look away, Janet reached for a chunky, red mug. "Let's get this girl her hot chocolate."

Ideal found himself entranced by Janet as she poured the rich liquid from a copper saucepan. After adding a heap of fluffy whipped cream, she sprinkled crushed candy cane atop its white mound. Every action she carried out, she did with enjoyment and care. Although she was a history professor, she simultaneously was a domestic queen. "You have a beautiful home."

"Thank you. That's a lot coming from someone with homes to spare."

"I sort of have a weakness for real estate."

"Nice weakness to have."

"Anytime you and your husband want to stay at any of them, just let me know."

"You rent them out?"

"No, but you can stay free of charge. As long as you want."

"Ideal, that is way too generous of you."

"It's not. Doing something special for you is doing something special for Ireland."

Again, Janet stopped and studied the man before her. At the beginning of his relationship with her daughter, she was as skeptical as Ireland. With each passing day, both women waited for things to fizzle out. However, week after week and month after month, Ideal remained devoted. There was nothing more the young man could do to show how much he loved Ireland. "I want to thank you for loving her, caring for her, and . . ." Janet paused. Searching for the right words, so she wouldn't seem intrusive, she then added, "being patient with her."

Ideal knew from her careful words that she was aware he hadn't made love to Ireland. "You're welcome," he said in a low tone.

"You're a special man."

Quickly, but meticulously, Janet returned everything to its rightful place then led Ideal back to the living room.

"Is there any pudding left?" Jonah asked, examining Ideal's full bowl. "That'll cost you ten dollars."

"Jonah, stop," Janet said.

"What? He's good for it."

"You're right," Ideal agreed, pulling a fifty dollar bill from his pocket and handing it to Jonah. "Keep the change."

"I certainly will," Jonah said, smiling at the picture of President Grant on the green currency.

"Daddy, are you serious?"

"You think I'm not?"

After swallowing his first spoonful of dessert, Ideal looked at Janet with adoration. "This is over-the-top good."

"I'm glad you like it."

Beaming from his recent monetary gain, Jonah began chatting with Ideal. "So I hear your latest song is number one."

"Yea, for four weeks now," Ideal replied.

"You wouldn't know it by looking at me, but I like your music."

"Well, that makes me feel a little bit safer. I've been looking around for shotguns ever since I got here."

"I didn't say, I don't have a shotgun for you. I just said, I like your music," Jonah said, sternly, before chuckling.

Relieved to see Jonah laugh, Ideal did the same. "I hope you like my next song. It's about how much I love Ireland."

"It's so embarrassing," Ireland announced, shutting her eyes.

"Gorgeous, when a man wants to proclaim his love for you, you let him."

"Now, I agree with your father on that," Janet confessed.

"So when are you going on tour?" Jonah asked.

"Next summer."

"Maybe I'll catch your show when you come to Philly."

"Daddy, I'm not sure you'll want to go to one of his shows."

"Why not?" he asked, assuming she thought he was too old.

"Hearing him on the radio and seeing him live are two different things."

"I'll prepare myself for the profanity."

"And the booty shaking dancers," Ireland warned.

"Your father won't have to prepare himself for that," Janet remarked.

"Yea, I'll manage," Jonah said, winking at his wife.

"On that note, you guys go get settled," Janet said. "I've got more cakes to bake."

"And I've got more movies to watch," Jonah said.

As Jonah went down to the basement and Janet rushed off to the kitchen, Ideal followed Ireland up two flights of stairs, while lugging all of their things.

Resembling a photo in a bed and breakfast brochure, the guestroom encouraged romance. A four poster bed, the shade of pecan, was covered in a taupe and red spread, and accented with rows of ruffled shams. Amaryllis dressed each bedside table and a fireplace was vivid with flames.

"You sure your father's okay with me staying in here?"

"Look," Ireland squealed, ignoring Ideal's question. "My mother bought us matching PJs," she said, pointing to plaid, flannel pajamas folded neatly on a bench.

"I think I've had Christmas pajamas only twice in my life," Ideal said, touched by Janet's thoughtfulness. She had been so welcoming that she eliminated his worries of intruding.

"You don't have to wear them if you don't want to."

"No, I want to," he said, reassuring her. Pulling out Janet's hostess gift of monogrammed, triple-milled soaps, he said, earnestly, "Your mother's amazing."

"Trust me, I know," Ireland replied, picking up her new sleepwear. "I'm going to go use the bathroom and put these on then we can go back down and hang out."

Suddenly all alone, Ideal realized all was calm. Stirred to move to the window, he arrived at its panes and watched the miracle of snow landing on ledges and branches. He had seen snowfall countless times, but it had never seemed so sublime. Perhaps it was because of where he was. The home felt fixed with love. He understood why Ireland made a point to return every single December. There couldn't have been a better place to be on the best day of the year.

Ideal was riveted by Ireland's mother, and Jonah Rochelle was exceptional. A Louisiana native, he was protective and present. He had been present for Ireland's entire life. As Ideal thought on Jonah's positive image, his own father's image stole his attention.

Thinking of his father was something Ideal did not do. If anything about the man ever crept into his mind, he shoved it away with a long-established rage. Unfortunately, on this night, visions of his father were unusually stubborn and the flood of painful memories, he could no longer obstruct. He recalled what he failed to have as a child due to his father's absence. Then he recalled the very night the absence came to be.

Receiving shelter from a snowstorm on Christmas Eve, Ideal, a decade old, rushed into the brown building of his family's one bedroom apartment. Along with his mother and little sister, he was excited to see his father who had been scheduled to get off early from work that afternoon. Expecting to see the older version of himself relaxing on the couch, Ideal pushed open his unit's door. Surprise fell upon him when he saw the place was empty. For a moment he froze as confusion crowded his brain, but soon it melted away like icicles dissolved from the sun. His conclusion arrived so robustly that he knew it had to be true. His father was sleeping in bed.

Ideal ran to the other room and with his twisted smile, flung open the door and yelled, "Daddy!" Hearing no reply, he found himself in another cold room void of his father.

Although he was disappointed, Ideal accepted his mother's theory that his father was out, trying his best, to find a gift for the following morning. They rarely had gifts on Christmas, a fact Ideal's father found deeply upsetting.

As they waited for him to arrive, Ideal and his mother gift-wrapped used books as well as empty boxes and placed them underneath their miniature tree as they had done many times before. It gave the dull room a festive flair and provided them with a much-needed fantasy that they lived in abundance. Annually, Ideal vowed to himself that one day he'd be able to put real gifts underneath a real tree.

Two hours passed yet Ideal continued enjoying his time with his mother and sister. He sang along to Christmas songs, playing from an old record player and after sneaking a swallow of raw cookie dough, helped bake a batch of cookies. Later, he sat on the sofa, covered by a heavy quilt and watched a collection of clay cartoons. Once another hour went by, he drifted off to sleep, but not before noticing his mother's glances at her stretch band watch.

He awoke to the sound of sobbing. Though his sister was asleep beside him, his mother had left the kitchen. Quickly, he tossed aside the quilt and traced the cries to the bedroom. Sitting at the foot of the bed was his mother, hunched over and shaking in despair. Ideal had witnessed stabbings and shootings, but his mother's desolation was the scariest thing he'd seen.

"What's wrong, Ma?" he asked, running over to her. In an attempt to hide her face, she turned away and didn't respond. Placing his hand on her jerking shoulder, he asked again, "Ma, what's wrong?" Though he didn't want to know what horrible thing had happened, he needed to know so he could take her pain away.

Without an answer, Ideal scanned the room and noticed a drawer of his father's chest was pulled out unusually far. Even more unusual was the fact that there was nothing inside. Normally, it was full as it was the only piece of furniture his father used to store his things. Ideal shut the empty drawer then pulled out the one above it. It was empty as well. Ideal's body felt sick, worse than when he had the stomach flu just weeks before. Crouching down, he grabbed the handle of the very last drawer and pulled it toward his body until its hollowness was revealed.

Ideal had heard the story repeated several times. Friend after friend had mentioned that their father had gone for good. Ideal's time had now come. He would have to face his friends and acknowledge that his father was no different from theirs. He had sworn on many occasions that his father would never leave, but he had just been proven wrong and the proof was unbelievably painful. He desperately wanted to find his father. He wanted to throw his arms around him, inhale his manly scent, and never let him go. He wanted to do what couldn't be done.

With tears plummeting from his narrow eyes, he looked up at his mother, and all the while praying that she would have an unforeseen answer, asked, "Did Daddy leave us?" They were the strangest words he'd ever spoken. They seemed to be a line from a film. However, the answer to his question was all too real. His mother sobbed harder, causing him to fall at her feet. With his arms wrapped tightly around her slim ankles, he wept.

Still standing at the window, tears streamed down Ideal's cheeks. Harshly, he rubbed them away. He hadn't felt tears in years.

Chapter 25

The instant Ideal opened his eyes, he saw Ireland's sweet smile.

"Merry Christmas," she whispered, her head resting on the pillow next to his.

"It's the merriest one I've ever had." His heaviness from the evening before had fortunately been lifted by Ireland's infectious joy, her father's blunt humor, and her mother's tender nurturing. Pulling Ireland closer, he added, "Merry Christmas to you."

"I'd ask how you slept but by the sound of it, you slept very well."

"Are you trying to say I was snoring?"

"I'm not *trying* to say anything. All of Philly heard you."

"I guess I needed some rest."

"Of course you did. You're the hardest working man on the planet. I can't believe I'm spending Christmas with you."

"Get used to it."

"Well, while you've been sleeping, I've been dying for you to open the gifts I got you."

"You must've gotten me some missiles the way you went and locked yourself away to wrap them last night."

"You kept trying to peek," she screeched, sitting up abruptly.

Rising from his resting position, Ideal grinned as he explained himself. "I told you, I was just peeping your gift-wrapping skills."

"Oh, please. You were looking at me so hard, you couldn't even wrap your own gifts."

"You know looking at you is what I do," he said, biting his bottom lip. "So are we going to stay in here all day or are we going to go open some presents?"

"Let's go."

While freshening up in the bathroom, they elbowed one another for sink space then tugged on each other's pajama sleeves as they made their way downstairs. When they entered the living room, the music was going, the candles were glowing, as were the spangled trees. Besides the blazing fire, they took Janet and Jonah's hands and recited *The Lord's Prayer.* When the prayer concluded, opening presents commenced.

Still, in awe of their family dynamic, Ideal observed Ireland exchanging gifts with her parents. From them, she received leather-bound collections of classic novels and stage plays, stacks of vintage bracelets, and exquisite, diamond hair accessories. She gifted them with elegant pen sets, cashmere scarves, suede jackets, and salsa lessons.

Next, it was Ideal's turn to untie the wired ribbons of his superbly wrapped packages from Ireland. Comic book subscriptions, silly graphic tees, and a gift card for go-kart racing made him hoot and holler. But a striped leather jacket, red luxury watch, and book documenting the history of hip hop had him uttering thanks. Impatient to launch Ireland into her own state of wonder, he placed her gifts around the reindeer socks covering her feet.

She, along with her parents, were baffled time and again, as she uncovered three rare, designer handbags. The handmade works of art were already excessive, but within each was a wallet as well as another gift. The first bag contained a bottle of perfume, the second possessed a gold necklace, and the third enclosed the grandest gift -

a key to her dream automobile. The white sports sedan had been delivered to Casey's home and hidden inside her garage for days.

Full of pride, Ideal pinched Ireland's cheeks to convince her the moment was real. He was caught off guard, however, when Janet surprised him with a shiny box. As a multimillionaire, he felt ridiculous opening a gift from Ireland's parents. His hesitancy caused him to delay, but at Janet's insistence, he lifted the top. Undoubtedly, a nod to his nickname for Ireland, he pulled out a red velvet photo album. Within its pages were endearing pictures of her from birth to the age of eighteen. While examining every image, he listened to stories of her childhood, and somehow valued her more with each page that he turned. He wouldn't dare tell Ireland, but the album was his favorite gift of all.

After experiencing two hours of gaiety with the man and woman of the house, Ideal sincerely felt close to them. They were benevolent, good-natured people, who were more than worthy of the gifts that they were about to receive. Handing Janet the last unwrapped box, Ideal explained its contents were for her and Jonah to share. Appearing more intrigued than her parents, Ireland stared intently as Janet revealed what was inside. Beneath two purple, hibiscus-strewn leis were gift cards affording them seven nights to a beachfront, Hawaiian resort. Additional gift cards to an airline, as well as a luxury car service, ensured the couple a carefree vacation.

Though Jonah and Janet were speechless, Ireland said in a deafening tone, "You gave them a trip to Maui?"

"I did," Ideal said, observing her astonished expression.

"What if they didn't like you?" she asked.

"If we didn't like him, we do now," Jonah answered.

"Daddy!"

"What?"

"Ideal," Janet whispered, feeling faint. "We can't accept this."

"Yes, we can," Jonah countered.

"He just met us, Jonah. We can't let him send us to Hawaii."

"Yes, we can."

"Your husband's right," Ideal said. "I really want you guys to go and enjoy yourselves. You're good people, great parents, and hard workers. You deserve this."

"Ideal, thank you," Jonah said, going to give the celebrity a hug. "Other than gifts from Gorgeous, this is the most amazing thing we've ever gotten."

"It truly is," Janet said, rising to hug Ideal as well. "We can't thank you enough."

Resting in Janet's embrace, Ideal replied, "It's the least I could do."

"So what's the most you can do?" Jonah asked, causing the women to admonish him.

Sipping caramel cappuccinos and freshly squeezed orange juice, the four of them ate a full breakfast with cinnamon rolls and croissants, while lounging around in sleepwear. When the day grew dark, they dressed in their Christmas best, enjoyed a sensational meal, and gorged on dessert.

Ideal's joy turned to fear so quickly, it left him wobbly. Disgusted with his damp palms, he rubbed them against his olive sweater then descended the stairs as slowly as he could. Regrettably, he reached the basement's media room in no time.

Nestled in a leather chair, Jonah studied a replay of the game he was watching. "Hey, Ideal," he said, glancing away from the television screen. "Have a seat."

Gnawing on his bottom lip, Ideal sat in an identical chair adjacent to Jonah's.

"What's Gorgeous up to?"

"She's on the phone with Casey."

"Checking on her new ride, no doubt."

"Yea," Ideal replied, tensely. With Ireland in the bedroom, Janet in the kitchen, and family on the way, Ideal knew he may not get another chance alone with Jonah. It was time to sink or swim. "Mr. Rochelle?"

"Yea?"

"I need to talk to you about something important."

Alerted by the serious look emitting from Ideal's eyes, Jonah placed the volume on mute. "What's going on?"

Recalling what he had so diligently rehearsed, Ideal stated, "I love Ireland. Being with her has made me happier than I thought was possible. I would give up all that I have just to keep her in my life. Our relationship is the most important thing to me and I don't ever want it to end. I want to be with her forever and I plan on asking her to be with me forever. I plan on asking her to marry me. So may I please have your blessing and permission to propose to your daughter?"

Seconds slugged by and Jonah said nothing until Ideal's desperation grew visible. "You've never been in love before so how do you know it's love that you feel for my daughter?"

"It's true that I've never been in love, but I know what love is. I have it for my mother and my sister and the fact that my feelings for them are surpassed by my feelings for Ireland proves that I love her. I would die for her." Looking away for a moment, Ideal continued, "I mean no disrespect, but I've spent time with a lot of women in my past. I know what attraction is. I know what lust is. I know what companionship is when you're bored. I've experienced all of that with other women, but not one of them even cracked the door to my heart. But somehow Ireland got it wide open and she's the only one inside."

"So do these women in your past stay in your past?"

"Yes, sir. I don't have contact with any of them."

"Not even ones in Miami nightclubs?"

Ideal shook his head at Jonah's reference. "That story was a complete lie. The only thing I whispered to that woman was to leave me alone. I don't speak to anyone from my past."

"So what about the future? Beautiful women throwing themselves at you will be a hard thing to pass up, especially years down the road."

"It won't be. I'll always be one hundred percent faithful to Ireland."

"You really believe that?"

"I know it."

"Of all the things I've accomplished, I'm most proud of staying faithful to Janet. I need Ireland to have a man that can do the same."

"I'm that man. I promise you." Ideal needed to be believed, but he understood why Jonah had doubts. Other than Dig, all of the men Ideal knew were liars and cheaters. Jonah had to have known similar statistics.

"You two haven't been together long. Are you sure you want to propose this soon?"

Ideal should've known the attorney would put him on the witness stand. Pushing past a flash of fever, he replied, "I'm positive. I've been around the world a few times. I'm not going to find another woman like Ireland."

"You've got that right." After rubbing the stubble on his cheek, Jonah smirked. "In a normal situation, I'd ask how you plan to provide for her, but you're already doing that."

"She'll be set for life. I won't have a prenup."

"Your lawyers will throw a fit."

"I don't care."

"Would you get her here more often?"

"Definitely," he answered, the question giving him hope.

"With my grandkids?" Jonah asked, confirming Ideal wanted children.

"All three of them."

"Then you have my blessing," Jonah said, extending his hand to shake Ideal's.

As the summit of relief washed over him, Ideal took a deep breath and shook Jonah's hand. "Thank you so much."

Rather than reply graciously, Jonah kept hold of Ideal's hand and nearly crushed it with excessive strength. With a menacing expression, he had one last thing to say. "You break her heart, I cripple your ass."

Immediately, they pulled away from each other as Ireland made her way into the room. Wearing a sweater dress, tights, and ankle boots, all the color of cranberry, she dazzled like the long, gold necklace dangling from her neck.

"Casey's as excited as I am about my car," she said.

"Well, don't let her drive it," Jonah warned. "She'll start thinking it's hers."

Chapter 26

Dig and Rona's private jet touched down in St. Martin with a glide as smooth as the flight itself. Behind Ideal, Ireland exited the plane with her bright summer dress blowing in the Caribbean wind. At the base of the stairs, they were greeted by a crew member of their soon to be chartered yacht.

After being driven to a turquoise bay, they were led down the docks of a marina, where Ireland's open-heeled sandals clicked against the silky soles of her feet. In awe, she ogled an array of enormous vessels. The fact that she was to board one was unfathomable, yet minutes later, she eased across a narrow gangway and walked onto a two hundred and one foot-long superyacht.

Standing on the magnificent aft deck, she heard an inner voice tell her that she was somewhere she didn't belong. Amid the carefree sound of calypso music, the voice began to lull her into apprehension. Yachting, in her mind, was something only rich people did. She was nowhere near rich. Instinctively, she pulled the island's air into her lungs and allowed it to gradually flow from her mouth. In need of redirecting her attention, she focused on the captain and officers, welcoming her aboard.

Once she and Ideal were handed mimosas, they followed a stewardess beyond automatic doors to pass through the saloon. Surrounded by dark wood, wide windows, and light fabrics, the space resembled a luxury apartment with handsome living and dining areas. After entering a foyer, they were led down a carpeted staircase and shown to their V.I.P. stateroom.

To Ireland's surprise, the room was princely. She assumed they would be sleeping in a somewhat cramped cabin. How wrong she was. Impressed with its grandness, she walked over to the desk and ran her hand upon its smooth, wooden finish while taking in the nautical view above it. As the deckhand stationed their bags near the foot of the king size bed, Ireland politely declined the stewardess' offer to unpack their things.

The moment the stewardess exited the room and the couple was left alone, Ideal opened one of his bags and pulled out a black gift box.

"Is that for Dig and Rona?" Ireland asked.

"No, it's for you."

"Christmas is over, Carrot."

"Open it."

Snatching the box from his hand, she did as he instructed. Unprepared for her latest gift, the item made her tremor. The epitome of tasteful elegance and undeniable sexiness, she held up an exquisite piece of lingerie. Cream and copper in color and seductively short in length, sheer silk joined delicate lace to form a gorgeous chemise. Looking back at Ideal, she saw a full-fledged fire in his eyes. Words escaped her.

"That's for tonight," he said in a deeper tone. With his eyes expressing certainty, he repeated himself. "Tonight."

Seconds later, they heard Dig shout, "Deal!"

"Yea!" Ideal shouted back.

"Let's do this safety thing so we can get on."

"Alright," Ideal replied, staring at Ireland once more before leading her out of the room.

A short time after their muster drill, the rocking boat set sail. Ireland's thoughts were hushed as her eyes indulged in the visual feast around her. Appreciating the stunning scenery of the glimmering sea, she felt her body let go and give in to the blessing that had been bestowed upon her. The sky seemed mysteriously close as if with an extension of her arm, she could touch the tips of the clouds and bring down a part of their cottony softness. The experience was thrilling, and the enjoyment gave her more chills than the cool winds running along her skin.

Though she preferred to continue standing at the bow, she followed her fellow passengers upstairs to the sun deck. On its table was a tiered centerpiece of red and green grapes, bordered by a pre-ordered breakfast. Not the least bit interested in eating or conversing, Ireland kept watch of the waves until they cruised into St. Barts.

The sands of unspoiled, crescent-shaped beaches resembled puddles of sparkly powder. Collections of grand rocks rose from the waters and morphed into majestic green hills. Buildings in the distance were topped by red roofs and though Ireland intended to venture into the structures, her primary objective was to accompany the anchor down into the depth of the sea.

Discounting nervous discouragement from Ideal and Rona, she suited up in scuba gear, took a lesson from the yacht's instructor, and left her friends on the deck as she disappeared into the bay.

Gratefully engulfed by the hue of blue-green, calmed by the rhythm of her even breathing, awed by the beauty of colorful coral reefs, and delighted by creatures in proximity, Ireland's spirit soared.

Among darkness, a glow of amber lights shone from the yacht's multiple decks. In the formal dining room, an exceptional dinner was served, but the meal's pinnacle was a decadent chocolate mousse.

Swallowing her final scoop, Rona declared, "That was so good."

"That was too good," Ireland added. "We can't keep eating like this."

"Hey, do you want to go run on the treadmills?" Rona asked, her eyebrows raised high from her spontaneous idea.

With lightning speed, Ideal answered on his girlfriend's behalf. "No," he said, giving Ireland a look that made it clear the thought was out of the question. Almost painfully, he had waited for the night to arrive.

"Excuse me, I'm asking Ireland, not you," Rona replied.

"Let's do it tomorrow," Ireland answered.

"You won't catch me working out on vacation," Dig said, leaning back in his chair.

"We won't catch you working out any time," Rona jabbed.

Dig rubbed his flat stomach and replied, "Ten times a year works just fine for me."

Ideal didn't want to spend one more second in the dining room. After staring intensely at Ireland, he rose to his feet and announced, "We're going to turn in."

"Already?" Rona asked, aware the night was still young.

"Yea," he said, pulling Ireland out of her seat.

"Well, don't forget we're going into town at nine-thirty tomorrow morning."

Ideal remained silent as he hurried Ireland to their room. When they stepped inside, she glanced at everything but him. Desperate to replace her worry with pleasure, he finally spoke when she began to sit down.

"Go change," he said, gently nudging her toward the bathroom, where he had carefully hung her gift. Like a hawk on high alert, he watched her leave his presence until she shut the mirrored door behind her.

On a mission, Ideal retrieved candles from a suitcase and placed them on each night table. Shaking, he struck a match and lit six wicks. After closing the window shades, he lowered the lights but left them high enough to secure a good view of Ireland's body.

Once he selected the perfect playlist, he gave attention to his own attire. Swiftly, he removed every article, including his black boxer-briefs.

Between the bed's cold sheets, he waited patiently. With his chest exposed and his back against the headboard, he fixed his gaze upon the bathroom door. Just a few minutes more and he would experience what he needed more than anything.

When Ireland emerged, the wind was knocked out of him. Regrettably, it was in an agonizing way. She stood before him wearing one of his t-shirts. Initially, he was confused until he recognized her rueful expression. Suppressing his anger, he asked, "Where's the chemise I gave you?"

"I don't think I should wear it," she replied, glancing at the candles he had lit.

Resentful, Ideal dug his teeth into his bottom lip. Yet again, she was attempting to delay him from being with her. He wasn't interested in her reason. He wouldn't listen to her explanation. He was done with her procrastination. With his eyes as serious as death, he said, "Go put it on."

Although she looked scared to reply, she did. "It's just going to make you more tempted."

"Make me more tempted to what? Make love to you?" he asked, sitting upright. After a strained pause, he continued. "That's exactly what I'm about to do, so go put it on."

Shaking her head, she replied, "No."

"Then take off that shirt."

"Ideal -"

"What Ireland?" he shouted, throwing back the covers and standing to his feet, making it known that not only his mind but his body was racked with palpable lust. As he waited for her to speak, he saw that she couldn't. An accumulation of too many seconds went by and her stillness made him demented with panic. Was she really going to deny him again? "I'm standing here baring my all to you," he said, with wet eyes. "Do the same for me."

It took her some time, but she denied his request, walked over to the bed, and hid in the sheets.

Ideal stood motionless. Consumed by a wrenching, pounding pain, the current rejection crushed him. Feeling defective, he slid to the floor where his hurt transformed into a powerful rage. There wasn't a chance in hell he would lie next to Ireland. He remained on the floor the entire night.

Ireland opened her eyes, and through her foggy view, noticed shrunken candles on the bedside table. They all too quickly reminded her of the previous night. She knew her behavior was deplorable. She knew asking Ideal to continue to wait was asking too much. Guilt-ridden, she expected him to be disappointed but hoped he wouldn't still be offended.

Hesitant to face him, she rolled over, timidly, and was surprised when she discovered that she was alone. Every time she spent the night with Ideal, she woke up with him right beside her. Confused by the odd occurrence, she concluded he was in the bathroom. Upon checking the time, she was distressed to learn she had only twenty minutes to get ready for their day in town.

Hurrying to the bathroom, she knocked on its closed door then turned the knob. "Ideal?" she called, entering the space and seeing he wasn't there. With no time to ponder her third surprise of the morning, she took a shower, did her hair and makeup, and dressed in an aqua tank and white shorts. Carrying her sandals and bag, she made her way to the aft deck, where she saw Ideal chatting with Dig, Rona, and the deckhand.

"It's about time you showed up," Rona remarked, placing her hands on her hips.

"I'm so sorry," Ireland said, self-conscious for arriving late.

Noticing her friend looked frazzled, Rona replied, "I'm just playing, Ireland. It's no biggie."

"Yea, we're good," Dig added.

After reaching Ideal's side, Ireland whispered to him, "Why didn't you wake me up?" Curious, she awaited his response but did not receive one.

"Alright, let's go," Dig said, picking up his camera.

Although Dig helped Rona into the tender, Ideal passed on doing the same for Ireland. Instead, he let the deckhand have the honor. Bewildered by his lack of attentiveness, Ireland studied her boyfriend as they sat in the small boat. No matter how much she looked at him, he would not look her way.

During the ride into the harbor, Ideal's anger failed to subside. He never once touched Ireland, and before long, she found herself hungry for his affection. It was the first time he withheld it from her and the absence of it made her feel isolated. After exiting the tender, she considered clasping his hand, but the possibility of rejection warned her against it.

Once the group met Chase and Sampson, who had flown in hours prior, the six of them walked the busy town of Gustavia. Candy-colored cottages popped among white, shuttered shops. French signs introduced slender streets and petite birds hopped among balconies. Although other celebrities roamed about, Ireland's comrades drew the most elated faces.

Ireland would have been disturbed by the fans following them, but her mind was far too occupied with Ideal icing her out. Not only did he refrain from holding her hand, but he also abstained from walking by her side. With his intent to linger several steps behind, none of her slowing caused him to catch up. In each boutique they visited, she pretended to browse, while he went on a shopping spree solely for himself. He purchased belts, watches, shirts, and sweaters, all to be added to his personal wardrobe. In an uncharacteristic fashion, he didn't buy her one item.

Soon embarrassment joined Ireland's torment. Out the corners of her eyes, she saw Rona and Dig keenly observing Ideal. Their observations eventually led to an exchange of hastened whispers. Without an ounce of doubt, Ireland knew what was being discussed.

Ideal's behavior was a startling contrast to the usual attention he gave her, and his concentration on merchandise failed to convince his friends that all was well. They were fully aware that for some unimaginable reason, Ideal didn't want anything to do with Ireland. Though they were sure a problem was present, Ireland was grateful for their charade of ambivalence.

Nearly two hours passed, and the wall Ideal built between himself and Ireland had yet to crumble. She was desperate for its demise and though seized with fear, gathered her courage and made an attempt to communicate with him. While at a bookstore, she asked for his opinion on which works to purchase for Casey. Without a word, he shrugged his shoulders and quickly walked away. His cold response left her with a hot stir of humiliation and solidified her need to steer clear of him altogether.

When the majority of shops closed at noon, they were driven to a restaurant nestled on a beach. Its pale palette prevented distraction from the white sand hugging the teal sea. Once they were shown to their table, Ireland instantly pulled out her own chair. Ideal couldn't be bothered to be civil so he for sure wasn't going to be chivalrous.

While reading the menu's description of a popular tuna salad, Ireland's attention was stolen by something she'd never seen. Three topless ladies lounged on the beach, soaking up the sun's ultraviolet rays. Taken aback, it took her a moment to switch the state of her mind to open, an adjustment no one else with her needed to make. She presumed Ideal and Dig would be engrossed in the partial nudity, but they didn't give it a third glance. It occurred to Ireland, the men traveling with her had seen bare breasts so often, the sight no longer left them beguiled.

Throughout lunch, Ideal kept true to his alienating actions and directed all of his dialogue to his two best friends. Unsure if he even remembered that she was sitting at the table, Ireland prepared for the likelihood that she'd be paying for her own meal. Perhaps only to avoid appearing heartless toward her, he took care of the bill for everyone.

After leaving the table, Rona and Dig strolled the shore, while Ideal and Ireland sat like stones on the sand. Drained from being ignored, Ireland was relieved when an ongoing downpour brought their outing to an end.

As rain rushed from periwinkle clouds, the group was driven back to the harbor. Ireland was sick in her soul. Ideal's withdrawal had grown more hurtful with each hour that crawled by. She not only felt invisible, she felt uncared for. While doubting his love for her, she fought back tears with a vengeance but failed to keep the salty liquid from drizzling down her cheeks.

Chapter 27

The sun was sliding down, filling the sky with a shade of orange sherbet when they, at last, returned to the yacht. Bags removed from their hands were replaced with much-needed cocktails. Impatient to swallow her tropical drink, Ireland shoved the pink straw between her lips and took a long sip. She needed something to lessen her pain and the wine she had with lunch proved to be ineffective. Unable to remain in Ideal's presence, she emptied her glass with a few gulps then raced to her room to be alone.

Slouched in a chair, she hardly had the strength to move but did so when there was a knock at the door. Prepared to dismiss a stewardess, she opened the door and saw it was Rona.

"Oh, hey," Ireland said, regretting she'd gotten up. "I'm really tired. I'm not up for talking right now."

"Well, get up for it," Rona demanded, strutting into the room. Turning back to examine Ireland's appearance, she asked, "What's going on with you and Deal?"

Rolling her eyes, Ireland replied, "I don't know."

"You don't know? You expect me to believe that?"

"I'll tell you about it later, Rona."

"This *is* later. I went all day watching Deal ignore you. What's going on?"

Certain Rona had no plans to leave, Ireland shut the door and simplified things. "He's mad at me."

"He's not just mad at you, he's furious."

"I know."

"Why?"

The truth refused to tumble from Ireland's tongue. "It's personal," she said, walking away.

"Personal?" Rona repeated, injured by the remark. She thought she had gained Ireland's confidence long ago. Close on her heels, she followed her to the foot of the bed and sat down beside her. "Ireland, I know I'm not your best friend, but I'm your good friend. I'm not asking about today, because I want to be in your business. I'm asking because I see you hurting. Casey's not here to help you, so why don't you let me?"

Warmed by the concern coming from Rona's eyes, Ireland let down her guard, and with a nagging fear of judgment, decided to confide in her. "Last night . . . I didn't let Ideal make love to me."

Rona found the admission appalling. Furrowing her eyebrows, she said, angrily, "That's it? He's walking around like you smacked his mother and all that happened was he didn't have sex last night? I'm going to kill him!"

"No, you're not."

"Yes, I am," she replied, nodding her head fiercely. "Does he always act like this when you're not in the mood?"

"No."

"Are you sure?"

"Yes."

"Has he ever treated you this way?"

"No."

"Then what the hell was wrong with him today?" Rona asked herself. Reaching for clarification, she gave her best guess. "Maybe something horrible happened with work and he took it out on you."

"His work is fine."

"Then maybe something happened with Sheila or Honesty."

Ireland couldn't continue listening to Rona's hypotheses. With each one voiced, the weight of shame pressed on Ireland's shoulders like a too-tight brassiere. "It's not them, it's me."

"It is not you. You are your own person with your own feelings. Deal can't expect you to want sex every time he does. He has to -"

"Rona," Ireland snapped, needing to stop the fast flow of words running her way.

"What?"

"We've never had sex."

The heat in Rona's body turned cold. Astonishing and troubling, the statement echoed in her ears, preventing her from obtaining any glimmer of doubt on what she had just heard. "What?" she whispered, solely out of habit.

Across Rona's face was the precise expression Ireland didn't want to see. Frozen, contorted, and eerily disparaging, it confirmed an explanation would be mandatory. Despite not wanting to speak any further, Ireland added, "He was hoping last night would be our first time."

Rona felt as if she had been flung against the wall and it took her a minute to mentally peel herself from its paneling. "How could you be with Deal all this time and never truly be with him?"

"I haven't been ready."

"I'm not following."

Ireland squeezed the slippery, pink flesh of her inner lips between her teeth. "I'm scared."

"Of what?" Rona asked, jutting her head forward.

"Of things not working out."

"Sexually?"

"No, generally," she replied, tightening her face like a toddler tasting a lemon.

"I have always believed things would work out with you and Deal, but if you keep denying him, they might not."

"I know, but at least I won't regret giving him all of me."

Rona was stunned by Ireland's warped reasoning. "Listen to yourself. You're worried about things not working out, but you're doing something that could cause them not to work out. Where's your logic?"

"I don't have time for logic," Ireland said, standing to her feet. "I'm trying to keep my heart from being broken."

"It's already broken. I saw you crying in the car and if Deal came to you later and said he wanted to break up, you would be devastated."

"But I wouldn't feel like a complete fool."

Realizing Ireland must have played the fool before, Rona asked, carefully, "So who made you feel that way? Your last boyfriend?"

The beat of Ireland's heart grew harder. It thumped as strong as a stricken drum on the football field of a southern college campus. "No, the last few left because they couldn't handle waiting."

"And the one before them?"

"The three before them," Ireland said, walking to the window, attempting to mask the pain of deep, ugly wounds. "They said they loved me and swore they would never hurt me."

"But they did," Rona concluded, familiar with the routine.

"Of course they did. I've only been intimate with three guys in my life. My first was an athlete that pursued me my entire freshman year of college. I finally went out with him my sophomore year and after we were together a couple of months, I decided I was ready. Thirty days later, he dumped me and bragged to his teammates that he was the first dude to crack my code."

"Oh, Ireland. That's horrible. What did you do?"

"I didn't let anybody else have me. But then I met a guy after I graduated. He was so patient and understanding. I had him wait six months before we slept together, and when we finally did, our relationship was beautiful. It felt like true love. But one day, I found out that he had been cheating the whole time we were together. Years later, I met somebody that seemed like such a good man so I gave it one more try. He turned out to be a liar just like the other ones."

"And you've been closed off ever since?"

"I can't go through that again," she said, her vision blurred with tears.

"Does Deal know all of this?"

"No."

"You have to tell him."

"Why, so he can triple the sweet talk, pour on the promises, get some then leave?"

"He wouldn't do that," Rona cried, storming her way over to Ireland.

"He's never had to wait before so you don't know what he would do."

"I know Deal. There is no way he would stick around all this time if he wasn't helplessly in love with you. He is not cheating on you, and if you gave yourself to him, he wouldn't think about leaving."

"I think he already is."

"Well, he's really mad, because he's really hurt. He has to know you not being with him, means you don't trust him."

"It's not an easy thing to do."

"Believe me, I know, but you have to. You can't keep punishing him for what happened in your past."

"You sound like Casey."

"Then Casey's right."

Ireland felt her past had been a tough but helpful teacher. It taught her to practice a foolproof method to prevent being hurt by someone she had sex with. The method simply called for her to not have sex. Granted, she missed out on a few good men who felt forced to move on after a couple of months, but she also filtered out countless guys who lacked any substance. As a result, she took great comfort in her system. It gave her a sense of protection and since its implementation, she was fortunate not to have experienced another overwhelming heartbreak. The thought of dismantling her reliable routine for a notoriously promiscuous celebrity was nothing short of petrifying. "I'm scared," she whispered, closing her eyes.

"Look at me," Rona said, taking Ireland's hands into hers. "Do not let your fear ruin this relationship. Stop shutting Deal out. Let him in."

In the openness of the aft deck, Ideal sat and watched the waves of the water turn dark. After shifting his focus to the brightness of the moon, a friend appeared by his side.

"Alright," Dig said, handing Ideal a glass of vanilla rum then sitting down across from him. "What's going on?"

"Nothing," Ideal replied, sourly.

"Deal, I'm your boy. Tell me what's up."

"I can't get into it with you."

"Since when you can't get into something with me?" Dig asked, raising his hands. In a flash, he answered his own question. "Since Ireland, right?"

Ideal peered into the blackness before him. "Yea."

"Why did you ignore her all day?"

"Because it's too hard to look at her."

"What? That's all you've been doing since you met her."

"Yea, and I need to learn how to stop," Ideal said, taking a swig of the liquor he held.

"Why? What did she do?"

"It's what she didn't do."

"Alright, what didn't she do?"

For a split second, Ideal thought of sharing his dilemma but realized it was futile. "I wish I could, but I can't get into it with you, Dig."

"You got to tell me something. We didn't invite you guys to come on this trip so we could watch you act like you don't know each other. You know what I'm saying?"

"I'm sorry, man. I honestly thought this trip was going to bring us closer."

"How could you guys get any closer? You're one of the closest couples out here."

"We're not," Ideal said, shaking his head. "It might seem that way, but we're not."

"What's wrong?"

Penitent for spoiling what was meant to be a carefree day, Ideal gave Dig the insight he requested. "She doesn't trust me."

"What do you mean? With other women?"

"With her."

"What do you mean, with her?"

"I mean, with her."

"Make some sense, Deal," Dig barked, growing more frustrated with Ideal's vagueness.

Following Dig's insistence, Ideal grappled with his decision to remain discreet. Perhaps sharing the situation would garner understanding and sympathy. Maybe his best friend could even keep him from exploding. "This got to stay right here. You can't even tell Rona," Ideal instructed, his face as solemn as a defendant's rising to hear a verdict.

"You forgot who you're talking to?" Dig asked, reminding Ideal that their conversations always remained confidential.

After taking an anxious breath, Ideal was as tactful as he could be. "Ireland won't let me *be* with her."

"What are you talking about? You are with her."

"No, she won't let me *have* her."

"Have her how?"

Ideal had never seen Dig so dense. It was as if his mind couldn't comprehend such an obstacle. The only way to make it clear was to say it clearly. "She won't let me make love to her."

"Since when?" Dig asked, entirely convinced Ireland imposed the condition on account of an argument she had with Ideal.

"Since I met her."

"What?" Dig replied, squinting his eyes, waiting for Ideal to correct himself.

"You heard me."

Dig's previously tightened eyes grew abnormally wide. "What?" he exclaimed, before falling silent. A minute of confusion bogged him down, but then a smile crossed his face and he began to laugh. "Man, be for real."

"I am."

Dig wanted Ideal to be joking, but there was no hint of a smirk or smile on his familiar face. Instead, he sat searing with anger. After glancing over his shoulder, Dig looked back at Ideal and mumbled, "You've never had sex with Ireland?"

"No."

"Shit!" Dig said, sitting straight up. "How long have you guys been together?"

"Seven months."

"Seven months. Shit. How in the hell are you doing that?"

"I don't know."

Prior to learning such startling information, Dig had been positive Ideal was faithful to Ireland. He was no longer sure. "You've been getting it somewhere else?"

"Hell no."

"So you haven't had sex in seven months?"

"No."

"Damn, Deal. I see why you're mad as hell. You should be flipping this boat over."

Ideal felt justified. Hearing his emotions affirmed, helped him to realize he hadn't been overreacting. Because of Ireland's kindness and gentleness, there were times he felt guilty for pressuring her to move forward. She often made him feel as if he was the one being unreasonable. "I just knew last night would be the night that she finally let me love her, but she didn't."

"Does she say why she won't let you?"

"She gives me this bullshit about not being ready."

"After seven months?"

"Yea, but one night she let it slip that she wants to make sure I'm going to stick around afterward. She thinks I'm going to treat her the way I did other girls."

"Those girls didn't even get to talk to you for forty-eight hours. Based on that alone, how can Ireland not see how special she is?"

"That's what I've been trying to figure out."

"Man, that's crazy," Dig said, staring at Ideal in awe. "I don't know how you got this far."

"Me either."

"You love her more than life."

"I wish she knew that."

"Do you still tell her how much you love her? Do you tell her you'll never leave her?"

"All the time, but it's like she can't believe it. I mean, why else would she keep me from her?" Lowering his head, he went on. "I was so excited about this trip. I thought we were going to reach a whole new level. I thought we'd be on that level when I . . ."

"When you what?"

"Nothing." Turning up his glass, he downed the remainder of rum then set the tumbler on a table. "She got me so messed up."

"Yea, I see that."

"I can't get over the fact that I'm putting up with this shit. Me."

"You," Dig said, equally astonished. Not many men surpassed Dig's playboy history, but Ideal was indeed one of those men. "So what are you going to do?"

"I don't know. I need time to think."

"Then I'm going to let you get to that. Hang in there, baby," Dig said, going over and gripping Ideal's shoulder then walking away.

Returning his attention to the light in the sky, Ideal soon remembered a moment in time. He was having dinner with his current companions when Ireland asked if there was a hotel on the moon. The cute recollection coerced him to grin until he recalled her refusal that night.

His hurt returned, pulsing like the ache of a delicate hand slammed in a car door. As if reliving the painful times over the past months, he heard her telling him no, felt her pulling away, and saw her offering the look of pity he fiercely hated to see. He acknowledged them all as expressions of rejection and he had experienced them far too often. They met him first in East Hampton. They found him in Las Vegas. They followed him to Miami. They joined him in Los Angeles. They resided with him in Manhattan. They amazed him in St. Barts. In the middle of the Caribbean Sea, in the luxury, safety, and privacy of a yacht, they had the gall to show themselves.

A sweltering heat charged over him, chased by the tremor of a chill. His desire made him ill. Knowing he'd receive no cure for his unfed hunger, he had to keep his distance from her off-limits body.

His expectations for the vacation were undeniably great. Aside from good times with close friends, he believed it would be the beginning of sexual intimacy with Ireland. He also believed that after loving her thoroughly, the retreat would provide the perfect time to propose. With his anticipations demolished, he couldn't help but ask himself, was he seriously going to propose to a woman that didn't have faith in him?

At an unpredictable standstill, he felt he had no other choice, but to cancel the rest of their trip. He and Ireland would pack their things, fly back to the states, and part ways. Uncertain of what would follow, Ideal was sure the depth of his sorrow went deeper than the sea on which he sailed.

Chapter 28

Heightening his strangling sadness, Ideal studied the exterior of his stateroom's closed door, viewing it as a symbol of Ireland's manner toward him. A long while later, he shoved it open. Expecting to enter a fully lit space, he was thrown by dimness and the burning of candles. Then his narrow eyes fell upon Ireland. The sight of her cut his breath short. She stood beside the bed, wearing the lingerie he'd given her.

As his heart rate sprung into acceleration, he shut the door behind him, never glancing away from the vision before him. Stunned to see Ireland in such a sexual way, he found the display of her body titillating, tantalizing, alluring, and spellbinding. He was irrefutably enthralled.

Although he originally wondered why she had dressed in the garment, he released his speculation and hoped it meant she was ready at last. Remembering his need to breathe, he inhaled sharply. Gradually, he moved closer to her but stopped a few feet away to ensure he had an unobstructed view. As his grateful eyes roamed sections of her flesh, he cautioned himself not to lose control.

Thin, dainty straps crossed her silken shoulders. Lace-covered cups presented her salient cleavage. Amidst the sheer fabric laying atop her torso was an appealing view of the indentation of her waist. Teasing Ideal mercilessly were the slim strings of her thong, which wrapped around the curves of her comely hips. Insistent on perceiving them from the other side, he voiced a command. "Turn around."

Relieved she had no reply, he watched as she turned her back to him. He hardly saw her back. Insanely aroused, he heaved while ogling the entrancing mounds that protruded below her waist. "Come here," he said, directing her to eliminate the few feet between them. With each step, her body swayed sensually, causing him to become lost in her aura. It wasn't until she spoke that he snapped out of the haze.

"Do you still want me?" Ireland asked, looking at him with uncertainty.

Her question was absurd, but the dubious way in which she waited for an answer reminded him of how horrible he had been. For far too many hours, he was unbelievably cold. He couldn't be surprised that his behavior confused her. He had to reassure her of how desirable she was to him. With the utmost sincerity, he replied, "Baby, I will never stop wanting you." Gulping every degree of his pride, he added, "I'm sorry for how I treated you today."

"I'm sorry I haven't trusted you for months."

Ideal hadn't expected an apology. He also hadn't expected a confession. Hearing the regret in her tone and seeing the guilt on her face, magnified his objective to make her feel more sensational than she had at any time in her life. Extending his hand to her face, he ran his thumb along her cheek. "I love you, Ireland."

"I love you too."

"I need you," he said, examining her with remarkable longing then pulling her mouth into his. Enjoying the life of her lips and the twisting of her tongue, he was satisfied with kissing for just a short time. Desperate for more, his hands traveled to her back, down to her waist, and lower to the twins of flesh he had been eager to feel. Tenderly, he rubbed them, gliding his palms and sinking his fingers, before gripping them firmly to pull her against him.

Like a second-story room, void of ventilation, on an August afternoon in Arizona, Ideal's body was trapped with heat. Feverish, he turned Ireland around, pressed her back to his chest, and while clutching her cushioned hips, sucked the slopes of her shoulders.

As her knees grew weak, he took her by the hand, led her to the bed, and helped her lie down. When he saw the want and willingness in her eyes, his heart rattled wildly. With rocket speed, he removed his linen shirt, dark shorts, and boat shoes, then positioned himself right beside her. No matter what she wanted and no matter how she wanted it, he was prepared to deliver.

When he undressed her, she didn't protest. When he caressed her, she didn't interfere. She allowed his hands and mouth to linger wherever they appeared. The lobes of her ears, the nape of her neck, the dip above her lips. The dark of her navel, the front of her wrists, the swell of her bust's tips. The all of her back, the nether of her knees, the top of her thighs, the sopping space in between. Her fingers and toes, along her ankles, there was no place he did not go.

Consumed with his exploring, Ideal was encouraged by Ireland's moaning. Raspy, low, sweet, and high, her sounds became his favorite type of music. Hard at work, he listened to her melodies and fell in love with their variations. Forever he would aim to produce more of the unique songs she sang.

An hour later, his supreme moment of gratification came when after asking Ireland to look him in the eye, he made his dream a reality and became one with her. He could have sworn the earth moved but perhaps it was the shifting of the yacht that simultaneously grew wrapped in wetness as rain poured then pounded against the vessel. To the sound of thunder, Ideal discovered what it was to make love. He yearned for it never to end. Prolonging its rapture became his main mission, a mission he accomplished masterfully well.

"Ireland," he continuously heard himself groan as if his pleasure depended on him stating her name. Being with her surpassed any ambition ever fulfilled. It was chaste passion. It was worth the wait. It was something he repeated twice more.

The next day was the happiest day Ireland was blessed to see. Just before opening her eyes, she felt the front of Ideal's naked body against the back of hers. Smiling, she began to stretch her limbs but realized there was no need. She was already loose and limber, free from any form of restriction. Ideal's lovemaking had eradicated her tension and given her a wondrous state of well-being. Light as a floating feather, she found herself enamored with the stamina and skillful attention he exhibited throughout the night.

Confident it was fatigue that kept him sound asleep, she listened to the hum of his breathing then decided to watch him dreaming. Careful not to disturb his slumber, she rolled onto her back, which landed his warm hand atop her soft abdomen. Stirred by the touch of his fingers, she recalled their recent powers and looked forward to another night of their sound and loving labor. Wishing she hadn't delayed experiencing her current joy, she studied Ideal's features and reverted to her disbelief that he was actually in her presence. As if he could sense she needed confirmation, he lifted the lids to his eyes and smiled.

"I must not have done my job last night," he said.

The huskiness of his voice made her hot. "Why do you say that?"

"Because you should still be sleeping."

"Trust me, you performed exceedingly well. I slept like a baby."

"So did I." With starry eyes, he observed Ireland for a long, quiet moment. He then glanced at the clock. "Good afternoon."

"Good afternoon," she replied, adoring the way in which he acknowledged the late hour.

"How are you feeling?"

"Better than ever."

"Yea?"

"Yea."

"Me too. That was the best night of my life." His serious expression morphed into a mischievous one. "You think we can top it today?"

Laughing, Ireland answered, "That would be hard to do."

"I'm up for it."

"Aren't you tired?"

"I'll let you know in a few hours," he replied, moving down to her feet.

His kisses traveled higher and higher until she had an urgent need. At the moment he ended her wait, the room's phone began to ring. Initially, Ireland ignored the noise, but it came again and again. Afraid something might be wrong, she ultimately reached for the phone, but her arm was brought back to the bed by Ideal's impeding hand. Eventually, the calls ceased and Ideal advanced with his agenda. Unfortunately, minutes later, there was a knock at their door. Ideal paused briefly then resumed his activity, but another knock caused Ireland to state an inconvenient suggestion.

"You should go see who it is," she whispered.

"I'm not leaving your body."

"Ireland? Deal?" Rona called, standing outside of the door. "You guys okay? You're not answering your phones."

"We're fine, Rona," Ireland replied.

"We're going to a restaurant in town. You guys want to go?"

"Uh . . ."

"No," Ideal said.

Unclear if the unanswered calls and unopened door were a good or bad sign, Rona replied, "Okay," before scuttling away.

"Are you sure you don't want to go out?" Ireland asked.

"I'm sure. I want to stay in."

***

Ideal was chest-deep in hot water when Ireland took hold of his hand to join him in the bubbles of the bathtub. Once she was settled between his legs, he rinsed her hair then lathered it with an ocean-scented shampoo. As streams of steam rose around their bodies, Ireland reflected on the day. Other than a recess for room service followed by a quick nap, the hours were packed with pleasurable motion. She was feeling carefree and blissful, but as foam coated her scalp, a bit of guilt entered her heart.

She and Ideal hadn't been the best of guests. They spoiled the previous day, passed on dining the previous night, and declined an invitation that afternoon. Like pain between pressure-filled eyes and throbbing beneath temples, they had been nothing but a headache. Intent on turning their behavior around, Ireland resolved not to miss more meals with their gracious hosts. Fortunately, Ideal agreed and after enjoying themselves in the bath, they dressed and left for dinner.

Ireland would have turned heads had others been present when she entered the saloon. Her dewy skin was glowing. The damp curls of her hair were flowing. Wearing a white dress with blue and red flowers, vibrant green leaves, and a dramatic, ruffled back, she looked extraordinarily beautiful, but not solely because of her appearance. This particular night, she oozed an internal radiance.

Sitting on one of three sofas, she and Ideal waited for their friends to arrive. Before long, they enhanced the perfect way to pass time. One slow, wet kiss soon became two, which grew into three, which hastened into more. It was while they were merrily occupied that Rona and Dig came into the room.

"Well, well, well," Rona sang, her eyes bright with enthusiasm. The affection she had just witnessed was a strong indication that her advice to Ireland had been taken. Teasing, she exclaimed, "What have we here?"

Assuming Ideal's apparent bliss meant things had lastly gone his way, Dig ragged on them as well. "If you guys are going to be doing all of that, you should just go back to your room."

Standing to shake Dig's hand, Ideal said, cheerfully, "What's up, man?"

"No, what's up with you?" Dig replied. "What's up with that big smile you got on your face?"

"Well, you know, life is good," Ideal answered.

"Oh, is it?"

"Yes, it is."

"Aw," Rona said, warmed by Ideal's sentiment. "I'm so happy my favorite couple is speaking again."

"Well, we didn't exactly see them speaking. You know what I'm saying?" Dig remarked.

"You do have a point," Rona replied, waving her index finger at her boyfriend. Looking at the reunited couple, she asked, "Are you guys speaking as well as uh . . . kissing?"

"Yea, we're speaking," Ideal said, returning to his seat by Ireland's side and prompting Dig and Rona to sit as well.

"We're sorry we didn't make it to lunch today," Ireland expressed, regretfully. "Where did you guys go?"

"This little place with the best crepes. I have to have some whenever we come here," Rona explained. "Did you guys get a chance to eat?"

"Yea, I ate," Ideal replied, grinning as if he were reminiscing on a delicious meal.

Mortified by his sly reply, Ireland's mouth fell open. Had her skin been pale, she would've blushed herself into a shade of fire engine red. "We had lunch brought to our room," she added, hoping to shroud the personal information he had just shared.

"Uh huh," Rona uttered, nodding her clever head. Unable to stop her good-humored torture, she posed another question. "So what else did you guys do today?"

"Just hung out," Ireland answered, before Ideal could do so.

"Just hung out? Where? The aft deck?"

"In our room."

"So you guys stayed in your room the whole, entire day?"

Chortling along with Rona, Dig threw in a witty query of his own. "Yea, you didn't want to get out and get some fresh air?" Although it was obvious Ideal and Ireland had overdosed on a day of intimacy, Dig wasn't aware that Rona also knew it was the couple's first day of familiarity.

"Ireland's going to dive back into the ocean if y'all don't stop," Ideal warned, putting his arm around her shoulders.

"We just want to make sure you guys had a good day," Rona said, modestly.

"Our day was good," Ireland clarified.

"Really good," Ideal confirmed.

In perfect unison, Dig and Rona replied, genially, "Good."

The sliding doors to the dining room quietly came ajar. A stewardess stepped into view. Opening her gloved palm toward the impeccably set table, she announced, "Dinner is served."

Ireland thought once dinner was over, Ideal would rush her back to their room. She was surprised when he suggested they watch a movie with Rona and Dig. In the comfort of the upper lounge, the four of them agreed on an action-packed flick, but midway through the film, Ideal disappeared for nearly an hour. Upon his return, he explained a business matter required his attention. When the film ended a few minutes later, he ushered Ireland to their room and pushed opened the door.

"Whoa," she whispered, suddenly hushed as her eyes took in the most enchanting scene.

Twin trails of miniature seashells bordered a winding path of rose petals along the floor. The path began at the base of the door, stretched across the length of the room, and met the elongated desk positioned beneath the window. The desk's surface was blanketed with more petals, exquisite seashells, and rhinestone starfish. Nestled on top of the delicate blanket was an assembly of hurricane vases. Each glass structure contained floating candles, which rocked in water above steeped tulips. In the midst of the splendor sat an elaborate jewelry box made of sterling silver. It begged to be opened.

"What did you do?" Ireland asked, dumbfounded by Ideal's undying willingness to create special moments for her.

"Who said I did this?" he replied.

"If you didn't do it, who did?"

"Your fairy godmother?"

"I don't have one of those."

"A lot of women would disagree with you."

Ignoring his shirk of responsibility, Ireland gazed back at the room. She needed him to know his work hadn't been in vain. "I am so touched by this. It is one of the most magical thing I have ever seen."

"Go see more."

Excited by the quest, she directed her bare feet to walk upon the piles of petals. As suave as a leading man in a nineteen-forties film, Ideal stayed by her side but only allowed her steps to fall between the beach-themed boundaries. Once she reached the desk, she noticed a slender key. Gracefully, she picked it up but paused before using it. "Please, tell me you didn't buy more jewelry."

"I can't tell you that."

Twisting the key into its slot, Ireland unlocked the ornate jewelry box and lifted its lid. Firmly pressed in the velvet-lined space was pure white sand. Placed upon its glittering grains was a queen conch shell, silver-lipped oyster shell, and the mysterious shell of an antique pocket globe.

"How pretty," she pronounced, eyeing the fine trio. Obeying his nudge for her to proceed, she took hold of the conch shell.

"There's something inside," he said, eagerly.

"Of course there is." Reaching into its glossy aperture, she uncovered an article she didn't know existed - a naughty but nice G-string, threaded with pink pearls.

"I want you to wear that tonight."

No longer needing to smother the flames that always rose between them, she matched his weighty stare and replied, "Okay." Certain the remaining shells held gifts of their own, she seized the oyster then pulled out a strand of elegant, white, South Sea pearls.

"I want you to wear that tomorrow."

"It's beautiful," she whispered, admiring the natural beads as she ran them across her hand. Although tempted to wear the necklace that night, she set it aside and grasped the pocket globe. Raising its northern hemisphere, she peeked inside the lower, concaved shell, and after hesitating, gradually brought out a breathtaking, diamond ring.

"I want you to wear that forever."

The term *forever* rippled in Ireland's mind, resembling waves produced by pebbles hurled into a pond. Fear galloped through her, but she complied with her intuition and stood perfectly still. While absorbing the critical look in Ideal's eyes, she felt him take the ring and globe from her hands. As if the floor beneath him opened up, she saw his body sink until he landed on one knee. The room began to spin with a speed she could not slow. Luckily, his grip on her left hand prevented her from swooning on top of him.

Beaming a brilliant light, the ring contained a platinum band paved with rows of diamonds. In spite of all their shimmer, they were rivaled by the sparkling of a diamond halo encircling a center stone, which was a dazzling, oval-shaped, twenty-two-carat diamond. Baffled by the gemstone's dimensions, Ireland looked at Ideal in wonderment.

With trembling in his voice, he spoke from his soul. "Ireland, you're my world. I don't ever want to live my life without you. I can't stand the thought of being with you for just five or fifteen years. I need you to be mine for a lifetime. Will you marry me?"

Like space above a lake at dawn, Ireland's mind was filled with fog. Trying to think clearly through the murky haze was utterly unfeasible. Her senses were conveying what she had supposed would only pertain to her most grandiose dream, but the quiet Ideal kept, compelled her to acknowledge the reality of his proposition. Convinced he hadn't fully contemplated his request, she was unsure of how to answer.

"Did you hear me?" he asked.

"Are you sure?" she muttered.

"Baby, don't I look sure?"

"Don't you need more time with me? Years with me?"

"All I need is for you to say you'll marry me." When his wait for her response grew longer, he lowered his head. "Unless you don't want to."

"Ideal, it's not that," she said, bidding him to look back at her. "I just don't want you to regret asking me so soon."

"I'd never regret holding on to my happiness."

"But what about when the happiness stops?"

"That won't happen."

"It happens all the time."

"It won't happen to us."

"Everybody thinks that and then they end up nose-deep in misery."

"Listen to me," he said, sternly. "I know there will be rough times, but on the days our happiness is hard to find, our love will still be there and it'll keep us there, committed to each other. You promised me today you were done letting your past and your fear keep us apart. Don't go back on your word." He then lifted the ring higher. "Will you marry me?"

Relinquishing her caution and linking her faith with his, Ireland stepped into the vastness of the unknown. "Yes," she said, nearly losing her breath.

Hurriedly, Ideal slid the ring onto her finger, unaware of the uneasy expression it brought to her face. "I love you."

"I love you."

Tenderly, he kissed her until she felt each of his emotions. He then held up her hand and glanced down at the ring. "Do you like it?"

Ireland recognized the ring was gorgeous, but it was also enormous - too enormous for her taste. Timidly, she prepared to share both her gratitude and preference for something much smaller. "It's beyond beautiful. I don't even know how to describe how glorious it is. Thank you."

"Thank you for accepting it."

The lump in her throat enlarged. Pulling her hand away and dropping it along her side, she broke the news as gently as she could. "Well, that's the thing. It's so big. It's sort of too big."

"What?" Ideal asked, the cheer gone from his tone.

"I love that you wanted to get me something spectacular, but it's humongous."

"Our love is humongous."

"That doesn't mean my ring has to be. I wouldn't even know how to function with it."

"You'll figure it out."

"Honestly, I'd rather have something more modest."

Ideal looked as though the wind was jostled out of him. Bitterly, he digested her words until their motivation hit him like a brick. "You mean something invisible," he replied. "Instead of you loving the ring I just gave you, you're worrying about what everybody's going to say about it. If I gave you a plain band, they would still talk and take pictures of it."

"But it wouldn't get as much attention as this one. It's so flashy," she said, feeling guilty for finding fault with the most stunning piece of jewelry either of them had ever seen.

"I didn't spend days with a jeweler, designing a ring, just to turn around and get you something else. That's the ring I proposed with. That's the ring I want you to have."

Ireland truly did not want the ring. Its ostentatious quality was a turnoff for her. Unfortunately, it was painfully obvious how much her having it meant to Ideal. "Okay, I'll keep it, but I don't want people seeing it."

"It's going to be kind of hard for them to miss."

"Not if I don't wear it in public."

"What?"

"I'll wear it with you when we're alone, but I won't wear it when I'm out."

"So you want to be secretly engaged?"

"It'll be easier that way."

"Not on me. I want you to wear your ring."

"I will. I just won't wear it out."

"You have to go out all the time. If you stick to that plan, you'll hardly wear it."

"Why does it matter how often I wear it if we both know I have it? Our engagement is supposed to be about you and me. We're the only two people that need to know about it."

Ideal placed his hands on her waist and pulled her closer to him. "I don't want to hide the fact that I'm marrying you."

"Why?"

"Because I'm proud of it."

"Be proud privately."

"Ireland," he said, ignoring her advice. "We're engaged. We're not hiding it." Ending his frustration, he placed his lips on the warmth of her mouth. He then walked to the bed, where on a polished tray were berries and chilled champagne. "Let's celebrate and set a date."

"Set a date? Now?"

"Right now."

Sickened at the prospect of voicing another complaint, Ireland suppressed her whining and made herself concede, but quickly added a stipulation. "Since I'm agreeing to wear this massive ring, you have to agree not to tell anybody our date."

"Alright," he said, smirking.

"I'm serious, Ideal," she said, sharply. "Promise me you won't tell anybody. Not even friends and family."

"Fine, I promise," he said, amused by her refusal to take her glass of champagne until he agreed. "So how does tomorrow sound?"

Rolling her eyes at his silly recommendation, she introduced a sensible one. "How does a year sound?"

"It sounds crazy."

"I think we should be engaged at least a year before we get married."

"I think when we decide to get married, we should get married."

"We will . . . in a year."

"I'm not waiting that long to marry you."

"What about ten months?"

"What about three?"

"We need at least six."

"I'll do five."

"Five?" she said, annoyed he was being unreasonable.

"It's either five months or tomorrow."

"You are so impatient."

Ideal sat in a nearby chair, pulled Ireland into his lap, and stared into her eyes. "You know I'm the most patient man you have ever met."

Ireland couldn't argue with his statement. After making him wait extensively for the night before, his point was altogether accurate. Following a pause, she sighed. "You're right."

"To five months," he said, lifting his glass.

While lolling at the sundeck's pool with her best friend, Dig, and Ideal, Rona took another look at Ireland's newest accessory. "Only you would have a problem with the size of that ring."

Sitting on the edge of the pool, Ireland glanced at the diamond dancing in the daylight. "Plenty of women would feel crazy wearing this rock of Gibraltar," she argued.

"Where they at?" Rona replied. "I'm dying to meet them."

Before Ireland could respond, her cell began to ring. Regretting her decision to turn it back on, she looked and saw her publicist was calling. "Hello Amanda," she answered.

At an office building in Los Angeles, Amanda sat at her desk, gawking at her computer. "Ireland, did you get engaged?"

Astounded by Amanda's question, Ireland froze. "What?" she asked.

As if speaking to an elder that was hard of hearing, Amanda spoke even louder than she already had. "Did you get engaged?"

The dense weight of doom compressed Ireland's body, making her curl into the fetal position. "Why would you ask me that?"

"Because I'm getting calls from the press requesting confirmation of your engagement."

"Where would they even get that from?"

"Where else? Online," Amanda replied. "Paparazzi got a shot of you this morning on a yacht with a gigantic rock on your finger."

"Oh, no," Ireland cried, scanning the boats in the distance, feeling like a guppy in a sea of sharks.

"What's wrong?" Ideal asked, swimming over to her.

"Well? Is it true?" Amanda said, tapping her high-heeled pump. She loathed nothing more than being bombarded with questions she wasn't prepared to answer.

"Uh . . . yea," Ireland confessed.

Amanda's irritation swiftly converted to jubilation. A client of hers marrying Ideal Morris was richer than gold. It would catapult Ireland's career. "Congratulations," she said, careful not to sound too invested.

"Thank you."

"Well, I know you don't care for excessive attention, but you'll have a load of it when you get back. Media sources are already contacting jewelers to find out about the ring. We should release a statement. What would you like to say?"

"Nothing."

"The cat's out of the bag, Ireland. You should say something or at least confirm it on your social media."

"I'm not going to say anything and neither is Ideal."

"Does his publicist know that?"

"Look, I've got to go."

"Alright, fine. Stock up on rest. You're going to need it."

When Ireland set down her phone, Ideal suspected she received bad news. "What happened?" he asked.

"We've only been engaged three days and the media already knows because of this," she said, flipping her ring finger. "Are you happy now?"

Kissing her left hand, Ideal replied, "I am."

Chapter 29

On the sound stage of a Hollywood studio, Ideal wrestled with the urge to put his fist through a freestanding wall as he watched another repugnant take of Alberto Domingo kissing Ireland. The five takes prior, had been acerbating enough, but for some idiotic reason, Michael Weston had them do it again. Although Ideal knew love scenes were part of Ireland's job, it didn't make watching them any easier. They were torture for him, but undoubtedly, pleasure for Alberto. In Ideal's biased opinion, the leading man was getting his jollies touching Ireland's body.

After an assistant director shouted customary demands, Weston said, "Action."

Lorenzo: When are you going to stop thinking the worst?
Lena: When you stop telling me one thing and meaning another.
Lorenzo: That's not what I do.
Lena: Then why are we here?
Lorenzo: I wanted us to get away and have a nice time.
Lena: Save the crap for the tables downstairs.
Lorenzo: That's the truth.

Lena: No, the truth is, you want me to end the night at the spa so you can bet your brains out in the casino.

Lorenzo: The truth is you're beautiful.

Lena: That's not the truth we're discussing.

Lorenzo: It is now. (He moves closer to her and runs his hands along the sides of her body.)

Lena: Stop trying to distract me with your hands.

Lorenzo: I'm not trying. (He lifts the hem of her dress to her waist, caresses her thighs, grips her backside, and kisses her passionately.)

"Cut," Michael said, standing to his feet. "That was it. See you in the morning."

Although the day had been long, Ireland zipped over to Michael, full of adrenaline. "Thanks for the tip," she said. Noting the wink and slight smile he gave her, she added, "See you tomorrow."

Admiring the cheerful expression on her face, Ideal watched as she walked toward him. When she arrived at his side he gave her his honest opinion. "You were incredible today."

"Thank you," she replied. "I'm loving this."

"Looks like Alberto's loving it too," Ideal said, glancing at the film's leading man. "I'm sure he asked Weston to do extra takes of that scene."

"You are so silly."

"I am so serious."

After being driven to her trailer, Ireland removed her character's wardrobe and put on her own. Dressed warmly in a black sweater, long skirt, and high boots, she signed paperwork, handed her bags to Ideal, and headed for the door.

"Aren't you forgetting something?" he asked, pulling her engagement ring out of his pocket.

"Oh yea, the cannonball."

For the past sixteen hours, Ireland retreated into her work, but it was time to return to the horrid truth of reality. Ever since she came back from vacation, days earlier, the media had been hounding her shamelessly. When there were volumes of important stories around the world, so-called journalists made her engagement front-page news. Sadly, the madness had no end in sight as Greg drove her off of the studio's lot and to her home where paparazzi camped out.

In the cold of the night, she stepped out of the SUV and into the throng of photographers surrounding her on the sidewalk. Holding Ideal's hand, she followed behind Chase and did her best to disregard the questions being hollered her way.

"Were you shocked when Ideal proposed?"

"Is the ring heavy?"

"Are you marrying him for his money?"

Seconds later, a chiefly aggressive man charged at her like a Nile crocodile.

"Man, back up," Ideal shouted, shoving the man's camera.

"Keep your hands off my camera, Ideal."

"Keep your ass back."

Flinching her way through the meddling maze, Ireland's energy quaked on a massive scale. Her eyes remained glued on Chase's wide waist as she waited for him to reach her gate. At last, when he did, she entered the courtyard and didn't look back to tell him goodbye. Without pause, she raced to the master bathroom and locked the door behind her, executing her time-honored tactic to hide her feeling of terror.

With the exception of a golden-hued night light, she disrobed in darkness then stepped into the shower. Clouds of condensation swarmed her tense body like strangers had done all too recently. In critical need of being upheld, she leaned on a limestone wall and pressed her face against its clammy tiles. Although attempting to soften the bellowing of her heart and slow the scuttling of her breath, she was taken over by low volume sobs. She cursed her hurt and longed to turn it off like she would a leaky faucet. Regrettably, her smeared eyes continued to drip as she thought of men lurking outside her front door. The warm resort that was her home was now an arctic prison.

When she could cry no more, she scrubbed her face free from makeup and tears, cleansed her skin with a beaded bar of soap, and rinsed her grime with a portion of her pain down the chrome-covered drain.

Wrapped in a white towel, she walked into the bedroom where Ideal was sitting in his boxers, updating his social media. Reclining beside him on the bed, she let out a light sigh. "This paparazzi thing is getting old."

"I'm sorry, baby," he replied, setting aside his phone. "They'll be gone when the next story comes."

"Yea, but when will that be?"

"Maybe next week," he said, hoping they wouldn't remain at her place any longer than that. Taking from her hand a jar of chamomile cream, he rubbed the moisturizer onto her shoulders.

"If you hadn't asked me to wear my ring, I wouldn't be dealing with this."

"Let's not get into that again. All of this was inevitable."

"But a delay would've been appreciated."

"Are you trying to make me feel worse?"

"No, I'm just frustrated. I hate these idiots following me. I don't know how I'm going to get in and out of here after you and Chase fly back to New York."

"Well, you won't have us, but you'll have Luke."

"Who in the world is Luke?"

"Your new security."

"What?"

"He covers for Chase. He'll be here in the morning before I leave."

"Wow," Ireland muttered, leaning back to stare at the ceiling. Although she was relieved to have help with the press, she was depressed about what her life had become. Her freedom and privacy had already been limited, but now they were officially extinct. "I can't believe I'm going to have someone with me everywhere I go."

"He'll be with you more than that."

"What do you mean?"

"Around the clock. Overnight."

"What?" she shrieked. "Isn't overnight overboard?"

"No, it's not," he answered, promptly. "My job is to protect you so that's what I'm going to do. When I can't be with you, a man I trust will be."

"Okay, y'all. In the studio today, we have a man that is so hot it's a wonder that the building is not on fire," Leticia exclaimed, fanning herself with a pamphlet. The female co-host of a New York-based radio show, Leticia sat at a desk across from Ideal, marveling at his physical appearance.

"Yea, and it's a good thing I'm near an extinguisher because it looks like I'm going to have to hose Leticia down," her co-host, Carlos added. Completing the introduction, he announced, "Alright, we're not going to make you guys wait any longer. We have in the studio, the one and only, off-the-charts talented, Mr. Ideal Morris. Ideal, welcome back to the show."

"Thank you," Ideal said, adjusting his headphones.

"It's been a minute since we've seen you."

"Yes, too long," Leticia remarked. "Thank you so much for taking the time to come through."

"Yep," Ideal replied.

"So how are you doing? How have you been?" she asked.

"I've been good."

"Clearly, you've been busy and we know your schedule stays hectic so what else you got going on today?"

"I got a few more interviews to do and a couple of meetings to run then I'll have my show tonight."

"Well, we definitely want to get into the show as well as your current album and how it's dominating the world right now, but first things first. Congratulations on your engagement."

"Thanks," Ideal mumbled, aware his response confirmed reports.

"Yo," Carlos said. "You've always been that dude that didn't want to get serious with a woman, so what happened, man?"

Ideal tilted his head. "Looking back, I don't know if it was that I didn't want to get serious with a woman. I just never met a woman that I felt serious about."

"Well, that obviously changed."

"It did."

"So what was it about Ireland that got you? I mean, other than the fact that she's fine."

"Uh, I can't say too much or she'll kill me, but, she's just a really good person. She's honest, caring, creative, and sexy as hell. You know what I'm saying?"

"Oh, I definitely do," Carlos replied. "No offense, but when I saw her movie I couldn't stop looking at her."

"Man, I feel what you're saying more than you know," Ideal said, shaking his head. "She's an incredible actress and she's loyal to her family and friends, but I guess what I love most about her is the fact that she's not with me, because of what I do or what I have. She's into me for who I am." Shrugging his shoulders, Ideal voiced one last thought. "I've never met anybody like her."

"Damn, Deal, that's deep. So you're all in?"

"I'm all in," Ideal repeated with pride.

"Ireland's a lucky girl," Leticia declared.

"I'm a lucky man," Ideal replied.

"So have you guys set a date? When is the wedding?"

Ideal knew Leticia hoped he would let the information slip, but he'd already broken a promise to not speak about Ireland publicly. He couldn't break another one. "I'll let you know once it's passed," he joked.

Laughing, Carlos jumped back in. "Alright, well let's get nice and nostalgic with Ideal's 2016 hit, *Down and Good,* then we'll be back to ask him about his latest single, *My Heart*, which rumors say is about his fiancé. We'll also be giving away free tickets to his show tonight so keep it locked right here."

Chapter 30

Waking to the light of day was an experience Ireland missed dearly. Arriving on time for work meant leaving her home before dawn. Grateful to have finally slept in, she remained in bed and stared between the parted curtains of her bedroom window. While observing jade leaves, a jet-black bird glided in the air. As it began to speak in its strong, distinctive tone, Ireland recalled she wasn't alone.

Across the hall, in the guestroom, was a young man named Luke. Tall with deep blue eyes, fair brown hair, and suntanned skin, he arrived at her gate the previous morning ready and willing to work. Upon introducing himself, he expressed that he was self-sufficient and required no tending to. He was there to look after her, not the other way around.

In addition to helping her pass through the press, he explained he would do his best to help her maintain some sense of independence. When she was home, he'd stay put in the guestroom. When she was on set, he'd be a few yards away. When she visited friends, he'd wait outside their door. When she walked in public, he'd linger steps behind. As long as there weren't people attempting to steal her personal space, he would watch over her from a nearby distance.

The more Luke spoke, the more comfortable she felt. She appreciated that he was vastly trained, kind, professional, and personable. At the end of their first conversation, she had quickly grown to like him, and on his first assignment, he provided precisely what Ideal promised - protection and relief. She had been left in very capable hands.

The hands, however, she was currently hankering after, were miles away outside of the country. Luckily, their owner's timing was right on cue with her thoughts.

"Hi," Ireland said, accepting his video chat call.

"So you're having my baby?" Ideal asked.

"What?"

"I hear you're having my baby."

"Is that what you hear?"

"That's what my publicist just told me. Reports say you're pregnant with my child."

"Ugh, of course," Ireland said, dropping her head back onto her pillow.

"You could've at least told me first."

"Shut up."

"I mean, I am the father," he said, allowing the corners of his mouth to turn up.

"You'd think these stupid magazines would at least come up with some original lies. They just circulate the same dumb stories for whatever couple's in the news."

In his Paris hotel suite, Ideal sat with his boot-clad feet on top of a French Provincial desk. "Seriously, baby, when do you want to start having kids?"

Caught off guard, Ireland blurted, "Huh?"

"You heard me."

"I don't know," she said, sitting up. "When do you want to?"

"A few months after we're married."

"Really?"

"Really. Your turn."

Becoming Ideal's wife still seemed like an improbability so planning to have his children felt a bit absurd. Saying what sounded best to her ears, she answered, "I guess after we're married a year."

"Okay. Three or four, right?"

"No, I told you I wanted two or three."

"We'll plan on three and let the fourth one be a surprise."

"I'm surprised you want that many kids. They're expensive and I know how much you love your money."

"Yea, well my love of money won't come close to how much I love spending it on you and our kids."

"That's a scary statement."

"Why?"

"Because our kids can be spoiled, but they can't be brats. They'll have to feel what it's like to go without sometimes and they're going to have to be involved in multiple charities."

"You're going to be such a good mom," he said, smiling. "So how did you sleep with Luke there?"

"I guess well because I just woke up."

"That's because of those long hours you've been putting in."

"I'm just trying to keep up with you."

"You shouldn't have today off if you're trying to do that. While you're lounging around, I'll be working."

"You mean, watching your staff work," she joked.

"Hey, I'm always busy making big decisions."

"Well, I have my own big decisions to make and for your information, I won't be lounging around today. I have a lot to do including picking my mother up from the airport."

"Whoa, your mother's flying in?"

"Yep."

"Man, I wish I was still there. I'd love to see her again."

"Well, I better get ready to go. I have to pick up Casey too," she said, rising from her bed.

"Okay," he said, putting a file in his leather satchel. "I can tell you haven't watched my interview yet. Watch it before you leave."

"How can you tell I haven't watched it?"

Ideal bit his bottom lip. "You're not mad at me."

"Why would I be mad at you?"

"I answered some questions that I shouldn't have."

"You kept your mouth shut about me, right?" she asked, studying his sheepish expression. Hearing no response, she repeated herself at a much higher pitch. "Right?"

"Wrong."

"Ideal!"

"Baby, I'm sorry. It's hard not talking about you."

"What did you say?"

Checking the time on his watch, he replied, "Look, I got to go. Just watch the interview and we'll talk about it later. I love you."

Teeming with concern, Ireland went to her laptop and forced herself to log on. There was nothing left to do except watch.

While driving at an alarming speed, Ireland's concentration swung from her rear-view mirror to the boulevard before her. Frantically, she changed lanes unaware of how long she'd been holding her breath. She was far too busy escaping paparazzi to be bothered with the routine of inhalations and exhalations. The collection of knots lodged in her stomach grew tighter as she slowed to approach a golden light. Defying her better judgment, as well as the law, she waited for the appearance of a neon red beam then slammed the sole of her shiny shoe against the accelerator.

Boldly, she sped through the café-lined intersection and lost all but one vehicle, which pulled alongside her. With a deafening screech, she jerked the steering wheel to the right and veered onto a quiet, residential road. Crisp leaves lying upon the ground were carried into the rush of wind her fast-moving car created. Ignoring stop signs with caution, she darted past homes and drifted around curves until she no longer saw the SUV. Once she gave the area one last assessment, she parked in front of a charming bungalow.

In sync with the rest of her body, her hand shook violently as she reached into her car door to retrieve much-needed napkins. Dabbing away perspiration pooled around her neck, she searched for her breath, fearful its calming ability may have expired. Gradually, its quick shallowness became slow, steady, and deep. Eager to float into a scene of serenity, she shut her eyes and just began to see the lavender tips of a jacaranda tree when she heard a voice ask, "Are you okay?"

The unexpected sound caused her to jolt. In some freakish way, she forgot Luke was sitting beside her.

"Yea," she responded, mechanically, staring straight ahead.

"Are you sure?" he asked, unconvinced. The day before, he watched Ireland take on the paparazzi with a brave face. This day, however, she fled with all her might. Although she got away, it was painfully obvious how much the ordeal upset her. It was the first time he was moved to compassion for a client. Perhaps it was because she was the first to seem genuinely displeased with the attention.

"I'm sure," she replied, finding it difficult to look him in the eye. "I'm sorry."

"For what?"

"For how I was driving. I shouldn't have put you in danger."

"I was actually impressed with your tactical skills behind the wheel."

"You were?" she asked, finally looking his way.

"Yes, but don't ever use them again. In fact, let me handle the driving for a while."

In his eyes, Ireland saw not only gravity but pity. He witnessed her having a panic attack and now must have viewed her as fragile. Embarrassment began to bind her like the laces of a corset. Avoiding his gaze again, she toddled to the other side of the car, where he helped her into the passenger seat as if she were a feeble elder. Feeling as small as a speck of lint, she surrendered control and allowed him to drive. The press had taken so many of her freedoms.

Now, they had abducted her driving privilege too. Rummaging for any distraction, she turned on the radio and soon heard the raspy tone of a station's feisty deejay.

"Hey, this is your girl, Vanessa. It seems we know why our favorite celebrity crush, Ideal Morris, is engaged to Ireland Rochelle, his girlfriend of just seven months. Ladies, let's go ahead and cry it out," she said, pressing a sound machine button that played audio of women weeping. "Ireland is reportedly pregnant with the superstar's first child. That's what made him pop the question so soon. By the way, have you guys seen her rock? If you haven't, I suggest you stop whatever you are doing and find it online. All I can say is, whoa," she added, pressing another button where a mob of men echoed the same sentiment. "Well, we congratulate the couple on their little one on the way. Here is Ideal's song, *My Heart*. We all know who he's talking about on this track, don't we?"

As the prevalent song began, Ireland paid no mind to the loving lyrics written about her. Disgusted by the deejay's irresponsibility in spreading the pregnancy rumor, her face remained stuck in a scowl. Knowing the lie would subject her to further scrutiny, she grew more infuriated with each second that passed. So involved in wondering when the media's nose would be removed from her affairs, it took her a moment to realize the car had stopped in front of Casey's home. Upon recognizing her location, she leaned over and honked the horn.

A moment later, Casey emerged, strutting in a pair of ankle boots the same shade as her beige dress. Although she glanced at Ireland, she spent most of her time studying the ambiguous figure in the driver's seat. Increasingly intrigued, she opened the rear door, settled herself behind Ireland, and gave the stranger another once over. Observing the man that was guarding her best friend was a pleasure she hadn't anticipated. Smiling, she reached her hand toward him. "Hello, I'm Casey. You must be Luke."

Wrapping his large hand around hers, Luke replied, "Nice to meet you, Casey."

After tugging her gaze from Luke's rugged good looks, Casey leaned forward and rubbed Ireland's stomach. "Any morning sickness?" she asked, giggling.

"That's not funny," Ireland said, sourly, flinging Casey's hand away.

"What isn't funny is you not telling me when and where you're getting married," Casey said, putting on her seatbelt. "A website just posted that a staff member of a mansion outside of Philly said you and Ideal are getting married there. Is that the plan?"

"You're actually asking me if that trash is right?"

"Yea," Casey replied, plainly.

"Why are you even still reading those sites?"

"It's not like if I stop reading them, they're going to take the stories down. The whole world reads them."

"Going online to be told lies is one of the dumbest things people do," Ireland said, glaring out of the window as Luke drove off.

"Just because some of the stories are lies doesn't mean all of them are. For example, have you heard about your current director, Mr. Weston?"

"I'm not interested."

"The sites say he has a mistress in France. That could be true."

In an instant, Ireland lost her patience. Void of any composure, she yelled, "Even if it is, it's none of our business!" Screaming louder than before, she repeated herself. "It's none of our business!"

Though Ireland's reaction shocked Casey and Luke, it stunned her most of all. As her heart pounded, she felt like she was invaded by a foreign force of fury. With her frustration unleashed, the three of them went mute and thus listened intently to the wind whizzing by and the hypnotic hum of the tires rolling upon the gritty ground.

To keep warm from the winter breeze, Ireland wore a high-collared, slim-fitting, black suede jacket. Along its sides were square studs, which balanced the wide, distinctive flaps above the faux pockets of her skinny, gray pant. Continuing her edgy vibe were oxford shoes with spiky heels in which she walked toward the entrance of a Beverly Hills bridal salon. As Luke held open the door, Casey and Janet hurried inside, ahead of the bride-to-be.

The sweet scent of gardenias welcomed them to the boutique. Other than shades of silver, it was saturated with light due to tall, immaculate windows framing headless mannequins. The lean, black and white figures stood bedecked in awesome creations. Parallel to bare walls were meticulously hung dresses, each one so breathtaking it seemed they shouldn't be touched. Nearly naked tables, topped with white flowers, sat next to velvet sofas set throughout the shop. A vision of stoicism, Luke remained near the door while the ladies waltzed over to the front desk.

"Good morning," the receptionist said, her gray eyes brightening as she recognized Ireland.

"Good morning," Ireland replied.

Although pleased to see Ideal's fiancé, the woman was taken aback. The salon had an appointment-only policy and while reviewing the calendar that morning, she failed to see Ireland's name. "May I help you with something? Perhaps you'd like to schedule an appointment?"

"I have one."

A look of fright arrested the woman's face. "You do?"

"Yes, it's at eleven o'clock."

Nervously, the woman began thumbing through books, hoping to discover an overlooked note.

"It's under Sondra Elise," Ireland said, informing the woman of the alias she used.

"Oh," the woman said, the fire draining from her pale cheeks. "I understand. Please have a seat and Marion will be right with you."

As Casey roamed around gawking at dresses, Ireland and Janet chose a place to sit. Once they were side by side, Janet examined her daughter's less than enthusiastic mood. Gently, she asked, "How are you feeling, Ireland? You've been quiet."

"I'm okay."

"Tell me the truth," Janet replied, lowering her chin.

"I'm just tired."

"Of filming?" Janet asked, running her hand along Ireland's thigh.

"Of the press. They chased me through the streets this morning."

"What? Was Luke driving?"

"No, I was."

"Don't you or Luke ever do anything crazy trying to outrun them," Janet warned, her eyes severe with concern. Demanding acknowledgment of her instruction, she said, "You hear me?"

"Yes," Ireland answered, having learned her lesson hours earlier.

The sound of a violin's pizzicato, drifting from overhead speakers, was suddenly drowned out by the squeals of two women entering the salon. Accompanying them was a bald male who stood a few feet from Luke. Ireland realized the woman with platinum extensions was a pop-singing sensation named Ashlyn.

Soon Casey appeared, sitting so close to Ireland, she was practically in her lap. "Look who's here," she whispered, having recognized the singer as well.

After scanning the space, Ashlyn noticed Ireland. Her injected lips stretched into a smile. Without hesitation, she marched her purple boots over to the trio of ladies. "Hello, Ireland."

"Uh, Hello," Ireland replied, surprised Ashlyn knew her name.

"We haven't met, but I'm Ashlyn."

"Yea, I know," Ireland said, standing to her feet and shaking Ashlyn's hand.

"I've been wanting to meet you. Ideal is the absolute best. He's produced a ton of my music."

"He told me."

"Congratulations on your engagement. I'm so happy he finally found someone."

"Thank you. I heard you found someone too."

"I did. Our wedding's next month. When's yours?"

"We haven't decided," Ireland lied. It was a date she and Ideal continued to guard for themselves. However, one reasonable day, they discussed telling their mothers. Ireland was certain Janet could keep the secret, but Ideal knew Sheila would tell Honesty. As a result, Janet was the only other person who knew the day they would marry. Everyone else, including vendors, wouldn't be privy to the information until a week prior.

"Let me see your ring," Ashlyn screamed, raising Ireland's left hand. "Wow, it's even more amazing in person. It's beautiful."

"So is yours," Ireland said, envying the understated elegance of Ashlyn's four-carat solitaire. Her dwelling on the ring was interrupted by a not to subtle kick she felt on her ankle. "Ashlyn, this is my best friend, Casey."

Eager to speak, Casey sprung onto her feet. "Hello, Ashlyn. I really admire your work. You have the most exciting performances."

"Thanks, I try."

"And this is my mother, Janet."

"Hello," Janet said, standing also to shake Ashlyn's hand.

"Hi," Ashlyn said. "May your talented daughter and talented son-in-law bring you some talented grandchildren."

"Ooh, you know exactly what to say."

Giggling, Ashlyn introduced them to her sister then took another look at Ireland. "Well, enjoy your marriage."

"You do the same," Ireland replied.

Just as Ashlyn walked away, another woman emerged. The picture of sophistication, she wore a shell top, pencil skirt, and slingback pumps. Her highlighted hair was swept into a bun, which showcased long earrings beside her long neck. "Good morning, I'm Marion," she said. "Shall I call you Sondra?"

"Ireland's fine."

"It's a pleasure to meet you, Ireland. Arielle happens to be here today for a fitting with another celebrity client, but she'd love to meet with you to discuss a couture gown."

"Ooh, couture," Casey moaned, placing a palm on her chest.

"That won't be necessary," Ireland said.

Waving her hand, Marion offered reassurance. "Oh, it's no trouble at all. Designing is a joy for Arielle. It's the reason she created the company."

"I'm sure it is, but I'd rather choose something off the rack."

"Well, then," Marion mouthed, slowly, the creases on her forehead exhibiting her confusion. "Let's get you settled in a room. Right this way."

As Ireland trailed Marion further into the boutique, the reality of becoming a bride began to sink in. Lastly, she looked forward to the upcoming hours and released the hellish thoughts of the recent ones. Little did she know, the information on her whereabouts had just been shared with millions through Ashlyn's social media. The singer's post read:

Just met Ideal's fiancé at Arielle in Beverly Hills! Such a nice person! She's going to make a beautiful bride!

In Ireland's ample dressing room, she stood on a carpeted pedestal, wearing her sixth selection. Form-fitting with an asymmetrical neckline, it was made of silk shantung and stopped above her knees.

"You can't be serious," Casey complained. "It's a cocktail dress."

"No, it's not," Ireland retorted.

"Yes, it is. It'll have you looking like a guest at your own wedding."

"Not if I'm the only one in white."

"Janet, will you please talk some sense into her?" Casey implored, taking a guzzle of her champagne.

Granting Casey's request, Janet asked Ireland, "Are you really considering this dress?"

"Yea," Ireland replied. "Why?"

"Because I've known you your whole life and you've never liked a wedding dress like that." Janet examined the nearby gowns she chose for Ireland to try then lifted one by its wooden hanger. "This is the kind of dress you've always wanted to wear."

"That's because I always wanted a big, lavish wedding. I don't want that anymore."

Making sure to keep tensions low, Janet said, softly, "I know you're exhausted from the media attention, but playing this wedding small and pretending it's not a big deal isn't going to make the situation any better. I don't want you to look back on your day and regret that you wore something you could've worn on Easter."

"Thank you," Casey murmured.

Leaning in closer, Janet told Ireland an undeniable truth. "No matter how hard you try, you're not going to disappear. Your light is too bright."

Janet's words moved them all to silence, but soon Marion recalled she still had work to do. Seizing the gown from Janet's hands, she stated the obvious. "Let's try this one on."

Ireland barely had time to blink before the dress was on her frame and clips were being attached to excess fabric along her back. As her audience gasped, she took a look in the mirror.

A vision of genuine romance, she seemed to be missing from an ethereal land. Draped in exquisite, Chantilly lace, embroidered with sequins and crystal beading, the trumpet gown's bodice was the essence of lovely. Classic was its sweetheart neckline as well as its delicate straps, but the flourishing skirt was a prevailing work of art with elaborate waves of the softest organza. On and on the abounding skirt went, reaching and rippling across the floor. The epitome of femininity, the ivory dress was incredible.

While listening to Casey's moans, Ireland caught a glimpse of her mother's tears. "Don't cry. You'll make me start."

Restraining the flood at the brim of her eyes, Janet gushed, "You look so beautiful."

"You truly do," Casey confirmed, additional words escaping her.

"I think I feel a bit like a fairy," Ireland joked, nervously.

"I think you feel that dress is the one," Janet said.

Ireland swayed from side to side, growing more lost in its beauty. "It's amazing. It really is," she admitted. "But, it's so glamorous. I want to try a few more that are less fussy."

Casey added her two cents for the third time. "You are wasting our lives with this simple dress search."

Before Ireland could reply, she heard the calming chimes of her ringtone. Stepping off of the pedestal, she grabbed her cell from her handbag. "Hi, Luke," she answered.

"Sorry to interrupt, but I knew you'd want to know."

"Want to know what?"

"Photographers are out front."

"No," Ireland groaned. "Oh, wait. They're probably here to see Ashlyn."

"Do you want to stay?"

"No, but I need to," she said, glancing over at Janet. "My mother's rarely in town and I want to do this with her."

"Alright, just be prepared when we go out."

"Okay, thanks."

"What's wrong?" Janet asked after Ireland ended the call.

"The paparazzi are here. Hopefully, Ashlyn will leave soon and they'll be gone by the time we leave."

In spite of what was growing outside, Ireland returned to trying on dresses. Eight creations later, an elegant, satin slip dress and the gown they all adored, rested on her heart. As she tried to choose between the two, Arielle arrived to introduce herself and personally take Ireland's measurements. In the end, Ireland was deeply conflicted and chose to wait until morning to make her decision.

An hour had passed since Ashlyn's departure, but the paparazzi and public remained. Ignorant of how anyone learned she was there, Ireland left the salon wrapped in Luke's arm. Normally, when bombarded by a group of grungy men, she was consumed with her own safety. At that moment, however, Janet's security was her sole concern. Holding her mother's hand firmly, with their fingers stiffly intertwined, they moved along the sidewalk. Right, left, pause. Right, left, pause. Tediously, they inched toward the severely blocked curb and eventually reached the car.

Once Janet was inside, Ireland crept to the passenger seat. The second she sat down, her heart nearly stopped as a wiry, young paparazzo dove on top of her feet before she could place them in the car.

Boiling with adrenaline, Luke yanked the man up and shoved him a few feet away. After crashing into fellow photographers, he tumbled to the ground. Lying on top of his camera, the man grappled for his bearings while his peers yelled obscenities at the bodyguard behind the wheel. At an unexpected speed, Luke pulled away, forcing the self-righteous vultures to rush aside.

Chapter 31

Over the past two weekends, Ireland felt like a deficient spare wheel, wobbling along with her celebrity friends doing celebrity things. Most recently, the four of them sat courtside at an All-Star basketball game at which Ideal was the halftime entertainment. The former week, they attended music's biggest award show, where both Dig and Ideal were winners and performers. Though Ireland enjoyed the music of the evening, she suffered acute discomfiture each time Ideal thanked her during his acceptance speeches. Resulting in close-up shots of her in the audience, she struggled to hide her irritation with his publicized gratitude.

Currently, Ideal was in Tokyo, but Rona and Dig were in Los Angeles, allowing Ireland to see them for the third consecutive week. The couple was in town for the world's most renowned award ceremony, which honored motion pictures the film industry deemed deserving.

Despite acquiring high earnings and dominating the box office, *Less Loyalty* failed to be nominated for *Best Picture*. Most individuals associated with the film, including its director and actors, also weren't nominated. Only a select few within the technical categories had the possibility of winning one of the handsome trophies.

While others were in an uproar the movie wasn't recognized, Ireland had an awful secret. She was relieved. She had zero desire to get gussied up, pose on a carpet, and schmooze at parties. Having already done so for luncheons and shows that had nominated her for Best Supporting Actress, she took comfort in knowing she could watch the grandest event at home in her warm robe and socks. Although *Less Loyalty*'s cast was snubbed by the academy, producers wanted to broadcast a show with star power. As a result, Rona was set to participate as a presenter.

Among rehearsal, meetings, and pre-show bashes, Rona and Dig could only see Ireland late Friday night. Although Rona wanted to meet for dinner at a restaurant linked to paparazzi, Ireland demanded they eat elsewhere. She made reservations at a moderate place, miles away in Redondo Beach. Optimistic she'd experience a hassle-free night, she arrived precisely on time.

Once Luke pulled up to the valet, a hasty attendant opened Ireland's door. Routinely, the employee helped her out of the car, but Luke was by her side before she took another step.

Defining elegance, Ireland wore a satin dress that above the waist was the color of champagne and below the waist, a deep gray. Two slim belts, one silver, the other gold, encircled her hips and emphasized her shapely figure. As she walked toward the entrance in the night's breezy air, she heard a man yell her name. Promptly, she turned around and saw Dig's smiling face. With the exception of a navy cardigan, he was wearing his trademark uniform of sneakers, jeans, t-shirt, and a chain.

"Hey, Dig," she said, happy to see him approaching her.

"Hey," he replied, reaching out his arms. After kissing her on the cheek, he gave her a hug. "It's been a long time. How have you been over the past five days?"

"Good," she answered, giggling at his joke. Looking behind his tall frame, she only saw his bodyguard. "Where's Rona?"

"She's running late so she's going to meet us here," he said, glancing at the establishment Ireland had chosen.

"Oh, okay," she muttered.

"What's up, Luke?" Dig said, shaking Luke's hand.

"Hi, Dig," Luke replied, always pleased to see the man who was secretly his favorite artist. When Luke saw Dig touch the small of Ireland's back, he allowed him to guide her inside.

Taupe walls, low lighting, and a fair amount of people, offered the very calm that Ireland was seeking.

"How many in your party?" the young host stammered, unnerved by Dig's presence.

"Three," Dig answered.

Although others expected to be seated next, Dig and Ireland were led to a table with a view of boats docked in the adjacent harbor. After pulling out Ireland's chair, Dig sat across from her. They then set aside their menus and waited for Rona.

"So what did you do today?" Ireland asked.

"Went to the studio and put down some rhymes."

"You and your friend never stop."

"And that's why we on top, hey," Dig rhymed, bobbing his head as if he were performing. Pleased he made Ireland smile, he asked, "You have a good week of shooting?"

"I did. I got to slap Alberto a few times."

"Whoa, that is a good week."

"I know."

"You are definitely on the come up when you get to start smacking legends around."

As they laughed, a waitress appeared. Eager to serve, she filled their glasses with water then hurried away to fulfill Dig's request for a bottle of wine.

"This meal is going to be my treat," Ireland announced.

Dig did a double-take then shook his head. "No, it's not."

"Yes, it is."

"We're not going to let you do that."

"I never pay when we go out."

"Because you don't have it like us."

"Well, I can afford this place."

Dig closed his eyes and spoke with assurance. "Deal would kick my ass if I let you pay tonight."

"I didn't know you were scared of Ideal," she taunted, hoping the remark would make him reconsider.

"When it comes to you I am," he said, emphatically. "On my watch, you're getting taken care of."

"Well, at least let me get the tip."

"Nope."

"Come on, Dig."

"Nope."

"Fine," she said, giving up on an argument she clearly couldn't win.

The sound of an alert chimed from Dig's phone. As he checked the device, Ireland scanned the room. Although she noticed some people gawking, she was so pleased to have avoided a packed place with paparazzi, the stares from Dig's fans didn't disturb her as much that night.

"Bad news," Dig said, putting his cell back down. "Rona can't make it."

"What?" Ireland replied, scowling. "Why?"

"Some sort of catastrophe with the dress she planned on wearing to the show."

"Oh, no," Ireland said, imagining Rona in a state of panic.

"She said to tell you she's sorry."

"Well, what she wears for the show has to be flawless so I understand." Thinking Dig may want to cancel the meal altogether, she asked, "So, do you want to just go?"

"I'm hungry," Dig said, slapping his chest. "I'm ready to order and I'm ready to eat."

"Me too," she said, cackling at his relentless candor. "I've been waiting all day to have their seafood linguine."

After taking their order, the waitress poured them each a glass of the wine Dig carefully selected. When Dig held up his goblet for a toast, Ireland followed suit. "To good health, good food, and good friends," he said.

"Good health, good food, good friends."

Typically, Ireland went to bed early, ensuring she was well-rested for her sunrise call times during the week. Sunday's award show, however, kept her awake far past her bedtime. Watching Rona grace the stage in stunning, canary jewels and a matching gown, made the late night worth it, but Ireland felt sluggish upon rising Monday morning. Despite the lethargy, she arrived at work on time.

In her studio trailer, she sat mumbling the lines for her third scene of the day. Nearby was Keith, typing absorbedly on his laptop. In due time, his ringing phone interrupted their concentration.

"How was your night?" Keith asked, answering his call from Amanda. "You have a hangover?"

"Not this time," Amanda replied, standing in her home office.

"Lucky you."

"Hey, Ireland's phone is off. Is she shooting?"

"No, she's right here."

"I need to talk to her."

Amanda's urgency and lack of small talk were impossible to miss. "Is everything alright?"

"I'll let her fill you in. Put her on the phone."

Appearing clueless, but curious, Keith handed his phone to Ireland. "It's Amanda."

"Hi, Amanda," Ireland said. "Shouldn't you be resting?"

"That was the plan."

"What happened?"

"Well, the biggest celebrity news site decided to sit on a story so they could post it today - after the awards. It made an even grander splash that way."

"Oh, so it involves one of your clients?" Ireland asked, leaning her head to the side in order to stretch her neck.

"Yes, it does. It involves you."

"Huh?" Ireland replied, whipping her head back to its natural position.

"Listen," Amanda said, "I hate to have to tell you this, but it's about you and Dig having dinner the other night."

Ireland rolled her eyes. "They don't have anything better to report?"

"Well, it's major breaking news, because they're saying it was sort of a . . . romantic dinner."

"Excuse me?" Ireland asked, genuinely confused.

"Ireland," Amanda said, pausing before proceeding. "Are you and Dig seeing each other?"

Disgusted by the question, Ireland exclaimed, "Have you lost your mind? It was dinner."

"It looks like it could've been more. Aside from the snug hug and kiss you guys shared when leaving, there was red wine, candlelight, and a lot of smiling. He even pulled out your chair."

"So what? He was being a gentleman."

"Dig's not really known for being a gentleman."

"Well, he is. He's gentle with Rona all of the time."

"Yes, with Rona. That's why this looks suspicious."

"What is wrong with you? You sound like you believe it," she said, glancing at Keith as he searched for the story.

"I'm just saying I can see how people could jump to the wrong conclusion."

"Look, Dig is with Rona and I'm with Ideal."

"Which is why they say the two of you went out of your way to sneak out of L.A. and dine at a smaller scale restaurant."

"This cannot be happening to me," Ireland whispered, her voice trembling. "I just went to have dinner with Dig and Rona, but she wasn't able to make it. That's all it was.

"I'm sorry, Ireland, but the media's turning it into something else. It's going to spread to all of the sites and the world's going to be talking so if you want to address it -"

"I don't," Ireland snapped, abandoning her softer tone.

"Honestly, you are a very hard person to work with."

For an unforeseen moment, guilt overshadowed Ireland's turmoil. She knew there was some truth in Amanda's statement. Recognizing the fact that she caused her publicist steady grief, she altered her rash decision. "I'm sorry. Can you at least give me time to think about it?"

With her eyebrows held high, Amanda replied with surprise. "Alright, I'll call you in the morning."

In disbelief, Ireland moved in slow motion as she set Keith's phone aside.

"This looks really bad," Keith warned, rotating the screen of his laptop to face her.

"I don't want to see it," she said, quickly turning her back to the device. Trapped in a corner, she was squarely confronted by her overall loss of control. Fearing the risk of catching a glimpse of the web page causing her body chaos, she scampered for the door. "I'm going to wardrobe."

Although work usually muted Ireland's thoughts, her scenes on that tumultuous day did nothing to silence her mind's deliberation. Relieved to be alone at last, she entered her bedroom at midnight, removing her coat and sheepskin-lined boots. After stripping off her jeans, she suddenly felt faint. Sinking onto the edge of her bed, she contemplated skipping her nightly shower. She hardly had the energy to do anything, including listening to voicemails that undoubtedly filled her mailbox. Preferring to remain irresponsible, she chose not to turn on her cell phone, but oddly enough, found herself turning on her laptop.

Internally, she pleaded with herself to cease logging on. Unfortunately, she continued pressing the buttons of the keyboard until she arrived at the homepage of a major website. Her heart raced then her eyes widened. The caption required attention. It read:

Dig Caught Cheating! The rapper betrays Rona and Ideal by romancing Ireland Rochelle!

Astounded, it took Ireland a while to look below the vile headline. Eventually, she did. Chronicling the night that she and Dig had dinner were pictures of them smiling and sharing a toast, as well as hugging and kissing before parting ways. Appalled by the insinuations of the innocent photographs, Ireland dreaded reading the accompanying text. She managed to scan a few sickening lines, but inadvertently dropped her laptop as she began to bawl. Soon there was a loud knock at her door.

"Ireland?" Luke yelled, waiting fixedly for a response. "Ireland?" he repeated. Met again with silence, he opened the door then rushed to her side.

Almost as soon as Luke appeared, Ireland ran away. Unable to make it to the restroom, she reached the nearby wastebasket and braced herself above it. Promptly, vomit escaped her throat and poured itself into the dark bin. Following a brief gag, she hurled more matter, which sounded like heavy rain splattering dry pavement. When she was done, she lifted her head and saw a shirtless Luke holding her hair.

"Are you okay?" he asked.

"No," she said, numbly.

"You need a doctor?"

"I don't know what I need."

"I do," he said. Scooping her up into his arms, Luke carried her into the restroom and sat her on the counter beside the sink. After wetting a hand towel and wiping her mouth, he gave her mouthwash to rinse with. He then carried her back to the bed and placed her body between the sheets. Once the duvet was over her shoulders, he stared down at her. "What you need is sleep."

Looking up into the seriousness of Luke's blue eyes, Ireland began to cry. As much as she wanted to halt her tears, they hurried down her powder-caked cheeks. "I'm too upset to sleep," she cried, aware that she again appeared unstable in front of him.

Lowering himself onto his knees, Luke leaned over and wiped one of her tears. "It's okay."

"It's not."

"Well, it's going to be okay. One day soon."

"Do you babysit all of your clients?"

"You're the first," he said, grinning. "Want me to sing you a lullaby?"

Grinning in return, she replied, "Something tells me you can't sing."

"I'm willing to try."

Their interaction was interrupted when the home phone rang.

"It's Ideal," Ireland said, peeking at the caller I.D.

Luke stood and moved away. After picking up the wastebasket, he walked to the door, but before closing it behind him, he gave Ireland a direct order. "Get some sleep."

Chapter 32

Never one to delay anything, Amanda called Ireland the moment she could. "First off, you haven't posted anything on your social media in weeks. If you don't start posting, I will." Certain Ireland was rolling her eyes, Amanda continued. "Secondly, and more importantly, have you come to your senses about a statement?"

"I thought about it," Ireland replied, racing around her living room, tossing items into a carry-on bag.

"Well, I hear Dig, Rona, and Ideal will be posting their statements tomorrow."

"Then shouldn't theirs be enough? Maybe I shouldn't say anything at all."

"That would be the worst thing you could do," Amanda said, pounding her petite fist on her home office desk. "You'll look guilty as sin. Sometimes silence is golden, but sometimes it's suicide."

"Dating a celebrity is suicide."

"Well, you chose to do it so now you have to learn how the game is played. I actually think it would be helpful for you and Ideal to sit down and do an interview together. Then you guys can squash all of these lies at once."

"I'm not inviting the world into my relationship."

"Dig and Rona have done many interviews together."

"That's Dig and Rona."

"Alright," Amanda replied, sighing heavily. "Let me read you the statement I worked up."

"Amanda, I'm in a hurry. Can't this wait until after my flight?"

"No, it can't."

Stilling herself to listen to a manufactured statement,. Ireland scowled while pondering the madness surging in her life.

Production of Weston's film was relocating to New York, which unfortunately forced Ireland out of her home and into the public. Feeling trepidation, she moved through the airport with her head hung low, insistent on not locking eyes with anyone. Sandwiched between Luke and Keith, she walked briskly behind the concierge until reaching the priority security lane. Despising her environment, she stared at the floor, hoping she wouldn't be noticed.

Her hope was practically futile since she happened to be the main topic on a variety of shows that morning. While painting her in the most unflattering light, reporters speculated if she was indeed pregnant, and if so, by which of the two hip hop artists she spent quality time with. Amused, many of them wagered that Dig was the father of her unborn child.

While waiting in the short line, judgmental quotes replayed in her mind until she heard a rise in hushed chatter. Convinced the talk surrounding her had to do with her poor morality, she was halfway thankful her neighbors had the decency to whisper. Her luck ran out, however, when three stylish women arrived at the line and recognized Ireland instantaneously.

"Oh yea, that's her," the thinnest one said. "I can't believe she did that to Rona. After everything Rona did for her."

The boiling of Ireland's center radiated to the layers of her skin. Although scalding, she stood frozen from embarrassment. It genuinely felt as if the mortifying moment would never pass. As Luke examined the women, Ireland transferred her gaze to a belted machine, but still could feel the piercing eyes of nearby strangers upon her.

Wanting to have a say, the tallest woman of the group chimed in. "She already had a good man, but she just had to sleep with Rona's. She is so nasty."

Although the third woman was tight-lipped, her grunts of approval allowed the other voices to proceed.

As a cell phone began filming, the first woman spoke again, her high nasal tone filled with disdain. "I hope that dirty whore is flying far away."

Keith had heard enough. Fuming, he turned around to respond to the hecklers, but before he could rip into them, Ireland clutched his arm.

"Don't," she murmured, shooting him a look that could rival a flame.

Honoring her wish, Keith turned back around and kept his profane mouth shut.

Causing a scene, outside of acting, wasn't Ireland's style. Even though her time at security was excruciating, she wouldn't make it worse. The hurt of degradation traveled through her body, but she fought against revealing any emotion. Conversely, once she was seated on the plane, all that she held in came gushing out.

When the plane touched down in New York, Ireland had one thing on her mind - getting to Ideal's place as soon as possible. Crashing her heels against the airport floor, she rushed through the terminal, doing her best to ignore the curious faces she passed. When she finally stepped outside, Luke found the car Ideal sent for them. Since Luke's orders were to escort her directly into Ideal's arms, he entered the vehicle with Ireland while Keith took a cab to his hotel.

Grateful for the vehicle's curtains, Ireland kept them closed during the ride to Manhattan, but had to abandon their covering when she reached Ideal's building. With a mountain of media waiting, she was welcomed by the lightning of cameras. As her nerves were on the brink of extinction, Luke led her through the cyclone of jittering bodies. Regrettably, she couldn't close her eyes or her offended ears.

"Ireland, are you here to apologize?"

"Is Dig the father of your baby?"

"Why would you betray Rona?"

The questions being yelled were so obnoxious and intrusive, only a foolish reporter would have expected a response. Although it took longer than it should have, she eventually arrived beneath the canopy and walked into the lobby.

Once the doorman retrieved Ireland's luggage from Greg, he followed her and Luke to the private elevator. The ride was tense and unusually quiet. The doorman often engaged in small talk with Ireland, but this day he stood stiffly, staring at the wooden wall. When the doors slid open, he moved with haste, parking her things in a corner then pressing the button to return downstairs. It wasn't until he was gone that Ireland supposed he believed the lies swirling about her.

Within seconds Ideal was in the foyer, pulling her into his arms. "Hi baby," he whispered, kissing her lips and forehead.

"Hi," she said, sinking into his body, appreciating the feel of stubble on his cheek.

A minute later, Ideal reached out his hand to shake Luke's. "Thanks for keeping my girl safe."

"Anytime," Luke replied.

"I know things are crazy right now. You need some help?"

Pulling back from Ideal's embrace, Ireland interjected, "I do not want *two* bodyguards."

"It's not about what you want, it's about what you need."

Responding to his employer, Luke answered, "I got her covered right now. I'll let you know if things change."

"Immediately," Ideal instructed.

"Yes, sir."

"I leave for Europe in a few hours so be back at ten tonight."

"Ten sharp," Luke said, walking away.

When Luke disappeared, Ideal's eyes swelled with concern. "How are you doing?"

"You have to ask?" Ireland replied. "I'm miserable."

"Don't be miserable, baby."

"How can I not be? Everybody thinks I'm a terrible person."

"The people who matter don't."

"Well, everybody else thinks I'm a backstabbing hoe."

"Forget about all that noise out there and focus on being here with me."

Ireland looked away. "I'll try."

"What do you mean, you'll try?"

"It's easier said than done."

"Then let me help," he said, leading her down the hall. "I know how to cheer you up."

"Good luck with that today." Before long, she stepped into the living room and saw the most familiar faces.

"Surprise," Janet sang, joyfully, sitting next to Jonah.

Shocked, Ireland held her chest as she observed her parents on the nearest sofa. Seeing her mother gaze at her with warmth and compassion made Ireland feel as if she were drifting into an ocean of love. On the day she was most vilified, she never expected to smile. Ideal was right. He knew how to cheer her up. He gave her joy and shelter in the midst of a treacherous storm.

Thank goodness for wrong assumptions. Though Ireland believed her day off would involve suffocating in sad isolation, it turned out to be a time of companionship and support. For more than twenty-four hours, her parents were right by her side and their company ultimately prevented her from wallowing in despair.

While Jonah initially gave uplifting lectures, he later forgot to continue the practice as he was distracted by his luxurious surroundings. Like a child in a candy-lined toy store, he raved about details of the penthouse from the views, square footage, and meals, to the sheets, showers, and towels. The technology alone not only rocked his boat but sent him happily overboard.

Janet was the blessing she'd always been to Ireland. Her presence was a source of aid and strength. She spoke encouraging words that brought light into the darkness. Along with loads of affection, surprising bouts of laughter, and somehow, inspiration, Janet gifted her daughter with what she needed to face the next day.

On the busy streets of New York City, Ireland returned to work with her head held high. Among the crowd of expected bystanders were both exuberant cheers and hypercritical sneers. While the former was expressed for Alberto, the latter was reserved for Ireland. Awaiting another take, she stroked the faux mink of her character's long coat until she heard Weston yell, "Action!"

(Lena stomps down the stoop of a brownstone as Lorenzo chases behind her. He catches up to her and grabs her by the arm.)

Lena: Don't touch me.

(Lena flings his hand away and continues to walk.)

Lorenzo: Would you please hear me out?

Lena: No.

(Lorenzo takes hold of her arm again.)

Lorenzo: Listen to me.

Lena: I tried that already. I listened to you for months, telling me you were done, but obviously, you weren't.

Lorenzo: It's not what it looked like.

Lena: That is such a cliché.

Lorenzo: It's true.

Lena: (Lena yanks her arm away.) I'm not your fool anymore.

"Cut!" the assistant director yelled, gripping an aged megaphone.

Done with the scene, Ireland hurried to her trailer to escape the cold weather and corresponding expressions.

During the first week of filming in New York, Ireland gave herself pats on the back for surviving the public and press. Sadly, during the subsequent week, her resiliency waned and her plan to soldier on collapsed. Mentally, she was waving a flag of surrender, wounded by hateful remarks. As if she and Dig hadn't denied allegations, and Rona and Ideal hadn't proclaimed their support, the media coverage multiplied, asserting the foursome's statements were lies to save face.

When a much-needed Friday night arrived and Ireland's workweek came to a close, she returned to the penthouse feeling haggard. Hunched over with a hood covering her head, she shuffled her way into the living room. Sitting in the softest chair, she recalled the hardest times in recent days. While staring into space, Tut appeared.

"Good evening, Miss Rochelle."

"Hi Tut," she whispered.

"Would you like dinner in the dining room or the kitchen?"

Regretful she had no appetite for the meal Tut prepared, she stalled in her reply. "Uh. . ."

"Or I can bring it in here."

"Tut, I'm sorry," she winced. "I'm not hungry."

"No need to apologize."

"I hate that I wasted your time."

"Don't give it another thought."

"I wouldn't mind a glass of wine though."

"Red or white?"

"It doesn't matter."

"Right away," he said, departing in his spotless white uniform. True to his word, he returned in a flash, holding a generously filled goblet.

"Thanks," she said, taking it from his hand. "Have a good night."

"You do the same," he replied, surveying her as she closed her eyes and took a long sip of merlot. After a short stammer, he spoke cautiously. "I'd like you to know that I don't believe any of the things the media is saying about you."

Surprised by his opinion, Ireland stared up at him.

"I don't know you very well, but I know that you're kind, thoughtful, and appreciative, not only to me but to the entire staff. We're always glad to see you and to serve you. There have been other visitors here and none of them came close to being as respectful as you are. So I feel like I know that you aren't capable of such disloyalty. No one has ever made Mr. Morris this happy. So please hang in there. This will all blow over at some point."

Stunned by his faith in her, Ireland was touched. "Thank you so much for saying that."

Tut slowly bowed his head then excused himself.

Perhaps it was Tut's words that sparked her desire to get some air, but Ireland wrapped herself in a throw and moved to a chaise on the terrace. Once she downed most of the merlot, her mind drifted to a not-so-distant moment in her past.

Seated on a bench in a large bookstore, Ireland and Casey flipped through magazines.

"Wait, why in the world is she messing with him?" Ireland asked, snarling at an image of a songstress walking hand in hand with a male actor.

"Obviously, she's lost her mind," Casey replied, glancing at the picture.

"He caused all that drama last year and she's looking at him like he's Mr. Wonderful."

"He's more like Mr. Pitiful."

"If she thinks they're going to last, she's crazy." Thumbing through more pages, it didn't take long before she found another point of interest. "Ryan and Tess are getting a divorce?" she asked, looking appalled.

"Yep, they say he's been cheating on her with Marguerite."

"No."

"It's been going on for months."

"That is terrible. Marguerite is such a skank."

Hauntingly, her last remark echoed in her head. Her estimation of Marguerite arose quickly and without any details or facts. A story was reported, therefore, it was true. Though Ireland later abandoned this warped way of thinking, for years she believed what she read and heard. How could she fault others for doing what she had done? She passed harsh judgment on many people - people she had never met. In an instant, it all became clear. She was reaping what she had sown.

Humbled, her soul was pervaded by a bottomless sting of shame. With hypocrisy staring her squarely in the face, she didn't notice Ideal approaching her.

"Oh, I see," he said, smiling, his eyes shaded beneath the bill of a navy cap.

"You see what?" she asked, elated he was finally home.

"How you do it when I'm on tour. You come out here, get all cozy, lounge, and sip some wine. You didn't even miss me while I was gone, did you?"

"Every once in a while."

At Ideal's initiation, they shared a slow, tender kiss that had been a long time coming. "So how was today?" he asked, sitting in the chair beside her.

"The same."

"It wasn't any better?"

"If anything, it was worse. I hate my existence right now."

"Don't say that."

"It's true. The press is on pregnancy watch. When I go to work, they're there and when I come home, they're here."

"Then let's get out of here."

"And go where? Antarctica?"

"Somewhere like that," he said, standing up. "Go pack a few things."

"What?"

"Go pack a few things."

"For what?"

"I just told you we're getting out of here."

"I can't go anywhere. We have one more week of shooting. I have a call time Monday morning."

"We'll be back by then."

"We're going to go somewhere tonight -"

"Actually, the crack of dawn," he interjected.

"Oh, excuse me. We're going to go somewhere at the crack of dawn, stay one night, and then rush right back?"

"You want to get away or not?" he asked, silencing her. After pulling her onto her feet, he added, "Pack light. Our clothes are already there."

Taken aback by his statement, Ireland appeared puzzled. "You already had this planned?"

"Yep."

"Since when?"

"Since Wednesday. Happy Birthday."

Ireland didn't know why she was surprised. As often as she tried to grow accustomed to Ideal's care, it never happened. He didn't just love her with his words. He loved her through his actions. For a moment, she stood there admiring him. Then she remembered, she had some packing to do.

Chapter 33

At nearly six o'clock on an April morning, Ideal walked Ireland onto a private jet. A few hours later, he closed all of the window shades. He didn't want any landscape to give her the slightest clue as to where they were going. Luckily for him, she didn't protest and ended up sleeping most of the flight. During her slumber, he gazed at her often, hoping she'd enjoy the excursion he planned. He felt fortunate to be able to provide her with the privacy she desperately craved.

When the plane began its descent, he woke her from her sleep. As she slowly sat up, he adored her groggy expression. She looked pure and innocent like a cute, young child.

"May I please look outside now?" she asked, fastening her seat belt.

"You may," he replied, smugly.

Excited, she lifted a cream-colored shade then peered at her surroundings. What commanded her attention immediately were the numerous collections of mountains. Beautiful green and gold hills rolled just beneath brown, snow-capped peaks. "Where are we?" she asked, a split second before giving her best guess. "Colorado?"

"Wyoming."

"Wyoming?" she repeated, loudly. Of all the places she thought they might be going, the state of Wyoming never crossed her mind.

"How many people do you think will look for us here?"

Flashing him a giddy smile, she replied, "None."

"Exactly," he said, winking.

Taking in the scenery, she soon noticed their proximity to a winding river. "This is the prettiest view."

Her statement was music to Ideal's ears. They were still in the air and she was already pleased. He loved that she took pleasure in the tiniest things. A sunrise, a single rose, the sound of rain all gave her joy. He supposed it was why he enjoyed spoiling her in grand ways. She appreciated every detail of whatever he chose to do and he never once felt taken for granted.

Once they landed, they followed Chase off of the aircraft and into an awaiting vehicle. With Chase taking on the dual-task of security and chauffeur, he eased behind the wheel and drove off of the tarmac. Many miles later, after rolling down dirt roads where log fences seemed to be never-ending, they arrived at a gate with a charming sign that read, *Get Lost Ranch.*

"Punch forty-seven, fifty-nine, enter," Ideal instructed.

Chase entered the code into the security box and the tall, iron gate crept open. Once they passed under an archway of logs, they were introduced to the loveliness of an immense ranch.

Ideal was dumbfounded by the property. It far exceeded his expectations. Nearly as animated as Ireland, he looked around, trying his best to study all that encircled him. Expansive views of jade and bronze brought about serenity. Gorgeous grasslands waving in the wind and magnificent pines standing at attention were reflected in the darkness of ponds. The prairies provided no end in sight. They stretched to forever, defying boundaries, except for the outlying mountains Ideal knew he'd never reach.

Once a few minutes went by, they approached a giant home that was made of red cedar logs. Grandiose, but in a warm kind of way, it resembled a luxurious lodge. A hundred yards in front of the house was a fish-filled lake, and along one of its sides, a free-flowing creek. As the visitors hopped out of the car, a bona fide cowboy emerged, thumping his boots on the home's wraparound porch.

In an endearing accent with plenty of twang, he called out, "Welcome to *Get Lost Ranch*." When Ideal and Ireland reached him, he stretched out his right arm. "I'm Gary, the ranch hand."

"Howdy, Gary," Ideal said, shaking the cowboy's moist hand. "I'm Ideal Morris and this is Ireland Rochelle."

"Pleasure meeting y'all," Gary replied.

"So I hear you don't know who we are."

"Well, no, Mr. Morris. I can't say that I do."

"She really appreciates that," Ideal said, tilting his head toward Ireland.

"Relieved to hear it," Gary confessed. "I'd be more than happy to give y'all a tour of the place if you'd like."

"No, that's alright. We'll see ourselves around."

"Alright," he said, assuming the couple was itching to be left alone. Handing Ideal and Chase a legal size piece of paper, Gary added, "These are your maps of the property. It's got twelve thousand acres. The main house here is twenty thousand square feet. Your clothes were delivered yesterday. They're in the master bedroom's closet. The kitchen is fully stocked." He then pulled two keys from his pocket. "Here's the key to the house and here's the key to the ride," he said, directing their focus to an open-air vehicle parked at one end of the porch. "Other than our own security, I'll be the only person on the ranch for the next twenty-four hours so rest assured y'all with have all the privacy in the world. About a mile down this road right here are a collection of fully-loaded cabins. That's where I and your security will be staying."

"Nice," Chase interjected, dropping Ideal and Ireland's bags near their feet. Having been told that with the exception of an emergency, the rest of his day would be free from duty, Chase looked forward to being paid to eat, sleep, and view movies.

"Your security's extension will be four, two, two. My extension is four, two, four. Give me a call if you need help with any gear or if you want to take the horses out for a ride."

"Will do."

"Oh and one more thing. Don't approach any wildlife. I repeat, don't approach any wildlife. You see them coming your way, move out of the way."

"Enough said," Ideal agreed, nodding. "Thanks."

"The boss is happy to have you here. His house is your house. Enjoy your stay," he said, tipping his hat then walking off. After formally meeting Chase, Gary jumped on a horse and rode away with Chase following behind in the rental car.

"Who's Gary's boss?" Ireland asked, overly curious.

"The person that tells him what to do," Ideal said, slyly.

"You know what I mean. Who is the owner?"

"A friend of mine."

"*You* have a friend that owns a ranch in Wyoming?"

"What are you trying to say? I'm too gutter to have friends in Wyoming?"

"You said it, not me."

"Look, I got friends in high places all over the world. You know what I'm saying? You should know that," he warned, shaking his finger at her. "On a sweeter note, look around." Under the wide sky, specked with cotton-like clouds, he watched her make a full turn while examining the ranch. "You see any fans or paparazzi?"

"No," she shouted, launching herself into his arms.

After swinging her from side to side, he picked up their bags and pulled open the front door. "Come on."

Iron hooks, holding faded hats and worn, shingle jackets, shared space with weaved baskets in the rustic entry. The great room exceeded its name. Mammoth in size, its cathedral ceiling was punctuated by hefty, log beams, consistent with the ever-present logs of the walls and random columns. Aztec rugs upon dark, knotty floors, mimicked blankets on the backs of brown, leather sofas, accented with tartan pillows. Mounted on each side of a towering, stone fireplace were eye-grabbing elk heads, however, even they paled in comparison to the arresting views showcased through seamless windows.

While the dining room boasted a chandelier of antlers and the kitchen impressed with saddle-topped stools, both rooms contained imported sunflowers stuffed in galvanized buckets.

After climbing up hulking stairs and moving down a lengthy hall, Ideal ultimately found the master retreat. The room had interesting points, including handmade quilts, but Ideal was most intrigued by a coil of rope that hung from one of the bed's posts.

"I'm going to put that rope to good use tonight," he said, seductively. "But right now, let's get dressed and go out."

Slightly different in color and style, their ensembles included jeans, plaid shirts, denim jackets, and cowboy boots, topped off with cowboy hats. Ireland also donned a quaint pair of turquoise earrings. Inspired by her new threads and jewelry, she styled her hair into a loose, side braid then freed plenty of strands to frame her face.

Ready for the ranch lifestyle, they returned downstairs, cooked a country breakfast, then ate while resting their bones in rocking chairs on the front porch. Silently, they gazed at the inspiring landscape, the only sounds being the creaking from their chairs and the gurgling of the stream. Minutes passed before Ideal finally spoke.

"It feels like we're some old married couple," he said, looking over at her.

"It does. It feels nice."

"What do you want to do for our fiftieth wedding anniversary?"

"Well, considering we'll be in our eighties, I think skinny-dipping would be fun."

"It's on. That's what we're going to do," Ideal said, fully determined.

"Okay," Ireland agreed, laughing as she imagined it.

"You know, unless I develop dementia, I won't forget."

"Yea, I know."

Itching to drive the car with no roof and no doors, Ideal stood and made an announcement. "Time for a safari." Moments later, he was behind the wheel with Ireland by his side.

They rode through the morning mist, which hovered delicately among the land, providing it with a dreamlike glow. The meadows were sometimes highlighted by patches of newly-bloomed flowers and vivid green trees that brought a sense of wonder. The natural, untamed beauty was strikingly unique from the precisely planted gardens they were accustomed to viewing.

Not long into their exploring, they spotted wildlife moving. Quickly, they snatched the pair of binoculars between their seats and peered into the magnifying lenses. A herd of elegant deer walked gracefully through the plain while antelopes leaped above the tall grass. Though the couple was mute while watching the activity, their breathing grew loud and rapid. In an instant, they became students, studying each move the animals made. After such a remarkable experience, they went on the hunt for more sightings.

It took some time, but next, they happened upon a bachelor herd of shaggy coats and wide frames. As if they were anything near wildlife experts, an engrossing argument ensued on whether the animals they were observing were buffalo or bison. Only when Ideal realized Ireland refused to be convinced, did he drop the matter altogether. When their attention returned fully to the grass-grazing species, they delighted in watching a few of them wallow in water. Consumed with their surveillance, they failed to notice an elk that was busy surveying them. Initially, moving as if it planned to stroll by, it suddenly altered its pace and severely picked up speed.

Stirred to steal another glance at the land, Ireland shifted her gaze to the right, but rather than seeing the magnificent terrain, she saw the elk's antlers charging toward them. Aside from involuntary trembling, she froze with fear then let out a scream.

Alarmed by her outburst, Ideal lowered his binoculars. "What's wrong?" he asked, his heart pounding with concern. The worry in her eyes said it all. He followed the direction in which they were focused and saw the elk preparing to ram them. Ideal's adrenaline took over. In seconds, he managed to restart the vehicle, change gears, and jolt them from harm.

Amazement stole their voices as they road to a safer spot.

"Do you think we'll get off this ranch alive?" Ireland joked, once Ideal parked.

"I'm sorry, baby," Ideal replied, rubbing the side of her neck.

"What are you sorry for?"

"For not seeing that moose sooner. For putting you in danger."

"First of all, it was an elk," she said, correcting his wildlife terminology again. "Second of all, you can't see everything."

"I'm supposed to," he said, adamantly. "Are you alright?"

"I'm fine," she assured him, pulling his hand from her neck and holding it."

"You know that I'd lay down my life before I ever let anything happen to you, don't you?" Barely giving her time to respond, he asked, "Don't you?"

"Yes."

"I'll always protect you with everything in me." Staring into her eyes, he couldn't understand how his love for her continued to expand.

"Whoa," Ireland whispered, nearly breathless, looking behind Ideal as something moved into her view.

"What?" Ideal replied, fearing he failed again at keeping watch. Indeed there was another animal roaming about, but luckily for them, it was a great distance away. "Whoa," he whispered, just as Ireland had done. "A bear."

"A grizzly bear."

"If it so much as looks our way, we're moving on."

Fortunately, the fuzzy-furred creature paid them no mind and for a good, awesome while, they watched it saunter along a marsh. More than satisfied with their sightings, they headed off for a nice, long drive, which later brought them to a trail in the most picturesque setting. At the base of the escalating path was a wooden marker that read, *Go take a hike.*

"I guess we should," Ireland said, a glimmer in her eye.

"Should what?" Ideal asked, furrowing his eyebrows.

"Go take a hike."

"We're not going up that trail."

"Why not? Are you're scared?"

"I'm not scared. I'm smart."

"You're scared we're going to be eaten by bears," she said, laughing.

"We just saw one and we got charged by a moose."

"It was an elk."

"Yea, whatever. We can roam around in here or on a horse, but we're not roaming on foot."

"Well, since it already happened today, the chance of us getting charged by another animal is extremely low." After stating her case, she hopped out of the vehicle.

"Ireland, get back in this car," he demanded.

Laughing harder, she went and stood by the sign. "Come on, scaredy-cat."

"I said, get back in this car." Horrified, he watched as she waved goodbye then began heading up the trail. "Damn," he said, turning off the car. "I knew I shouldn't have stopped carrying a gun." A thought then occurred to him. "There's got to be something in here," he mumbled, reaching in the glove compartment. Fortunately, he found bear spray and a pocket knife.

After getting out of the car, he raced to reach Ireland. Once he arrived at her side, he matched her stride. "I can't believe you're out here walking in the jungle after what we just went through. We don't have a backpack, flashlight or water."

"We have each other," she replied, taking his hand into hers.

They kept a steady pace as dirt wafted beneath their inappropriate boots. Though an abundance of beauty surrounded them, they held their focus low, intent on avoiding rocks scattered throughout the course. As a result of the lasting cold, their fingers and toes grew numb, and the climb in elevation caused their breathing to become labored, but sometime later, their steps were rewarded with a glorious view.

Panting in unison, they stood in disbelief. They were far higher than they ever expected to be. Wrapping their arms around each other, they saw mountains upon mountains, some dark and some bright, but all purely majestic. Lining their slopes were a multitude of pines, while the valley below contained a sliver of water so clear its stony floor was easily seen. Calmed by the incredible sight, Ideal and Ireland took deep breaths of the clean, fresh air.

Without warning, there was rustling in the bushes behind them. Whipping around then tensing up, Ireland whispered, "What was that?"

"Oh, now, look who's scared," Ideal teased.

Whatever was concealed in the collection of leaves didn't sound as if it were small. Briefly, the rustling left, but then came again. It grew louder. It grew closer.

Before Ideal could blink once more, Ireland began bolting downhill. Although worried as well, he was amused by her speed and couldn't contain his laughter as he ran after her. Soon she was laughing also, noticing their haste made their surroundings a blur. It wasn't until they approached the car, that they were brave enough to peek behind them. After seeing there wasn't a beast on their heels, they looked at each other and howled hysterically.

Hyperventilating from the sprint, Ideal put his arm around Ireland's shoulders. "I thought there wasn't anything to be scared of."

"I wasn't scared."

"You weren't scared. Then what do you call what you just did?"

"Being careful."

***

Ideal gripped the back of Ireland's knees as she rode him piggyback style to the center of an open field with a view of the main house. Although the air remained cold, sunshine rained throughout the ranch, which prompted Ideal to plan a picnic for lunch. In the basket Ireland held, he packed roast beef sandwiches, barbecue kettle chips, and a local, apple wine, which he unveiled after placing layers of quilts upon the chilly ground.

In the midst of nature, Ideal couldn't ignore that Ireland was glowing. She was the smiling, joyful, bright-eyed beauty, he'd spoken to after Dig's fundraiser. Over the past weeks, while he was away on tour, he noticed during their video calls, she seemed absent from herself. Seeing her full of life and vibrant again, energized him as well. "I've never been on a picnic with a woman."

"Not even once?" she asked, appearing skeptical.

"Picnics weren't exactly my thing."

"Oh, yea. You would rather pay for a quick dinner and then get right down to business."

"Yea," he confessed, shrugging his shoulders and glancing away. Ireland knowing the truth about his promiscuity still made him feel uncomfortable, and surprisingly, ashamed. "Well, you're the type of woman a man wants to romance so how many men have taken you on a picnic?"

"Um. . . maybe five."

"So this is just like any other picnic to you," he said, trying to hide the sting he felt by her response.

"Not even close. This picnic is with you and I've never loved a man as much as I love you."

"Let's see if that's true," he replied, picking up the sunflower he'd brought from the kitchen. Taking off his hat, he laid on his back and began pulling the yellow petals from its core. "She loves me, she loves me not."

"That's not going to tell you anything."

"She loves me, she loves me not."

"Give me that flower," Ireland said, failing at her attempt to take it from him.

"She loves me, she loves me not." In no time, there were just two petals remaining so the verdict on Ireland's love would soon be revealed. "She loves me. . . she loves me not." Though Ideal was certain his feelings for Ireland surpassed her feelings for him, he knew wholeheartedly that she loved him. Pretending to be crushed, he put on a gloomy expression. "I guess that settles it."

"That settles nothing."

"You're marrying a man that you don't love."

"Would you stop?" she said, kicking his leg with her boot.

"You're just like all those other chicks. In it for the money."

"I'm in this for you."

"Prove it," he said, biting his bottom lip, letting her know how she should prove herself.

Moving closer to him, Ireland laid her body on top of his and began kissing him. It was exactly what Ideal wanted. After removing her hat and tossing it aside, he cupped the back of her head then moved his hands lower to press his palms against her back. Rolling her over onto the ground, he trailed kisses down her neck until he noticed something small traveling upon her décolletage.

"Looks like I'm not the only one that wants to touch you," he said, leaning back so she could sit up.

As soon as she glanced down, Ireland smiled with delight. "Ooh, a ladybug."

"Hey, ladybug, do you mind? I'm trying to have some time with my girl."

Admiring the beautiful beetle, Ireland allowed it to crawl on her skin, but in the blink of an eye, it took flight and disappeared.

Forced to move their attention elsewhere, they enjoyed the meal Ideal prepared, then chose to visit the two-story barn. Gary introduced them to several horses, but Ireland was particularly fond of Winter and Wonder. Impeccably groomed, they were chestnut in color with auburn hair, white strips down their faces, and warm, almond-shaped eyes. Once Ireland asked to take them for a ride, Gary led the brave creatures outside, and helped the nervous couple mount them.

"I never thought I'd see your butt on a horse," Ireland said, laughing at the image of Ideal in a saddle.

Though Gary was their guide, he rode his horse far ahead, in order to provide the tourists with a sense of privacy. Initially, they moved timidly, tightly gripping their pommels, but sooner rather than later, they relaxed and rode with ease. More often with Ireland in front, but at times side by side, they traveled the land with fresh eyes, listening to the sound of horseshoes punching the ground. Each moment of trotting on horseback was more invigorating than the last, and in the end, they were sad to see their spirited ride come to a close.

With sunset on its way, Ideal rushed to spend time on the lake. At the end of the dock, they entered a small boat then rowed their way through pristine water. Settling on a spot at the lake's calm center, they were stilled by the stillness around them. The fishing gear at their feet remained untouched as they cherished how substantial the face of the earth was and remembered how trivial their daily tasks were. Content to stare at reflections on the water's mirror-like surface, they barely made a move until dusk slipped away.

Upon returning to the glow of lights in the house, Ideal cooked wild rice, a colorful mix of vegetables, and a mesquite-seasoned trout. By candlelight, he dined with Ireland and discussed the adventures of their day. Then he banished her from the kitchen to prevent her from helping with the dishes.

"You got to be freezing out here," he said, later finding her on the front porch. He knew she adored lovely things, but the temperature had taken an impressive dive.

"I am but the sky is too great to walk away from."

"That's how I feel about you." Picking up a nearby blanket, he wrapped it around her body.

In the peacefulness of the blackest night, they listened to zealous crickets while staring at what seemed to be a bazillion dancing stars.

"This was the most perfect day," Ireland whispered.

"I think so too," Ideal agreed, kissing her on the cheek. He then looked at her with surprise. "You're cold as ice."

"I'm okay," she said, aware of what he'd say next.

"Let's go inside."

"In a few minutes."

"Now," he said, turning her body to face the house and walking her toward it. "It's time for dessert anyway."

When Ireland entered the great room, she was relieved to be cocooned by warmth. She went directly to the blaze within the fireplace, oblivious to the bowl that sat on top of the mantel. Distracting her view from the flames, Ideal held the bowl beneath her chin, and in a French accent said, "Your dessert, Mademoiselle."

Pleased, she saw that the wooden bowl contained four jumbo-sized marshmallows. "You baked marshmallows?" she joked.

"From scratch," he said, playing along.

"They're extraordinary. Look at that form."

"Wait until you taste one."

"I can't wait," she said, watching him slide one onto a steel, roasting fork. "You know, this is supposed to be done outside on an open fire."

"Well, your California bones can't handle the cold so we have to do it in here."

"I do not have California bones! I'm from Philly."

"You've been gone too long."

After placing the treat in the fire, he twirled it about, expecting to charm her by its gradual transformation into a golden-edged goo of softness. When it was just as he desired, he removed it from the fire, and while its flame burned bright, he sang his rendition of a popular birthday song. Laughing along with Ireland, he finished the song then held the marshmallow to her lips. "Make a wish."

Closing her eyes for a second, she did as he instructed, and blew a cool stream of air onto the glimmering mound. "Thank you, Carrot," she said, ever so sincerely.

"You're welcome," he replied, smiling. "I got you a real cake. It's in the back of the fridge."

"Really?"

"It's red velvet." Handing her the roasting fork to move directly behind her, he asked, "Is your butt still sore?"

"Yes," she answered, intrigued by his change of subject. The horseback ride had been wonderful, but the hardness of the saddle had not. Slowly, he reached in front of her waist and unbuttoned her blue jeans. "What are you doing?"

"Wait and see." Carefully, he pulled down her zipper, slid the waist of her jeans to her hips, adored the panty she wore, and placed his palms on her derriere. Firmly, he began massaging her round, tender rear. After kneading her flesh for a while, he asked a simple question. "You like that?"

"I do."

"I can't wait to hear those words at our wedding."

"I can't either," she said, holding the back of his head. Wanting to free her other hand, she took the first bite of her treat. "Mm, you were right. This is good." Interrupting her massage, she turned around to face him. "Would you like to taste my marshmallow?"

His eyes peered into hers. "I really would."

When she lifted it to his lips, he took every bit of it into his mouth. After lowering her to the floor, he concluded the massage then gave her so much more.

Chapter 34

After putting in hours at the studio, Ideal hurried to his penthouse to prepare to escort Ireland to her film's wrap party. He had been counting down the days she would officially be done with the project that kept him from seeing her often. At last, the night arrived.

Even though the past weeks, including recent days, were filled with merciless media coverage, Ideal was eager for his frequent dates with Ireland to resume. It seemed like ages since they'd gone out, and quite honestly, he missed it. He loved seeing her dolled up, sitting in the best restaurants, enjoying extravagant meals while sharing her thoughts on hot topics. Such times with her made him feel alive and proud that he could court her in superior ways.

He knew early on, she could do without the opulent treatment he was dependent on bestowing. Their time in Wyoming was additional proof that mountains, moonlight, sunshine, and stars, were what made her most blissful, however, those were things his money couldn't buy. They were God's creations, nature's beauty, things he couldn't take credit for giving her. Unfortunately, credit was something he craved. Only to himself, was he able to admit that buying her expensive things and taking her to expensive places made him feel like more of a man.

Holding a hand-tied, spring bouquet, Ideal entered the master suite, expecting to see Ireland wearing a dress. Instead, he found her in jeans and a cream, cardigan sweater.

"I thought you'd be dressed to the nines by now," he said, glancing at his watch. Joining her on the sofa, he gave her a kiss as well as the flowers. "Congratulations."

"Thank you," she said, positioning her nose near a stargazer lily.

Noticing the weary expression on her freshly-washed face, he said, gently, "You look tired."

"I am."

"Was today a tough shoot?"

"No, everything went well. We wrapped on time."

"Then what is it?" he asked, running his thumb along her cheek. He watched as she kept her focus on the flowers and merely shook her head. Seeing that she didn't want to answer caused him to take an educated guess. "The media?"

"Yea."

"The wrap party will take your mind off of them."

"No, it won't."

"It will if you let it," he said, before rising to his feet. As he walked toward his closet, he contemplated just how smooth he should dress for the event. "Are you still going to wear black?"

"No."

"What color?"

"I'm not going."

Ideal paused then turned back around. He couldn't have heard her right. "What did you say?"

"I'm not going."

"Why not?"

"I'm not up for it."

Surprised by her reason, he tried to reason with her. "Baby, you have to go. You've been working on this film for months. You have to celebrate what you accomplished with Michael, Alberto, and everybody."

"I can't."

"What you can't do is let another bad day with the media stop you from going tonight."

"Ideal, I made up my mind," she said, looking him squarely in the eye. "I'm not going."

"You're making a mistake," he replied, looking at her just as directly as she did him. With nothing to do, but accept her decision, he returned to sitting next to her. "You should call Michael and tell him you're not going."

"I told him already."

"When?"

"When we wrapped."

Ideal recalled how happy Ireland was when she received the role in Weston's film. During every phase of the project, she demonstrated drive, determination, and dedication. Now that her time on set was complete, he couldn't believe she wasn't enthused about celebrating with the cast and crew. Her decision to pass on a work-related function was out of character for her. For the first time, he worried about her state of mind. "So you're just going to let the media run your life?"

"No, not anymore."

"Then let's get ready to go," he said, standing and attempting to pull her up as well.

"Ideal," she said, removing her hand from his then setting the flowers on a table. "I need you to sit down."

"Why?" he asked, reclaiming his spot on the sofa.

She took a long breath then made a grueling confession. "I can't do this anymore."

"Do what?"

"Live in a fishbowl. I'm just not wired for it."

"How many times do I have to tell you to stop worrying about what other people think?"

"I've tried."

"You got to stop trying and do it."

"That's so easy for you to say. You get off on people watching you and talking about you. Everything you do has to be done in a big, flashy way."

"That still bothers you? You want me to tone myself down?"

"No, that's how you are. But that's not how I am."

"You like to blend in and I like to stand out. Opposites attract."

"Yea, and that's exciting in the beginning, but it doesn't last in the long run."

"So we're the exception."

"No, we're not," she said, shutting her eyes, her face trembling from a swell of tears.

Alarmed by her sudden sadness, Ideal leaned in closer. "Baby, what's wrong?"

"Ideal, I love you."

"I love you too."

"I love you, but," she said, stammering before grasping her engagement ring. After sliding it off of her finger, she added, "I have to give this back to you."

"What are you doing?" he asked, richly confused, refusing to take the ring from her wobbly hand.

A tear spilled from her left eye. "I can't marry you."

Her words took seconds to process. Stunned, Ideal sat there, unable to stop his eyes from viewing the guilt in hers. Disbelief stole his voice, but soon it was returned. "What the hell are you talking about?"

"I can't marry you," she repeated, placing the ring beside the flowers.

Outraged by the absurdity of what she was saying, Ideal catapulted onto his feet. "What the hell are you talking about? The wedding's a few weeks away. We get our license on Wednesday."

Relieved the staff had gone home and weren't privy to his thunderous reply, she murmured, "I'm so sorry."

"You're sitting here, trying to cancel our wedding and you're telling me that you're sorry?"

"I am," she said, lowering her head. She couldn't be judgmental of his response. He had every right to shout. She'd thrown him a damaging blow that for him came out of nowhere. In truth, she had been pondering the decision for the last few days.

Taking a moment of silence, Ideal tried to slow his harshly beating heart. His volume then changed to barely audible. "Why don't you want to marry me?"

"It's not that I don't want to. If we were ordinary people that the world didn't pay attention to, I'd marry you in a second."

"You think the world's going to stop paying attention to us if we don't get married? They chased us around before we got engaged. It's not going to stop whether we're married or not."

"I know."

"You know? Then why are you trying to stop our wedding?"

"It's not just the wedding." Her breathing grew shallow. "We need to stop us altogether."

Ideal's heart seemed to race beyond its capability. Nausea raided his torso. As emptiness began to replace his soul, he realized his greatest fear was happening.

"Just like you said," Ireland continued, "they'll never stop chasing us. As long as I'm with you, I'll have to live with being followed and scrutinized everywhere I go. I can't deal with it anymore. I can't be with you anymore."

Abruptly, Ideal turned away, unprepared for her to see the tears flooding his eyes.

Aching, Ireland looked at the man she loved and aimed to garner his understanding. "I need a simpler way of life. I need the life we just had in Wyoming. I felt so free and at peace there."

As if she'd thrown him a life preserver, Ideal swiveled back around, filled with hope and solutions. "Baby, we can go back there. I'll buy us our own ranch. We can go whenever you want."

"With your schedule?"

"I'll make it a priority."

"It wouldn't be enough. It would only be on vacations. I want to be able to breathe on a daily basis."

Instantly, Ideal noticed something unattractive about Ireland. She was a professional grumbler when it came to her observers. Her complaining was relentless. It was a trait he found repulsive in others, but until then, he hadn't recognized her inclination to gripe. Whining that private, platinum vacations a few times each year lacked enough isolation, made her sound self-absorbed. "We can't live in a cocoon our whole damn lives. We have things to do, art to create, and people to help. We can't sit around every day staring at the sky. We have to work. The more we work, the more we accomplish, the more we accomplish, the more people we help with our money and our influence. You need to focus more on how your gifts can serve others because focusing on your petty problems is selfish."

"Selfish?" she said, quickly standing, clearly insulted.

"Yea, selfish."

"I have always and will always help people in need. I don't have to be in the public eye to do it."

"You act like I'm the only reason you're in the public eye. What about your career? You chose to be an actress. You chose to go to France. You walked on red carpets in fancy dresses, posing for the paparazzi. Cameras didn't bother you then, did they?"

"Yes, they did."

"No, you were fine with all of that when it was all about you, but since the attention's been about you being with me, it's too much to handle."

"You have no idea how hard it was for me in France."

"Well, I don't see you quitting acting. I only see you quitting me."

"I'm done with acting too."

"What?" he asked, arresting his movement. "You can't stop acting. It's what you love to do more than anything."

"But I hate the business of it. It's a circus and I feel like a clown."

"You can't have great blessings and not have great trials. You have to deal with them."

"I can't!" she yelled, beginning to cry, feeling like a weakling, shattering under pressure. When Ideal arrived at her side and committed to rubbing her back, she finally found the courage to reveal what she'd been hiding. "I never wanted you to know this, but I get extreme anxiety before certain social situations. The thought of being watched at parties and premieres, even crowded restaurants, is much worse for me than you think. It's terrifying and overwhelming. I've always worried about people viewing me in a negative light so being put down in the news day after day for weeks has been a nightmare come true. Even though I know, this story will die down, they'll be another story next year, and another the year after next. I can't learn to live with that."

"Yes, you can. Let me help you. Let me find somebody to help you." Astonished by what she shared, Ideal cursed himself for not knowing the hell she was often in. He knew she preferred private times with him and special occasions with family and friends, but he had no idea other social events caused her great fear and dismay.

"I have to go," Ireland announced, walking out the door. As much as it was hurting to leave, she had to go through with it. She couldn't remain in a lifestyle that would regularly break her down.

Ideal's mind was void of any other option. He chased her down the hall and stopped her at the staircase. Driven by the foreign feeling of desperation, he prevented her from descending the spiraling steps. "Don't do this to me," he said, peering into her eyes. "Don't give me your love then take it away."

"You'll always have my love, Ideal."

"If we're in love, we should be together."

"There are people all over the world who love each other, but can't be together."

"Those are people who don't have the guts to fight for what they want. I get what I want and I want you as my wife."

"I am positive you're going to find somebody that loves you and the limelight. Somebody that won't hold you back. That's who you need."

"I need you," he said, his body heat dampening him with sweat. Once he watched her move around him, he blurted something shocking. "What if I gave up music?"

Ireland's eyes began a flurry of blinks. "What?"

"What if I stopped singing and rapping and producing and performing?"

"You're not doing that," she said, rolling her eyes at the insanity of his question.

"You're leaving acting."

"I don't have twenty years of success under my belt and millions of fans who identify with me. I can leave my career. You can't leave yours."

"Music is in me as much as acting is in you. If you can leave, I can leave."

"I'm not listening to this," she said, managing to make her way down three steps.

"You didn't answer my question!" he yelled, causing her to halt. Gradually, he walked toward her until he arrived at the step on which she stood. "If I gave it all up, would you marry me then?"

"No."

"No?" he said, devastated by her response. He was willing to give up everything and it still wasn't enough.

"The world is entertained by you whether you're trying to entertain them or not. You leaving your work wouldn't change much."

"It might take a while, but it would change."

"Ideal," she said, clutching the rail. "It's over." She raced down the stairs at the highest speed her sandals would permit. When she reached the first floor, she hurried to the foyer's closet and pulled out a suitcase and carry-on.

"What the hell is that?" he said, storming over to her. "You packed your bags?" Another current of pain encased him as he realized she knew that morning that she would leave him. "How long have you been planning this?"

"Stop making this harder than it already is," she said, placing the strap of her carryon onto her shoulder.

Snatching the strap back down, he repeated, "How long?"

"Since last night."

"Before or after we made love?"

Ashamed, Ireland replied, "Before."

"So while I was making love to you, you were thinking it would be the last time?"

"I didn't know how to tell you."

"No, you didn't want to give me any time to change your mind. You wanted to tell me and then run out the door."

With his world deserting him, he wondered if she ever truly loved him. A lump, seemingly the size of a softball, formed in his throat. "I thought you loved me," he said, tears coursing down his smooth face. "I thought you wanted to be my wife."

"I did."

Grabbing her by the waist, he said, "Don't let other people keep us apart. Stay with me."

"I can't."

"Please."

"I can't."

"Please," he howled. Swallowed up by emotion, he began to sob fiercely. In a slumped position, he hid his face, embarrassed by his lack of control.

Hurt by his demeanor, Ireland tried to console him by rubbing the back of his neck. She wished she could change her mind, but was far too convinced her action was the right one. Afraid of saying the wrong thing, she figured it was best not to speak. Discreetly, she used her free hand to push the elevator button. Soon there came a beep, alerting her of its arrival.

Alarmed by the sound, Ideal shot straight up. "Ireland, I need you. I need you with me. I'll quit my work. We can move to a small town," he promised, as she collected her things.

The elevator door slid open, and with every ounce of her might, Ireland fought against Ideal's groping hands and pressed her way into the small space. As she predicted, he followed her inside then wrapped his arms around her tightly.

For nearly a year, Ideal gave Ireland his heart and soul. He trusted she'd treasure them the way he treasured hers. Though he offered her all that he had, in the end, it didn't matter. He wasn't good enough. He failed at keeping her happy. In heart-wrenching despair, he leaned on her shoulder, dreading the moment she would force him to let go.

Knowing it was goodbye, Ireland gave in to her yearning and draped her arms around Ideal. Clinging to each other amidst heavy breaths, he begged for her to stay as she whispered her regrets. Their cycle of misery persisted as they descended floor after floor then landed at the lobby level.

Immediately, Ireland broke away from their embrace. She then grabbed the handles of her bags and walked off of the elevator. Careful to remain close to its door, she turned around to gaze at the love of her life. The deep shade of burgundy tinting his eyes hurt her more than he could know, but with a necessary sternness, she said, "If you love me, you won't follow me and cause a scene."

"If you love me, you won't go."

"Please," she uttered, a look of terror seizing her face.

Somehow her last word got through to him. He wouldn't follow her through the lobby and into the street, providing the world a satisfying view of his and her private pain. Although he was living his worst nightmare, he couldn't worsen hers. With their eyes locked more intensely than any time before, the elevator door began to close. Glancing down, Ireland wiped her wet face, slid on her sunglasses, and turned away. It was the last image he saw of her before the wooden door shut.

Overtaken by grief, Ideal slid to the floor, weeping only the way he had when his father abandoned him. Wrecked with rejection and feeling discarded, he was unable to cease the continuous groans deriving from his gut. With his famous face crumbled in distress, he longed for yesterday.

Chapter 35

It was late in the midnight hour when Chase and Ideal parked at Ireland's home. Luckily, the paparazzi were nowhere to be found. The so-called photographers stopped haunting her place while she was away in New York, but due to current news that Weston's film had wrapped, it wouldn't be long before the scoundrels lined the sidewalk. Relieved they were elsewhere, harassing another life, Ideal stepped out of a rented vehicle with his ruined heart in his hands.

Prior to boarding a plane, he made five calls to Ireland's cell. All of them went to voicemail. Twice, he hung up and three times, he left a message, but at no time did he divulge that he was following her home. Determined to show up without warning, he was able to do just that, but when he rang her bell, she never came to the gate.

For twenty-eight hours, with the exception of restroom breaks and a hefty meal for Chase, Ideal waited for a glimpse of Ireland, coming out or going in. Unfortunately, neither occurred. It was obvious she was avoiding his calls, but obscure if she was refusing to open her door. When an entire day of despair went by, he sensed she hadn't returned to Los Angeles. Cuffed by the painful reality, he went a more conventional way to track her down.

As embarrassing as it was, he picked up his phone and placed a call to Casey. After much convincing on Casey's part, he believed she wasn't hiding her best friend. Eventually, due to pity, he extracted a confession that Casey had heard from Ireland. Although Ireland refused to share her whereabouts, she said she was somewhere safe and sound. The moment Casey spoke the familiar phrase, Ideal knew where he needed to go. He had come to know a place that embodied both safety and soundness. Shortly after, he was boarding a plane bound for Philadelphia.

Six hours later, he stood on the porch of the Rochelle residence. He apologized to Janet for showing up unannounced, then after explaining his reason for doing so, fell into her open arms.

In the living room, the two of them sat tensely as Janet sadly conveyed she did not know where Ireland was. Although her daughter sent a text stating she was far from harm, Janet's mind wasn't eased. Yet in the midst of her own worry, she took time to express her sympathy for the heartbreak Ideal was feeling. It was the most genuine compassion he had encountered, which reminded him of how much he craved to be Janet's son-in-law.

When his visit came to an end, Ideal was at a loss. Other than hiring an investigator, which he gravely considered, there was nothing more he could do. Clueless of where to go next, he returned to his heartless home and continued his barrage of obsessive phone calls. Though ashamed of his psychotic behavior, he could not restrain it. The hurt he felt drove him to do things he previously viewed as pathetic. At last, he understood losing control as a result of desperation. Hour by hour, he grew weaker, and in spite of the torture he was living, days had the audacity to still go by.

Although he was sitting at a conference room table, surrounded by *Try Real* executives, Ideal barely heard a word.

"Our sales aren't up, because our marketing went down. It's as simple as that," Brian argued, tossing up his dry hands.

The Vice President, Jill, begged to differ. "It isn't our marketing, it's our products. Our consumers want edgier design."

"Our line is perfectly edgy, but people can't buy what they don't know exists."

"What do you think, Ideal?" Jill asked.

Ideal stared down at his open folder and gave no reply.

"Boss?" Jill repeated, awaiting a response.

Danielle, who was sitting closest to him, stopped scrolling through her emails. "Ideal," she said, touching his forearm.

With a flinch, he looked at her then walked out of the room. Oblivious to his staff's confusion, he went straight to his private office, unable to prolong the charade of caring about the meeting's agenda. All that crammed his mind were unremitting thoughts of Ireland. He hadn't heard from her in days and remained clueless as to where she was. Feeling ill, he leaned over his desk, as a pair of tears ditched his eyes.

"Ideal?" Danielle said, poking her head past his door, which he foolishly left slightly ajar.

Overwrought to be caught crying, Ideal wiped the wetness on his chin. "Yea," he replied, not glancing her way.

Opening the door wider, Danielle stepped inside. "Are you okay?" she asked, nervously. Having never seen him cry, the sight scared her significantly. Clearly, he was in pain. "Do you want us to break from the meeting?"

"No, have Brian run it."

"Okay," she whispered.

"I need you to cancel my studio time with *Crooked Drive*."

Danielle appeared even more baffled. "They just flew in all the way from Australia. You can't cancel it."

"I said, cancel it," he said, finally looking at her.

"The only reason they are in town is to work with you."

"Danielle!" he shouted, his chest heaving. "You do what I say, I don't do what you say. Now, cancel the sessions then get back to the meeting."

Frightened by the ugly glare in his handsome eyes, Danielle fled from his presence. In all the years she worked for him, he had not yelled at her once. The novel occurrence had her trembling, and although she felt humiliated, she worried more for him than for herself.

All week, his demeanor had been out of character. He arrived at the office late, failed to return calls, and bowed out of appearances. Now, he was canceling studio time. In addition to just watching him desert a meeting, Danielle actually witnessed him shedding tears. In the past, there had been deaths among his family, but even during his grief, she hadn't seen him cry. His work had always brought him solace and joy, but lately, it seemed to drain him. He was deteriorating before her eyes, and for the first time in her career, there was nothing she could do to assist him.

So eerily quiet was the front of her home, Ireland felt a chill as if she were feeling an evening breeze from the ocean that waved a mile away. It was midmorning and unexpectedly, she stood alone on the unspoiled sidewalk. Grown men in dark clothing weren't collected upon the grass, blocking her gate with blinding cameras. The only bright light shining was that of the blazing sun. Observing swaying palms, she took a full breath then entered her courtyard. After dropping her bags at the front door, she kicked off her sandals and wandered the outdoor area.

She had been away from home for far too long and although she could have returned a week earlier, she decided not to do so to avoid being followed. Upon leaving New York, she flew to Rhode Island, where she spent seven days at an elegant bed-and-breakfast. On the first night, she sobbed herself to sleep, but the next morning, she recognized a shocking truth. She had completely forsaken her imagery meditation.

For weeks on end, she went from film sets to meetings to an assortment of engagements, all without taking the time to be still and breathe deeply. It was with breath and stillness that she calmed herself through imageries, which silenced the negative voice that kept fear clenched around her soul. In hindsight, it was clear. The longer she went without meditating, the louder the voice grew. As a result, in recent weeks, it was roaring at a deafening tone. It made her believe, she couldn't handle life. It made her believe, she couldn't simply be.

Although she knew it was imagery that helped her cope with anxiety, during her darkest and busiest days, she abandoned the practice. At the times she needed it most, she chose an alternate course and indulged her mind by reliving the past and imagining the future. This locked her in a perpetual state of misery and worry. She forgot she couldn't control others actions and many of life's circumstances. She could only control herself and her thoughts. Thankfully, for seven straight days, within her guestroom and its adjacent garden, Ireland reintroduced herself to habitual peace.

She immersed herself in silence. She banned business, television, radio, and even communication with those she held dear. Her days were like charming dreams, void of things she cared not to hear. Being unplugged and out of the public eye was so enormously liberating, the benefits outweighed her irrefutable case of heartache.

Upon returning home, she felt refueled and refreshed. While sitting on a bench, she listened to the birds, but once an hour passed, she noticed something peculiar. Her satisfaction with solitude seemed to suddenly vanish. Replacing the contentment was an epiphany. No matter how often she acquired peace and quiet, there would always arise a need for human connection.

At that moment, Ireland acknowledged returned phone calls were past due. She grabbed her bags, went inside, sat on her sofa, and turned on her cell. She had an obscene amount of missed calls. Aware the high number meant upcoming interrogations, she chose to further delay her most pressing responsibility.

As she scrolled through the phone, she came across future meetings scheduled with her agency. Staring at the appointments, she contemplated whether or not to cancel or attend them. Should she carry on with the intricate life she'd been living or create for herself a much simpler one? If she was going to choose a new career path, there was no time like the present.

Via the search engine at her fingertips, she examined lists of various professions. Many caught her eye, however, none grabbed her heart. Counseling, teaching, marketing, and engineering were all wonderful callings, but they didn't call her. After whizzing by every vocation known to man, she realized she was incapable of choosing one other than acting. Acting felt like home.

An image of herself at the age of nine emerged in her mind. In full makeup and costume, she stood center stage in her school's auditorium, at the end of her first play. Her mother, who was front row center, and beaming more than her daughter, began the applause that every audience member contributed. Ireland scanned the people then took a gracious bow. The praise was great, but what was much better was her sense of accomplishment. She felt proud of how well she delivered her lines and conveyed the directed emotion. Proud of the time she rehearsed with the cast as well as alone in her room. She loved every step of the process and when her performance came to a close, she felt life couldn't be sweeter. While standing on the brightly lit stage, the fourth-grader knew within her young soul, she wanted to act again and again. Though Ireland was now a grown woman, she knew the very same thing. She wanted to act again.

Suddenly, her home phone rang. Prepared to face some admonishing music, she answered the call after identifying the caller. "Hi Ma," she said, softly.

"Oh, thank God," Janet replied. "Your father and I have so been worried about you."

"I sent you a text every day, letting you know that I was okay."

"Where were you?" Janet asked, impatient for the answer she'd been agonizing to know.

"A bed-and-breakfast in Newport, Rhode Island."

"Why didn't you just tell me that?"

Reluctantly, Ireland admitted the reason. "I didn't want you to tell Ideal in case he called you."

"Oh, he did more than call me. He showed up at the house."

"What?" Ireland replied, her heart skipping a beat.

"He waited outside your place for an eternity then he flew here."

"I can't believe he did that."

"I can."

"What did he say?"

"What do you think he said, Ireland? He said he misses you. He said he loves you. He said he wants to marry you." After a brief pause, Janet added, "He's really hurting."

The thought that he could be just as distraught as the day she left New York, made Ireland feel cruel. "I'm sure he's better now," she muttered, attempting to convince herself.

"I'm sure he's not. Are you?"

Ireland struggled to find an answer.

"I didn't think so," Janet said, ending the silence. "With all the meditating I'm sure you've been doing, you haven't realized that you made some poor choices?"

"What I realized is that I hadn't been meditating at all."

"Hmm, so that's how you got so overwhelmed. You know you need to sit yourself down in order to balance your busy schedule."

"I know, I got back to that this week."

"Well, it's easy to do it when you stay isolated with zero distractions, but that's not real life. You have to take care of yourself even when you've got a lot going on."

"That's what I was doing until people started vilifying me."

"When you're hurting, you have to love yourself more not less, so when people spread lies and say ugly things you can keep on going with your head held high."

"I'm still not sure I can do that."

"Look, you have to accept your fame. You don't have to like it or agree with it or get high on it, but you have to accept it so that you can move on with your life. If you would do that instead of fighting it so hard, you'd be much, much happier."

"Happier being scrutinized?"

"Happier letting go. I know it's not easy, but Ideal, Rona and Dig manage to do it."

"I'm more sensitive than they are. Fame affects me deeper than it does them."

"Ireland, you have always wanted a successful career in film, an honest husband that loves you, the gift of children, and a beautiful home. I'd hate to see you give all that up because you're tired of unwanted attention. Don't let other people's opinions prevent you from reaching your destiny. You're stronger than that."

"No, I'm not."

"Yes, you are," Janet said, forcefully. Allowing her reassurance to touch her child's spirit, she stayed mute for a moment. "Now, one last thing then I'll let you go."

"What?" Ireland asked.

"I know imagery helps you a lot and you should keep doing it, but you need to get down on your knees and pray to God right now. Ask Jesus for strength, courage, and wisdom then let the Holy Spirit lead you. You hear me?"

"Yes."

"And remember to count your blessings. I love you."

"I love you too."

The truth of her mother's words sank into her soul, and without hesitation, she allowed her body to slide to the dusty floor. Positioned on her knees, she went to the Lord in prayer, confessing to Him her self-absorption, thanking Him for her innumerable blessings, and asking Him for the strength, courage, and wisdom she needed for her future.

As she prayed, a few thoughts zipped through her mind, but Ideal was the constant squeezing her heart. Soon, she was unable to stop the determined tears dropping from her eyes. Her bottled emotions had been uncorked and they spilled from the depth of her.

Consumed by her surge of tears, she was frightened when the doorbell rang. Expecting no one, she rose to her feet then moved to her security camera. Once she recognized her visitor, Ireland couldn't believe her wet eyes. After another ring of the bell, she dried her face, walked out the front door, and pulled open the gate. She stood face to face with Danielle.

"What are you doing here?" Ireland asked, doing nothing to disguise her displeasure.

Wearing her customary cold expression, Danielle replied, "I need to talk to you."

"About what?"

"Can I come in?"

As much as Ireland wanted to deny the request, she led Danielle into the living room. "You know, you could've just called," she said, turning around to face her.

"I did, but both of your voicemail boxes are full."

"Oh," Ireland mumbled, looking away.

"I'll just cut to the chase. I'm here because of Ideal."

"He sent you?"

"No, he doesn't know that I'm here, but I am on his behalf."

"Meaning?"

"I want you to take him back."

Stunned by Danielle's boldness, Ireland's jaw hung open.

"I know it's not my place to get in your business, that's why I never have. I've known where you guys have dined, traveled, and stayed, and I've always kept my nose out of it. But I can't do that now, because Ideal has fallen apart."

"I'm not talking to you about this."

"Then how about you just listen?" Danielle replied. "It's obvious that you left him because he would never end things with you. As much as I hate to admit it, you made him happier than anybody. You made him happier than his music and that was impossible to do. I have no idea how you did it, but you did. But since you dumped him, he can't function. He's this miserable mass of depression. I don't recognize him anymore and soon his fans won't. At the rate he's going, he could lose his career."

"Oh, I see," Ireland said, nodding her head.

"You see, what?"

"Danielle is worried about Danielle. Well, relax. Nothing is going to happen to his career so nothing is going to happen to yours. There was no need to swing by my place seeking job security."

"That's why you think I'm here?"

"That's why I think you're here."

Wringing the leather straps of her handbag as if it were Ireland's neck, Danielle made her presence more clear. "I'm here because my boss finally fell in love with a woman, and he was one hundred percent faithful to her, but for some reason, she lost her damn mind and broke his heart. He will never get over you, and by the looks of your red, puffy eyes, you won't get over him either." In an instant, her brazen attitude switched to one of genuine care. She then whispered something so softly, her words seemed to linger in the air. "Please, Ireland . . . go back to him."

Chapter 36

Despite Ireland's perpetual gulping, her throat remained dry like the sands of Dubai. Regardless of its parched condition, the moment she would be required to speak loomed insistently. With the spare key she somehow failed to return, she stepped onto the elevator and began her ascension to the penthouse. Between imagining scary scenarios of how her arrival would be received, bitter memories of her last time in the home came sprinting back to her. Fortunately, her attention was diverted when the elevator reached its highest point and the dark doors slid open.

Almost led by the temptation to turn around and bolt, Ireland knew it would profit her nothing, but a brief relief from the worry of appearing pitiful. Putting one stiletto in front of the other, she entered the foyer. Straight away, she regretted wearing the strappy heels. Although they looked great with the dress she wore, they risked announcing her presence prior to when she had planned. She hoped to catch the homeowner off guard, not grant him an audible warning.

Within her short time in the entry, something dawned on her. What if he wasn't alone? What if he was currently being comforted by a woman all too pleased to be in his bed? The torturous vision made her sick. Unable to continue her pace, she stood there immobilized, searching for an answer on what to do next. Then all of a sudden, at the end of the hall, Ideal stepped into view.

The sight of him stupefied her. She literally had forgotten just how attractive he was. Not only his physical features, but his aura and essence had her yearning to be close to him. She remembered what a privilege it had been to be in his arms, his heart, and his bed. As much as she wanted to rush over to him, she didn't dare. After ignoring him for far too long, she wasn't certain a part of him didn't hate her.

Although his face was initially inquisitive when it peeped into the hall, it transformed into an aspect of amazement, then shortly after, vacuity. He didn't seem to be looking at her but through her, as if she was a phantom or flawless piece of glass. Ireland struggled to read his reaction, unable to tell if he was happy or furious. He said absolutely nothing, making what she had to say even more difficult and humbling.

"Hi," she whispered, feeling an irrepressible tremor.

A multitude of seconds crawled by then, at last, he gave a reply. "Hi."

After glancing at his shirt then back at his face, she began to speak. "I feel ridiculous being here, but there's something I have to say to you and I needed to say it in person."

She waited for him to offer something – a word, a smirk, a nod, but nothing came her way. In spite of his lack of encouragement, she had to lay her heart at his feet. If he chose to trample on it, he would have every right to do so.

"I was wrong to walk out on you the way I did," she admitted. "I got so overwhelmed with everything that I was desperate for it all to stop. I thought the main way to make that happen was to end things with you. I thought it was the right decision, but now, I know it wasn't. I should've stayed with you and leaned on you and accepted the help you offered me."

Ideal didn't part his perfect lips, comfortable with continuing his stoicism. Ireland would have welcomed the buzzing of bees if it meant terminating the demoralizing silence. Embarrassed by the one-sided conversation, she was ready to depart in shame.

"Well, I didn't come expecting you to take me back or anything. I just wanted to look you in the eye and say I'm sorry." Having said what she needed to say, there was one thing she needed to ask. Abjectly, she uttered, "Will you forgive me?"

Ideal remained silent. He didn't, however, remain in the spot in which he stood. Slowly, he took a step toward her then another and another, his black socks aiding him in the quiet way he approached her. After what felt like an hour, he arrived directly in front of her. A haunting concentration radiated from his eyes. In the same cadence and melody Ireland had just used, he responded to her question with a question of his own. "Will you marry me?"

It took her a moment to comprehend what she had been asked again. Once she was certain it was a proposal, she had no doubt in her mind. Calling off her marriage was a decision based on fear. Being given another chance was a hope come true. "Yes," she answered, freely.

"Tomorrow?" he asked, his expression unmistakably serious.

"Tomorrow?" she mouthed, her voice stolen by surprise.

"Tomorrow," he repeated, firmly, annihilating any way for her to misconstrue his intention.

Ireland's mind swirled with the outrageous amount of tasks that would need to get done in twenty-four hours. Although she believed it was impossible to pull off, it was worth an honest try for Ideal. Smiling, she agreed with one simple word. "Yes."

Though the presence of the press was not requested, they arrived anyhow. Struggling for a glimpse below the tops of two tents positioned on the lawn of Ideal's East Hampton home, they circled the evening sky in helicopters.

Set during the hour of sunset, the wedding's site held an awesome glow. Sunlight shimmered across the ocean's belittling surface. Shining from the pleated fabric adorning the tents ceilings were warm-hued bulbs in sparkling chandeliers. White lights burned bright in towering, potted trees and an excessive amount of flames flickered atop white candles. Some enclosed in hurricane lamps and some in gold-trimmed lanterns, each collection of scented pillars was attached to an assembly of flowers.

French tulips, callas, and Casa Blanca lilies intertwined with roses, hydrangeas, and orchids. The all-white ensembles embellished every area including the altar's arbor, the center aisle's borders, the backs of elegant chairs, and the reception's tables. Naturally, they were the focal point of boutonnieres and bouquets, which were wrapped in satin ribbon accented with crystal pins.

Clutching the hand-tied arrangements and wearing pale gold dresses was the generous bridesmaid, Rona, and the supportive maid of honor, Casey. On the other side of the altar, sporting a tux and gold tie, was the best man, Dig, standing beside his best friend. In a black tuxedo, white vest, and white tie, the good-looking groom was terribly eager to see his bride. Braced for her entrance, he stood with the bridal party, before a modest total of fifty inspired guests.

The invited had been delighted to receive impromptu instructions to pack then board private planes to witness the couple's nuptials. Enamored with the luxurious beachfront location, they felt as if they had roamed into a seaside hotel. Merely a leap from the altar, rightly seated in the front row, were Janet, Sheila, and Honesty subconsciously holding their breath.

As a female quartet began playing gold flutes, Ireland appeared and Ideal began to cry. Others followed his lead while watching her glide down the aisle on the strong and protective arm of her tearful father. Wearing the beaded lace and organza dress of her dreams, Ireland modeled the gown that Janet and Casey adored. Having let go of her inhibitions about the spectacular gown, Ireland wore it proudly with pearl and diamond jewels.

As romantic and dazzling as everything was, nothing surpassed the beauty of the couple exchanging their vows. Tenderly they recited every line, perceiving each phrase as sacred. With the gentleness of handling an infant, they placed bands on each other's ring finger then anticipated the next statement to be made.

With pleasure, the tall, bald minister declared, "By the power vested in me by the state of New York, I now pronounce you husband and wife." Smiling at Ideal, he added, "You may now kiss the bride."

To an exuberant cheer from all, Ideal quickly grabbed his wife then slowly wrapped his lips around hers. After a while, he pulled away, needing to see her again. He worshiped the way she looked and wanted the image forever seared into his memory.

"Ladies and gentlemen," the minister continued, "It is my honor to introduce to you Mr. and Mrs. Ideal Marvin Morris."

Rose petals rained on them as they made their way back up the aisle then crossed over to the neighboring tent. Pursued by a photographer and videographer instructed to take candid shots, Ideal and Ireland were captured in the center of a white dance floor. To an airy, flute version of Ideal's hit, *My Heart*, the married couple moved to the music. They kissed throughout their first dance, then released one another so Jonah could sway with his daughter and Sheila could rock with her son.

When the tears stopped flowing, the champagne began pouring and everyone dined on the feast Tut created. After wiping his satisfied mouth, Dig picked up his glass of bubbly and rose from his chair to give the customary toast.

"Alright, first off, I got to say to Deal and Ireland, thank you for the fastest start to a wedding reception I've ever seen." The guests, in total agreement, lifted their loaded forks and shouted gleefully. "Secondly, I got to say, I never, ever, ever, thought this day would happen. Believe me when I tell you, Deal didn't think so either. But it has and uh, I'm in a bit of a daze knowing that he's now a married man," he said, glancing at Ideal. "Him falling in love took us both by surprise. I mean, when it happened, he didn't know what to do. He was shaking and hyperventilating," he shared, gaining more laughs. "I'm not exaggerating. He took one look at Ireland and before he even met her, he was gone. So I'm proud of him for stepping up to the plate and deciding to faithfully love this woman. I've gotten to know her and she's a beautiful, smart, talented person that not only makes my boy happy, but my girl as well. So I can honestly say, Ireland, I love you."

Blowing Dig a kiss, Ireland replied, "I love you too."

"I wish you both a lifetime of happiness. So with that, run off to your honeymoon and make a baby named England or Scotland or something." Hoisting his glass, Dig concluded. "To *I* & *I*."

"To *I* & *I*," the attendees repeated, before guzzling the delicious champagne.

Recalling his tight schedule, Ideal led Ireland to their three-tier wedding cake. He forced her to taste a piece of carrot and she forced him to eat a hunk of red velvet. Once he finished licking the frosting from her fingers, he handed her a flute of champagne and picked up his own. Without a glitch, they linked arms and took a brief sip then Ideal addressed the applauding guests.

"Ireland and I really want to thank you guys for making it to our wedding. We always planned on giving you short notice, but we know this short notice was extreme. We appreciate what it took for you to drop everything and be with us today."

"Hey, anytime you need us to swing by here, just let us know and we'll make it happen," Jonah added.

Exhibiting his crooked grin, Ideal focused his attention on Jonah and Janet. "To my father-in-law and mother-in-law, thank you for creating my world. Today is hands down the happiest day of my life. I'll spend the rest of my years doing all that I can to keep your daughter happy. She'll never want for anything," he said, before quickly catching himself. "Well, except privacy. I can't give that to her always, but I will as often as I can. And actually, I can give her that now so I hate to eat and run, but we've got a plane to catch."

"Well, don't let us keep you, son-in-law," Janet said, her smiling face exuding the radiance she was known for.

Winking at Janet, Ideal continued. "Alright, we're going to toss the bouquet and garter then take off, but Dig is going to stick around and give you guys a show."

There was an eruption of joy, primarily from grown men, excited they would receive a private concert from their idol. To the sound of jubilation, Ireland walked to the dance floor with an attractive group of single women. Although Rona, Honesty, and Sheila, were ready to make the catch, Ireland was tickled to see her bouquet land in Casey's hands.

After the groom spent quite some time under Ireland's magnificent skirt, he re-appeared with the garter fixed between his teeth. Ignoring other men, he zeroed in on Dig and flung the blue band directly to him.

The newlyweds were mobbed with farewell hugs, but Sheila and Janet's were treasured most. A good mother's love was like no other. Rich, deep, and incomparably true, it was free from conditions and always there for submergence. Full and forever it went on and on. Ideal and Ireland had no doubt to whom they would turn during difficult times.

Ideal took Ireland's hand and stepped out from beneath the tent. Determined to escape the media's beams from above, they walked at a brisk pace but didn't get far.

"Mrs. Morris," someone called, causing Ireland to pause.

When she turned around, she saw Danielle, hurrying to reach her.

With an actual smile, she said to Ireland, "Congratulations. You make a beautiful bride."

Ireland smiled in return. "Thank you, Danielle."

"No, thank you."

Without hesitation, Ireland gave her a hug that was happily received.

Thrown by their warm interaction, Ideal stood by speculating. He had always felt the tension between them. Now, that they were hugging, he didn't know what to make of it. He did know, however, the change was a good thing.

As the couple trotted off to the front of the house, they laughed until they were settled in a white limousine. Stocked with slices of cake, and champagne flutes filled to the brim, they fed each other once more as Greg pulled away.

"So where are we going?" Ireland asked, her eyes bright with anticipation.

"A little castle I rented."

"A castle? Where?"

Ideal smiled from ear to ear. "Ireland."

Chapter 37

As to be expected, the honeymoon was heavenly. Within the ancient walls of an extraordinary castle, Mr. and Mrs. Morris slept in, ate well, and made love. When outdoors, they took strolls in green pastures, while bearing their souls about their childhoods, failures, and triumphs. The glorious days were gratifying, but as with all times of leisure, they were much too brief.

It was high time they return to their daily grind, but not before embarking on some serious house hunting. After departing the island, they flew to California, and in less than thirty-six hours, chose a newly constructed French Country estate.

A couple of weeks later, when rooms of the home were filled with boxes, fabric swatches, and landscape paintings, Ireland struggled to carry her loaded suitcase down the wooden stairs. Wearing a romper and *Try Real* sneakers, the lady of the house finally reached the foyer and parked her heavy bag near the rustic front door.

"Hey, baby. I need you to come and do something," Ideal said, appearing by her side.

Ireland rubbed the sting from her hands. "Where were you a minute ago?" she asked.

"In the back," he replied, taking hold of her waist then leading her to the backyard. They stepped out onto the loggia, passed a sparkling pool, and entered his recording studio.

"Well, well, well, I see everything got hung up in here," Ireland remarked, scanning the framed platinum albums on the walls. "I wish you'd spend a little time in the living room."

"I'll hang the painting when we get back," he said, guilty for not doing so the day prior. After sitting in front of an imposing board, he returned to his agenda. "Go in the booth and put on the headphones."

"Why?" Ireland asked, scowling.

"I want you to sing something for me."

"No."

"Come on."

"I told you, I don't want to sing."

"You can't sing one little hook for me?"

"You're not going to be able to use it."

"How do you know?"

"Because I said so."

"What if I said, since you're going on tour with me next month, you should be ready to sing in case I pull you up on stage?"

"What if I said, I change my mind? I'm not going on tour with you anymore."

"Go in there and put on the headphones," he said, grabbing her rear end and pushing it in the right direction.

Sighing in irritation, Ireland walked into the vocal booth and did as she was instructed. "What do you want me to sing?"

Amused to see her standing behind the glass, Ideal sang:

> "*You the one for me, the one for me, yea, you the only one.*"

"That's it?" she asked.

"Yea."

"Original."

"Just sing it."

After rolling her eyes, Ireland sang it back to him, delivering the pitch and tone he was hoping for.

"Yea, just like that. Sing it again," he said, gleefully, pressing buttons and recording her as she sang. "Ooh," he grunted. "Okay, I'm going to play the track." After singing the lyrics to the music, he turned it over to her. With his eyes closed, he listened to her sing the hook continually. Because he loved Ireland, it enchanted him that he loved her voice too. Future plans of what to do with it began flooding his mind until he heard her stop singing.

"That's enough," she declared, pulling off the headphones.

"Just one more time."

"No, that's enough," she said, walking out of the booth.

As Ideal prepared to negotiate, he received a text message. "Man, our ride is here," he said, rising from his chair. "I'll have to make you a recording artist another time."

"Would you stop with the recording talk?"

"No," he replied, running his hands through her hair. "You got a gift and I'm going to make sure you use it."

As if each of the past twelve months had been gathered and flung backward due to fate's mission to have them pass by, time seemed to vanish. Bewitched by her French surroundings, Ireland's onyx-lined eyes stared through the window of the chauffeured vehicle making its way down the boulevard. Present with her thoughts, yet experiencing déjà vu, she viewed billboards, banners, and posters, as well as throngs of people hurrying, but what she noticed most was her reaction to them all. They brought her a hum of excitement, and more surprisingly, joy. In contrast to her first journey to the splashy festival, her focus was not on herself, but on the art she would experience. As a result, she looked forward to attending its events.

After a healing hiatus, ongoing imagery and stillness, intentional breathing, and mornings with her creator, at last, she felt capable of stepping into vulnerability.

Content being Ideal's guest, she rode beside him, quietly, as they approached the liberal, crowded theater. Recognizing her husband's support, shown by his negligence of speech, she closed her eyes, took a full breath, and went to an imagined place.

A familiar tune drifts from an aged accordion. Her feet, in flat sandals, carry her over an arched bridge. A dark row of water rests below. The sun shines upon unlit lampposts dotted throughout the town. She reaches the base of the bridge then crosses onto cobblestones. Walking beside the decorated doors and windows of pretty boutiques, she gets a whiff of sweetness. She slips inside a pastry shop and buys a chocolate croissant. She takes a bite and the warm, brown goo glides between her teeth. She smiles at its goodness. She floats out onto the sidewalk then comes to a handsome building. The doorman tips his high-sitting hat and welcomes her back in the loveliest of languages. She proceeds through a revolving door and arrives in an elegant lobby. Her ears are pleased by the keys of a piano. Passing assemblies of floral arrangements, she glances to her left, where well-dressed diners eat gourmet cuisine. She hears a toddler exclaim, "Mommy!" She moves her attention to the right and sees her child, with his infectious smile, running quickly toward her. Ideal is behind him, wearing a smile of his own.

"It's time," Ideal said, gently.

Slowly, she opened her eyes and saw what she expected - a mass of flashing lights, documenting her arrival. Wearing a bold, elaborate, red gown, Ireland gracefully stepped onto the carpet then remembered her mother's words.

"You don't have to like it, but you have to accept it."

Ireland didn't like the obsessive attention, but by accepting it for what it was, she was able to discern what mattered. What mattered was peace, which is what she had with herself. What mattered was love, which is what she had with Ideal. Hand in hand, they traveled the carpet, stopping time after time to pose. She was no longer preoccupied with the alarm of being seen and he was much less preoccupied with the need to be seen.

With each step Ireland took, she held steadfast to a decision she made the morning of her wedding. Nevermore would she grant her fear the authority to steer her life. Nevermore would she allow it to hold her from her dreams. The invasion of fame had caused her to examine all that was wrong in lieu of all that was right. She had good health, a trustworthy man, a stimulating career, and financial security. With all that she possessed, her attitude cried for an adjustment, and from her wedding day forward, she made one.

Her outlook on life was through a lens of gratitude. In spite of unwanted attention, she lived with appreciation and when tempted to complain, focused on those who had far less. Such people she committed to serving, and through more service, her pity parties plummeted.

Although her most frequent activity evolved into counting her blessings, she recognized social media, fans, press, and paparazzi would be entities she'd continually have to withstand. Their adoring or derogatory words and obtrusive behavior would swell, but she wouldn't let them deter her from living a wonderful life. Walking a street, roaming a beach, kissing her husband, and raising her children would be actions captured by cameras for all the world to critique, but she couldn't continue being tormented by insatiably curious minds.

Motivated by the strength of her mother, Ireland kept on going. With all of the fame she encountered, she knew there were people, past and present, whose experiences eclipsed hers. She often said a prayer with thanksgiving, petitioning God to bless those souls that endured more scrutiny than she.

CPSIA information can be obtained
at www.ICGtesting.com
Printed in the USA
LVHW031146281220
675195LV00026B/545/J

9 781734 699708